COLIN FALCONER

CRY JUSTICE

Constable

An imprint of
Little, Brown Book Group
Carmelite House
50 Victoria Embankment
London EC4Y 0DZ

An Hachette UK Company
www.hachette.co.uk

CONSTABLE

CONSTABLE

First published in trade paperback in Great Britain in 2021 by Constable
This paperback edition published in 2022 by Constable

A CIP catalogue record for this book
is available from the British Library.

ISBN: 978-1-47213-274-1

Typeset in Sabon by Initial Typesetting Services, Edinburgh
Printed and bound in Great Britain by Clays Ltd, Elcograf S.p.A.

Papers used by Constable are from well-managed forests and
other responsible sources.

MIX
Paper from
responsible sources
FSC® C104740

This one's for you, Charlie. Thanks for keeping me company when I'm writing and for the free publicity shots on my Facebook author page. If they ever make the movie, yes, you can play yourself.

'Where will it end? –
where will it sink to sleep and rest,
this murderous hate, this Fury?'

Chorus

The Libation Bearers (lines 1075–77),

from *The Oresteia* by Aeschylus

DAY 1

CHAPTER ONE

The head had been impaled on a railing outside the Royal Courts of Justice in the Strand in the early hours of a cold November morning. There was a fine dusting of frost on the corpse's hair and eyelids which gave it a festive touch.

The dead man looked disconsolate. Reasonably so, in the circumstances, Charlie thought.

Jennings, a DC with the Homicide Assessment Team that had been one of the first police at the scene, stood at Charlie's shoulder, his hands in his pockets, his breath forming little clouds in the air. 'We've ruled out suicide,' he said.

'On what basis?' Charlie said, going along with it.

'He didn't leave a note.'

According to Jennings, the couple who called it in thought it was a prank, and one of the young women had even taken a selfie with it. Alcohol will do that to you. When her male companion put his fingers in the deceased's mouth, he sobered up quite quickly and then fainted. His girlfriend put him in the recovery position and dialled 999.

Jack, the head of Crime Scene, saw Charlie and headed over, pulling back his mask. 'Well,' he said. 'This is very medieval.'

'Not your usual,' Charlie said, and wondered what his DCI was going to say when he found out about this. It was going to make the dailies. His boss hated being in the papers unless it was in a photograph taken at a Masonic dinner.

Jack's team had put up a tent to stop people taking videos and posting them on YouTube. The influencers on Instagram

3

would have had a field day. Use them to promote weight-loss programmes. People were like that.

Charlie stepped outside and took a deep breath. There was a real bite to the air this morning. Red and blue strobes flashed up and down the street, Charlie could see people milling about beyond the cordons. Half of London would grind to a standstill if they didn't get this sorted and out of the way. It would be rush hour soon, long before the sun came up.

He stamped his feet against the cold. At least there weren't any flies, not in this weather. He didn't think he could do this job if he lived somewhere hot, like India.

He was desperate for a coffee. Jack came out and joined him on the pavement.

'Anything?' Charlie said to him.

'There's something in his throat.'

'What is it?'

'Looks like a scrap of paper. When the photographer's done, one of my lads is going to extract it and bag and tag it for you. Five-star service, this.'

They went back inside the tent and waited. Finally, one of Jack's Scene of Crime Officers retrieved the piece of paper, unfolded it, and placed it inside a clear plastic evidence bag. It was smeared with blood and fluid, but the printing was clearly legible. It was a page, torn from a book, and two lines had been highlighted.

This is the reason that you see this man fallen here.
I am he who planned this murder and with justice.

'Sounds like Shakespeare,' Jack said. '*Macbeth* or something.'

'It's Aeschylus,' Charlie said. 'From an old Greek play. *Agamemnon*. Part of a trilogy called *The Oresteia*.'

'Fuck me. Whatever you say, Charlie.'

'How do you know this stuff, guv?' Jennings said.

'Google,' Charlie said. Because it was easier than explaining.

'Who was Aga Memo?' Jack said.

'Agamemnon. He was a king. Got drowned in his bath by his missus.'

'What for?'

'Usual thing. Jealousy. Also, I think she had a better offer.'

'So this note, Charlie. How is it relevant?'

'It's complicated, Jack. What happens, the son murders the mother for killing his father.'

'Sounds like a Tarantino movie.'

'An early version of one.'

'So how does it finish?'

'Lots of people die. Finally, the son is pursued by the Furies, the three infernal goddesses of vengeance.'

'*Kill Bill* with togas.'

Charlie was about to say, no, only the Romans wore togas, but he let it go.

'There you go,' Jennings said. 'They left you a clue. Dead simple this. You'll have this all written up and the file closed by lunchtime.' Jennings thought he was being funny.

Charlie closed his eyes. One step at a time, Charlie son. Treat it like it's another stabbing on one of the estates. First principles.

'Where are our eyewitnesses?' he said.

Jennings nodded at an ambulance parked outside the Pret on the other side of the Strand. Charlie went over.

There was a clown with an axe through his head sitting in the back. A nun in a tight black skirt was with him. Her face was made up to look like a skull. He reminded himself it was Halloween. Not everyone worked impossible hours and had no time for messing around, like him.

The clown was shaking and throwing up into a sick bag. The nun had her arms around him, stroking his orange wig in a kindly way. There was a paramedic with them. He gave Charlie a look, like: *I've got better things to do.*

Charlie showed the nun and the clown his warrant badge

and the paramedic got out and let him sit in his chair. 'I won't be long,' Charlie said to him.

'You take your time. I need a gasper.'

It amazed Charlie how many paramedics smoked. You'd think they'd know better after the lung cancers and emphysemas they had in the back of their vans. Perhaps it was the stress.

Charlie settled himself, took out his notebook, in case the clown said something that was worth writing down. 'Do they know who it is?' the nun asked him, nodding towards the white tent on the other side of the road.

'Too early to tell. Can I have your names, please?'

'Sophie. Sophie Lyons-Hatton. This is Will. Will Tarrant.'

'You were the ones that found the . . . remains.'

'We thought it was a joke, you know? Here.' She held out her iPhone. It was a selfie of Sophie and Will proper mugging it for the camera, in front of the railing and what they now knew to be the deceased, or what was left of him.

'You took a selfie?'

'We didn't know the head was *real*.'

It crossed Charlie's mind to ask her if that would have made any difference, but he let it go. 'Do you mind if I take this?' Charlie said, holding up the phone. 'We might need it as evidence.'

Sophie nodded. Jennings was standing outside with an evidence bag, and Charlie leaned out and dropped it in. 'Sophie, before you came across the remains, did you see anything, anyone? The person responsible for this might have run past you or near you.'

'There were a few people. Dressed up. We'd been drinking. I don't really remember anything.'

Will looked up from his sick bag. 'There was a witch,' he mumbled, and then he threw up again.

'A witch?'

'That was Katie, Will,' Sophie said. 'She went home early.' She turned to Charlie. 'Sorry, he's not much good at the moment.'

'When you saw the head,' Charlie said, 'what did you do?'

'I stuck my finger in his mouth,' he said, and started blubbing again.

'You did what?' Charlie said.

'I didn't know it was a real head, did I? I thought it was a joke.'

'It's so horrible,' Sophie said, and she started to cry as well.

'We'll need statements later,' Charlie said.

He got out of the ambulance, stood there a moment, watched the light leaching back into the night sky, what stars there were over London fading away. He looked up at the towers of the Royal Courts. It was a beautiful building, if you liked over-the-top Gothic. Like something God might use as a townhouse.

He saw his outside DS, Grey, making his way through the cordon. About time. Charlie went over, walked him through the crime scene, showed him where to find the rest of Sophie and Will's friends, huddled in their zombie costumes next to a patrol car, still yet to be properly interviewed; he pointed up at the CCTV cameras on the Gothic facade. That evidence could be key.

'Why would someone do something like this?' Grey said.

'To make a statement, I suppose,' Charlie said.

He told him about the note the SOCOs had found in the dead man's remains.

He said they would need statements from Sophie and Will and the rest of the zombie apocalypse, as well as DNA swabs as they had tampered with the remains and would need to be excluded from the investigation. And he wanted that CCTV footage urgently.

He left him with it and went back to his car. His caffeine debt was reaching emergency levels. He wondered if anywhere would be open in the centre of London at half past four in the morning. Bugger reversing cameras and climate control, what he needed in his car was a barista.

CHAPTER TWO

When Charlie walked into the incident room, he spared a glance at the flat screen at the far end. There was a live report from the law courts, a talking head with the white tent prominent in the background. The reporter was providing a salacious description of the murder scene for the rest of Britain to enjoy while they scoffed their breakfast; but then this was London, and most Londoners wouldn't look up from their fry-up for anything less than a multiple stabbing.

Jayden Greene was back from stress leave and Charlie had assigned him as his new office manager. His long-time inside DS, Dawson – 'the skipper' – had taken a turn at his desk a few days before, heart attack they said. So, he'd got Greene back, strict orders to keep him off the street because of his post-traumatic stress. At least that's what Greene was calling it.

Greene was busy, marking out a column in black felt tip on the whiteboard, putting crime scene pictures under Charlie's name.

'That's what I missed about being on your team,' Greene said. 'You get all the good ones.'

'I don't know that's quite what I would call it, Jay.'

'Who's the pathologist?'

'Middleton.'

'Hope he's going to bill the post-mortem at a reduced rate.'

'Give it a rest, Jay,' Charlie said.

'All right, no need to bite my head off.'

DCs Wes James and Rupinder Singh looked up from their

8

desks, but no one laughed. Greene didn't seem to care. Charlie was missing the skipper already.

The rest of the crew gathered in a semicircle around the whiteboard for an informal briefing. Charlie told them what he knew so far: at around three o'clock that morning, person or persons unknown had placed a male human head on the railings of the Law Courts in the Strand.

'First thing we have to do is ID the . . .' Charlie stopped himself. He nearly said 'body'. Greene would have had a field day. 'The victim. The remains have been transported to the mortuary, hopefully we will be able to make an identification through dental records. The DCI has promised me that it will be fast-tracked through the system, but as you all know it could still take some time.' Weeks, possibly. Or never. Charlie was hoping that someone would find the rest of their John Doe long before then.

'We're going to give the media an identikit reconstruction of the deceased,' Charlie said and held up his iPad so they could have a look. 'Perhaps someone will recognise him.'

'Looks like that bloke from *EastEnders*,' Greene said. 'What's his name?'

'Tony King,' James said.

'Every corpse looks like Tony King,' someone else said, from the back. James said to Singh, in a voice loud enough for them all to hear: 'Police are looking for a man between thirty and forty years with a vacant expression, dead from the neck up.'

'Half of London fits that description,' Greene said.

'Enough, people,' Charlie said. 'Concentrate. Let's talk about the note.'

Singh's head shot up. 'He left a note?'

'A piece of paper had been placed in the victim's throat, presumably post-mortem. It's been sent to Lambeth for further investigation, but it appears to be torn from a book.'

'What did it say?'

Charlie pretended to consult his notebook, though he had

9

already committed the lines to memory. '"This is the reason that you see this man fallen here. I am he who planned this murder and with justice."'

'Very poetic,' DC Lubanski – Lube – said. She'd been 'Lube' to everyone in the squad for so long, he wasn't sure anyone even remembered her first name any more.

'It's Aeschylus,' Charlie said.

'Who's that? A rapper?' Greene said.

'No, Jay. He's Greek. He is considered the father of Tragedy.'

'Never heard of him,' Greene said.

'That's impressive, guv,' James said. 'I mean, that you know this stuff.'

'I may not have had a private school education, Wes, but it doesn't make me a complete Neanderthal.'

Charlie looked at Grey, who had just walked in. 'You know about Aeschylus, right? You and the DCI must have done the classics at St Michael's.'

Grey looked uncomfortable. 'I was never all that interested in the Greeks.'

'Well, all you need to know, people, is that the words are from an ancient play about revenge. Now it's very important that no one starts blabbing about this note outside of this room. We don't want the media getting to hear about it. My gut feeling – we are going to have every nutjob in London confessing to being the perpetrator after it goes public. So this little detail we keep to ourselves.'

He looked around the room, made sure they understood. They all nodded.

'Until we have established the victim's identity, we can't draw up a list of suspects. So that's a priority. And as soon as we get the CCTV from the Law Courts we have to establish the exact time that the head was impaled on the railing. 'Wes, you and Rupe canvass the area around the Law Courts for more CCTV. Take it wide, very wide. The first responders found a witness who claims he saw a bloke with a backpack fleeing the scene on foot. We need to verify this and establish where this person came from. There should be hours of viewing pleasure in that part of London. Check the local ANPR cameras, see if we can get a visual. We need to track any motors in the vicinity at that time, interview the drivers, find out if they saw anything.' Charlie turned to DS Grey. 'What else do you have, sergeant?'

'We have statements from the five young people who found the . . .' He glanced at Greene, who was ready to pounce. 'The remains. They don't remember seeing anyone else near the Royal Courts at the time. But they were all pretty drunk.'

'Well, it's Halloween,' James said. 'Our man could run down High Holborn with the head under his arm, people would think it was a joke. They'd pay no attention.'

Charlie tapped the map on the whiteboard behind him. 'The question we have to answer is: where did he or she come from and how did they get away? Was it in a car, on a bike, on foot, what?'

'The CCTV should tell us that.'

'It's the Law Courts,' Lubanski said. 'They must have more cameras than Steven Spielberg.'

The phone rang on Greene's desk. He snatched it up and put it to his ear.

Charlie went on: 'We are about to issue a press release that will include a dedicated hotline number. Hopefully, that will give us some more leads. We will have a formal briefing this evening at six o'clock and by then I anticipate that the investigation will have a clear focus. Until then . . .'

Greene raised a hand to beckon him over, the phone still to his ear.

'Just a minute, Jay,' Charlie said.

'No, you'll want to hear this first,' Greene said. 'We've got our murder scene.'

Everyone in the room turned and looked at him.

'HAT have a headless corpse in a flat in Kentish Town. It was rung in about an hour ago.'

Charlie put his jacket on.

'Is it the victim?' one of the trainee DCs said.

'Don't worry, the guv'nor will be taking the head with him,' Greene said, 'to see if it's a match. Like Cinderella.'

The poor bastard gave Charlie a look. He was only two weeks out of CID and he wasn't sure if Greene was messing with him. Charlie clapped him on the shoulder. 'Take no notice, son. Jay, stress leave has done you no good at all.' He turned to Grey. 'Grab your car keys. We're going to Kentish Town.'

CHAPTER THREE

Grey turned the wipers on. As they drove down the Essex Road, plastic bags and bits of newspaper swirled across the street in a sudden gust. A street cleaner in a dirty fluoro vest sucked on a cigarette and threw the butt in the gutter. That's the way, Charlie thought. Love to see someone taking pride in their work.

'Where were you this morning, sergeant?'

'Sir?'

'Half an hour I was at the crime scene and no deputy to help me out.'

'Sorry. I realise I was a bit late getting there. Won't happen again.'

'I hope not. I don't expect my outside DS to be last out the door when we've got a major flap on. Doesn't set a good example.'

Grey didn't say anything. No explanation, nothing.

'You look worn out. Everything all right at home?'

'Everything's fine, thank you, sir.' Grey was a rotten liar. But if he didn't want to talk, that was his business.

Charlie looked out of the window. London, on a cold November morning. Buses nudged their way through the mist, black bin bags spilled rubbish into the streets. A sleeping bag littered a shop doorway, surrounded by lager cans and take-away boxes.

'The human stain,' Charlie said.

'What's that, guv?'

'Does my head in, all this. Stop here, I need a coffee. Want one?'

'No thanks, sir.'

'Suit yourself.'

Grey parked on a yellow line outside a Costa.

'Why are you stopping here? There was a proper coffee shop back there.'

'Coffee's coffee, isn't it, sir? There was nowhere else to park.'

There was no way to explain coffee to people who didn't understand, Charlie thought. It was like trying to explain democracy to Donald Trump. Charlie took his coffee cup out of the console and went in, ordered a flat white with a double shot.

As he came out, he saw the entrance to the Wetherspoons next door was occupied. Poor bastards were everywhere these days. He could make out a dirty mop of ginger hair sticking out from under the zipper of a red nylon sleeping bag. He had change from a tenner in his hand, so he tucked it under the zipper.

'What did you do that for?' Grey said, when he got back in the car. 'He's only going to spend it on booze.'

'What do you think I was going to spend it on?' Charlie said. He took his first sip of coffee for the day and groaned. Coffee, beer, the Arsenal. Made life worth living. And a good woman, of course. But where was he going to find one of those?

'Get 50p off, did you?' Grey said, nodding at Charlie's keep cup.

'I don't do it for the 50p, I do it for David Attenborough.' He took out his phone and read out: '"But there where criminals are slain or mutilated is meet abode, and the feast ye love, ye loathsome goddesses!"'

'Jeez guv,' Grey said. 'What website are you on?'

'It's Aeschylus,' Charlie said. 'It's when Apollo urges the Furies on to vengeance.'

'Right,' Grey said. 'Well done. Impressive.'

'You mean impressive for someone who never went to a

public school?' Grey coloured up and Charlie wished he hadn't said it. He wasn't a bad lad, really. He should get off his case. 'I read a lot.'

'I actually meant impressive for an Arsenal supporter.'

'Thanks.'

'Well, you know.'

'Nick Hornby's an Arsenal supporter. So is Piers Morgan.'

'Piers Morgan,' Grey muttered. 'Proves my point.'

'"There is no pain so great as the memory of joy in present grief."'

'Is that Aeschylus as well?'

'No, that's every Arsenal fan you'll ever meet. At least we beat Blackpool last night. Spurs next, in the quarter final. Any luck, we'll catch the psycho who put the head on the railing in the next couple of days and then I'll be off the roster and me and Ben can go and watch it. See this?' Charlie held up his phone.

'Not when I'm driving, guv.'

'It's a picture of my niece. Just came through on my WhatsApp. My sister had another baby a couple of months ago.'

'Nice. What did she call her?'

Charlie didn't want to say. A bitter pill, this.

'Sir?' Grey said.

'Jocaster.'

A beat. 'That's unusual.'

'Unusual. Code for "stupid". You're right, why couldn't they give the kid a real name? Why does everything have to be a fucking statement? If you call your kid Jaxon with an X or spell Lucee with two EEs, you might as well put "CHAV" on their forehead with a branding iron and mark them for life.'

'Takes all sorts.'

'Jocaster. It's about as clichéd as a pikey in Burberry. She's going to grow up to have fake boobs and hair extensions. She has no chance. Watch where you're driving. Where did you get your licence, sergeant?'

***

15

Kentish Town was London in spades, all garages and garden centres: white collar professionals in Georgian terraces on one side of the high street, with Remain posters in their sash windows; council blocks and Poundstretchers on the other side, landlocked by railway lines and building sites. Charlie and Grey drove past the stone turrets and chimneys of a Gothic church. There was a sign with 'Jesus Answers Knee Mail' outside and a Neighbourhood Watch sticker on one of the glass windows. A clutch of delinquents were hanging around one of the street corners, getting ready for a casual afternoon of shoplifting at Tesco.

Their crime scene was a ground floor flat on one of the estates, a spit in the wind from the Queen's Crescent Market. There was the usual flotsam hanging around the cordon, even a couple of tourists looking thrilled and taking selfies.

'Wait up,' Charlie said as they pulled up outside, 'what's that geezer doing?'

'Who's that, sir?'

'That dodgy looking bloke over there.'

The character Charlie had clocked looked a bit like Rhys Ifans from his *Notting Hill* turn. He was wearing a long khaki overcoat with most of the buttons missing and his ratty hair was hanging off his collar in greasy strips. But it was the way he was prairie-dogging over the heads of the crowd around the cordon that made Charlie look. When he saw Charlie get out of the car and start towards him, he took off. Only blokes with plenty of priors know a cop in plain clothes that fast, Charlie thought, and he went off after him.

In the movies Charlie watched when he was a kid, cops yelled 'Stop, police!' when some low life hoofed it, but personally he never saw the point of that. If they were intending to hang around for conversation, they wouldn't have scarpered in the first place. The bloke was nimble on his feet, he'd give him that.

Charlie was about to give up and let him go when he heard

16

someone steaming up behind him and DS Grey shot past. Not often he saw anyone who could run that fast, certainly not when he was watching Arsenal every week, and the rugby tackle Grey followed up with was sheer poetry. He had the bloke down and the speed cuffs on before Charlie could get his warrant card out.

The two uniforms standing at the end of the street barely had time to react.

'Well come on then,' Charlie yelled at them. 'This is your job, this.'

'Sir,' Grey said, 'look at this.' He had already done a quick body search and held up a baggie of white powder.

'Get in,' Charlie said, but privately he was a bit disappointed. A few grams of coke was all well and good, but what he had been hoping to find on the geezer was a bloodied knife. Still, that wasn't the way life worked.

The flat smelled faintly of mould tainted with the distinctive coppery smell of blood. Charlie stood in the middle of the carpet, in his plastic bodysuit and boots, and watched the CS team at work. The photographer was still shuffling around, making a video record of the scene, and two fingerprint techs were dusting the windowsills; the filmy grey dust they used shimmered in the halogen gleam of two arc lights.

Their victim had been done for in the kitchen; the landlord would never get that stain out of the linoleum. The place was pretty much as Charlie had anticipated before he walked in, not too many surprises: empty vodka bottles, some drug paraphernalia, video games. A life well lived.

No Jack today, he was still busy down the Strand. The CS manager was a heavy-set man with a moustache and bifocals, Lewis. He nodded at Charlie and pulled down his mask.

'Hello Nick,' Charlie said. 'This is my new deputy, Matthew Grey. What do we have?'

Lewis held up a plastic evidence bag; inside were three parts of the locking mechanism from the front door. 'Looks like the

17

killer used an adjustable wrench and a screwdriver to get in. Something like this, if you know what you're doing, would take you less than ten seconds. We found the body in the kitchen, looks like he was eating his tea when it happened.'

It was a tiny flat and there were SOCOs everywhere, there was hardly room to move. The CS photographer swore at two DCs who were too slow to get out of his way. There was a sheen of luminol on the doors and the kitchen bench. The Formica table had been overturned, baked beans and bits of toast had stuck to the tiles in pools of blackening blood.

'Lovely,' Charlie said.

'Puddles of Blood,' Lewis said. 'Be a good name for a punk band.'

'No one listens to punk any more,' Charlie said.

Fenwick, one of his fellow DIs from the team at Essex Road, was already there. He had been called in by a HAT team when the body had been found. It hadn't taken him long to work out that the body was part of Charlie's case.

Charlie nodded to him. 'How are you then, all right?'

'Not really. I'm ambivalent, Charlie.'

'Ambivalent, that's a good word.'

'Looks to me like this is your crime scene now. Pity, it looks interesting. So me, I'm back to the domestics and the gangbangers in Tottenham.'

'Some guys get all the luck. Who found him?'

'It was an anonymous tip-off. Someone rang it in to the local nick.'

'That's nice of them.' They went outside. Two paramedics and the mortuary crew were smoking cigarettes, joking with one of the borough detectives. A uniformed sergeant was standing to one side, with one of his constables, watching them. Charlie introduced himself. 'The bloke in there. Do you recognise him?'

The sergeant gave him a look. 'Not without his head.'

'I mean, you or any of your boys ever been called to this address?'

He shook his head. 'We've rung the council for you.' He took out his notebook. 'It's rented to a Michael Richard Grimes.' He tore out the page and handed it to Charlie. 'I checked. He has previous. His prints will be on file.'

'Any luck tracing whoever called it in?'

'Unregistered phone. We'll go through the motions but my guess is the SIM is at the bottom of a canal somewhere. What you reckon this is all about? We haven't got any of them ISIS in Kentish Town, have we?'

'No, mate. We do not believe this is terrorist-related.'

'What was the little set-to outside? Hope you're not upsetting the local citizens?'

'Some bloke got as far as the cordon and ran for his life. He had some blow in his pocket.'

'Round here, the only surprise would be if he didn't.'

'Well,' Charlie said to Grey, 'let's see what that bloke you nabbed has to say for himself.'

CHAPTER FOUR

It was the usual circus in the custody suite; the duty sergeant was punching information into the computer like he was beating it into a confession, a plastic gangster with blood on his face was shouting threats in an Irish accent while two young constables fresh out of college tried to pin his arms. There were lunch trays balanced on the platform like a Jenga game played with dirty plates. One of his fellow inspectors was pacing up and down, whispering into his iPhone.

The duty solicitor, Garner, had been waiting patiently for his client and accompanied him into the interview room. He was wearing some decent aftershave, which was pleasant. Charlie's suspect, now identified as Alan Chapman, wasn't wearing any kind of personal fragrance. At least he didn't look quite so much like a kiddie fiddler in his custody tracksuit. Still, the mélange of scents in the room was distracting.

Garner had prepared a statement. 'My client is willing to cooperate in your investigation in any way he can,' he said.

'That's very nice of him,' Charlie said.

'He wants you to know the drugs you found in his possession were for his own personal use. He knows nothing about the alleged homicide of Michael Grimes.'

'We'd still like to ask him a few questions. Clarify a few things.'

'Wait a minute,' Chapman said. 'Who's dead?'

The brief shook his head. Charlie felt a bit sorry for him. 'We've been through all this, Mr Chapman,' he said.

'The deceased – that means the bloke who's dead – is a Michael Richard Grimes. You didn't think we'd need three squad cars, a CS van and two detectives for a minor drug bust?'

'Fuck me.'

'First of all, Mr Chapman, can you tell us why you ran away when you saw the police at Mr Grimes' house this morning?'

'Well, wouldn't you, if you saw a whole load of coppers?'

Charlie glanced at Garner. Oh, this was going to be a long afternoon. 'No, I wouldn't. I see a whole load of coppers every day.'

'You know what I mean.'

'Not really.'

'Well I knew I had a bit of gear on my person, so to speak. I thought it would be misconstructed.'

'Misconstrued in what way? That we would think that you had come to Mr Grimes' house to sell him cocaine? Or that you had come to Mr Grimes' house to see if his body had yet been discovered?'

'I didn't know about no body. I was there just minding my own business, like.'

Garner leaned forward. 'I think my client has been clear,' he said. 'There is absolutely no evidence to suggest that he was running because he was involved in Mr Grimes' homicide. Asked and answered.' Charlie glanced up at the digital clock in the corner. Time was getting on. He wasn't sure they were getting anywhere with this.

'Is he dead, then?'

'Yes, Mr Chapman.'

'You sure?'

'We've had experts look at him. Trust me.'

'It wasn't an overdose?'

'He was murdered.'

'You don't think I did it?'

Charlie wondered if Chapman was really that stupid, or if he was faking it. 'Can you describe for me the nature of your association with Mr Grimes?'

21

'What?'

'How did you know him?'

'Who says I did?'

'Mr Chapman, from our initial enquiries it seems you were a regular visitor to Mr Grimes' flat.'

'No, not really.'

'Two of his neighbours say they saw you there several times last week. Yesterday evening they heard you screaming at him from the street. Your words were –' Charlie consulted his notes and dropped his voice to a monotone: '– "Give me the two hundred you owe me, you fucking maggot, or I'll rip your fucking head off." Interesting turn of phrase.'

'It was only friendly banter. I didn't mean it.'

'So, it is only a coincidence then, that this morning Mr Grimes was found decapitated on his kitchen floor?'

Chapman looked at his brief. Garner pointedly ignored him.

'What's decapitulated mean?'

'Decapitated. Somebody ripped his head off.'

'What? No. That's barbaric, that is.'

'Want to tell me what the argument was about?'

'You are under caution, Mr Chapman,' Garner said. 'As I have previously advised, you do not have to answer.' For a moment, Charlie wondered if Chapman was going to fold his arms, sit back and shrug. But the 'no comment' routine wasn't as common as it used to be. These days juries tended to construe silence as a tacit admission of guilt, bless them.

'The argument, Mr Chapman?'

'Wasn't what you'd call an argument. Just a disagreement.'

'And how long were you disagreeing with Mr Grimes last night?'

'What?'

'How long were you inside his flat?'

'I never went in. We just stood on the doorstep and chatted.'

'What did you chat about?'

'You know. Things.'

'What things? Philosophy? Football? Existentialism?'

'What?'

'Can you be more specific. What did you talk about?'

'He owed me money.'

'For drugs?'

'I don't know what he spent it on.'

'No, why did he owe *you* money? What was the nature of the debt?'

'It was a loan, like.'

'How much did he owe you?'

'Two hundred. He owed everybody money, didn't he?'

'Did he? I don't know. That's what I'm trying to find out.'

'He was . . .'

'What was he, Mr Chapman?'

'Insolvent.'

Garner coughed to cover a laugh.

'I ask you again. Were you supplying him with narcotics?'

'Me? No. Never. The gear, it was . . .' He took a moment, trying to remember what his brief had told him. 'It was for my own personal use.'

'Let's start again,' Charlie said. 'What were you doing last night between midnight and four a.m.?'

'Is that when they did for him?'

'When who did for him?'

'Whoever.'

Charlie opened Chapman's file. He'd had three custodial sentences, the last time the judge had given him six-and-a-half years in Pentonville for GBH. That was a surprise. Charlie didn't think Chapman looked like he could win an arm wrestle with a six-year-old, but blokes were different when they got drugged up. You could never tell.

'Let's start from the beginning. How long had you known Mr Grimes?'

'We met in prison.'

'Ah. That's nice. Like *Shawshank*.'

'Like what?'

The brief smiled. At least one of them is on the same page, Charlie thought. 'Never mind.' Charlie consulted his file in front of him. 'It says here you've done some serious time for GBH.'

'That's not me, that. I'm not a violent person. It's just I don't know what I'm doing when I'm off my head.'

The solicitor's eyes flickered. Bet he wished he'd stuck with 'no comment' now. 'Is that what happened this time?'

'This time?'

'Were you off your head, and didn't know what you were doing when you attacked Mr Grimes?'

'No. No, like I said, I never went in. We shouted a bit, down the path outside his gaff. It might have sounded a bit tasty, and all that, but it was only messin'. You know.'

'So why did you go back to Mr Grimes' flat this morning?'

'To apologise.'

'Apologise?'

'For all the things I said last night. I was worried I'd hurt his feelings, like.'

'Were you? Worried.'

'Sometimes I get a bit carried away. Who found his body?'

'I'll ask the questions, thanks. Why did you tell Mr Grimes that you were going to rip his head off?'

'Like I said, I was only mucking about.'

It's us you're mucking about, Charlie thought. He tried to imagine this low life decapitating Michael Grimes and sticking his head on the fence outside the Law Courts, but he couldn't.

'Do you know anyone who might have wanted to harm him?' He put up a hand. 'Do not say everyone loved him.'

Chapman looked crestfallen, like a chess master whose opponent had foiled a signature move.

He shrugged. He said he didn't know.

'You know what I think, Mr Chapman? I think you were supplying Mr Grimes with prohibited narcotics and he owed you money and so you did for him.'

24

'I never.'

'It's what it looks like to me. I reckon it would look that way to a jury as well.'

Sweat beaded on Chapman's forehead. He leaned across and whispered to his brief, 'It wasn't me, I swear to God.'

Charlie leaned back, folded his arms. 'Then who was it?'

'He said . . .' Another glance at his solicitor. 'He said the bikers were after him.'

'Which bikers?'

'That lot over Harrow. They're all Poles and fuckers now, half of 'em haven't even got a motorbike. He owed them big time. The few quid he owed me wasn't anything compared.'

'Why did he owe them money?'

'What do you think?'

'I have an open mind.'

'He was on the gear, big time. They wanted their money. He said one of them told him he was going to break his legs if he didn't pay up. That's why he couldn't pay me back my loan, I reckon.' He smiled, finally pleased that he could be helpful.

'Who was it that threatened him?'

Chapman looked at his brief, then back at Charlie. 'If I tell you, can I go home?'

'That depends a lot on you.'

'I know my rights.'

Charlie shook his head and nodded at Garner. 'No, you don't. *He* knows your rights, and he thinks you're going to be in a nice, snug little cell tonight, cuddling up to a big hairy biker with tatts and a beard, just like the one you say did for your mate Grimes. Unless you cooperate.'

Chapman's Adam's apple bobbed in his throat like a cork on a stormy sea. 'Name,' Charlie said.

Garner was in the waiting room with his iPhone on his lap and earbuds in his ears, a fragrant oasis of tranquillity among the chaos. He had a legal pad on the chair next to him, and he was scribbling notes with a silver Parker ballpoint.

'How are you, all right?' Charlie said.

Garner took out his earbuds. 'Hello Charlie. Got another one in five minutes.'

'Hope he smells better than the last one. How's the wife and kids?'

'She's off at her mother's in Bristol. Had the last few days to myself. You must be happy, man.'

'Why's that, then?'

'Your lot barely scraped past Blackpool. Won't do you much good. You're going to get a hiding next round.'

'Get off it. We're going to give your spuds a good walloping.'

'That was nicely done in there. Didn't think you'd get much out of him and I'm his brief.'

'All down to my personal charisma and charm.'

'Yeah, must be that.' He grinned. 'Keep taking the pills, Charlie.'

CHAPTER FIVE

There was a look that his guv'nor sometimes gave him, like everything that went wrong was somehow his fault. 'Look,' Charlie wanted to say, 'this isn't down to me. There's a roster system, I just happen to be up when some of these nastier cases come in.'

He hadn't asked for this one. He would have been much happier with a shooting in Tottenham or a knifing in Brixton. Their run-of-the-mill didn't make the nationals or the nightly news; there was a couple of days of basic if rather tedious watching of CCTV and knocking on doors and it was all sorted.

Blame chance. Blame coincidence. Blame God, if you're of the religious persuasion. Don't blame me, boss. DCI Fergus O'Neal-Callaghan, or FONC as people liked to call him when he wasn't listening, looked at him over the rim of his teacup, and made a face like he'd found an amputated finger in his French fries. 'I blame you, Charlie.'

'Sir?'

'I don't know. You're like one of those blokes the casinos employ to stand next to gamblers on a winning streak and bring them bad luck. What do they call them? Coolies.'

'Coolers. That seems unfair, sir.'

'Harsh but true, Charlie. Go on, then,' he said, 'do your worst.'

'Sir?'

'What have we got?'

Charlie passed some printouts across the desk. 'These are the CCTV captures we have so far.'

The DCI shuffled through them, blurry images of a figure in black, wearing a ski mask. 'He doesn't look like he's in any hurry.'

Charlie passed him a USB. 'He's actually moving quite fast. Just easy on his feet.'

The DCI put the USB into the port on his computer, watched the clip from the CCTV mounted above the gates of the Royal Courts, winced when the shadowy figure jammed the head on the railing. 'Where did the perpetrator come from?'

'We've pieced together this timeline from the CCTV cameras in the area,' Charlie said. He pushed an A4 sheet across the desk, a map of the streets around the Royal Courts, with arrows pointing out the CCTV captures and the times. 'We have vision of a motorcycle entering Star Yard at 3.12 a.m. Two minutes later the figure in the ski mask emerges, wearing a backpack. We have two more captures in Bell Yard, and then the vision of our perpetrator in front of the Royal Courts, impaling the head on the railing, as you saw. He then goes back the same way. At 3.18 a.m., we have further vision of the motorcycle exiting Star Yard heading towards Chancery Lane. Last positive image we have is from an ANPR on High Holborn.'

'Plates?'

Charlie shook his head.

'What about Star Yard. Don't we have any vision?'

Charlie shook his head. 'There's a shop down there, makes wigs and academic robes. They have some major renovations going on – there's a hire cabin parked outside, obscures the vision. He must have known about it, because he parked his motorbike on the other side of it.'

'You said "he". It could be a woman.'

'I somehow can't imagine a woman ripping a bloke's head off and impaling it on a steel fence.'

'Ever been married, Charlie?'

'No, sir.'

'There you are, then. Never mind. Moving along, what have you done to try and trace the motorcycle?'

'I've had the best of the images enhanced and sent them to the Transport boys to have a look at. They should be able to give us the make and model. That will only help us if we can find a suspect.'

'Eyewitnesses?'

'The 999 call came from a Sophie Lyons-Hatton. She and her young friends had been clubbing, they can be seen on the CCTV arriving at the Strand one minute and thirteen seconds after the head was placed on the railing. Unfortunately, they haven't been able to provide very much. They were under the influence of alcohol.'

'Lucky them. So where are you with the investigation right now?'

'We're looking at ANPR, trying to track down the owners of vehicles who were on the Strand around the time of the incident, one of them might have seen something. Wes and Rupe also took a statement from a homeless man who was sleeping in a doorway in Bell Yard.' Charlie referred to his notebook. 'He thought he saw someone run past him a couple of times during the night. Couldn't give us much more than we have from the CCTV, I'm afraid. He also saw Jesus Christ standing on top of the Law Courts, saying he was coming back to Earth next Sunday for the Day of Judgment.'

'Well, it doesn't give you very long, you'd better look busy. Anything else?'

'Yes, sir. There's the note.'

'The note?'

'The pathologist found a bit of paper lodged in the deceased's throat.'

'You've got me on the edge of my seat, Charlie. Come on, what did it say?'

Charlie opened his file and pushed a 6x8 glossy across the desk. The DCI raised both eyebrows. '"This is the reason that you see this man fallen here. I am he who planned this murder and with justice." Is it Shakespeare? I'm sure you'll tell me if I'm wrong.'

'Aeschylus.'

'Never heard of him.'

Charlie thought, but didn't say, it's the Greek classics, didn't they teach you or DS Grey anything while you were being buggered by the prefects in the home room at St Michael's?

'Whoever did this went to a lot of time and trouble. They don't want us to guess the motive, they're giving it to us on a platter.'

'Or a railing.'

Charlie nodded.

'What about the murder scene? You arrested someone outside the deceased's house, I believe.'

'Yes, sir. DS Grey apprehended him.'

'I heard he was quicker on his feet than you.'

'He has an impressive turn of speed.'

'He'll never play for Arsenal, then.' The DCI seemed to think that was funny. 'Good man, that. Have to keep an eye on him.'

Charlie felt a pang that he liked to think wasn't jealousy.

'Get anything out of him?'

'DS Grey?'

'The absconder.'

'His name is Alan Chapman, he has previous for various drug offences.' Charlie pushed a file across the desk. 'He also did serious time for GBH. Apparently, he was involved in a heated argument in May 2013 over an unpaid drug debt, and he hit someone with a house brick. The victim was in a coma for two months.'

'What's his relationship with the deceased?'

'Grimes owed him money.'

'You think this is our Grim Reaper then?'

'He certainly has motive. He was heard making threats to

the deceased on the night he was murdered. I'm holding him on suspicion.'

'Where does he live?'

'He has a flat on the same estate as Grimes. I've got a search warrant, the CS team are there now.'

'But?'

'Unless we find something really damning, I don't think he's our boy.'

'What makes you think that?'

'Whoever did this was organised. I'm sure our Mr Chapman wouldn't shrink from casual violence, as his record shows, but this crime involves a level of planning and premeditation I doubt he's capable of.'

'Let's not be too quick to put a line through him. Have you done house to house?'

'Still working on that, sir.'

'Anything?'

'A couple of Mr Grimes' neighbours thought they heard a motorbike in the early hours of the morning, about the time we believe he was murdered.'

'Does Mr Chapman own a motorbike?'

'No, sir. He did offer up the name of someone else who does. He thinks he may be able to help us further our enquiries.'

'Did he now? That's convenient.'

'His name's Stanislav Podborski. More commonly known as Shovelface. He's not a taxpayer.'

'Go on.'

'We've checked him out and he has form. He's an enforcer for a biker gang. According to our Mr Chapman, the deceased also owed money to Mr Podborksi's associates, for a separate drug debt.'

'Are you going to bring him in?'

Charlie shrugged. 'Bikers don't usually read a lot of Aeschylus. They're more about biting the heads off live chickens than reading the Greek classics.'

'Let's not get too fancy about this, Charlie. You're not Sherlock Holmes. Stick with the facts.' The DCI pushed a pile of newspapers across his desk, the *Sun*, the *Mirror*, the *Telegraph*. 'You've seen these?'

'I read the *i*.'

'We have the eyes of the nation on us, Charlie. Apparently, the case has even made the front pages of newspapers in Australia, and they can barely read comics down there.' He leaned forward. 'The assistant commissioner is taking a personal interest. He has promised us all the resources we need. So let's show him what we can do.' He fixed Charlie with a stare. Am I supposed to be intimidated? Charlie thought.

All you have to do is give me one of those chocolate bourbons in your secret drawer and I'll do anything you ask.

CHAPTER SIX

He didn't say much, Grey. Taciturn. Not like Lovejoy, Charlie thought. He could talk to Lovejoy about anything. Grey, it was like pulling teeth. He didn't like football, he didn't want to talk about his wife or his family, he didn't have a dog, he couldn't even talk about the weather. The drive to Harrow seemed as long as the Dakar Rally.

It wasn't that he actively disliked him. He didn't have homophobic or racist opinions, like Greene. It was just that he was always so fucking intense.

'How are you settling in?' Charlie said, when he couldn't take the silence any longer. 'Do you like being part of the team?'

'Yes, sir. Very much.'

Sir, Charlie thought. Not 'guv' or 'guv'nor' like everyone else.

'The DCI seems to like you,' Charlie said.

'Does he, sir?'

'Especially impressed with the way you rugby tackled Mr Chapman. So was I, by the way.'

'I've caught blokes faster than him. Chapman is never going to play on the wing for England.'

'I can see why you were good at rugby.'

'Not that good, or I wouldn't be a copper.'

'Well, you're a better failure than I was, then. No one would have ever mistaken me for a good football player.'

He thought that might get at least a smile. No, nothing.

He gave up. They drove the rest of the way in silence.

***

33

Podborski didn't live in what Charlie would have called a biker-friendly area. It was relentlessly suburban. All the front gardens had been paved in so people could park their Ford Fiestas off the street. A shame. England must have been a pretty place, once, Charlie thought. Well, outside of Hackney; he couldn't imagine Hackney had ever been pretty, even in the Stone Age.

Podborski's entire street had bay windows and porches, the only way you could tell the houses apart was the colour of the wheelie bins. He got out, clocked the motorbike in the front yard. Then he went up the front path, knocked and took out his warrant card.

In Charlie's experience, bikers came in two types: your bog standard, wearing leather cut-offs and faded Levi's, sporting a big gut, rat-tail and cottony beard; and your cutting edge, dressed for court, they might have passed for errant bankers.

Podborski was from the first variety; his head looked like a bowling ball with a beard.

'You must be Mr Podborski.'

Podborski took a long look at their warrant cards.

'Not going to invite us in for a cup of tea, then?'

'What you want?' He talked slow, with a strong Eastern European accent.

'I am Detective Inspector George, this is Detective Sergeant Grey. May we have a word?'

'What about?'

'We're investigating a homicide. A *murder*.'

Podborski pretended to think about it. 'Not murdered anyone for months.'

That was good, Charlie thought. He liked a bloke with a dry sense of humour. They were going to get on famous. 'Look, I'm not going to stand out here all day like an encyclopaedia sales-man. Can we come in or do you want to come down the station house and we can do this formal?'

Podborski sighed and went back into the house. He left the door open. 'Delightful,' Charlie said, and went in.

There was a large front room, empty except for a pool table and a plywood bar with a Jack Daniel's sign hung on the wall behind it. They passed a bedroom. Through the half-open door Charlie clocked a mattress on the floor and a mess of sheets on top of it.

They followed Podborski into the back room. There was a stained velour sofa and a plasma television bigger than Charlie's kitchen. One wall was entirely taken up by a stuffed moose head and several samurai swords.

Podborski threw himself onto the sofa. Charlie looked around. There was nowhere else to sit, unless he wanted to hunker down next to him. He didn't fancy it much.

'Love what you've done with this place,' Charlie said.

'You are very funny man.'

'Thank you. Hard to get by in life without a sense of humour. Nice sword collection. Are they legal?'

'Yes, legal. Handmade, using traditional method. I import from Japan.'

'Ever used one?'

'What do you think?'

'Where were you last night between midnight and four a.m.?'

Podborski took his iPhone out of his leather waistcoat and made a show of going through it. 'What date we are today?'

'The first,' Charlie said.

He pointed to the calendar function on the screen. 'Day of Dead in Mexico.'

'Bank holiday in Cancun,' Charlie said. 'We should have it here.'

'Where were you last night?' Grey said.

'Last night? Maybe I was here. I am sleeping, you know.'

'Can anyone verify that?'

'Three girl. I don't know their name. Never seen them before. They all gone home now.'

'So you don't have an alibi,' Grey said, sounding testy.

35

No, don't lose your beans, Charlie thought. He's only playing with us. We've got plenty of time if we want to get serious with him.

'Why do I need alibi?'

'What do you do for a living?' Charlie said. 'You know, job. Do you have one?'

'I am businessman.'

'And what line of business would that be?'

'I help people, you know, with cash flow.'

'Debt recovery.'

'Yes. See, you understand. You are very smart fellow.'

'Thank you,' Charlie said, brightly. 'It's good to be appreciated sometimes. Do you know a Michael Grimes?'

A shake of the head.

'He had a lot of debts. At least, that's what his friends say.'

'I do not know this person.'

'One of Mr Grimes' associates says you do know him, and has given us a statement to that effect. He says you were round there all the time. So we spoke to some of the neighbours and one of them said she heard you a couple of nights ago, kicking Mr Grimes' back door in and shouting at him that you were going to –' Charlie took out his notebook, '– "rip his balls off and feed them to your dog". Do you have a dog?'

A nod. Charlie looked out the window. There was a mastiff, chained to a post in the back yard. 'He looks well fed.'

'Testicles. They have very lot of protein.'

Charlie liked that one and laughed along.

'What this is about?' Podborski said.

'It's about this man you don't know, Grimes.'

'Look, whatever this guy say to you, I never touch him.'

'You're on remand, aren't you?' Grey said.

'What is this remand?'

'You're on bail awaiting trial. Grievous bodily harm.'

'Was not me. They cannot prove.'

Charlie looked at Grey. 'How easy would it be, do you think,

36

to have Mr Podborski's bail conditions revoked?'

Grey fixed Podborski with a stare. 'Very easy.'

'You know what I think, Matt? I think he did it. We should call him a brief.' Charlie took out his phone. 'Do you have a brief, Mr Podborski? I'll get one for you, he can be at the station by the time we get there, save everyone a bit of time.'

'What you talking? I don't do nothing.' He jumped to his feet. Grey had been leaning against the wall. He pushed himself away and stood loose-limbed, up for it. That's it, Charlie thought. I like that in a copper. Bit of old school.

When Charlie and his sergeant didn't back off, Podborski cooled down a bit.

'It's like this,' Charlie said. 'Mr Grimes was found dead this morning. No great loss to the world, I appreciate, but murder is still illegal in this country last time I checked. So, how about you cooperate with us?'

'What are you saying, dead?'

'You know, as in no longer alive. How many other ways can you be dead?'

'Cannot be dead. He owe us money.'

'Us?'

'Me and my associates.'

'Ah, so you do know him. You know, a lot of people are mourning his passing today, just like you are. Maybe he'll remember you and your mates in his will.'

'You think I kill him?'

'Did you?'

'What for? Guy owe you money, you chop a finger, maybe some toe. You don't kill, is bad business.'

'Well, that's all very interesting, Mr Podborski, but I'll tell you the way this works. I need to bang someone up for this and you look like a likely young lad. Now, are you going to help us or do I have to read you your rights?'

Podborski lost all his belligerence. He slumped back onto the sofa.

'Where were you last night between midnight and four a.m.?'

'I was at clubhouse.'

'Which is where?'

'Slough.'

'Lovely. That's where they make the Mars Bars, innit? I suppose the local chapter will vouch for you. What time did you get home?'

'Two. Maybe three.'

Charlie tossed him his notebook. 'Write down which route you took, we'll reference it against ANPR. I also want the names of any of your associates who are prepared to give you an alibi for last night.'

Podborski clutched the pen and paper and did as he was told.

They got back in the car and Grey started the engine. 'What do you think?' Charlie said.

'He could have used one of those swords. They're the real deal, you could take someone's head off with one of those, easy.'

'What about the note?'

'Warning to others?'

'Too poetic. The bloke can barely speak English, he's not going to go around quoting ancient Greek playwrights.'

'So, what are we thinking?'

'We're thinking the answer to our little conundrum lies somewhere in our Mr Grimes' murky past. We've followed the obvious leads. Now it's time to look for some avenues of enquiry that aren't quite so obvious. Let's get back and do a bit of digging.'

DAY 2

CHAPTER SEVEN

'Well, you look like shit,' Jack said.

Charlie sat up, looked at his watch. Half past six. He'd slept in, not easy having a lie-in in a camp bed in your own nick. He ached all over. He swung his legs out of the cot, groaned as he got to his feet, and stretched. He'd only meant to sleep for three hours. Four felt like self-indulgence.

'Want coffee?' Jack said and held out a jumbo plastic cup.

'I'm dreaming this, right?'

'Jumbo flat white with a double shot.'

'Where did you get that this time of the morning?'

'Little place I know, they're not open yet but they serve me out the back door – I'm a regular. Thought you'd need cheering up.'

'I was going through witness statements and staring at CCTV files until one in the morning.'

'Wish I could be your little ray of sunshine today, but I fear I am another dark cloud.'

Charlie looked at the forensics report Jack had in his hand. 'That bad?'

'I know you were hoping for more.' Jack threw it on the desk and took a seat. 'This is only the interim report, mind.'

Charlie flicked through the pages, trying to focus.

'Didn't find anything on the Strand,' Jack said, 'didn't think we would. We found some fibres in the deceased's hair, but they came from a towel in his bathroom.'

'What about his flat?'

'Still waiting on results but don't hold your breath. It'll take us a while to identify all the prints we found, he wasn't exactly Mr Sheen.'

'What about footprints? There has to be something.' Charlie pored through the report, looking for something that afforded hope. 'Blood spatter?'

'Spray pattern up the wall facing away from the window. Looks like the deceased didn't even hear the intruder come in. Grabbed him from behind halfway through his beans on toast and did the deed. The pattern indicates the deceased was leaning back, like this.' Jack mimed it, to demonstrate the point. 'We found spatter on the ceiling near the light fixture.'

'Anything else?'

'Couple of fresh grooves in the floor, looked to me like they were made by a sharp blade. There was blood and tissue embedded in the linoleum. That must have been where the perpetrator hacked his head off.'

'Christ Almighty. And then he put it in a bag and took it to the Law Courts. Who does shit like that?'

'One shred of hope on this dark November morning. We found a fragment of metal embedded in the linoleum. It's still in the lab being analysed, but it's a fragment of the blade from the weapon used in the assault. If you can find the knife, we should be able to match it.'

'I suppose that's something,' Charlie said.

'Sorry I couldn't be more help. This isn't *CSI* where they find a microbe peculiar to someone's unique biome and clone it into a perfect suspect. Whoever did this was careful.'

'Thanks for the coffee,' Charlie said.

'Chin up,' Jack said as he left. He didn't say, 'because you're going to need to', but it was implied.

CHAPTER EIGHT

Most of the team were in the office and on the phone or at their monitors by seven o'clock. DC Sanderson was the only notable absentee. 'He called in ten minutes ago,' Greene said. 'Said he's running late.'

'He's supposed to be coming with me to the post-mortem, he's the evidence officer.'

'I'll come,' Greene said. 'Wouldn't mind getting out of the office for a bit.'

'All right,' Charlie said, 'but no jokes. This new pathologist, Middleton, he's got no sense of humour. Know what I mean?'

'Don't worry about it,' Greene said.

Charlie let Greene drive, hoped he wouldn't run over any old ladies on zebra crossings, and looked out of the window, watching the world go by. The world; that would always wipe the smile off anyone's face, especially when you had to look at it from London. He clocked a filthy blanket in the doorway of a Boots chemist, all the depressing Starbucks and Tesco and Costa Coffee signs. This whole city was a franchise now. No matter where you were in London, you were always in the same street.

'So, how's life treating you, guv?' Greene said.

'All right,' Charlie said.

'The Arsenal are winning, I see.'

'Since when have you been interested in football?'

'I've got Sky.'

'For the cartoons, right?'

43

'I watch the sports sometimes. If your lot are playing, I always have a close look, see if I can spot you in the crowd, with your scarf and your little red and white beanie.'

'You're getting football mixed up with *Where's Wally?*'

'Getting plenty?'

'Let me run through something here, Jay. What's your rank again?'

'Sergeant.'

'And I am?'

'Inspector.'

'So, one, mind your rank, and two, mind your own business.'

'Only I heard you had a new girlfriend. Real looker.'

'Who told you that?'

'People talk. Round the office, like. When you're out.'

'Well, don't. Watch where you're going, Greene. You just cut off that bloke on a bike.'

'I didn't see anything.'

'My point. Now concentrate on your driving and let's get there without adding to Professor Middleton's workload. And remember—'

'No jokes. I got it, guv.'

The Iain West Forensic Suite was an extension to the Westminster Public Mortuary on the Horseferry Road, near Victoria Station. Professor Middleton was waiting for them outside one of the autopsy rooms. When he saw Charlie and DS Greene walking towards him, he looked at his wrist and tapped his watch. 'You're late.'

'Only three minutes,' Charlie said.

'Go without oxygen for three minutes, inspector, and then tell me it's not a long time.' He handed him a file. 'The post-mortem results.'

'You matched the head to the right body?' Greene said.

Middleton gave him a hard stare. 'Your senior officer may not have informed you, but I don't do jokes.'

'Sorry, professor,' Greene said.

44

Charlie tucked the report under his arm but didn't look at it. Middleton would tell him everything he needed to know.

'The initial wound was made with a sharp blade in a lateral motion. It's consistent with someone standing behind the victim and holding the knife to the throat. I would hazard that the assailant was taller than the victim. The initial injury started below the ear at the upper third of the neck and ran downward and medially, with severance of the left carotid artery. The wound ran straight across the midline of the neck, and ended on the opposite side, lower than its point of origination. The right-sided end of the injury was at the mid third of the neck with a tail abrasion. This indicates that the assailant was right-handed. There were no other injuries, including hesitant cuts or defence injuries. Lungs showed aspiration of blood. The initial wound severed both carotid vessels, unconsciousness would have followed very rapidly due to a catastrophic fall of intracranial perfusion leading to brain ischaemia.'

'That was enough to cut his head off?'

Middleton shook his head. 'In my view, decapitation occurred post-mortem. The blows that severed the cervical vertebrae and the larynx came while the victim was supine. It takes quite a lot of force, you know. That the third cervical vertebra was fragmented suggests a heavy downward blow. A chopping motion, if you like.' He pantomimed for them what he thought had happened, an assailant approaching Grimes from behind, delivering the first and fatal wound to the neck, then leaning or kneeling over the body to deliver secondary blows forceful enough to decapitate the head.

'Thanks, professor,' Charlie said.

'Of course, all of that assumes I managed to match the body to the right head,' he said, 'Like Cinderella.' He smiled at Greene and walked away.

'Bastard,' Greene muttered, under his breath.

CHAPTER NINE

Someone had left a copy of one of the dailies lying on his desk. There was a picture of the Law Courts splashed all over the front page; it had caught the public imagination this one. Perhaps it was a good thing, he told himself, lots of publicity meant lots of calls on the hotline.

It wasn't every day that someone planted a head on a spiked fence in London, though he supposed it was only a matter of time before it caught on. A couple more referendums should do it.

But these questions had been burning him and everyone involved in the investigation for the last twenty-four hours: why did they do it? Why the Royal Courts? They had interviewed Chapman and Podborski, it would have been negligent not to. But he'd never really thought either of them would turn into prime suspects. The pertinent question remained: if someone hated Grimes enough to kill him, why not just do it.

Why all the stuffing about, sticking his head on a spike on the Strand? What was the reward for the additional risks?

Charlie put his takeaway coffee on the desk and sat down. There was a knock. Parminder from Intel put her head around the door. 'Got a minute, guv?'

'Come in, Parm. Hope you've got something interesting for me.'

She put a printout on the desk. 'This was posted on Facebook a few minutes after you left this morning. It's been taken down now, but every journalist in the world must have seen it.'

Charlie stared at it. It was a high-quality image of Grimes' head, with blood leaking down the railings. It looked to have been taken from the other side of the Strand, but the appalling image was in sharp focus; death-glazed eyes, a gaping mouth, blood-smeared teeth. It was almost as if it had been posed. It had an eerie beauty, with the blurred lights of a passing car in the foreground, the floodlit Gothic arches of the Law Courts behind.

'It appeared on a Facebook page called Cry Justice,' Parminder said. 'The page had been set up two days ago and all there was on it was a picture of the Royal Courts and the same quotation from that Greek poet we found in Grimes' mouth.'

'Dramatist,' Charlie said. 'He wasn't a poet, he was a dramatist. What's happened to the Facebook account?'

'As soon as we were aware of it, we had it closed down.'

'Do we know who posted this?'

'Our people in Lambeth are trying to trace the IP address, but they say it's going to be very difficult, if not impossible. Whoever did this used a Wi-Fi connection with a Tor exit node.'

'I'll pretend I understand what you just said and take that as a "no",' Charlie said. 'When was this taken?'

Parm put another printout on the desk, a block of thumbnail image captures from the CCTV at the Law Courts, with handwritten notes down the margin indicating the progression of events. 'We know from CCTV that the head was placed in situ at 03.15.23. We have vision of Sophie and her group approaching the head at 03.17.08. There is no blurring of the footpath in the photograph, which would indicate pedestrians, so it has to be between those times. The quality of the image indicates a camera capable of low ISO values and a lens of f/4 or less. The shutter speed would have been at least ten seconds. Also, there's no metadata.'

'An SLR,' Charlie said, 'not a mobile camera, then?'

'Someone was standing on the other side of the Strand with a tripod-mounted camera to get a shot like that. They used a delayed exposure. You can see the shadow of a car driving past in the foreground.'

Charlie thought about Jack and his CS team, wondered if they were still at the scene. If they'd opened the footpath on the other side of the Strand, it would be too late to capture any forensics the photographer might have left behind.

'Someone impaled Grimes' head on the railing, then ran across the road, set up a camera, took a photograph, then went home?'

'They must have an accomplice.'

'A killer with a media director. That's something new. How long was this up for?'

'It was online for less than two hours, but it was shared thousands of times. All the major news agencies were alerted via the hashtags. You can still find the photograph on Google if you know where to look. Whoever did this wanted to make sure we weren't able to keep the reason for Grimes' murder out of the media.'

Right, Charlie thought. Not the greatest of news, but at last we're getting somewhere. Parm was holding another manila folder, he could see by the look on her face that she'd left the best for last. She was trying not to show it, but she was excited.

'You finished the full background check on Grimes?'

She put the file on the desk, turned it around and opened it. Charlie found himself staring at a photocopied page from one of the national dailies. The date was 21 May 2014.

WHAT PRICE A LIFE?

Underneath, there was a photograph of a four-year-old girl, pictured with her parents, taken on a beach somewhere. Beside it, there was another photograph, of the girl's father wearing an army uniform.

He skimmed down the page:

The parents of a young girl killed while sitting in a parked car by a drunk driver have said that the sentence handed down to 34-year-old Michael Grimes is 'laughable'.

They are calling for his jail sentence to be reviewed.

Grimes was already banned from driving for life when he was involved in the crash. He was yesterday sentenced to eight years in jail, but is likely to be released on licence in less than half that time.

Charlie reached for his coffee. It was cold. He drank it anyway. Parm handed him the police report on the accident. Charlie read it through quickly. Zoë Miller and her mother had been parked at the side of the road when Grimes' car hit them. Zoë was strapped in to a booster seat in the back. Mrs Miller had got out of the car to take her out of the vehicle. Grimes had recorded a blood alcohol reading of .124 at the scene, and toxicology tests later found traces of methamphetamine in his system. Traffic estimated his speed at somewhere between fifty and sixty miles per hour in a thirty miles-per-hour zone.

The car had been stolen from a car park in Barnet about an hour before. The report said he'd run from the scene and had been detained two hours later at a house in Camden. He had been released from prison for drug offences a month before the crash.

Charlie reached for the other file. 'Is this his rap sheet?' he said.

Parminder nodded. Charlie opened it. The document was over forty pages long.

'A pillar of the community. What was the little girl's name again?'

'Zoë.'

'Did Zoë die straight away?'

'She was in a coma for two weeks. She didn't regain consciousness. The doctors finally declared her brain dead and she was taken off life support.'

49

'What about Mrs Miller?'

'She was treated for serious injuries to her pelvis and spine, as well as an open fracture of the femur in her right leg. She almost lost her right arm. She was in hospital for five weeks.'

'It says here she still has psychological counselling.' He put the file down. 'How long ago did Grimes get out of stir?'

'Six months, guv.'

Finally, it's all starting to make sense, Charlie thought.

Parminder tapped an index finger on the file. 'He pleaded guilty to eight offences; aggravated dangerous driving causing death, four counts of aggravated dangerous driving causing grievous bodily harm, two counts of aggravated dangerous driving causing bodily harm, and failing to stop and provide assistance.'

'What did the judge say about that?'

'He told him that he hoped he would learn how to live in society while behind bars. He was given a seven-and-a-half-year sentence, backdated for time already served. He was eligible for parole two years before the end of his sentence.'

'So how long did he get for killing a little girl? I'm no good at sums. What was the bottom line?'

'Four years.'

Charlie fiddled with the Met police paperweight on his desk. He would have liked to have something to throw it at. Made him angry this job; the minute he thought he was jaded enough to just come to work and get on with things and not let them bother him, along came another Zoë Miller.

'What about dad?'

'Thomas Miller was with Special Forces in Afghanistan when the incident happened.'

'Did they fly him home?'

'They couldn't.'

'Couldn't?'

'Not straight away. He was in a field hospital. He only found out about the accident after his daughter was taken off the respirator. He was in a medically induced coma at the time. He had been wounded by an IED in Helmand province the day before the car accident. Ended up losing both his legs.'

'Oh, fuck me. This gets better and better.'

Charlie stood up, put his hands in his pockets, went to the window. He parted the blinds and stared at the rain beading on the window.

'Tell me about the Millers,' he said.

She flicked through the file. 'Tom Miller, born 1983, Bromley. No immediate family. No siblings, parents are both dead. Wife is Jennifer Miller, born 1985; she has two sisters, Margaret, born in 1988, and Tracy, 1990. Tracy is a constable with a CO19 squad based at Heathrow. Margaret is in the Guards. She's based in Aldershot, recently returned from a tour in Afghanistan. Jennifer's brother is Gordon Lennox – he was in the same SAS squadron as Tom. He's the oldest, born 1984.'

His iPhone rang on his desk. He picked up.

'I want to suck your cock.'

A quick glance up at Parm. 'Who's calling?'

'South Kensington CID.'

'Very funny. If you'd said West End I might have believed you.'

'What time will you be home tonight?'

'Late.'

'Perfect. I'll be waiting. Bring wood.' She hung up.

'Thanks, Fi. Yep, see you later then. You have a good day, too.' He put the phone down.

'Anything else?' Parm said.

'That should be it for now. Tell DS Greene to get everyone together. I think we finally have a clear focus for the investigation.'

'Yes, guv.' She got up to leave. 'Was that your girlfriend?'

'Hmm,' Charlie said, reaching for his jacket.

'She sounds nice,' Parm said, and walked out.

CHAPTER TEN

Charlie stared at the whiteboard, at the photograph of their early suspect, Alan Chapman. He tore it down, crumpled it in his fist and threw it in the waste bin. He had never really been convinced it was him. He was sure he had it in him to murder someone, but putting their head on a spike outside the Royal Courts? That required imagination.

That left Podborski, on bail with a GBH trial hanging over his head, and an extensive Samurai sword collection. A debt collector for a biker gang certainly wouldn't blanch at murdering a scrote like Grimes. But what would be the point of sticking the geezer's head on a railing? That made no kind of sense.

The team gathered round and he brought them up to date.

He tapped a link on his iPad. 'For those of you who have missed the finer details, this is what we have. Between twelve and three a.m. yesterday morning, someone broke into the flat of a thirty-four-year-old IC1 male, Michael Richard Grimes. He had a standard Yale lock on the door, so it wasn't hard to gain entrance. The pathologist's report says he was held from behind and his throat was severed, using a bladed instrument. The initial wound was so deep it severed the larynx and trachea and all the major blood vessels. Death from exsanguination would have been almost instantaneous. When he was supine on the floor, the assailant decapitated him. Parts of the metal blade were found embedded in the linoleum floor and will provide us with a match if we can find the murder weapon. The attacker then transported the head to the Strand where it was found in situ at 3.17 a.m.'

Charlie tapped another link on his iPad and footage from the Royal Courts CCTV cameras appeared on the screen behind him.

They saw a shadowy figure appear on the left of the frame as the digital clock ticked over in the other corner. The figure was dressed in black and wearing what appeared to be a ski mask. They retrieved something from their backpack and placed it firmly on top of the railings and then ran off. The entire action lasted less than ten seconds.

There was a beat, and then McCullough, Lubanski's partner, said: 'That is one of the most disgusting things I have ever seen in my life.'

'What about the two suspects who were heard shouting threats at Grimes?' James asked.

'Alan Chapman does have form and he does not have an alibi. However, I cannot believe he has the abilities, mentally or physically, to commit a crime such as this. He is also six foot three inches tall with the physical attributes of a kebab stick. He is not the individual in that CCTV footage.'

'Did we check out the alibi for Shovelhead, or whatever his name is,' James said.

'The guv'nor sent us out to Slough for that, all expenses paid,' Lubanksi said. 'His hairy mates said he was with them drinking shandies and eating crisps until three in the morning.'

'Even better,' Charlie said, 'we checked the registration of his motorcycle on ANPR. He was recorded by a camera on the M1 at 3.41 a.m., which puts him in the clear. Parm, will you share with everyone the latest intel?'

Parminder stepped in and ran through everything she'd told Charlie earlier that morning, together with images of the Cry Justice Facebook page, then scans of the various newspaper headlines from 2014, and transcripts from the trial, Regina vs Michael Richard Grimes. She then went through Tom Miller's service record as well as his wife's medical history since the accident.

When she'd finished, there was a long silence. Charlie tried to read the mood in the room. He had never seen his team so subdued.

'They're practically telling us they did it,' Singh said.

'He's in a wheelchair,' McCullough said. 'He couldn't have done.'

'Let me get this straight,' James said. 'These people, they lose their kid to this waste of oxygen Grimes, the system lets them down, so someone else sorts it for them. Now we have to step in and clean up the mess the courts left behind. Not sure if I want to do much overtime on this.'

'We have a job to do,' Grey said. 'If everyone starts taking the law into their own hands, we might as well all go back to the . . .' Charlie knew he was about to say 'jungle'. Didn't mean anything by it, more than like, but he should think before he opened his mouth.

James glared at him. 'Careful, sergeant.'

Charlie put a hand on James's shoulder. 'Wes, I think DS Grey was making a philosophical point. Admittedly, he didn't do it the best way.'

'No, he's stealing my best lines,' Greene said, who seemed to think it was funny.

Charlie ignored Greene, focused on James, who had pushed his chair back from his desk, looking edgy. 'Look, I think DS Grey was trying to say that we are here to uphold law and order, whether we agree with it or not. And Wes, you were saying that in this case the forces of law and order have got it proper wrong. See, you both have made your point and, as it happens, I agree with both of you. Let's leave it there, fellas.'

'So do we have a main suspect?' Lovejoy said, parachuting in, trying to rescue the situation.

'As yet, no. But it seems evident that our focus now has to be on the Miller family and their close associates. I'm going to interview Tom Miller and his wife now. He has a sister-in-law, Tracy Lennox, who happens to be a proud member of the

Metropolitan Police Force, same as us. Her sister, Margaret, better known as Meg, is in the army, based at Aldershot, and her brother, Gordon Lennox, was also in the SAS. Finding these people and either implicating or eliminating them from the inquiry is now our priority. We have to know everything there is to know about Tom Miller by the end of the day, who his mates were in the army and who he hangs out with in civilian life. Same with his wife. Lovejoy, you come with me; Sergeant Grey, you and Sanderson find Tracy Lennox. The rest of you, DS Greene will action you all your jobs for the day. We'll hold evening prayers at six o'clock. Questions? No? Right, let's crack on.'

Charlie clocked some people queuing at a bus stop, they all looked like they were waiting for the firing squad. A woman tried to hold down her coat while she battled with her umbrella, which had turned itself inside out in the cold November wind. A cyclist hurled a string of abuse at a lorry driver who casually gave him the finger. London, in all its glory.

'What did you think about what happened at the briefing this morning?' Charlie said to Lovejoy.

'You mean Wes and DS Grey?'

'Yeah, that.'

'Well, to start, I don't think DS Grey's a racist.'

'Neither do I. But I think Wes was right to be pissed off.'

'He's like that, isn't he? Sergeant Grey. A bit tone deaf. He's definitely by the book.'

'We're all supposed to be by the book.'

'But not all of us are, though. Are we?'

They turned into the Strand, by the RAF church. The CS team had cleared up and gone home; they'd even got the painters in to fix up the railing where they'd found Mick on a Stick, as Greene had now unofficially dubbed the operation. It disturbed him, a bit, how his team dealt with this sort of thing. Would sound callous to outsiders, he supposed. But the truth of it was, Grimes wasn't a true victim. Charlie had seen his file. He didn't deserve their tears.

The spot had become a tourist attraction already. A squealing group of Korean tourists were lining up, waiting their turn to have a selfie in front of the railing spike. It looked like platform 9¾ at King's Cross station.

Charlie got out the beacon, slapped it on the roof, and told Lovejoy to park on the double yellow lines. He got out, ran across the Strand to a half-timbered pub, The George. He stood under the porch, looked back across the road at the Royal Courts, pulled out the printout of the Facebook page Parm had given him, unfolded it. The photograph must have been taken right about here.

No one would have seen them in the shadows at night. They knew what they were doing all right, must have planned this like a military operation. This wasn't murder.

This was theatre.

CHAPTER ELEVEN

The Millers lived in a Victorian terrace, not far from the Westfield. There was a ramp up to the front door. Charlie took a deep breath and knocked.

A woman opened the door, leaning on a cane. His first thought was that she hadn't washed her hair since punk music; she wore a shapeless jumper and a long skirt that looked like it came from a Primark sale. But it was her eyes that bothered him most. So much pain. It hurt to look into them.

'Jennifer Miller?'

He got this look, maybe it wouldn't have sunk ships, but it might have bent a few propellers. 'Who wants to know?'

Jennifer Miller was thirty-five according to her file, but she looked twenty years older, just worn out with life. There were lines on her that shouldn't have been on a young woman's face.

He showed her his warrant card. 'DI Charlie George, this is DC Lesley Lovejoy. Might we have a word?'

'What about?'

'We want to talk to you about Michael Grimes.'

She didn't seem surprised.

'Can we come in?' he said.

She shrugged, turned away and went back inside. Charlie waited a moment, then followed. He heard her shout: 'Tom, it's the cops. I owe you a fiver.'

Tom Miller was a triple amputee; he had a prosthesis on his right arm but if he had them for his legs, Charlie couldn't see them. He was sitting in his wheelchair, watching the morning news. He was wearing grey tracksuit pants and a black Metallica T-shirt. The handlebar moustache gave him a mean look. Charlie supposed it was meant to.

'There you are,' he said, his eyes still on the screen. 'I bet her five quid you'd be round this morning. She said you'd have the decency to wait until tomorrow before you started hassling me. I said, no, they couldn't give a toss about decency.'

'Well, at least I earned you a fiver,' Charlie said.

Lovejoy held out her right hand, habit. Tom Miller held out his left. Lovejoy fumbled a handshake. Tom didn't even look at her, kept his eyes on Charlie. 'If you've come to tell us the good news, you're a little late. It's all over the news.'

'I thought you'd be pleased.'

'I'm fucking over the moon. What do you expect? Want a seat, do you?'

Lovejoy flopped onto a tatty brown sofa and almost disappeared. It had the consistency of jelly. Charlie decided to stay on his feet. Jennifer Miller had lit a cigarette, was standing by the fireplace, giving him the evil eye.

Charlie glanced at the framed photographs on the mantelpiece, soldiers in combat gear in a desert somewhere, leaning against a camouflaged Humvee.

'You were SAS,' Charlie said.

'Two tours of Helmand. Best years of my life.'

'What happened?' Lovejoy said.

Tom rubbed at a small scab on his jaw. 'Cut myself shaving.'

'What I meant was . . .'

'He knows what you meant,' Charlie said.

Tom turned and looked at her for the first time. 'IED. You know what that is?'

'Not really.'

'Improvised explosive device. The Taliban use them all the time. The one I found, they buried it near a wall, outside this village. Some fucking raghead waited until I was almost on top of it, then set it off. They use mobile phones. Modern technology, it's brilliant, isn't it?'

'You're lucky to be alive,' Lovejoy said, and Charlie sort of wished she hadn't.

'Yeah, God was really smiling on me that day.' He turned to Charlie. 'Two blokes crawled a hundred metres over open ground with the Taliban firing at them from three sides to bring me back. Never even got a citation for it.'

'You didn't come here to hear war stories,' Jennifer said.

The look on her face. Hard as a frozen chicken. Still, he supposed, the things she'd seen, what she'd been through, she had the right.

'No, you're right,' Charlie said. 'That's not why we're here.'

'Did he suffer?' Tom said. 'Grimes.'

'Hard to say.'

'I'd like to think he suffered,' Jennifer said.

'Any signs of torture?' Tom said.

'I'm not at liberty to tell you that, Mr Miller,' Charlie said.

'See, thing is, if I was involved, there would have been a lot of that. I would have slowly pared him back with nail scissors, starting from his toes. If it was quick, it had nothing to do with me.'

'Stop yapping and give the bloke a chance,' Jennifer said. 'He wants to ask us questions. Don't you, inspector?'

'It's routine,' Charlie said. 'We need to eliminate you both from our investigation.'

'Do you?' Jennifer said. 'Why would you want to do that?'

'Look, Mrs Miller, this is my job. I may not like it, but I am going to do it anyway. An individual has been murdered in his own home, and I am charged with finding the person or persons responsible. Now, at his trial—'

'Four years, he did, in the end,' Tom said. 'Four years for killing my little girl and almost killing my wife.'

'Yes, I read about that in his file.'

'Did you? Well, that's good, if you read all about it, then

59

you'll understand the pain and anger we feel. I won't have to try and describe it to you.' He looked at his wife. 'Show him.'

Jennifer Miller pulled up her jumper. A scar arced from below her navel to her ribs. It had hardened into a raised, white cicatrice. Then she lifted up her fringe so Charlie and Lovejoy could see another scar, this one extended from just above her eyebrow and disappeared into the hairline at her temple. 'Three operations and one hundred and twelve stitches later, they saved her life,' Tom said. 'She was still in a coma when they turned off our daughter's life support.'

Charlie didn't look away. 'If that was me, I think I would have wanted to kill him.'

'Fucking right, we did.'

'Did you?'

'Yeah. I chased him down the street in my wheelchair and battered him to death with my prosthesis. Anything else you want to know?'

There was a retriever beside the chair, every now and then Tom reached down and stroked his ears.

'Nice dog,' Charlie said.

'His name's Joe. After my best mate.'

'One of the blokes that saved your life?'

'As it happens, yeah. A real racing snake, Joe. Lean and very fucking mean. A good laugh when you were out for a drink but when shit went down, he was as cold and collected as they come.' Tom put his hand over the side of the chair and Joe sat up and let him scratch the back of his head, leaning in. 'This Joe saved my life, too, but in a different way. When I came out of the hospital, I was so bloody angry at the world, wouldn't let anyone get close to me. But somehow you let dogs in to places where you won't let people. He's my best mate, now. Aren't you, Joey?' Tom looked up at Charlie. 'You'd have seen some things in your time, right? Murder squad.'

'I've seen a bit.'

'Ever seen anyone with their limbs blown off? No? I didn't

bleed as much as you'd think. I looked down, the blood was just sort of oozing. But you can still lose enough to go into shock and die. That's what should have happened to me. I mean, I was lying out there, in the open, helpless. But Joe and Big Gordie, they wouldn't leave me. Otherwise I wouldn't be here.'

'Who's Gordie?' Lovejoy said.

'My brother,' Jennifer said. 'I'm sure he's on your list.'

'What happened to Joe?' Charlie said.

'Topped himself six months ago,' Tom said. 'He couldn't handle civvy life. That and the nightmares, I suppose. Happens a lot. I've lost more mates since I've been back than I did when I was there.'

'How did he die?'

'Threw himself off a cliff. He loved all that jumping out of planes, suppose he decided to try it one last time, only without a parachute. See what it felt like.'

'What do you reckon it felt like?'

'A relief, probably.'

Interesting answer, Charlie thought. 'Where were you on Thursday night?'

'I was here, watching Netflix, like I always am.'

'Mrs Miller?'

Before she could answer, Tom said: 'She was here with me. Weren't you, love?'

'I was here watching Netflix,' she said, deadpan. 'With him.'

There was an inch of ash on the end of her cigarette. Her hands were shaking. Don't let the ash go on the carpet, Charlie thought. Flick it in the ashtray.

It fell on the carpet. She ignored it.

'Want to see a picture?' she said. 'Of Zoë?'

Charlie didn't want to see a picture of Zoë. He'd already seen a picture of her in the newspaper in Grimes' file and seeing another one of her was only going to make his job harder, but he didn't see how he could say no.

'All right,' he said.

61

There was a nest of photographs on the stand in the hallway, like a shrine, he had clocked it when he came in. Now Jennifer went through the photographs for him, one by one: *this is Zoë when she learned to walk; this is Zoë's second birthday party; this is Zoë in the hospital, the day before they turned off the machine.*

'You know, people say, even if he had got the death penalty it wouldn't have brought Zoë back, wouldn't have made things better. But they're so wrong. See, that's what judges and parole boards and do-gooders don't understand. Knowing that piece of filth was walking around free again, that made the grief so much worse. When you let someone like that go, you crucify us all over again.'

Not me, Charlie wanted to say. I wasn't the one who let him off easy.

'Did you read what he did?' Jennifer said.

'Yes, Mrs Miller. It was all in the file.'

'Sixty miles an hour they reckon he was going. Down the high street. He was out of his head on some shit. I'd got out of the car, I was leaning in the back to get Zoë and I heard this noise, not brakes, I don't think he even tried to stop, he still had his foot on the accelerator, so the cops reckoned. There was this roar, and last thing I remember was looking up and seeing this . . . shape. It was an SUV, the car he'd stolen, and I only had this little hatch thing. I got thrown across the pavement into a wall. But Zoë was trapped inside the car. Took the fire brigade almost an hour to get her out. She was conscious some of that time. People at the trial said they could hear her screaming.'

Charlie nodded. What was there to say? She'd lost more than he'd ever had.

'When I heard on the news that he was dead, I wasn't happy, not jumping up and down, like you'd think. I was just, like, still. I thought, well, good. Finally.'

'Come on, Jen, the inspector doesn't want you making him gloomy.' Charlie looked around. Tom was right behind him, hadn't even heard him. He didn't think it was possible to be stealthy in a wheelchair, but somehow he'd managed it. He wheeled himself into the study on the other side of the hallway. 'Want to see my souvenirs?' he said to Charlie.

He followed him in. There was a bookcase, a desk with a computer and a printer, and stacks of paper lying everywhere, it was a bigger mess than his office at Essex Road.

'Like it?' Tom said. 'This is my little den.' He spread his arms. 'Spent day after day in here, sending letters, writing petitions, trying to persuade someone in the fucking system not to let him out.'

'Grimes would have been safer inside.'

Tom shrugged. 'Looks like it.'

There were more photographs around the walls, soldiers in uniforms, leaning against armoured vehicles, outside tents, all of them smiling, fierce, bloody invincible. There were mountains and deserts in the background.

'Helmand,' Tom said. 'They got the "hell" part right.'

Charlie pointed to one of the photographs, Tom leaning against a jeep with two blokes mugging for the camera either side of him. 'Who's this, then?' Charlie said.

'That's Gordon, the stocky one. The long streak is Joe Cole.'

'Where was it taken?'

'I don't know, somewhere over there. I was in shape then. Look at me, all muscle. Not an ounce of fat on me. I was a fucking fighting machine, man. Thought I was fucking bulletproof.'

'Just not bomb proof.'

Tom looked up at him, to see if he was taking the piss. He decided he wasn't, so he said: 'Thing is, they teach you all this stuff, you have all these brilliant weapons. Some of it, it's like out of *Star Wars*. I thought I was Captain Marvel, fuck sake.'

'Sounds like you miss it.'

'Of course I do.'

'Of course? A minute ago, you said it was hell.'

'Yeah, well. Even hell has its good points. Mostly I miss my mates.'

63

'How long were you in?'

'Feels like forever. Twenty-two I was when I joined up. Loved it. Gave me a purpose, know what I mean? I would have ended up in prison if it wasn't for the army. My mates from school, most of them were already inside, usual shit, drugs, stealing. The army straightened me out. I was good at it, too. Always turned out, spit and polish, you would have cut yourself on the creases on my dress uniform. So I miss being part of it, you know? Being elite, being dangerous.'

'You still in touch with any of the other squaddies?'

'Only Gordie. He's family. Not the others. Seen this? It's called a *pesh kabz*.' There was a knife on a stand, it was almost lost among the clutter on his desk. It had a leather scabbard engraved with Arabic.

Charlie bent down to take a closer look. It had to be almost a foot long.

'It's a close combat knife. They used it for finishing off wounded Russians after the Soviet invasion.'

'Nasty.'

'Or beautiful. Depends how you look at it. Damascus steel. I got it off a dead Taliban, he was the local executioner. The villagers say he used to take people's heads off with it in the market square.' Tom slid the knife out of its sheath. He handed it to him. 'Here, feel the weight of it.'

'Must be worth a lot of money.'

'Oh, I'd never get rid of it.' He took it back and put the knife back in its scabbard, but not before Charlie had satisfied himself there were no bloodstains on it. Still, he wouldn't mind Jack's boys having a closer look at it in the lab at Lambeth. 'Then there's this one,' Tom said. He spun his wheelchair around and went to the wall next to the bookcase. There was another knife, hanging by a well-worn leather strap from a nail in the wall. 'It's a slayer *kukri*. Also known as a "zombie head". They're used for sacrifice. Good for taking the heads off animals.'

'That's not a knife, that's a sword.'

'Eighteen inches. Handle's made of rosewood.'

'Did you get this from a Taliban as well?'

Tom smiled. 'No, I got it online. A hundred and seventy-five US.'

'What did you need it for?'

'I like knives,' he said, and grinned.

He's fucking with me, Charlie thought.

'Mind if I take these souvenirs of yours with me? It will help us to rule you out as a suspect.'

'Actually, I do mind, inspector. And I don't care if you rule me out of your little bad boy list or not. Not my problem. You want them, you'll have to get a warrant.'

Right, Charlie thought. Got that. He spared a glance at the bookshelf: Clancy, McNab, books about the SAS, about history, about the Afghan wars. A few books by Jung. And then a couple of books he wasn't expecting to see: Homer, Ovid. 'Which one of you reads the classics?' Charlie said.

'That would be Jen. She's the smart one in the family.'

'What's that one you've got there? *The Art of War*, Sun Tzu.'

'Every soldier should read it.'

'Good is it?' Charlie said.

'Sun Tzu was a master tactician.'

'Like pincer movements, stuff like that?'

'No, not the fancy stuff – the fundamentals. Warfare is the art of deceit. Did you know that?'

'Is it?'

'If you can make your enemy look the wrong way, you have the greatest chance of success. Like D-Day, like Sicily.'

'A gap in my education,' Charlie said and reached out to take it down from the shelf, but Tom put a hand on his arm. 'I don't like people reading my books,' he said. 'They curl the pages.'

When they got back to the living room, Lovejoy was talking to Jennifer Miller, trying to be a good cop, a professional. 'You do understand why we have to ask you these questions?' Lovejoy was saying. 'Don't you?'

65

'You do understand why we don't give a fuck,' Jennifer said, 'don't you?'

'Jen, are you still raining on their parade? That's no way to treat our guests. Laugh and the world laughs with you, cry and you cry alone.'

'Funny, my old mum used to say that all the time,' Charlie said.

'Did she, inspector?' Tom put his head to one side and studied him. 'You're still a believer, aren't you?'

'A believer?'

'You've got this innocence about you.'

'Really. No one's ever said that to me before.'

'You know what I mean. When you're a kid, growing up, you believe certain things. It's like the films and television you watch, the books they give you, the things the teachers tell you at school, and yeah, the sayings you hear from your parents. They keep telling you that the world is, like, fair. "Good things happen to good people, bad things happen to bad people." "And they all lived happily ever after." Bollocks like that. But that's not the way it is. You go to the Stan and everything you ever thought about people, it's just shattered. Fucking *shattered*. You see people doing shit they'd never do in a million years at home. I saw one of our blokes shoot this Pashtun woman, he thought she had a vest, a suicide vest. Turns out she was pregnant. We all saw him do it, but nobody said anything. Because you know what? We all would have done the same thing. The day before we lost one of our best mates when some raghead blew himself up in the road, so we all thought: yeah, why take chances? Fucking shoot her. Ask questions later. At the time I thought nothing of it. Now I think about it all the time.'

'Who was it that fired the shot?'

'Like they say, what happens on tour, stays on tour.'

'Only I wondered if it might have been this Joe. The one that threw himself off the cliff.'

'Maybe. Maybe not. No one will ever know.'

'What about you,' Charlie said. 'Ever kill anyone?'

Jennifer Miller laughed. It was a brittle sound, like glass breaking. 'That's deep. You trying to catch him out? You think you're clever?'

'You're wasting your time here,' Tom said. 'All you'll get out of her is bitter irony. All you'll get out of me are war stories.'

'Thanks for your time,' Charlie said and nodded to Lovejoy. They left.

They drove in silence until they were almost back at Essex Road. Charlie felt dirty, and not just because he'd slept in his clothes.

'So, what do we think, Lovejoy? Any theories?'

'They have the motive,' she said. 'And their alibi is each other, which is no alibi at all.'

'So, how did they do it?'

'I haven't worked that out yet.'

'I'm trying to picture Miller's wife in a jumpsuit and a ski mask, pushing him as fast as she can along the Strand in his wheelchair. Tom's got Grimes' head in a bowling ball case on his lap, he hands it to her as they get outside the Law Courts and she plonks it on the railing, like a cocktail cherry. No matter how hard I try, I can't see the CPS going along with me on that one.'

'The CCTV rules that out anyway. There was only one plonker, as you so vividly described it.'

'And yet they are the ones with the motive, not only for killing him, but making the statement.'

'And there's what happened at the trial.'

'Enlighten me. I didn't read all the transcripts.'

'After sentencing, Jennifer Miller ran to the front of the courtroom, shouted at Grimes that she'd be waiting for him when he got out of prison, that he was as good as dead. She also tried to attack the defending lawyer and had to be restrained by the bailiffs.'

'So we've doubled down on motive. That's still not evidence.'

'Anyway, why now? Grimes has been out more than six months.'

'Yes, but Tom Miller is army,' Charlie said, 'those blokes like to plan. What we need is something putting one of them at the crime scene or the murder scene. And we don't have either, yet.'

'I feel for her. I feel for both of them. What happened to them, it wasn't right. Four years? Society spat in their faces.'

'Have you heard of the trolley problem, Lovejoy?'

She shook her head.

'Imagine this, all right? You see a runaway train carriage moving toward five people who are tied to the railway line. You are standing next to a lever that controls a switch. If you pull that lever, the carriage will be redirected onto a sidetrack, and you save the lives of those five people. What would you do?'

'I'd pull the lever, guv.'

'Of course you would. But what if I tell you there is one person tied to the other track. You have two choices. You can do nothing, and five people will die. Or you pull the lever and save five people, but you kill one person by your actions. Now what do you do?'

Lovejoy hesitated.

'I don't know.'

'Come on, you've got five seconds. Four, three—'

'I can't.'

'Two, one, too late. Five people are dead. Is it your fault, Lovejoy?'

'I didn't do it.'

'Yes, you did. Your *inaction* caused the death of five people. But by most people's reasoning of the trolley problem, inaction is morally excusable, but taking positive action isn't.'

'Your point, guv?'

'My point is this: the reason Zoë died is because of the trolley problem. This Grimes bloke was a runaway train. But we, as a society, don't want to do what needs to be done, and eliminate the problem, so we let him go careering down the track and clean up a mother and a four-year-old kid. But not our fault, right? If we don't touch the lever, we're not to blame. I wouldn't like to be the one making those decisions either, Lovejoy, but until we solve the trolley problem, there's going to be a lot more Zoës. And everyone will say it's not their fault.'

CHAPTER TWELVE

Tracy Lennox had brought a union lawyer with her. Charlie hadn't been expecting that. He watched her on the screen in the viewing room, weighing her up. 'Nothing like I imagined her,' Grey said.

'What were you expecting?' Charlie said.

'I don't know. Something a bit more . . .'

'Macho?'

'Well she is in Armed Response.'

'She can check my weapon for rounds any day,' Greene said.

Charlie turned around. Greene had joined them. Brilliant. 'That's the best you can do, is it?'

'She doesn't look that tough.'

'Neither do you. But in her case, looks are deceptive.' He turned back to the screen. She hadn't even bothered with her uniform, had turned up in her civvies: white t-shirt and jeans, hair in a ponytail, no make-up. She sat back, with her arms crossed and a 'fuck you' look on her face.

Charlie nodded to Grey and they went out into the corridor, left Greene on his own in the viewing room to laugh at his own dubious jokes. They got coffees from the vending machine, then Charlie touched some numbers on a keypad on the wall and the door to the interview room clicked open.

Charlie didn't know the lawyer, and the bloke didn't look up and didn't introduce himself. Right, Charlie thought, so that's how it's going to be, is it?

Charlie went through the formalities and started the

recording. Before he asked his first question, Tracy's brief sat forward and placed both hands on the desk. 'First of all, can we clarify something, inspector? Should my client be under caution?'

'She is not a suspect at this stage. She is assisting us with our enquiries, that's all.'

'If at any stage you believe her to be a suspect, then may I remind you that under the PACE legislation, you have to put her under caution and the interview must then proceed on a different footing.'

'I am fully conversant with the PACE laws, thanks,' Charlie said.

The brief sat back. Charlie returned his attention to Constable Tracy Lennox. He had been expecting her to be defensive at worst, but she stared at him as if he'd shot her dog. It took him off balance for a moment.

He looked through her file, though he already knew most of it by heart: she'd been in the force eleven years, joined almost straight out of school, had spent the last four years on an Armed Response Vehicle out of Heathrow. She'd won a Queen's medal for bravery during a terrorist incident when she was an off-duty DC at Southwark.

He took a sip of his coffee and immediately regretted it. It tasted like bleach.

'Thanks for coming in,' he said.

'Why am I here?'

'I am leading an investigation into the murder of a man called Michael Richard Grimes. The name would be familiar to you.'

She didn't answer.

'You are aware of what happened to him?'

'Someone stuck the scumbag's head on a fence. What has it to do with me?'

'We are talking to everyone who might have had reason to want him dead. We want to eliminate as many of those people from our enquiries as soon as possible.'

71

'I imagine it's quite a long list you have there, sir.'

'Reasonably extensive.'

'I think it's a waste of police resources. If you don't mind me saying. Sir.'

'Where were you between midnight and three a.m. on the morning of 1 November?'

'I was on duty. You can check with my sergeant. The whole squad will tell you where I was. I beat Tank at pool, then I got some sleep. Went home at six thirty after our shift. Anything else?'

'Who's Tank?'

'DC Young. We call him Tank because he's built like one. You didn't have to drag me in here for this. A simple phone call would have sufficed. Sir.'

The look on her face. I wouldn't like to see those eyes looking at me down the wrong end of a Heckler & Koch, Charlie thought.

'Can I go?' she said.

'Couple more questions,' Charlie said. 'We are trying to trace your sister, Margaret.'

'Meg. We call her Meg. Everyone calls her Meg.'

'Have it your way, constable. Do you know where Meg is?'

She leaned back, gave a twitch of her shoulders. 'No, I don't.'

'We rang her regimental commander in Aldershot and he told us she has been missing for ten days. That's quite serious, isn't it, going AWOL for that long? Never been in the army but I imagine they don't take kindly to that sort of behaviour.'

Nothing, just a sullen look.

'I would have thought her disappearance might also be of great concern to the family.'

'Yes. We're concerned. Sir.'

'She hasn't been in touch with you or your siblings in the last ten days?'

'If she'd been in touch we wouldn't be concerned. Would we? Sir.'

72

'No. Right.'

Grey had been leaning back, arms folded, mirroring her. He suddenly leaned in. 'You have a very military family, don't you?'

'He speaks.'

'Careful how you address a superior officer, DC Lennox. This is just a friendly chat at this stage, but I can and will bring a disciplinary charge if you don't mind your manners.'

She chewed her lip. 'Sir.'

'Why the attitude, Constable Lennox? What's going on here?'

She glanced at her lawyer. He shrugged back at her.

'Maybe I'm missing something,' Charlie said. 'I get hostility twenty-four/seven from some of the people I have to deal with, and I don't expect any different. But I thought this morning was going to be different. You know, a friendly chat, another member of the thin blue line, a cup of tea and a biscuit. I was looking forward to a break from all the language and the bad behaviour.'

Tracy leaned forward. 'Let's get this straight, sir. I didn't kill Grimes. But I'm happy that someone else did for him. I hope he died slow and screaming, all right? It really makes me sick, you know?'

'What makes you sick?'

'You people. What you're doing.'

'Us people? Are you referring to DS Grey and myself? We're just doing our job.'

'What is your job, sir?'

'Excuse me, DC Lennox?'

'Your job, right, is to find who killed Grimes, and put them in prison. Like they did something wrong.'

'They did do something wrong,' Grey said. 'It's called murder.'

'That depends on how you look at it. I'm authorised to kill people, DS Grey, in certain circumstances. You see, murder isn't the act of killing, it's a licensing issue. My brother, for instance. He shoots a Taliban in Afghanistan, they give him a service medal. Frankly, whoever stuck that cunt's head on the railing outside the Royal Courts, personally I'd give him a service medal, too.'

'That's a dangerous attitude, DC Lennox,' Grey said.

'With respect, sir, if I had dangerous attitudes they wouldn't let me near an ARV. I'm speaking theoretically. Your inspector asked me why I was hostile. I would think that's obvious.'

Grey was about to say something else, but Charlie silenced him with a glance. This was an interview, not a philosophical argument. Save those for the pub after a few bevvies.

'Have you talked to my brother-in-law?' Tracy said.

'You know we have. Your sister would have rung you and told you the moment we left the house. Right?'

'Then you've seen what happened. Can you imagine what that's been like for him? He wakes up in a military hospital in some stinking hot shithole on the other side of the world and the doctor tells him he's lost both his legs. Then someone else comes in half an hour later and says, "Oh, by the way, some scumbag has killed your daughter and put your wife in a coma." What's that about?'

'It's about bad luck,' Grey said, and Charlie suddenly wished he had a rather large sock he could put in his sergeant's mouth.

'Is it? Bad luck? Was it bad luck that the judge only gave Grimes a slap on the wrist for what he did? Naughty boy, you shouldn't be driving with no licence and four times over the alcohol limit. Four years he did, in the end. My niece was just coming up to her fifth birthday. If you look at life expectancy in this country, she lost seventy, eighty years. How is that fair?'

Charlie didn't answer straight away. She'd built up quite a head of steam. Her lawyer looked worried, like he was thinking about intervening. Charlie was worried, too, but more for himself, because he agreed with her.

'What would have been fair?' Charlie said.

'Eighty years. That's what he took from Zoë. Even better,

74

I reckon they should have put him down. They do it to dogs, don't they, if they go mad and maul someone? They don't say: *the dog might get better behaved tomorrow.* Because you know he won't. So you do what has to be done, before anyone else gets hurt.'

Charlie could feel Grey squirming in his chair beside him. 'You're a police officer,' Grey said to her. 'How can you say things like that?'

'I joined the police force because I believe in things like law and order. I believe in them very much. Like you do. But I don't know that the legal system in this country equates to . . . well, justice. That's my opinion – sir.'

If she didn't have a cast-iron alibi, Charlie thought, she certainly would be on my suspect list. We would be finishing this interview under caution, just as her brief had wanted.

He wondered if her sister, Margaret, felt the same way.

Tracy leaned back. 'As I said, I'm very happy Grimes is dead. About time. But I was on duty that night. Are we done here, sir? May I go?'

'Thanks, DC Lennox. I appreciate you making time to come in to see us.'

She left with her lawyer. Grey asked Charlie what he thought. He didn't answer; decided to keep it to himself. He couldn't speak his mind, like he could with Lovejoy, and speaking his mind was what always got him into trouble.

CHAPTER THIRTEEN

Charlie parked in the street. He turned off the engine and was tempted to stay there, get some kip in the car. He felt too exhausted to move. Should have bunked down on the cot in his office. Fi always expected more than a cup of cocoa and a quick cuddle.

He crossed the street and stumbled up the stairs. He couldn't see her in the dark, knew she was there, heard her throw back the duvet and sit up. *Just let me sleep, sweetheart. For once.*

'Are you all right?'

'Out on my feet,' he said.

'I saw it on the news tonight. Intense.'

'Yeah.'

'Fancy seeing . . . that.'

His brain wasn't keeping up. He realised she meant seeing that bloke's head on the railing. 'Yeah, terrible,' he said, because that was what she expected him to say. Fi had accused him once of overdoing the hard man routine. Only it wasn't a routine. Dead bodies and all the bits of bodies didn't bother him all that much. It was the families, talking to the people they'd loved and listening to their grief and desperation, that was what did him in.

Michael Grimes didn't fit into that category.

'I don't know how you do it.'

'You get used to it,' he said, and sighed and stretched out on the bed. His whole body felt numb, even his brain.

'How do you do that?' she said.

'What?'

'How do you get used to it?'

'Well, when it's a kid or a woman it's worse.'

'Why?'

'Because most of the time, they're innocent. It's not how they die, it's who it is.'

'I don't get how that matters.'

He was drifting off. He had a micro-dream about penguins. 'Hmm?'

'He was somebody's son. A human life. No one deserves to die like that.'

'Some do. You'd be surprised.'

He wanted to sleep but she kept on at him. 'Everyone has a story,' she said. 'Everyone deserves a chance.'

Everyone deserves a chance? Do they? Best not to refer to Grimes as Mick on a Stick, then.

'I read what they said in the newspaper.'

Let it be, he thought. Just agree with her and close your eyes. You need some sleep, another long day tomorrow. 'If you read it, has to be true then.'

'Even if half of it is right, sounds pretty diabolical to me. It said his own father started giving him heroin when he was a teenager. He never had a hope of a decent life. A lot of these kids don't.'

'He wasn't exactly a kid any more.'

'He'd never known any better life. He was a victim himself.'

'Was he a victim? Because I thought the dead girl was. She was sat in her booster seat in the back of a car when he ploughed into her doing sixty miles an hour in the high street.'

'You worry me sometimes, Charlie.'

'How do I worry you?'

'Some of the things you say. No talking to you sometimes. There's this part of you that's dead cold.'

'Sorry. Does it scare you?'

'A bit. And you know what happens when I get scared.' He

77

heard her reach into her bedside drawer, looking for something. He heard buzzing. She told him her last boyfriend had felt threatened by it, thought he should be enough.

Did he feel threatened? Actually, he didn't. Most of the time he was so knackered he was glad of the auxiliary support.

She nuzzled his neck. She smelled musky, a heady musk of sleep and the lingering residue of whatever fragrance she'd been wearing through the day. She put a hand under the sheet, ran her fingers over his old appendix scar. 'Tell me how you got this,' she murmured.

'Knife fight with a Bulgarian gangster, he was a member of the Black Hand.'

'And what did you do to him?'

'I pulled out the knife, beat him unconscious with the blunt end, and handcuffed him to the last carriage of the three fifteen to Leeds.'

'I could just see you doing something like that,' she said, and cupped his balls in her hand.

'I'm so tired, Fi.'

'*You* may be,' she said. 'He isn't.'

When he woke up it was dark, and he was still inside her. Falling asleep on the job, they called it. He rolled onto his back, felt something hard sticking into his kidneys. It was her vibrator. He put it back in the drawer.

He unbuttoned his shirt and kicked off his socks, slipped them off with his toes. Hadn't had sex fully dressed since he was sixteen. Who said romance was dead?

He reached for her in the dark, but she groaned and rolled away from him. Oh well, nothing was ever perfect, was it? He wondered for a moment if he'd ever find a woman that meshed with him the right way, and decided it must be him, he was just a difficult bastard and always would be. He face-planted back into the pillow but he couldn't sleep.

It only seemed like a few minutes later when his alarm went.

He sat up and walked naked into the shower. When he came out, Fi was sitting up in bed, her knees drawn up to her chin. She had on his Alexis Sánchez Arsenal shirt. Buying that had been one of the regrets of his life. It seemed to him like there was a certain synchronicity to life, seeing her in it now.

'Sorry,' he said. 'Got to head straight back in. You know what it's like.'

He studied his rack of suits in the walk-in. He might have to do media today, it called for something a little more tasty than one of his knock-offs from TK Maxx.

'I worry about you, Charlie.'

'I'll be all right. The first seventy-two hours are the worst. I never expect to get much sleep anyway.'

'I don't mean that.'

He came out, laid his navy Ermenegildo Zegna carefully on the bed, struggled into his Calvin Kleins and rummaged through his drawer for socks. 'What is it you mean, sweetheart?'

'It's scary. You don't even sound all that bothered.'

'About what?'

She shook her head. 'See what I mean?' she said.

He finished getting dressed and kissed her goodbye. She was already on her phone, tapping away, maybe to a girlfriend, or perhaps to her next boyfriend. He had no illusions. Wasn't that what he wanted? Someone with a house key and a vibrator who would come and go as she pleased and wouldn't steal anything out of his wallet?

On the way back to Essex Road, he thought about what she'd said, but he didn't have time to think about it for long. They had to find Corporal Margaret Lennox. If the army couldn't find her, either something had happened to her, or she must have decided to stay well hidden for a reason.

DAY 3

CHAPTER FOURTEEN

Morning prayers on the third day. There was a lethargy in the squad that Charlie wasn't accustomed to. It didn't sit right with him. They were supposed to be professionals. They were also human beings, he supposed, which was the biggest disadvantage about being a copper in the first place.

'Okay people, this is where we're at. Tracy Lennox presented herself here yesterday evening and has been interviewed and eliminated from our inquiry. Our main person of interest is now her sister, whose whereabouts remain unknown. We must make every effort to find her but leads are elusive. Her family are being especially uncooperative in this regard. Meanwhile Parminder is compiling a list of other KAs for the Millers. Thomas Miller's former squad members in the SAS are of most interest, due to the organisation and violence exhibited in the execution of the crime. Our job is to trace, implicate or eliminate in turn. DS Greene will action those interviews among you today. DS Grey and myself are going to interview Gordon Lennox as soon as this briefing is over. Mr Lennox was not only Thomas Miller's closest associate from the army, he is also his brother-in-law. Any questions?'

'What about the knife fragments the CS team found in the lino in Grimes' flat?' It was Grey, the only one in the team who seemed to be wide awake.

'If we can find the murder weapon, it could prove crucial.'

'Didn't Miller have a number of Afghan knives on his wall?'

'He refused to surrender them voluntarily. I'm working on it.'

A couple of the squad yawned and stretched their arms. Lubanski was staring out of the window. This is what it must have been like for my teacher when I was in high school, Charlie thought.

'Lube, I'm over here,' he said.

'Sorry, guv.'

'How's the skipper?' James said.

'Not great. Doctors have told him his coronary arteries look like the Whitechapel Fatberg.'

'But what about all that watermelon he ate?'

'Did you really think that was his diet, Wes? He was going into McDonald's and getting a double cheeseburger with extra bacon on his way home every night. He used to eat it at the bus stop.'

'The flaky bastard. Did you know?'

'Of course I knew, Wes, it's my job to know. I also know you like to dress up as a schoolgirl on Saturday nights but, like I promised you, I will not tell another living soul.' There were hoots and cheers around the squad room. 'Serious, Wes, I'm not his mother, am I? He's a grown man. We all make choices.'

'Is he coming back to work?'

'Not if he's got any sense. He's considering doing a job with less stress, like running air traffic control at Heathrow.'

'Poor bastard,' Singh said. 'We used to ride him about his weight. He should have listened.'

'Don't think anything you could have said would have made any difference.'

'All that bigging himself up about going to the gym,' Wes said. 'Was that all bollocks as well?'

'No, he went to the gym, religious, every morning before work. Then he'd reward himself with a thick shake and a muffin afterwards.'

'Does that mean DS Greene is now our permanent inside DS?' McCullough said, addressing the elephant in the room.

'Well, I've been holding off telling you all, I was keeping

it as a special surprise. But yes, Jay is now confirmed as our permanent inside DS. I'm sure you'll all join me in congratulating him.' DS Greene swivelled his chair around, and raised his hands in the air, kissed his shirt like he was Harry Kane scoring for England.

There was silence. 'Aw guys,' Greene said, 'I know you all love me, really.'

It seemed to Charlie that Greene was the only one who actually thought that.

Charlie had seen a lot of corpses in his career and when he walked in the skipper's room, he thought DS Dawson looked for all the world like another one. His mouth hung open and his skin was a mottled and dusky grey. He lay on a bed in a shared ward, staring out of the window at the car park. He turned a baleful stare on Charlie and Grey. 'What's this, the burial party?'

'If it was, we'd have brought bigger shovels,' Charlie said. 'What have they been feeding you in here?'

Charlie glanced at the monitor next to the bed. He watched the numbers tick over on his pulse rate.

'Don't keep looking at that bloody thing,' the skipper said. 'If you want to know how I'm feeling, ask me.'

'How are you feeling?'

'Like shite.'

'You don't look too bad.'

'Bloody tubes in and out of me, even got one up me whatsit. Everything's out on display. Anyway, what are you doing here?'

'Came to see how you are.'

'What did you bring him for?' he said, nodding at Grey. 'Thought it was the Grim Reaper.'

'Hi, Skip,' Grey said.

'Brought you some grapes,' Charlie said.

'Don't like grapes, it's like chewing water with bits in.'

'Right. On a brighter note, how have they been treating you?'

'Got plaque, the doctors reckon. Knew you could get it on your teeth, not in your bloody arteries. I said, did I have the heart attack because I don't floss? They reckon I have to change my lifestyle. I said I haven't got a lifestyle, I've got a wife and a job.'

'Lifestyle means watching what you eat, Skip. Getting exercise.'

'I've got a gym membership.'

'Yeah but just having the card in your wallet isn't going to stop you having a cardiac. You actually have to go to the classes. Setting up a direct debit to Virgin Active and then forgetting about it doesn't count.'

'No pop, no chips. Walking every day. Call that living? Doctors said I've got to stay away from bloody McDonald's too. I mean, what's the use? I'm a bloody addict. They should go to the source, go after the big boys, like they do with drugs. No good just penalising the users. Shut down all the McDonald's and then maybe I'd stand a chance. They sent this nutritionist whatsit round to see me, I asked her if there's cheeseburger patches like there is nicotine patches. What are you up to now? Leave the bloody flowers alone.'

'From your daughter. That's nice.'

'Don't read the card. It's private.'

'We've been missing you at work,' Charlie said. 'It's not the same without you. DS Greene doesn't complain about everything as well as you do.'

'Well, nice to know I'm missed. Sit yourselves down, mind my catheter tube.'

Grey sat but Charlie preferred to lean on the windowsill. A nurse came in and drew a curtain around the patient in the next bed. Charlie hoped there wasn't going to be screaming.

'When's your op?' he said.

'Tomorrow morning.'

'Brilliant what they can do these days. You'll be good as new in no time.'

'Bollocks.' The skipper's fist screwed up the edge of the sheet.

'My brother, he smokes two packs a day and he's still pansying around like there's no tomorrow. I like my food and a couple of beers, but never once have I touched tobacco. And I'm the one that has the heart attack. Where's the justice?'

'Well that's life, innit? No such thing as fair.'

'Haven't you got somewhere else to be?' the skipper said to Grey.

Grey looked at Charlie, who nodded. 'Get a couple of coffees out of the machine, will you, sergeant?'

Grey took his cue and left. 'That was a bit blunt, Skip,' Charlie said.

'Intimations of mortality will do that to you. When you realise you could be dead this time tomorrow, you get overtaken with this, like, wave of regret, for all the people you haven't told to fuck off.'

'He's harmless enough.'

'Remains to be seen, guv. That's not the consensus in the squad.' He lay back on the pillow and blinked. 'Have you told them all I'm not coming back?'

'This morning.'

'I don't want no fuss, no leaving party. I'll fade away quiet, if you don't mind.'

'We'll be sorry to lose you, Skip, but your health's more important than the job. You've got the rest of your life to think about.'

'Rest of my life is all watermelon cubes, wholegrain rice and personal trainers, according to the missus. She says it like it's a good thing. How's things down at the nick anyway?'

'I wouldn't know where to start. You've seen what's happening, it's been all over the news. The papers love a good vigilante. They're calling it an attack on the justice system.'

'There's no such thing as justice. If there was, Boris would have got his knackers stuck in an industrial grade juicer when he was still at Eton.'

'It's been hard to keep the team motivated. Been hard enough

87

to keep myself motivated. Michael Grimes was hardly an innocent adrift in the world.'

'His picture's been all over the TV. He looked like a right
scrote.'

'Yeah, he was. File on him thicker than a cheeseburger.'

'Now then. You can't say the "C" word in here, you'll set off
an alarm. How's it working out with Greene?'

'He hasn't changed. He's not you.'

'What about Lovejoy? She'd be better than Greene any day.'

'Lovejoy? She's not long out of probation.'

'Rate her above everyone else in the squad. I still reckon you
should get her transferred out.'

'What for?'

'Better you don't spend too much time working together.'

'Why not?'

'You're always banging on about how you can't have relations
if you're in the same squad. So having Lovejoy hanging off your
shoulder every day would put you in a right fix, wouldn't it?'

'There's nothing between me and her.'

'You should tell her that. I've seen the way she looks at you.'

'You're imagining things.'

'Maybe. Did I tell you, I think I had one of those out-of-body
experiences?'

'You?'

'Yeah, when I had the heart attack. I'd read about them, you
know, thought it was all fairy dust and bollocks. But I'm telling
you, that's what happened. I can still see it now, clear as day. It
was like I was hovering over myself while the ambulance john-
nies were banging away on my chest.' He leaned in. 'I saw God.'

'Yeah, right.'

'I did. He wasn't like a bloke with a long beard or anything,
not like in his photos in the church. He was more like this really
bright light. I thought, here's my chance, ask him a few things
that have been on my mind, like. So I said to him: "Why is there
so much pain and sadness in the world?"'

'And what did he say?'

'He said: "None of your fucking business, son."'

Charlie left the grapes on the table beside the bed and told him he'd be back the next time he had a break, probably after they caught whoever killed Michael Grimes.

'Guv,' the skipper said as he was leaving.

'What, Skip?'

'I'm going to miss it.'

'You'll be all right.'

He shook his head. 'No, I'm going to miss being on the side of the angels. Being a copper, it made me feel like that bloke Hodor in *Game of Thrones*. I knew the evil fucking horde were going to break down the door one day, but I liked being on the other side, trying to hold them back. I might not be much, but I was the heroic fat bastard that everyone was cheering for.'

'Just stop eating cheeseburgers,' Charlie said, and left.

CHAPTER FIFTEEN

'Why doesn't he like me?' Grey said.

'He doesn't like anyone.'

'That's not true. He idolises you.'

'Well, he's from Yorkshire. They're all weird up there.'

They were driving along the B112, heading towards Stratford. Charlie stared out of the passenger side window at the Hackney Marshes, the acres of Sunday league football pitches. It was a national obsession for all the millions of blokes who had ever played the game, but you could count on a handful of amputated fingers how many got a contract in the Premier League, and their share of the WAGS and the Bentleys and the exposés in the Sunday papers that went with it. Sometimes he wondered what it would have been like, to be his namesake. But they were different days then; twenty quid a week and go home on the bus with the supporters.

'You miss it?' Charlie said.

'Miss what, guv?'

'Playing. *Rugger*, in your case.'

'I do, actually.'

'Never understood rugby, myself. A load of blokes with cauliflower ears and their bums in the air. Like mud-wrestling, only for geezers.'

'I suppose you have to grow up with it to understand it.'

'And did you? Grow up with it?'

'My father was pretty good. He encouraged me. Came to all the games.'

'What made you stop?'

'I broke my leg. Quite badly, as it turned out. I was playing for England schoolboys.'

'England schoolboys,' Charlie said. 'You were that good?'

'I was quick. Obviously not quick enough that one time.'

'I thought you just played for Durham University.'

'I did. I kept playing after it mended, even though the doctors told me not to, you know how it is. But I was never the same after that. I don't know if it was leg speed I'd lost or if it was – you know – bottle. Anyway, I broke it again, in the same place, and that time the doctors insisted. They said if I wasn't careful I'd end up in a wheelchair. Like Tom Miller.'

'Well, you both took one for the team, I suppose. For England.'

'Not quite the same.'

'I wasn't suggesting it was the *same*.'

'What about you, sir? How far did you get? In your football career.'

'Crown and Anchor Sunday team. I was first reserve. They reckon I would have made the first team one day, but I broke a nail when I got home pissed after watching Arsenal lose to Tottenham and I was never the same after that.'

Not even a smile. At least with Greene he could banter a bit. Missing Jayden Greene's sense of humour, now that was a slippery slope.

'So, sergeant, what do you think? You used to be a lawyer. How does this case make you feel?'

'Do you want me to put my lawyer's hat on?'

'If that is what it takes. But that's the problem, right? Should we have two hats? Should we be able to put personal feelings aside and talk about the law as if it's something separate to daily life?'

'Don't mind me saying, sir, that's not even a question. Of course we do.'

'That's what you think, is it?'

91

'Well, the law is the law, whether we agree with it or not.'

'But who makes these laws, sergeant? Is it all up to a handful of judges and politicians who, quite frankly, are insulated from real life and what goes on? Because I'll tell you this, some of the people I've met from the legal profession are more concerned with winning cases than whether the laws they are defending are right. That is the disadvantage of the adversarial system. It's also why you gave it up, right?'

'There's no such thing as a perfect system.'

'That's not an answer. Now you definitely have your lawyer's hat on.'

'So, what's the alternative?'

'Well, sergeant, there has to be one because I am trying to do my job right now but all the time I am looking at Tom and Jennifer Miller and thinking: if that was me, I'd want to knock Grimes off as well. I think sticking his head on a railing outside the Royal Courts of Justice has a certain symmetry to it.'

'It's not our job to put society right, sir. We have a murder to investigate. We have to find the culprit.'

'I don't know if I totally agree, sergeant. If I'm not on the side of the angels, I'm just a civil servant with handcuffs.'

A freezing November day, grim and overcast, like God had picked up a grey blanket and thrown it over London, couldn't stand to look at it any more. Gordon Lennox lived in East Ham, not that far from the Millers, but when they called round, he was already at work. His wife didn't seem surprised to find two cops on her doorstep, looking for her husband. She told them he was working over in Larkhall. They had to backtrack right across London, another hour and a half of his life he wouldn't get back.

When they got there, they finally managed to find a space behind an Amazon delivery van. Good to know that Jeff Bezos was a few quid richer. Charlie put his hands deeper in the pockets of his Stone Island and took out his warrant card. The house they were looking for was halfway down a row of Edwardian terraces. Hard to tell whether the owner was renovating or just doing some stopgap work to keep it habitable.

A yummy mummy in pink Lycra jogged past, pushing twins in a buggy bigger than his first car. She got tangled up with a dog walker coming around the next corner, there was a lot of yapping and screaming. Need someone from Traffic down here to sort that lot out, Charlie thought.

'Don't get your shoes dirty,' Grey said.

'What was that, sergeant?'

'I know how you love your shoes.'

The sarcasm from DS Grey was duly noted. Was it because of the case or was it a response to their disagreement about the country's legal system? In the meantime, he actually did take care not to get his shoes dirty. He was a major crime detective not a builder and he had on his new Thom Brownes with the pie crust stitching.

They followed the sound of Capital Radio played at a volume that would have made a heavy metal band put their fingers in their ears. There was a bloke standing with one hand on a rubbish chute, yelling instructions at someone at the window on the top floor as bricks and plaster crashed down the chute in a cloud of white dust. All he had on was a t-shirt and a pair of camo shorts, a massive pair of steel-toed boots on his size twelves, like his old man used to wear for the football. Didn't look unlike his old man either, Charlie thought, a head like an unwashed potato and tats up and down his arms. They were old-school tats, too, not the designer sleeves the young blokes got to accessorise their beards.

'Gordon Lennox,' Charlie said.

'Who wants to know?'

Charlie flashed his warrant badge. 'Your missus said we'd find you here.'

'You been round home?'

'Well, it's where you live, we normally start there. They

93

teach us that in detective school, proper clever it is. You don't seem surprised to see me.'

'I can read. It's about that piece a shit, Grimes. Tommy said I'd be getting a visit from you blokes sooner or later.'

Charlie recognised him as one of the blokes in the photo on the Millers' wall. Gordon yelled up at his offsider that it was time for Rosy Lee and went to his van, threw open the door and took out a thermos. He poured some coffee into the mug.

'Go on then,' he said.

'We're investigating the murder of Michael Grimes,' Grey said. 'We'd like to ask you where you were on the night of 1 November between midnight and four a.m.?'

'That would be Halloween.'

'That's right,' Charlie said. 'Get dressed up, did you? Go walking round the street with a decapitated head under your arm?'

'In my younger days I did,' he said, straight-faced. 'Too old for that now. Stayed home with me wife. I don't live a very exciting life these days. I've had my share of fun and games for one lifetime. Like to keep my head down now, know what I mean?'

'Can anyone else verify that?'

'Got two kids. But they were in bed asleep. Anything else you wanted?'

'Do you own a motorbike?' Grey said.

'No. What would I want with a motorbike?' He rummaged under the seat of the van, produced a packet of digestives. 'Want one?'

'Don't mind if I do,' Charlie said. 'Lovely these. What did you think about what happened to Zoë Miller?'

'Bloke who did it got off too easy. That's what I think.' He held both hands in front of him. 'Are you going to take me in?'

'Only doing our job,' Grey said.

'And I'm here trying to do mine.' He turned back to Charlie. 'After you finish gobbling my morning tea, mind telling me if

I need a lawyer? If I'm a suspect, you're supposed to caution me, aren't ya?'

Charlie took his time finishing the biscuit. 'My mum used to give me these when I was a kid. When I was good. If you've been good, Gordon, like you say, there's no need to get the silks down here.'

'I need to take a piss,' Gordon said, and went inside the house. There were dust sheets up and down the hall. Charlie liked a careful builder.

His labourer was standing in the doorway, leaning against the jamb. He was a skinny bloke with long hair and a beard, in a tie-dyed t-shirt. 'Got a light?' he said to Charlie and held out a hand-rolled cigarette. Charlie stared at it, an ache in his gut. He really wouldn't mind a drag right now.

'Why are you asking me?' Charlie said.

'You look like a smoker.'

'I've quit.'

'Good for you, man.'

'How long have you worked for Mr Lennox?'

'Six months. Maybe.'

'What's he like?'

'You're cops. I shouldn't be talking to you.'

'Why?' Grey said. 'What's he got to hide?'

The bloke grinned and pointed the unlit cigarette at him. 'I see what you did there.'

'Seems like a good bloke,' Charlie said.

'He's a bloody nervous wreck. Too long in the army.' He lowered his voice to a stage whisper. 'I reckon he was the one who did it. Three tours in Afghanistan.' He made a looping motion with his finger at his temple. He mouthed, 'Absolute. Fucking. Nutcase.'

'We'll take that on board,' Charlie said.

'Nice shoes,' the bloke said to Charlie. He heard the toilet flush and looked over his shoulder, saw Gordon coming back. He came down the steps and got a bottle of water out of his backpack in the front of the van. He winked at them and went back inside.

'Still here?' Gordon said.

'Have you heard from your sister?' Grey said.

'Tracy? Spoke to her last night. She said you blokes had been hassling her as well.'

'What about Margaret?' Charlie said.

'Meg? She's in the army, down in Aldershot.'

'She's supposed to be. But you know she isn't.'

'Can't help you there.'

'Can't or won't?' Grey said.

'Did you know,' Charlie said, 'that we have had complaints from some of the people in this street that you have been starting work prior to eight a.m.?'

'Bollocks.'

'Under the Control of Pollution Act 1974 you could be fined a maximum of twenty thousand pounds.'

'What is it you want?'

'What do you think I want?'

'Look, I told you. The night Grimes was knocked off, I was at home with the missus. You want to take a look at my phone? Check the GPS?'

He reached into one of the zip pockets in his shorts and offered Charlie his mobile.

'All that proves is where your phone was. Your Android is not under suspicion.'

'How long have you been doing this work, Mr Lennox?' Grey asked him.

'Since I left the army. I'm helping out a mate for wages.'

'Making a few quid?' Charlie said.

'It pays the bills.'

'You could make a lot more in private security. I thought that's what a lot of you blokes did when you left the army.'

'Wife doesn't want me doing that shit any more. Look, arrest me or stop harassing me. I'm trying to do a decent day's work here.'

'This is a murder inquiry,' Grey said. 'A man was killed and decapitated.'

'He fucking deserved it,' Gordon said.

'Excuse me?'

'That arsewipe got four years for what he did. Four years! Think I'm going to cry floods of tears for him? Am I fuck. If it had been me, I'd have stuck him on that railing while he was still alive. Satisfied?'

'Thanks for your help, Mr Lennox,' Charlie said.

'Leave my sister alone. Her and Tom, they've been through enough.' He turned around and yelled for his offsider to get back to work. Charlie nodded at Grey and they went back to the car. That hadn't been much help, but he hadn't supposed he'd get too much in the way of cooperation there.

And frankly, he couldn't say he blamed him.

Grey's face was white. Charlie waited while he fumbled with the keys. 'Going to start the engine, sergeant?'

'Do we go back and talk to his wife?'

'We could.'

'Look at him. He's on the phone already, telling her what to say, I reckon. She'll back up his alibi, it will be impossible to corroborate it one way or the other, and we're back where we started.'

'Welcome to the world of criminal investigation.'

'You should have pushed him harder.'

'Excuse me?'

'You went too easy on him. He wanted to give you his phone, you should have taken it.'

'He was offering me his phone because he knows there's nothing incriminating on it.'

'He bluffed you, sir, and you went for it.'

He went to start the engine. Charlie reached over and stopped him. 'What's going on, sergeant?'

'I don't feel your heart's in it. Sir. Right from the beginning you've been lukewarm.'

'Because I feel for the situation the Millers are in?'

Grey didn't answer.

'Do you feel I have been negligent in any way?'

'Perhaps.'

'Well, if you've got a complaint about my performance, then you should take it to the DCI. Now can we get back to the nick? We have a lot of work to do. I have been negligent for eighty hours this week alone, but the work is still piling up on my desk.'

Grey looked Charlie hard in the face. 'I didn't leave the law to work against it.'

'Thanks for that, DS Grey, I'll bear it in mind. Can we get back to Essex Road now?'

CHAPTER SIXTEEN

The DCI put on his glasses and read the report Charlie handed him. Let him have first dibs, Charlie thought, make him feel important.

They were in the Incident Room with Wes James and Rupinder Singh, who had been busy doing the groundwork while he was being lukewarm in Larkhill with DS Grey. He tapped his iPad and an image flashed on the screen. He nodded to James, let him take over.

'This is a capture from an ANPR camera in Tower Hamlets. The car is a red Ford Clio registered to Jennifer Miller. As you can see the time is 2.11 a.m. Jennifer Miller told us in her statement that she was home all night with her husband.' Another tap on the screen, another grainy image. 'Here is the same vehicle, at the same location, heading back to Stratford. The image came from the same camera, and the time is now 4.23 a.m.'

'The question is,' Charlie said, 'where the hell was she all that time?'

'You think she killed Grimes?' the DCI said.

'I think she at least needs to explain to us where she was going and why.'

'Are you making Jennifer Miller your main suspect?'

'Well, not getting carried away too soon, sir. Jennifer has no military or weapons training, unlike her sisters or her brother. Her husband, Tom, is a triple amputee. To make either of them prime suspects in a case like this is a significant leap of the imagination. What I do believe is they may be complicit in the crime and, for sure, they know more than they're telling us.'

'You want a search warrant for the Millers' house?'

'Yes, sir. I think we should also bring her in for further questioning under caution.'

'This ANPR capture. It's suspicious, but on its own it's not enough to charge her.'

'There's also this,' DC Singh said. He passed a printout across the desk. 'The Department of Transport have been able to give us a make and model of the motorcycle seen leaving and entering Star Yard at the time of the incident. It matches the make and model of a machine registered to Tom Miller and which he claims was stolen several weeks ago.'

'Did he report it at the time?' the DCI asked.

Charlie nodded.

'There's one other thing,' Charlie said.

'Tell me this is a good, solid evidential lead.'

'The note that was found lodged in Grimes' throat. We know it was from a play by Aeschylus. The lines were spoken by one of the Three Furies, the sisters of vengeance. It can't be a coincidence that Jennifer Miller is one of three sisters.'

'Charlie, we're wandering into the *Twilight Zone*. I shan't be mentioning that when I apply for the warrant. Hopefully the ANPR evidence and the evidence from Swansea about the motorbike will be enough for a search and seizure. If I start talking about Greek goddesses, I'll get sectioned. Thanks everyone.' He was about to leave, gave Charlie a look over his shoulder. 'You have no idea the grief I'm catching on this one from upstairs. Get this sorted, everyone. And no more bodies.'

'Or heads,' James said.

There would be days, not long into the future, when Charlie would look at Wes James and wonder what on earth made him say it. If you believed in curses, or tempting fate, that was as close as you could get.

CHAPTER SEVENTEEN

When they got to the Millers' place, there was already a crowd around the cordon, everyone in the street had come out for some free entertainment, holding up phones to get pictures, something to put on Instagram. McCullough and Lubanski were escorting Jennifer Miller to one of the squad cars.

'Have you put her under caution?' Charlie said to Lubanski.

Lubanski nodded, sullen. It wasn't like her to look stressed. She couldn't even look at him. 'This is not right, guv,' she muttered.

'It's the job,' Charlie said.

A copy of the search and seizure warrant lay on the hall table. Tom Miller sat in the middle of the living room, in his wheelchair, watching the SOCOs turn out drawers, go through bookcases, lift up cushions. One of them carried his laptop out of the house in a clear plastic evidence bag.

'Your people are very tidy,' Tom said. 'I thought you went around tossing drawers on the floor and ripping up people's clothes.'

'We're not the Gestapo.'

'Well, that's what you say.'

'You shouldn't have lied to me,' Charlie said.

'Lost my legs, lost my kid. Now you've arrested my wife. Any more misery you'd like to pour down on us?'

'I'm just doing my job, Mr Miller.'

'That's what the guards said to the Jews at Auschwitz. It's called the Nuremberg defence.'

'I know what the Nuremberg defence is.'

'We don't want to do this,' Grey said to him. 'But murder is murder.'

'No, it's not.'

'Excuse me?'

'My sister-in-law tells me she had this conversation with you already. Murder is a licensing issue. Isn't that right, inspector?'

'You can't take the law into your own hands,' Grey said.

'Depends what you think of the law.'

Grey jabbed a finger at him. 'If you're behind this, we're coming after you. You can't hide behind a wheelchair.'

Charlie took a deep breath. That was enough of that sort of talk. 'Shall we step outside?' he said to Grey. He put a finger on his sergeant's arm and propelled him through the door. 'What was that?' he said.

'Sorry, sir.'

'What's got into you, sergeant?'

'He wants us to feel sorry for him because he's lost his legs.'

'No, he doesn't. He is angry because of what he perceives as a grave injustice.'

Charlie saw McCullough leaning against the squad car, smoking a cigarette. He went over and asked him for the pack, took one. 'Got a light?'

McCullough took out his lighter.

'Don't do it, sir.' Charlie looked over his shoulder. It was Grey. 'You haven't smoked in months. It only takes one.'

'What are you, my mother?'

'You'll hate yourself tomorrow.'

'I hate myself now,' Charlie said and lit up.

'There is no justification for vigilante justice. Whether the courts got it right or not, we have to enforce the law, as it stands.'

After the first hit of tobacco, Charlie felt a little calmer. 'Stay out here and make yourself invisible, my son. We'll talk about this later.'

He went back inside the house. Tom Miller was leaning back

in his wheelchair and shouting instructions to one of the SOCOs, who was examining a vase. 'Careful with that, it's Ming dynasty.'

Jack came out of Tom's study. 'Anything?' Charlie said.

He held up a clear plastic evidence bag: there was a paperback book inside, it looked old, and there was no dustcover. 'What is it?'

'We found this at the back of one of the bookcases, tucked behind some old paperbacks. It's an old edition of *The Oresteia*. There's some pages missing.'

'Is it the same book?'

'Could be. Can't tell you that until we get it back to the lab.'

Charlie looked at Tom. 'Yours?'

A shrug. 'A mate lent it to me when we were in the Stan. Forgot to give it back.'

'Which mate?'

'Can't remember now. It's that long ago.'

'Why was it hidden?'

'I didn't hide it. It must have slipped down the back.'

'There's pages missing.'

'No shit, Sherlock. It had pages missing when I got it. It's fucking old.'

'We also found this,' Jack said, holding up one of Tom's Afghan knives in a plastic evidence carton.

'I already showed your inspector that. It's a *pesh kabz*. Part of my personal collection. Careful with it. Could be valuable one day.'

'It's positive for blood,' Jack said.

'Probably,' Tom said. 'I got it off a Taliban. Those fuckers don't wear them for decoration.' He looked back at Charlie. 'This is all bullshit.'

'I'm sorry about this, Mr Miller,' Charlie said. 'It has to be done.'

'Sorry? You don't have enough sorrys in you for this. What you're doing is criminal and you know it. It's written all over your face.'

'We're not persecuting you, Mr Miller. As my colleague said, this is a murder inquiry.'

'You think my wife cut off this dick-wipe's head?'

'I don't know. I do know she lied to us. I know *you* lied to us. And I know you're capable.'

'In this thing?' He slammed the palms of both hands against the wheels of the chair.

'How many blokes?' Charlie said.

'How many blokes what?'

'How many blokes did you kill? Over there.'

'I never kept count. Sometimes you don't know anyway. You give them a burst, you run, you take cover. Fire an RPG at something, there's no way of knowing the exact count, there's not much left of anything afterwards.'

'You must have a rough idea.'

'Ten. Twenty. Five thousand. A million.'

Charlie lowered his voice. 'I'm not saying I blame you for wanting Grimes dead. But it's illegal, and that's where I come in. Where did your wife go on Wednesday night, Mr Miller?'

'I don't know what you mean.'

'We have photographic evidence showing your wife's car on the B118 in Bow at 2.11 a.m. and returning at 4.23. As the vehicle has not been modified, we have to assume that she was driving it.'

'I have no idea where she was. I was asleep. Perhaps she's taken a lover. I wouldn't blame her. I can't do much any more.'

'Why don't you tell me what you know, and we can stop putting you and your wife through this?'

Tom stared right through him. Charlie had had a few hard cases stare him out in the course of his working life, but he didn't think any of them had ever looked at him with such contempt. 'I don't know what you're talking about,' he said.

They went through the formalities and Charlie reminded Jennifer Miller that she was under caution. Her solicitor sat there rigid like a mannequin in the front window of Selfridges. Jennifer stared at the desk, huddled inside the custody suite tracksuit.

'So, Mrs Miller, in your original statement . . .' He slid a piece of paper across the desk. 'In your original statement you said that on the night of 31 October you watched television until around eleven o'clock and then went to bed, and did not wake up until six the next morning.'

'No comment.'

'You don't have to comment, Mrs Miller, I was merely reminding you of what you said.' He slid a glossy photograph across the desk and placed it alongside the printed statement. 'For the tape, I am showing Mrs Miller ANPR stills of her car on the A11 heading south-west near the intersection of the B142 at Tower Hamlets. The time is 2.11 am on 1 November. If you were home in bed at that time, as you said in your statement, who was driving your car when this photograph was taken?'

'No comment.'

'We also have this. For the tape I am showing Mrs Miller an ANPR capture of her vehicle returning to Stratford at 4.23 a.m. What explanation do you have for this, Mrs Miller?'

'No comment.'

Charlie leaned in. 'Look, this doesn't have to be this hard. I don't think you killed Michael Grimes, but I do believe you know who did.'

Jennifer Miller looked up, her eyes fixed on a point somewhere above his left shoulder. The old thousand-yard stare.

Charlie reached for the clear plastic evidence bag on the desk beside him. It was the copy of *The Oresteia* that Jack Reid's team had found at the back of the bookshelf during the search and seizure.

'For the tape I am showing Mrs Miller a paperback book, a Penguin Classics edition of *The Oresteia* by Aeschylus, published in 1977. Mrs Miller, this was found on the bookshelf of your home. Can you tell me how this book came to be in your possession?'

'No comment.'

'You see, your husband said that a colleague in the army lent it to him when he was on duty overseas and he forgot to give it back. On examination, it was found that several pages were missing. Technicians in our Forensic Pathology department tell us that one of those missing pages matches exactly a page found in Michael Grimes' mouth after his murder. That is a very curious coincidence I think you'll agree.'

'No comment.'

'You can sit there and say no comment all day if you want, but you do understand that we, as police officers, are entitled to draw adverse inference from your silence.' He looked at the brief. 'You did tell her that?'

'My client is exercising her right to silence, as enshrined in the Police and Criminal Evidence Act 1984.'

'Mrs Miller, your solicitor has given you advice which in certain circumstances can certainly be to a suspect's advantage. If you were guilty of murder, for instance. On this occasion I would advise you to seriously reconsider your responses.'

'No comment.'

Charlie leaned his elbows on the table. There was a part of him that wished 'no comment' could be a part of his repertoire, too. 'I know you and your husband have been through a lot. I can't imagine what it must be like to suffer what you have suffered.'

The look she gave him. *No*, it said, *you have absolutely no idea.*

'The thing is, I don't want to put you through any more than you've already been through. But these inconsistencies have to be explained. If you could do that for me, then no one will be happier than me to see you walk out of here and go home.'

She leaned over and whispered something to her brief.

'We'd like a moment to consult, if you don't mind, inspector.'

Charlie nodded. 'Interview suspended, 3.41 p.m.'

He and Grey walked out.

DCs James and Singh had been watching in the viewing room.

'What do you think?' James said to Charlie.

'I think I would rather this was some gangbanger who knifed some other scrote in a stairwell. What do you think she's hiding?'

'Could she have been the one who took the photograph?' Singh said.

'Possibly. I don't know. You see the way she looks at me? I wouldn't want to be in a room alone with her, especially if she had one of those knives her husband collects.'

'I'm not seeing this,' James said.

'Neither am I. There's something here doesn't add up. And that one in there,' Charlie said, pointing to the screen, 'knows exactly what it is.'

CHAPTER EIGHTEEN

'My client wishes to state, for the record, that she wishes to revise her statement,' the brief said.

Charlie folded his arms and waited.

Jennifer Miller raised her eyes from the desk. 'I couldn't sleep. I decided to go for a drive. I parked down Grove Road, down by Victoria Park there.'

'That time of night. On your own?'

'I didn't get out of the car. I'm not stupid. I just wanted to be alone. Think, like.'

'You could have gone downstairs and made yourself a cup of tea.'

'Could have. I didn't.'

'What about the book?'

'Never seen it.'

'Your husband said you liked the classics.'

'Tom hasn't been right in the head since he got back from the army. Wasn't all that right before he went.'

'Your husband owns a motorbike. A 2014 S1000R. A black one.'

'It got nicked, didn't it? Have you found it? Didn't think so. Too busy chasing the hero who knocked off that dirtbag Grimes.'

Charlie turned off the tape. 'Interview suspended, 4.10 p.m.'

The brief started to pack up his papers. 'Are you charging my client?'

'I have to consult with my superior officer.'

'This is laughable.'

'The piece of paper in the deceased's mouth came from a book that was in your client's possession.'

'All that means is one of her husband's former colleagues in the army is responsible for the murder. You have no evidence putting my client at the scene. I think that's it.'

They got ready to leave. Charlie waved them back to their chairs. 'You are not free to go yet,' he said.

As he left the room he heard her say to her brief: 'What the fuck does he hope to achieve?'

'No comment,' Charlie said and went out.

'FONC wants to see you,' James said as Charlie walked into the incident room. 'He said, *straight away*. Unquote.'

'We said we'd let you know,' DC Singh said, 'soon as you came out of the interview.'

He felt them all watching him when he went towards the lift. He reckoned he knew what this was about, and in a way he wished he could save blokes like Grey from themselves. He had a pretty good idea what Grey had done and he wasn't angry about it. He just felt sorry for him.

'I've had a complaint,' FONC said when he walked in. Not even a: *Sit down, Charlie, how was your day?* He looked to be busy writing up a report, or just sending an email to his wife.

'Complaint, sir? About me?'

'Yes, about you.'

'Formal or verbal?'

'Only verbal at this stage. One of your team has been voicing their concerns about your attitude.'

'DS Grey.'

'He doesn't think you're showing sufficient zeal in pursuing the Grimes investigation.' The DCI still hadn't looked up from his laptop. Charlie supposed it was the closest his boss would ever get to looking embarrassed.

'He thinks I should start taking zeal supplements?'

'This isn't funny, Charlie.' He slammed down the lid on his laptop. 'Does he have cause to be concerned?'

'What do you think, sir?'

'I think the boy has a lot to learn, so be careful what you say around him in future. How was your interview with Jennifer Miller?'

'Unsatisfactory.'

'Is she talking?'

'She says she couldn't sleep and went for a drive the night of the murder.'

'What about the book?'

'Someone gave it to her husband when he was in the army. It's the only piece of evidence we have to tie her to the murder. I mean, it's feasible that the page was already ripped out when he got it.'

'What do you want to do with her?'

'Don't see any point to holding her. She's not going anywhere.'

'All right, let her go. We'll put her and Tom Miller under twenty-four-hour surveillance. Keep working on it. And watch what you say in front of DS Grey in future. I don't want to have to put an official reprimand in your file.'

Charlie took the lift back to the IR. He stopped at Grey's desk. 'Don't ask me to apologise,' Grey said. 'I stand by everything I said. I didn't say to him anything I didn't say to you.'

'When you played rugby,' Charlie said, 'did your team mates ever tell you that you didn't pass the ball enough?'

Grey stared up at him but didn't answer. Must have hit a sore spot, Charlie thought.

'Because some blokes, sergeant, they only play in a team so they've got someone to pat them on the back when they score.'

'I studied the law for four years, sir. It's not perfect, but I believe in it. What do you believe in? Sir.'

'Funnily enough,' Charlie said, 'I believe in angels.'

110

CHAPTER NINETEEN

He went in, threw himself down in his chair, which skidded halfway across the room on its castors. He hauled himself back to his desk, like a man pulling on a lifeline. Maybe some symbolism there, Charlie thought.

There was a tap on the glass and Parminder put her head around the door. 'The intel you asked for, guv.'

'Come in and sit down, Parm. What have you got?'

She had a file with her. She slid it across the desk. 'Tom Miller's military record, or as much of it as the SAS are willing to provide. His last posting was Helmand province in Afghanistan. He was part of a sixteen-man platoon, based in Hereford; his troop specialised in HALO and HAHO.'

'That sounds like fun, but I'm assuming it isn't.'

'Stands for High Altitude Low Opening and High Altitude High Opening. Jumping out of a plane at forty thousand feet and freefalling until you see the top of the Shard go past before you open your parachute.'

'Not something you do for fun on the weekend.'

'No, guv.' Parminder checked her notepad. 'Of the sixteen men in the squad, eight are still serving but Hereford will not tell us where they are, except to say they are on active service. Out of the seven other squaddies, besides Tom Miller, I have traced all but one of them. There's a Rodney Brinkley, thirty-two years old, invalided out of the army June 2015, unfit for duty. He's now living in Bolton, believed to have severe mental health issues. Detectives from Lancashire CID have interviewed him, he has a strong alibi – he was admitted to the psychiatric ward of the Royal Bolton on 29 September and was not released until yesterday. Then there's Gary Walsh, thirty-one, currently serving nine months in prison for assault.'

'What did he do?'

'He fired a flare gun at a group of teenagers in the street outside his house.'

'Go on.'

'Darren Jarvis committed suicide in 2016 after stepping in front of a Tube train at Parsons Green. At the time he was on remand for assault and possession of a prohibited substance. Joe Cole, found dead at the foot of cliffs near Brighton 23 May this year.'

'Two suicides out of sixteen blokes?'

'It's not that unusual, guv. After the Falklands in the 1980s, more blokes died from suicide when they came back than in the actual battle. As for Jarvis and Walsh, that's pretty consistent also. I did a little research. Figures from the National Association of Probation Officers puts around eight thousand army veterans in the prison system at any one time, another twelve thousand on probation or parole.'

'Post-traumatic stress?'

'Perhaps. But a lot of these guys had been violent before they joined the army. Like Gordon Lennox. Signed up at sixteen, already had a list of priors from the juvenile court. Basically, his future was the prison or the army.'

'That leaves two,' Charlie said.

'Christopher Pemberley and Anthony Marshall. Marshall, also known as Ant; he and Tom Miller were both in the 1st Battalion, Parachute Regiment and went through SAS selection together. Marshall left a year after Miller was wounded, went back to Afghanistan as a close quarter combat instructor. Killed two months later by an Afghan soldier, along with two other recruits.'

'Pemberley?'

'Left the army the same month as Marshall. Haven't been able to trace him. He's not married. I've been in touch with family members who say they believe he joined a private security firm and that he is somewhere in the Middle East. A lot of ex-soldiers do private work when they get out – five hundred in the hand every day, tax-free, working as bodyguards or military advisers.'

'The army doesn't know where he is?'

'When they leave, they leave. There's not much follow-up.'

'All right. Good work, Parm.'

'I'll keep working on Pemberley.'

'Good. As soon as you've got something, let me know straight away.'

Charlie went out to the incident room, stood in front of the whiteboard, stared at the photographs of the two crime scenes, and the mugshot of Grimes, the manky bastard they were all working to avenge.

Jack had emailed through the final forensics from Grimes' flat; not a single hair that matched the DNA on the database after Chapman and Podborski had been excluded. Since yesterday Greene had taken down their mugshots and put up three new photographs – Tom and Jennifer Miller, and one of Meg Lennox, in her army uniform. Who else? He took the marker pen and wrote *Chris Pemberley??*

Lovejoy got up from her desk and came over, handed him a printout.

'What's this?'

'The rap sheet on Gordon Lennox. Since he was discharged he's had two convictions, both for assault. One incident from last year when he was arrested at Westfield shopping centre in Stratford, the second six months ago at a pub in Brentford. Got in a fight with a bouncer. He was given a six-month suspended sentence.'

'Why was he arrested at the Westfield?'

'He was brandishing a knife. He never actually attacked anyone. Two uniforms used Mace to take him down. At the

113

trial, his psychiatrist told the judge it was a reaction to his medication.' Charlie added Gordon Lennox to their rogues' gallery on the whiteboard.

'We have to find Margaret Lennox. What have you found?'

'She's an IT specialist with the 1st Battalion, Grenadier Guards. She doesn't have any specialised combat training. Think she could do something like this?'

'The Yorkshire Ripper didn't have weapons training, but he did enough damage. Get a full list of her friends and KAs. Nothing come up on any of the traces?'

'She left barracks with a weekend leave pass to visit her parents in Hertfordshire. She never showed up and hasn't been seen or heard from since. I've checked with Licensing in Swansea and with Customs. Nothing. She's not used her mobile phone, her credit cards, or any email accounts registered to her. She hasn't shown up on any social media. She's not seen a doctor or claimed a benefit and there's nothing on our national database.'

'What about the rest of her family?'

'A couple of aunts and uncles up north. They all send Christmas cards once a year, they reckon. But they haven't seen her since Moses was a boy.'

'She can't have just dropped off the grid. Keep working at it.'

'You know, it might not be anyone we've got on the board. Could yet turn out to be a vigilante, someone who took up the cause after they read about it in the papers.'

'I'm going to rule that out. The page we found in Michael Grimes' throat came from a book belonging to someone known to Tom and Jennifer Miller.'

Lovejoy pointed to the board. 'Who's Chris Pemberley?'

'Another one of the squaddies from Tom Miller's platoon in Afghanistan.'

'Is he a possible?'

'Have to find him first.' Charlie rubbed his face with his hands. 'What's everyone saying about this case? You know, when I'm not there.'

'Honest, guv?'

'Well, you can lie to me, but that's not why I keep you around.'

She looked over her shoulder, checked the room. 'Wes and Rupe don't want to be on it, I heard them talking to each other this morning. Lube and Mac and the others, well they're getting on with it, trying not to let themselves think about it too much, but they're not happy either.'

'And DS Grey?'

'They're all really pissed off with him. If it was the army, they'd frag him.'

Lovejoy's mobile rang in her pocket, and she turned away to take the call. When she turned back, she was white as chalk.

'What's happened?'

'That was Dad. Something's happened to Charlie. Said he's had to rush him to the vet.'

'You'd better get over there,' Charlie said and nodded towards the lifts. 'Back as soon as you can.'

'Need a lift from someone. My car's broken down, I had to leave it at home today.'

Charlie thought about the bedraggled spaniel he had found on his front step all those months ago. 'What's wrong with him? You reckon it's serious?'

'Sounded like it.'

Charlie went back to his office and got his coat. 'I'll take you,' he said.

They jumped in Charlie's Sierra and went blues and twos out of the gates. The police commissioner probably wouldn't think a sick spaniel was an appropriate use of emergency protocols, but the police commissioner didn't own a dog. And anyway, as his ma used to say, what the eye doesn't see, the heart doesn't grieve over.

The vet's was in a pleasant street in St John's Wood; the white frontage made it look more like a florist's shop. The waiting room was rammed, even for a Saturday morning. There were harried-looking people with cat boxes and whining chihuahuas and one woman with what looked to be a fully grown macaw in a cage big enough for a Russian model to dance in.

Lovejoy's father, Howard, sat in the corner with his head bowed, dabbing at his eyes with a sodden clump of tissue. Lovejoy rushed over and put her arms around him. Charlie stood there, feeling like a bit of a knob, but no one else in the waiting room seemed to think this public display of distress excessive. Even the receptionist looked like she was going to burst into tears.

'What happened, Dad?' Lovejoy said. 'He didn't find the chocolate stash, did he?'

Howard shook his head. He couldn't seem to get any words out.

'Tell me what happened.' She shook him.

'He got outside,' he managed, finally. 'I found him under the car.'

'Under the car? You didn't run him over?'

'You've got a leak in the radiator. He was licking the antifreeze.'

'What?'

'Terrible, it was. I gave him some milk, thought he'd be okay, but then he started shaking and peeing everywhere. He was throwing up in the taxi, the bloke was right pissed off, I had to give another tenner to shut him up.'

'Is he going to be all right?' Lovejoy said.

But that was as much as Howard could manage. Another wipe of the nose with the sodden bit of tissue and then a gasp like he'd been gut-punched.

A large bloke with hair spouting out of his cuffs and the neck of his shirt came out of the door beside the main desk. 'Mr Lovejoy?' he said. 'Can you come this way, please?'

Howard almost ran after him, Lovejoy followed and, as she was going through the door, she turned and motioned for

Charlie to follow. He didn't think it was quite right, but he did as he was told.

Charlie the spaniel lay on an examination table, looking a right mess. There was a tube in his nose and an intravenous line in his foreleg, and they'd covered him with a blanket. He was panting, like he'd chased a Ferrari down the high street.

'How is he?' Lovejoy said.

The vet folded his arms and frowned. Charlie felt something slip, deep in his guts. It was a long time since he'd felt anything like raw grief, and it surprised him, more than a bit.

'This has to be one of the most unusual cases I've had since I've been working here,' the vet said. 'Basically, your Charlie has ethylene glycol poisoning. It is a common additive in radiator and brake fluids. It's usually a bright green colour and is very sweet. That might have been what attracted him. A couple of licks is enough to cause problems in most pets. The problem is, it's highly toxic and often causes kidney failure, which can be fatal.'

Charlie thought Lovejoy was going to faint. Howard put his hands over his face.

'Can you do anything for him?' Lovejoy said.

'We only have one antidote to hand. It may help to alter the chemical reaction and prevent kidney failure from occurring. You've got him in here pretty smartish, so we're optimistic. As you can see, I've inserted a tube through his nose to his stomach. Over the next forty-eight hours we're going to give him successive doses of alcohol.'

'Alcohol?' Lovejoy said.

'Vodka, actually. It's the easiest form to administer. He's not a very well dog right now, but we hope to see an improvement in his condition over the next few hours. We've sedated him, so the best thing you can do right now is wait at home. I'll call you with an update later on this afternoon.'

'You've hooked him up to a vodka drip?' Charlie said.

The vet nodded. 'Any other questions?'

'Just one,' Charlie said. 'Can I go next?'

Howard didn't want to go home. Guilt, grief, duty, whatever it was, he said he would wait at the vet's for as long as he could. Charlie and Lovejoy got in Charlie's car for the short drive back to Essex Road.

Neither of them spoke until they were almost back at the station. Finally, Lovejoy said: 'They get under your skin, don't they? Dogs. Something about them. Charlie's not just a dog, he's family. Most people don't get it.'

Family, Charlie thought. Someone to rush you to the A&E and chew their nails for you in the waiting room. Not sure I've got one of those. Ben, maybe. If he's not in Davos with a ski bunny.

They stopped at lights and he heard a strange noise from the passenger seat. Lovejoy was crying. She angrily brushed her eyes with the back of her hand. 'Bloody dog.'

'Look at you,' Charlie said, not unkindly. 'You didn't even cry when you stepped on that booby trap.'

'Different kind of pain, that. Physical pain is nothing next to thinking you're going to lose someone you love.'

'No,' Charlie said. 'I suppose not.' He thought about his little brother, Liam. She was right, that still hurt him, after all these years. He didn't even want to think about it now, in case he choked up, too. That was the thing, wasn't it, about love, and loss. Maybe he was better out of the whole thing.

DAY 4

CHAPTER TWENTY

His wife sat at the table in her dressing gown, waiting for him. Her eyes were hollow, red-rimmed. He hated her looking at him. He wondered what it was that she saw.

She had a look on her face this morning, like he was some stranger that had just walked in and she was trying to work out where she knew him from. He looked down to make sure there was no blood on his shirt. The girls were sitting with their backs to him, he could almost see them stiffen as he walked in. They all stopped talking.

It was so quiet. Before he left to go on deployment, they would have the TV blaring every morning, all the mindless breakfast television and breathless news, like it all mattered somehow. But he didn't watch television any more, didn't listen to the radio. It made him angry. People had no idea what he'd been through, what they'd all been through over there. He supposed he wasn't really sane any more, or at least not what people might call normal.

How could he be? One day he was face down in a *wadi*, watching a medic putting the bits of his platoon sergeant in a bag, forty-eight hours later he was in a shopping mall in Stratford, watching people play with their smartphones. He still had people asking him what Iraq was like; they didn't even know where Helmand was.

He couldn't sleep for more than a few hours, the slightest noise woke him up and then he'd spend hours wandering around the house, sweating and shaking.

He couldn't tell her about Helmand, the things that had happened, the things he'd done, the terrible things. He wanted to, but he couldn't. He went to the refrigerator, took out two eggs. He cracked a shell on the edge of the counter, swallowed it. Then he did the same with the other. Breakfast.

He brought his coffee to the table. They all looked down, wouldn't catch his eye. He knew they were scared of him. He'd go crazy if he didn't have them, but he couldn't seem to talk to them when they were right there. His own family.

'I'm sorry,' he said to her. 'I know I was a little crazy there for a while. But I'm better now. I'm straightening myself out. Really. I feel calmer.' He tried a smile. 'Got a few things to finish off, to sort it out. When it's all done everything will be fine, you'll see.'

He slammed his fist on the table.

'Don't look at me like that! I'm trying, aren't I?'

He went outside to smoke a cigarette.

They were out of Shuga, a mile north of their Forward Operating Base, Jackson. He could make out flower-speckled mountains in the distance, through the heat ripples. The ground was like concrete, the dust as fine as talcum powder. It got everywhere: your nose, your eyes, your throat. It was so quiet, he could hear his own heart beating.

They covered the dead ground through a wadi and crept through the narrow mud corridors of a medieval Afghan village, looking for insurgents, the safety catches on their C8s set to single shot. The sun baked his head through his helmet; he had to wear gloves or his rifle would have been too hot to hold.

They were supposed to capture a Taliban commander that intel said was hiding in the compound. They were wrong, as usual. Didn't take long in country to learn you could trust Donald Trump before you could trust army intelligence.

All they found were the severed heads of two Afghan villagers. They had been paraded around the compound on stakes, to frighten the locals. Whoever the poor bastards were, they'd had their eyes gouged out.

Some things, you could never get out of your head. No wonder he hadn't come back the same. He hadn't wanted to hear that at first, but in the end you had to accept it. You couldn't fool yourself.

There was something inside you keeping count.

Always.

CHAPTER TWENTY-ONE

Charlie had just started the morning's briefing when Lovejoy made her appearance, out of breath, flapping with her coat and gloves, nudging her way in. Jayden Green held up his watch and tapped it. 'What time you call this then?' he said to her.

'Sorry, sarge, my car's still out of action, I had to take the Tube.'

'Murder doesn't wait,' Greene said.

'Actually, it does, sarge,' James said. 'It's kidnappings that don't wait. Corpses aren't in a hurry to go anywhere.'

There were a few grins around the room.

'All right, settle down, everyone,' Charlie said. 'If you look at your briefing notes, you'll see we have four possible suspects for the Grimes homicide: Jennifer Miller, Margaret Lennox, their brother Gordon and an ex-SAS paratrooper called Chris Pemberley.' He got up and scrawled three question marks next to Jennifer Miller's photograph on the whiteboard. 'The page found lodged in the deceased's throat is a match for the book retrieved from the Millers' house during the search and seizure. Tom Miller says he was given the book when he was in Afghanistan, and that it was already in poor condition.'

There was muttering around the room.

'That's just weird,' Wes said.

'The technical analysis is all down there in your briefing notes, you'll probably make as much sense out of it as I did, unless you got an A in your chemistry O level. But the page is definitely from the same book.'

'Someone's having a laugh,' James said.

'It's the only evidential link we have between the Millers and the remains of the deceased. But it's not enough to proceed with charges.'

'Oh, well,' Singh muttered. 'Good for them.'

Grey gave him a look but didn't say anything.

'How did we go with this Chris Pemberley?' Charlie said.

'We think he's working for a company called DynaCorp,' Greene said. 'They hire ex-soldiers for private work in all the dodgy parts of the world. I'm sending DCs James and Singh off to the wilds of Paddington to follow up this morning.'

'Do we have any more on our elusive Margaret Lennox?'

Parm opened a file on her lap. 'I've accessed her service records. She's not quite the Action Man her brother is. Completed basic training in October 2012, moved on to Combat Engineer Class 3 at Gibraltar Barracks before getting her HGV licence. She had trade training at RSMS before going into the field army in 2014. Was deployed to the Falklands at the end of the year. Back to Aldershot in 2015 where she's been ever since. Her speciality is comms and IT. She represented her regiment at rugby on six occasions.'

'You never played against her, sir?' James said to Grey and a few people laughed. Charlie let it go.

'Still nothing?'

'I gave a list of all her KAs to DS Greene.'

'We're working our way through it,' Greene said. 'No joy so far.'

'That leaves Gordon Lennox,' Grey said.

'Mr Lennox is under twenty-four-hour surveillance. As you can see from your file notes, he has a record for violent offences, but his wife has been interviewed and she confirms his alibi for the night of the 31st.'

'But all the wives do that, don't they?' Lovejoy said. 'She's not going to shop her own fella.'

Charlie turned around and stared at the whiteboard, looking

for inspiration. He couldn't find any. He felt in his bones that he'd made a misjudgement; he just couldn't see where.

He had hoped that one of Miller's collection of knives would prove to be their murder weapon, or that the page found in Grimes' throat would yet yield something conclusive.

Who else might have had access to the book? Any of their family, clearly; or one of his former SAS mates, whose name they were yet to uncover. He only wished he could find sufficient enthusiasm for the task in front of them.

'DS Greene will action your jobs for today,' he said. 'Do your best.'

It was an unsettling thought, but he suddenly realised Grey was right; if their victim had been a child, or a woman targeted by a predator, an old man robbed and beaten, he would be tearing at the gates of hell for answers. But there was a part of him just going through the motions on this one. And his team were only mugging for the camera as well.

Charlie was sitting at his desk scrolling through the witness statements on his monitor when the DCI put his head around the door.

'Charlie.'

'Morning, sir.'

'Making progress?'

'Depends what you mean by progress.'

'Do you have a main suspect in the Grimes homicide?'

'Ah, that sort of progress. No sir, we don't.'

FONC came in and sat down, a bad sign. 'How are things between you and DS Grey after the other day?'

'We're both professionals.'

'That wasn't an answer to my question, was it?'

'What's done is done. He came to you voicing a valid concern, left no paper trail, so we'd best leave it behind us.'

'You know the squad has turned on him?'

'Sir?'

'Somebody left a dead rat in his drawer last night. He found it when he came in this morning.'

'There's no saying anyone put it there. It's an old building.'

'Someone had spray painted it grey.'

'I thought rats *were* grey.'

'No, the word "Grey". Someone wrote the word on it.'

'Right. Well, I don't hold with that. Do we know who it was?'

'If I knew who it was I'd be dealing with it myself, not in here talking to you. It's your squad, Charlie. You have to keep control of your own people. I'll leave it with you, shall I? I don't expect to have to bring this up again.'

'No, sir.'

He got up to leave. He stopped at the door. 'You haven't forgotten tomorrow?'

'Sir?'

'The lunch. To celebrate the awards you and Lovejoy are getting at the Dorchester.'

'Is that still on? I mean, we're in the middle of a high-profile investigation. How's that going to look?'

'We can't let this go by unrecognised, Charlie. It's not just about you, you know. These awards recognise the work done by this entire team.'

'Yes, sir.'

'It will give you a chance to wear one of your fancy suits,' he said, and walked away, his hands in his pockets.

Charlie waited until he'd got into the lift, then went into the incident room. Jayden Greene was on the phone, manning the hotline with a couple of trainees. Charlie signalled to him and went over to the corner, where they kept the kettle and the microwave. Charlie pretended to make himself a cup of tea.

Greene put down the phone and followed him over. 'Guv?'

'A quiet word, Jay.'

'Am I in strife?'

'What's with the rat in DS Grey's desk?'

127

'The what, guv?'

'I'm not accusing you of anything, Jay, all I'm saying is, I know it was you. I could send the rat to forensics and get prints off it, but they're busy enough. I appreciate the gesture, but I believe it to be misguided. This vendetta against DS Grey is to go no further. Understood?'

Greene shrugged. 'If I find the person responsible, guv, I'll let them know.'

'You do that. Here, have this cup of tea. I can't stand the stuff.'

As he was walking away Greene put a hand on his shoulder. He lowered his voice. 'I think DS Grey's got porn on his computer, guv. No idea how it got there. He wouldn't want to go opening it by mistake while there's people around.'

'Thanks Jay. I'll let him know.'

'He shouldn't have done what he did. You're our guv'nor. You can be a right pain in the jacksie sometimes, but you've always had our backs. Thanks for the tea.'

He went back to the phones.

CHAPTER TWENTY-TWO

Halfway through the afternoon Lovejoy put her head round the door, saw the bone sitting on Charlie's desk. 'Shouldn't that be in an evidence bag, guv?'

'It's for Charlie. When he's feeling well enough. He is getting better, isn't he Lovejoy?'

'That's what I came to see you about. They're sending him home today. Is it all right if I slip out of the office for an hour to pick him up?'

'Got your car fixed, then?'

'They had to put a new radiator in. At least it was under warranty. The worst part was Charlie drinking the coolant. That's the bit that's going to cost.'

'Charlie got a bottle of vodka out of it, I'm sure he doesn't mind.'

'Unlike you, guv, he doesn't know about the hangover that comes afterwards.'

'Are you going now?' She nodded. Charlie closed down the computer and put his jacket on. 'I need a break from all this. I'll come with you.'

'How's life, guv?'

'Not bad. Arsenal are playing Liverpool tonight, three points and we'll be in the mix for a top four finish.'

'I mean apart from that. Life doesn't revolve around football.'

'See, only someone who doesn't understand football would say something like that. You clearly don't understand the game at all.'

'But it *is* just a game.'

'No Lovejoy, it's a state of being. It gives life meaning. It's at the Emirates and I should be there.'

'Yeah, it's a shame you'll miss it.'

'No, I mean, *I should be there*. They might not win without me.'

'Sorry guv, I think there's something wrong with my ears. I thought you said: if you're not at the ground, your team might not win.'

'It's a proven fact. Don't ask me how it works. But like sometimes, if I look away for a second, the other team scores.'

'You could look away whenever you liked and the other team would score. It's Arsenal.'

'If you're going to insult my football team, I'm not going to talk to you. Mind out, you're too far over.'

'Who's driving, guv?'

'Nominally, you. But don't forget who's in charge here.' Charlie turned down the buzz and chatter on the Airwave. They were caught in traffic on the Marylebone Road; Charlie stared at the hordes of tourists pouring out of the Tube towards Madame Tussauds, to look at tailor's dummies that looked vaguely like someone they'd seen on television. Weird. He found himself humming 'Baker Street', couldn't help himself.

'Do you ever dream about giving up the booze and the one-night stands?' Lovejoy said.

'The one-night stands have given up on me, Lovejoy.'

'I forgot. You have a girlfriend now.'

'How do you know?'

'People talk. What's her name?'

'Fi. Fiona.'

'Like her?'

'I don't dislike her.'

'Wow. Head over heels, then?'

'She's . . .' He was going to say 'great in bed', then changed his mind. 'She's quite vivacious.'

'How long have you been seeing her?'

'About three months. Off and on. She works long hours, same as I do.'

'What does she do?'

'She runs a bar, in the West End. She works late almost every night, sees a lot of random violence. We have a lot in common.'

'I get the sense that she's not the one.'

'Or is it I'm not the one? You know, people go around, complaining about their love lives, saying things like "men are all the same", "women are all bitches", giving it all that. You never hear anyone say, "*maybe it's me*, maybe I'm the problem". Do they?'

'Is that what you think, guv? That you're the problem?'

'Course not, Lovejoy. It's women. All the good ones are gone.'

Charlie the spaniel was staggering like a drunk when he came out into the reception room at the vet's. Charlie had seen that expression countless times, but it was usually when he looked in the mirror after a big night. Lovejoy cradled him in her arms like he was a baby, and he yelped and clawed his way up her shoulder until he was upright. He peered at Charlie over her shoulder through pain-flecked eyes. His tongue was hanging at full stretch, and he was panting. Poor bugger.

Charlie rubbed his ear as gently as he could. 'I know the feeling, pal. Don't worry, it wears off.'

'He's a lucky dog,' the vet said. 'You got him here just in time. He spent all yesterday on a drip in our intensive care unit.'

'He's going to be all right?'

'No signs of kidney damage. He should be fine, once the hangover wears off.'

'I don't know what I'd do without him,' Lovejoy said. She looked at Charlie, for backup.

'Not my dog,' Charlie said. But even as he heard himself say it, he realised that wasn't entirely true.

131

They laid Charlie down on the back seat, and Lovejoy hardly got above twenty miles an hour all the way back to Primrose Hill. Charlie offered him the bone, but the spaniel turned his head away and whimpered. He left the bone at hand in case he changed his mind. His eyes were drooping, he looked more like Ozzy Osbourne than a cocker spaniel. It hit home to him where the word 'hangdog' came from. He looked like he could do with another drink.

'Poor little boy,' Lovejoy said.

'Needs another sip of vodka,' Charlie said. 'Hair of the dog.'

When they got to Primrose Hill, Howard was waiting for them on the doorstep. They pulled up and he went straight to the back of the car, scooped up the spaniel and took him inside.

'Why don't you take the rest of the day off?' Charlie said to Lovejoy.

'DS Greene wants me to follow up on Meg Lennox. I've got a list of numbers to call, I'm only halfway through.'

'It will keep until tomorrow. Drop me off at Chalk Farm and I'll get the Tube back. It's only three stops.' As they drove down England's Lane, Charlie said: 'Thought I might look in on Charlie on the way home,' he said. 'If I don't finish too late.'

'Yeah, sure,' Lovejoy said, but there was a hesitation in her voice that told him there was more. 'You can meet Harry.'

'Harry. Is that, like, another cocker spaniel or a bloke?'

'My boyfriend. You'll like him.'

I don't think so, came immediately to mind, but Charlie bit it back. All his double standards and ambivalence collapsed inwards, catching him off balance. 'So how long have you been going out with him?'

'He was one of the nurses at the hospital.'

Charlie remembered now, wondered if he was the one who looked like Chris Hemsworth. That was a depressing thought.

'He really loves Charlie.'

'Well, that's good.'

She didn't say anything until they got to the lights on

Haverstock Hill, and when she did, Charlie cut her off, claiming that he thought he'd seen Derek Jacobi outside the Chamomile Café. He told her a long, tedious story about having seen Michael Kiwanuka at the Enterprise before he was famous, and she said, 'Who's Michael Kiwanuka?' and by then they were at Chalk Farm.

'So, you still coming around to see Charlie after you finish up?' Lovejoy said, as he got out of the car.

'Got a lot to do,' he said. 'Maybe another time.'

Lovejoy looked – what? Relieved? Sad? He couldn't tell. He couldn't explain away how he felt either. He was a mystery to himself sometimes. He felt like he'd lost something that he really had no claim to. Was he jealous about Lovejoy, or jealous about the spaniel? Maybe it was both. He had no cause to be. It was his rule, after all: no fraternising with members of your own team.

But sometimes, like Tom Miller had said to him, dogs, people, they get under your skin, no matter how hard you try to be reasonable about it.

But rules were there for a reason and he always kept to his own rules.

CHAPTER TWENTY-THREE

Hannah at reception looked up from the desk as he walked in. 'Mr George! Your mother's been asking for you.'

'I got held up. Bit busy at work. How is she?'

'A little confused today. She's been asking for your father a lot.'

'Well, if he shows up we're all in trouble,' Charlie said.

Hannah led him across the foyer; the carpet was thick enough to wade in, good to know that Ben was getting something for his money. The lighting was turned down this time of the evening, all nice and peaceful except for someone yelling in the locked section. It all seemed slightly unreal and blurred at the edges. Old people sat around, it was like being at bingo night, only the one calling the numbers was God.

'You want a cup of tea?' Hannah said.

He hadn't been expecting that. 'I'd kill for a coffee,' he said.

'Only got instant.'

'I suppose a beer is out of the question? IPA?'

'This is an aged care facility.'

'I'll take that as a no. But thanks anyway.'

'Your mother says you're a policeman.'

'For my sins.'

'I never see you in a uniform.'

'Pity, I look good in one. I'm plain clothes now.'

'Drug squad?'

'Now why would you say that? Do I look like someone who would have a lot to do with drugs?'

Hannah gave him a cheeky smile, which was unexpected. 'Well, you don't look like a traffic cop.'

'You say that now, but you should check under your windscreen wiper when you get back to your car.'

'So, if you're not drug squad, what are you?'

'I go out to schools, talk to them about stranger danger, how to cross the road, that sort of thing.'

Hannah laughed and shook her head. 'Okay, don't tell me, then.'

'Don't you believe me?'

'I do not believe the Met Police would let you within a mile of a primary school. You'd have all the kids hiding under the desks clutching their teddies.'

There was a shadowed figure in one of the chairs. Hannah bent over and whispered: 'Mrs George, there's someone here to see you.' He was blessed with another cheeky smile and Hannah made her way back to the desk.

The sound on the television was turned up way too loud. He heard Big Ben. *News at Ten* was starting. The world was still going then, but not doing too well by the looks of things, as usual. 'Hello Ma,' Charlie said and sat down in one of the plush velvet armchairs.

'Hello Ben,' Ma said.

'It's not Ben, it's Charlie.'

'Of course it is. I know who you are. Do you think I don't know my own little boy?' She leaned closer and whispered, loud enough for the whole building to hear, even over the sound of the television: 'Those nurses have been stealing stuff from my room again.'

'No one's stealing from you, Ma. You do lose things sometimes.'

'No, I don't.'

'What's missing, then?'

'My wedding ring! Worth a lot of money, that is. I reckon one of these nurses has took it, pawned it off.'

135

'Ma, you lost your wedding ring about ten years ago. Don't you remember? You were fiddling with it when we were on the pier at Brighton.'

'I never been to Brighton.'

'We all went, Ben and me and Michael and you. It was not long before Dad died.'

'Before he what?'

Oh fuck, he'd said the 'D' word. That would proper set her off if he didn't distract her. 'It dropped off into the sea. Ben said he'd go out and look for it at low tide, but we couldn't find it.'

'You're doolally tap, you are. I never take my wedding ring off. Someone might steal it.'

'What are you doing up? You should be in bed asleep.'

'Oh, I can't sleep. I'm afraid of the dark. Keep hearing all these noises. Bad as you, I am.'

'What do you mean, "bad as me"?'

'You were always scared of the dark.'

'Me? I never was.'

'Course you were. Always had to leave a light on for you at night or you wouldn't go to sleep. Your dad was worried you were going to grow up and be a poofter.'

'Oh, for God's sake, Ma.'

'Funny little kid you were. Not like Michael. You were sensitive.'

'I was never sensitive.'

'A real cry baby, you. I remember when you were little, you coming home from school, you got in a fight with a boy in your class, black and blue you were. I said, "What happened?" and you said the priest told you if someone hit you, you had to turn the other cheek. Your father, he was fuming when he heard. He soon sorted that out.'

'What, did he go up the school?'

'No, he taught you how to headbutt.'

'He what?'

'Got sent home, you did, next day. I got a nasty phone call

from your headmaster, said you were violent and you'd get expelled if you did it again. I didn't know what to say to him. Your father was right pleased, took you to see Arsenal as a reward. Couldn't stop you after that, you used to go with him every week. I didn't hold with it. I never wanted you to be like that but there was no talking to your father.'

'I don't remember any of this.'

'Violence never solved anything, I always told you that.'

Charlie experienced a moment of unreality, sitting here in his mother's halfway house, talking about things that might never have happened with someone who wasn't quite all there. His history was full of shady and unreliable memories, the only people he could rely on for an accurate retelling were Ben and Michael, and these days he didn't talk much to Michael either.

The trouble was, his ma was gone and yet she wasn't gone. Listening to her was like interviewing a suspect without a lawyer present; none of it might be admissible later.

Perhaps it was him it had happened to, or one of his brothers. Or perhaps it was some flotsam thrown up on the tide of her fragmented memory; it could be a priceless treasure or a rusted bike.

'How are things at work? Are you still a policeman?'

'Yes, Ma. Still a cop.'

'You must get sore feet, all that walking they make you do.'

'I sit at a desk mostly.'

'Don't be daft. What you take me for? Policemen don't sit at desks. Are you all right for money? I've got some in my room I can lend you. I've hidden it, so the nurses can't pinch it.'

'No one's going to thieve from you here, Ma. They're all really nice and they take good care of you.'

She patted the handbag on her lap. Her whole life, passports, will, life insurance, everything, was in there. 'Well, that's what you say. I know different.'

He looked over at the desk, saw Hannah watching them. I

wonder what she makes of us? When he turned away, he felt his mother staring at him. She looked frightened.

'What's up, Ma?' he said.

'Who are you again?'

'Charlie.'

'Charlie who?' And there it was, she was gone again. Her spirit had made another fleeting visit, then run off like a distracted child. 'I want to go home now,' she said.

'You can't go home, Ma. This is your home now.'

'No, it's not. I know where I live.'

'You have to stay here, Ma.'

'Why do I? I don't like it here.'

'It can't be helped.'

'Why can't I come back with you? It's been a nice holiday, but I've had enough now.'

Hannah must have heard the anguish creep into his mother's voice and she came over to check on her. 'Are you all right, Mrs George?' she said.

'Where am I?' she said.

Hannah crouched down, put a hand on her shoulder. 'You must be getting tired, Mrs George.' She turned to Charlie. 'You should go, now. I'll make sure she gets to bed. It's very late for her.'

Charlie kissed Ma on the forehead, her skin felt dry and hot and paper thin. He said goodnight to Hannah and left the warmth of the foyer, braced himself against the November wind as he stepped outside. He put his hands in his pockets as he walked across the car park, closed his eyes, felt a mist of rain on his skin.

He quite liked the dark these days. Funny to think that once he had been so afraid of it.

Fi was sitting on his sofa watching television when he got home. Her eyes flickered, then went back to the screen. 'Hi, handsome.'

'What are you watching?'

'I don't know what it's called. It's about people living in

138

substandard housing coping with random acts of violence and habitual drug use. How was your day?'

'A lot like that.'

'The reviews said it was a commentary on the disintegration of our society.'

'Britain doesn't need a commentary. We're not a horse race. If we are, we're running last, by about ten lengths.'

'How are you doing with this case that's been all over the news?'

'No closer. We have to catch a break soon, I suppose.'

'You don't sound like you care much either way.'

'I don't.'

'As a member of the public, I can't tell you how reassuring it is to hear that.'

'What I mean is, if this turns into another Jill Dando, it won't be half the tragedy that was. Anyway, one in four homicides goes unsolved, there's no law that says we have to close this one because the papers say we should.'

He threw his coat on a chair, sat down on the sofa and shut his eyes, just for a second. Big mistake. Now he would have to find the strength to open them again.

'At least Charlie pulled through,' he said.

She looked puzzled.

'DC Lovejoy's spaniel. The one I found on my doorstep that time.'

'What was wrong with him?'

'He drank anti-freeze.'

'Would have thought it would do him a bit of good, in this weather.'

'It's not a joke. It could have killed him. We got him there not a moment too soon, the vet said.'

'You went to the vet's with her?'

'Yeah, over in St John's Wood.'

'Why couldn't Lovejoy take her own dog to the vet's?'

'She was having trouble with her car.'

139

'Right. So if this was one of your other detectives, and their pet goldfish had water retention or something, you would have put them in your car and raced off to the vet's with them with your little light on the roof?'

Charlie tried to focus. His brain felt numb. 'What?'

'Are you interested in the dog or in DC Lovejoy?'

'I'm not interested in DC Lovejoy. She's one of my team.'

'So, if she wasn't one of your team, would you be interested then?'

'I'm going out with you.'

Fiona gave a funny little laugh and reached for the remote. 'You really know how to sweep a girl off her feet, don't you?' She got up and switched off the TV. 'I'm going to bed. Coming?'

'I'll be right up.'

He wanted to follow her but couldn't summon the energy. He felt his eyes start to close again. He thought about Charlie and the vodka drip. Now that was what he called a proper medical innovation. He heard buzzing from upstairs. She'd started without him.

And then he passed out.

DAY 5

CHAPTER TWENTY-FOUR

Charlie sorted through his suits. Had to look the part for the lunch, even if it was a massive waste of time. Nothing there that quite fitted the bill. A bloke could never have enough suits and he didn't have nearly enough.

He finally settled on the Boglioli he had picked up at a charity shop in Woolwich, navy-blue wool with notched lapels, double-breasted, straight-legged. He'd taken it to a proper tailor to get it refitted, had only worn it the once. He decided on his Bottega Veneta belt. Not too shabby.

He got dressed and shaved and headed outside, half of London still asleep and he couldn't blame them, it was real brass monkeys. There was frost on the windscreen, had to scrape it off, another bloody London winter on its way.

He drove past the shuttered chemists and halal shops, a few shopkeepers rolling up their metal blinds, clocked some desperado rolling out of a twenty-four-hour convenience store, hands shaking as he lit his first gasper of the day.

Still quiet when he drove into the yard, just a few staffers from the night shift down in the naughty corner for a cheeky fag. Charlie punched in his code on the keypad and went in. When the lift doors opened on the third floor, he was expecting to be first in, but the DCI was already there, saints preserve us, talking to Grey.

Catching up on old times, Charlie thought, talking about how many first formers' heads they'd stuck down the toilet and seeing if they could remember all the words to the school song.

They stopped talking when they saw Charlie and the DCI nodded towards Charlie's office. 'Shall we?' he said.

He followed Charlie in and shut the door. 'Where are we on Grimes?' he said.

'Good morning, sir. Lovely day.'

'Come on, Charlie. Spare me. Five days and we still don't have a main suspect. You realise the grief I'm getting on this from upstairs?'

'We're doing everything we can.'

'It's not enough. You've got to be doing better than that.'

'Due respect, I don't see how that's possible, sir.'

'This isn't going to go away, Charlie. The nationals, all the TV channels, they're still running with this. A head on a spike in the middle of London? It's every news editor's wet dream.'

'It's nothing new, just went out of fashion for a while is all. It was all the rage back in Henry the Eighth's day.'

The DCI shook his head. 'It's amazing, really.'

'Sir?'

'I mean, what are the chances? You always get the gnarly ones, don't you?'

'I don't exactly go looking for them,' Charlie said. He threw his jacket on his visitor's chair, on top of the stack of files that were already teetering on top of it. 'What did Grey say? Does he think I'm still dragging my feet?'

'We weren't talking about you, Charlie. We were discussing the arrangements for lunch today.'

'The old boys get their own limousine and a red carpet?'

The DCI pretended to flick something off Charlie's shoulder. 'You've got a chip right there,' he said. 'Bloody big one.'

'Fair play. I'll get on with work now, shall I?'

'Cut him some slack, Charlie.'

'I do my best.'

'Besides what you think, he doesn't have it easy.'

'In what way?'

'Look, I know he never talks much about it. I'm not even

144

sure I should be talking out of school, so to speak.'

Charlie waited. Either tell me or don't, he thought. But stop fucking me about.

'Thing is, his wife had an accident a few years ago, in her car. She pretty much relies on her wheelchair. On top of that, they've got two young kids. Her parents help out, much as they can, as good as gave up their retirement to become full-time carers and babysitters, look after things while he's at work. But it's tough.'

'I'm sorry to hear that. So, what's he doing working murder squad?'

'That's what I said to him when he applied for the job here, but he's a pretty driven young man. He doesn't want a desk job and he doesn't want anyone feeling sorry for him.'

'That's insane,' Charlie said. He couldn't manage his own life with the hours he worked, and he was single. He couldn't imagine doing this job if he had a family.

That was why he didn't have a family. Perhaps.

'He's a good lad, Charlie. He'll work it out. Just go a bit easy.'

'I'm going as easy as I can. I did like you asked, I got in the pest exterminators. His workspace is now rodent free.'

'That's good.'

'I don't get it. Why didn't he ever tell anyone about his situation? We're a team. We can talk to each other.'

'Great souls suffer in silence.'

'Do they?'

'That wasn't me said that. It was Lincoln.'

Charlie bit his lip as the DCI turned for the door. Don't do it, he thought; let him walk out with his stupid aphorism intact, and let's leave it at that. But he couldn't help himself. 'Actually, it was Schiller.'

'What?'

'Friedrich Schiller. The "great souls" thing.' He clocked the DCI's blank look. 'He was a German playwright.'

'Thanks Charlie,' the DCI said. 'I knew I could always rely on you. Oh, one last thing. You haven't forgotten lunch today. You and Lovejoy are the honoured celebrities.'

'I didn't forget, sir. But I still think we'd be better off back here getting on with finding a lead in this Grimes murder. You know, that thing you just gave me the hurry-up on.'

'A couple of hours won't hurt. Catlin has organised for some of the press to come along afterwards for a photo op.'

'Really?'

'Times like this we need all the good press we can get.'

'It's embarrassing, sir. I'm not one for all this attention.'

'Come on, you deserve this, you and Lovejoy. Two people out of the same team getting bravery awards. What's the odds? Especially detectives. Usually the uniforms hog all the limelight.'

'So where are we going?'

'Some place around the corner. Catlin booked it. I think it used to be a laundry.'

Probably still is, Charlie thought, thinking about the recent budget cuts.

After the DCI left, Charlie looked down at his shoes. One of them had a scuff mark on the toe where he'd banged it on the kerb getting into his car. Wouldn't do if there was going to be Press with cameras.

He told Greene he was going out to interview a suspect, and drove to the nearest Sally's. There was a parking space almost right outside, took it as a sign from the Universe that he was doing the right thing.

'Hey Charlie,' the woman behind the counter said as he walked in. Shirley, her name was. They all knew him. He'd got his Kiton suit in here, he'd had to have the trousers taken in, but when you'd paid a hundred quid for a three thousand pound suit, it was worth it.

A couple of regulars were there already; the bloke who talked to himself in a high-pitched Scottish accent and wore a *Stars Wars* t-shirt no matter the weather; and the woman in the electric wheelchair who once ran over his foot and then yelled at him that he'd have to pay for repairs if he'd damaged the working parts.

Charlie found a pair of shoes he liked and took them to the counter. 'How much for these?'

Shirley shrugged and looked at the tag on the sole. 'Forty.'

'I'll give you thirty.'

Shirley nodded. 'As you're a good customer,' she said.

'And here's the other ten for your Christmas box,' Charlie said, and gave her two twenties.

'You're a gentleman.'

'That's what everyone says.'

He walked out with a pair of brown leather John Lobb Oxfords with an almond toe, stitched panels, leather lining and pie crust stitching. Absolute bargain. They'd be worth a grand new, easy.

Okay, now he was ready for the media.

CHAPTER TWENTY-FIVE

It was a big crowd for lunch, everyone brought their partners except Lubanski and Lovejoy. And Greene of course, who didn't have one. Charlie was the other Lonely Heart, Fi had cried off at the last minute, said she had an emergency at work, something to do with a problem with the gas lines at her pub. It sounded like an excuse to him.

The place was in Lo Ho, which was what they were calling Lower Holloway these days. It was set back from the road on a residential strip, noisy, hip and industrial, with a small gnarled olive tree in the brick courtyard outside, doing its best with its change of circumstances.

It was really flogging the laundry aesthetic, all bare brick and concrete floors, an open kitchen galley at the far end. There were long benches instead of tables, a handful of local business people eating at the counters and mostly talking property prices. Charlie took a quick glance at the menu. It wasn't cheap, which surprised him. Someone at the Met was taking all this seriously.

Their names had been scribbled on the tables in chalk in front of their seats. The DCI had made the seating arrangements according to his own arcane whims. Charlie was surprised to find himself sitting next to Grey's missus. She was already there when he arrived, her wheelchair near the courtyard and the nearest door. Ease of access, he supposed.

He had imagined a dour sort of woman, but she gave him a broad smile as he sat down, then said, 'You must be the fearsome DI George that Matt is always talking about.'

'Name's Charlie. Did he really say that about me?'

'My husband isn't scared of many things, but you seem to have put the fear of God up him.'

She had short dark hair and lively eyes. Where Grey was pretty much inscrutable, she was animated and quick to smile. She had on a knee-length blue woollen dress, and very little jewellery. Her most striking accessory was a bright yellow pashmina.

'Like the scarf thing,' Charlie said.

'Do you? I wear it to hide my surgery scars. No one wants to look at a woman who looks like Frankenstein, do they?'

'You don't look like Frankenstein.'

'That's the nicest thing anyone has ever said to me,' she said and held out her hand. 'My name's Whitney. Ages me, doesn't it? I was named after the singer.'

'The "I Will Always Love You" one? Drowned in the bath after a drug binge.'

'Yes, that one. I only ever take showers these days, in case I'm tempted. Parents don't think of these things when they pick names. We called our kids John and Jane, save them a lifetime of explanations.'

'I was named after a famous footballer. Fortunately he's still around and considered something of a living legend, unlike myself. Can you see the menu? I can't read the blackboard from this far away. I've got glasses for long distance but I'm too vain to ever bring them anywhere.'

'It's all right, I heard your boss ordering share plates.'

'That takes the worry out of that, then. My guess, he didn't want anyone choosing lobster.'

'What's for dessert?' she said.

'We haven't had the entrées yet.'

'If there's a dessert I like I want to make sure I leave room.' She put on her glasses.

'So, you're not vain at all then?' he said.

'I stopped being vain about the time I needed someone to put me on the toilet and take me off again. Sorry, too much information. There's rhubarb and ginger beer sorbet, citrus curd and rum baba—'

'Stop right there,' Charlie said. 'I used to love rum babas when I was a kid. I'd save up for weeks to buy one from the cake shop in the high street. Hardly see them any more.'

'I hear they're making a comeback.' She put her glasses back in their case. 'That's two rum babas then. So, this big lunch is all for you and DC Lovejoy?'

'More her than me. They had to give me an award as well – it was politics. They could either make me a hero or send me to the Outer Hebrides on traffic duty.'

'Do they have traffic up there?'

'Only five cars but they all go to the pub at the same time.'

She laughed and shook her head. 'You have the weirdest sense of humour, Charlie. Matt never told me that.'

'Well, he doesn't joke around much. He's very serious, your husband.'

'I know he's not everyone's cup of tea.'

'He's clearly yours.'

'He has a big heart. You have to get to know him.'

Charlie wondered how easy it was to get to know DS Grey. Had he told her about the complaint he'd lodged with the DCI, or the dead rat in his desk? Somehow he doubted it.

'He believes in what he does, Charlie. He's very . . . earnest.'

'Sometimes perhaps a bit too earnest?'

She gave him an apologetic smile. 'I've told him he has to learn to loosen up a little bit if he's going to fit in.' She looked around the table. 'Your team look like a pretty easy-going bunch.'

'I don't know about that.'

'Perhaps I worry too much about him. I try to be supportive.'

Charlie didn't know what to say to that. He wasn't inclined to talk out of school but she must know by now that having any kind of relationship with a copper wasn't all beer and skittles, even without two kids and a wheelchair. Lubanski had already burned off one husband, Wes James had a girlfriend with him, but she was the third one this year, and McCullough had brought someone he didn't recognise, could have been a Tinder date for all he knew. Rupinder Singh and his FLO, Malik Khan, were the only ones with their original wives, though he thought that might be cultural influence.

'You must be a good boss.'

'I try and foster a sort of . . . cohesion.'

'Matt says this lot will follow you anywhere.'

'Sometimes they follow me when they shouldn't. Look at DC Lovejoy. I have warned your fella. Everyone who comes out on jobs with me ends up either in the hospital or on stress leave.'

'Matt knows how to look after himself,' she said.

'That's good, then.'

'It doesn't mean that I don't worry every time he walks out of the door to go to work. But Matt says being a detective isn't dangerous.'

'He's probably right. When you're in uniform, it's a bit different. They're the ones who take most of the risks.'

'So how do two members of the same murder squad get nominated for bravery awards in the same year?'

'You can't legislate against bad luck. Nothing like that is likely to happen again.'

'You know, every time the phone rings, my heart's in my mouth, thinking it's Matt. When it's just one of the kids' teachers saying they've fallen off the play equipment or bitten some other child, I breathe a sigh of relief. It must be what it's like to be a soldier's wife, I suppose. Do you have a wife, Charlie?'

'Who'd have me?'

'Oh, I'm sure there would be plenty of takers.' The first share plate arrived. 'What are these?' she said.

'Pig's head croquettes,' the waiter said.

'Amazing how they can shrink a pig's head to this size.'

151

'You need a special kind of steamer,' Charlie said. 'You get them in Asda.'

She picked at one, raised an eyebrow. 'Not bad. I'll have to get one of those.'

Grey waited until after the share plates had finished, then came over and whispered something to her, and wheeled her towards the Ladies at the back of the room. Charlie clocked how she reached back over her shoulder to put her hand on his, and the look she gave him. For a moment there he felt jealous.

Then McCullough said something about Spurs being ready to thrash Arsenal in the League Cup and he was forced to wade in and put him straight.

When the Greys got back, the DCI tapped his fork on his glass and stood up. Charlie felt sorry for the other people in the restaurant. They'd probably come here for a quiet lunch, not to listen to some pompous copper gob off at the top of his voice. But there was nothing for it but to hear him out.

He thanked them all for coming, as if there was any choice, and congratulated Lovejoy and Charlie on their upcoming awards and made the point, jokingly, that he hoped this would be the last time the assistant commissioner would have to cream off the top of the budget to buy them all lunch, and that they definitely wouldn't be getting a new kettle for the squad room now. There was applause, even from some of the other diners.

Finally, he sat down.

'Matt says you support the Arsenal,' Whitney said, trying to pick up the conversation again after the DCI had finished banging on.

'I wouldn't say "support".'

'What would you say, Charlie?'

'Well, you know that bit on official forms where you have to state your religion? That's where I put "Gooner".'

'I'm Man U myself.'

'You? Get out.'

'Is that a surprise?'

152

'I don't mean to be rude, not to the wife of my own outside DS, but that's typical.'

'Why is that, detective inspector?'

'I have yet to meet a Manchester United supporter who actually comes from Manchester.'

'Well inspector, I'll put you straight. My grandfather played for Manchester United in the fifties as a defender. He's still alive, lives in Chester. That's why I support Man U.'

'Pull the other one.'

'No, it's true. Gospel, as they say round here. Not only that, he's promised me when he dies I can have all his United memorabilia. There's even a photograph of him with Duncan Edwards, Bill Foulkes and Matt Busby.'

'I take back every word then,' Charlie said.

Grey looked up, saw Charlie and his wife laughing, and looked utterly bewildered.

He hadn't even finished his double espresso when the DCI started ushering him and Lovejoy outside for the photos. Catlin had turned up with a posse of press photographers, and they were waiting for them in the courtyard.

Whitney put her hand on his arm as he stood up. 'It was lovely to meet you,' she said.

'Likewise.'

'It's good to know Matt's in good hands. I hope he does well. He loves this job.'

'I'm sure he'll be fine,' Charlie said.

'Be patient with him. I know he can be a bit prickly.'

'We all can.'

As he and Lovejoy and the DCI were posing for the endless group hugs under the olive tree, Charlie saw Grey standing on the pavement waiting for the taxi to take his wife home. His sergeant turned around and gave him a look. What was it? Gratitude? Remorse?

That look would stay with him, as it turned out, pretty much forever.

CHAPTER TWENTY-SIX

Charlie realised there was no way he could properly cope. On TV, the detectives worked one murder case at a time; here at Essex Road, apart from Mick on a Stick, he had five different murders on his desk, one of them waiting for trial, another up for jury selection on Monday in the Old Bailey, which would tie up Wes and Rupe most of the following week. One case was still open, a shooting in Tottenham; charges still hadn't been laid. It was frustrating him because he thought it should have been sorted by now. They had what he thought was a good case, but these days it still wasn't enough to please the CPS.

He hated talking to the CPS. The government had slashed a third of their jobs in the last few years; he could never get hold of the same case officer, every time he rang he ended up talking to someone different. There was no point emailing them any more, you might as well scribble a note and throw it in the waste bin. Get an email back from the CPS and he'd be off down the framers to hang it on his wall.

He thought he had good cases for the other two; there was the idiot who ran over three people standing at a bus stop, one of them happened to be his ex-girlfriend. He was driving so fast he demolished the bus shelter and half a front window of Tesco. His story was he sneezed and lost control of the car; unfortunately, he happened to say within earshot of twenty people at a party the night before that he was going to kill her for sleeping with his best mate.

The girl had died of her injuries a week later and the CPS

were now saying they didn't have enough to bring a successful prosecution. Made him think the Millers had been lucky to see Grimes go inside at all.

Then there was the sixteen-stone bloke who beat up his wife with a baseball bat. She was five feet four and seven stone dripping wet and he was claiming self-defence.

He had briefed a lawyer, gave him the evidence, sent all the necessary paperwork over as soon as it was finished. Just before the trial day, the barrister rang him up and said, 'Why didn't you send me the witness statements?' Somehow they'd got lost in the system, and the trial had been delayed again.

No matter what he did, the CPS always wanted more; more fingerprints, more DNA, more positive photo ID. He'd say, *Look, I've sent you fingerprints, I've sent you DNA from the crime scene, we've got him bang to rights, surely?*

James had walked in one afternoon and found him yelling down the phone, '*What do you want, a handjob?*'

While he was juggling all that, he had the DCI breathing down his neck about Grimes. It was bloody impossible, there was too much to do and not enough to do it with and all the odds were stacked against him. It was like managing the Arsenal.

He remembered he was supposed to be going to the theatre with Fiona after work. *Agamemnon*, if you don't mind. He'd bought the tickets months ago, long before this case. He knew he should go, for research if nothing else, but if he did he'd never get through all this backlog. So he rang Fi and told her he couldn't make it, that he'd meet her at the Trafalgar for a drink afterwards. She wasn't well pleased, but what could he do?

There was a knock on the door. 'You got to see this, guv,' James said.

'What is it, Wes?'

Charlie followed James outside. Amory, who headed up Surveillance, was with Greene, leaning on his desk, watching video footage on the monitor. Singh was with them.

155

When he saw Charlie, Greene rewound the video. Charlie went over to have a look.

'One of my team got this last night,' Amory said. 'They followed him down the local pub. He was in there for a while. Had quite a bit to drink, they reckon. One of them recorded this on their phone.'

Charlie watched Gordon stagger out of the front door of a pub, nearly tripping over his own feet. 'A bit to drink?' Charlie said. 'He's absolutely legless. He doesn't get in his car, does he?'

'No, but look at this,' Greene said, and pointed at the monitor.

There was a loud noise and Gordon threw himself flat on the pavement and stayed there.

'What was that?' Charlie said.

'A van backfired at the lights,' Amory said.

'What's he doing?'

Gordon seemed to suddenly sober up. He raised himself on his arms, sprinted to the nearest wall and waited there, in a crouch, his back against the bricks. Then he took off, zigzagging up the street, took cover behind a row of yellow bins outside an all-night laundrette.

The screen blurred and jumped as the surveillance boys followed. There was another short few seconds of video; Gordon running across the street, shouting at a young couple to get off the street, *now*.

'Where is this?'

'Down Hackney, by London Lane,' Amory said. 'Near the railway bridge. People were standing around staring at him, thought he was high on crack or something.'

'Watch this,' Greene said. 'He was playing soldiers all the way home.'

There was some more jumpy video; Gordon doubled back, took cover in a doorway, then ran at a crouch up the middle of the street. A taxi pounded its horn as it swerved to avoid him. The cabbie leaned out and yelled at him.

156

'Listen to your bloke puffing,' Singh said to Amory. 'He should join a gym.'

'Lennox may be crazy, but he's fit,' James said.

The video ended and Charlie straightened up, shaking his head. He'd never seen anything like it. Gordon Lennox had seemed so bloody normal, when he spoke to him, at least compared with Tom Miller.

'He's a bloody psycho,' Singh said.

'No, he's not a psycho, Rupe,' Charlie said. 'That's post-traumatic stress, that is.'

'You reckon it was him after all?' James said. 'It's only his wife backing up his alibi. He's clearly unstable.'

'Tell that to the CPS,' Charlie said. 'Unstable doesn't get us an arrest warrant.' Charlie turned back to Amory. 'Thanks Martin. Good work.'

Charlie went back to his office and double-checked his applications for additional covert surveillance on Gordon Lennox. He patched through an Airwave call to the officer on the overnight shift outside Lennox's house. Nothing to report.

He always wondered about surveillance teams, what it took to sit in a parked vehicle waiting for something to happen for thirteen hours without going brain dead. He supposed some of the time it must be interesting, coordinating with four or five other cars in a surveillance operation, that could be good, would require a high degree of skill. But the rest of the time, even though it sounded glamorous, it had to be one of the worst jobs in the world.

He started reviewing more witness statements on his monitor, but his eyes were sore and his head was throbbing. Hardly anyone left in the office by now, most of the strip lights were off, only the night duty staff left. He pulled out his cot from the corner, took off shoes and laid down. Just a couple of hours, rest his eyes.

He woke with a start a little later, remembered he was supposed to be meeting Fi in town. He grabbed his coat and ran for the lift. Outside, he saw lights glittering and falling over London. Either he was having a stroke from overwork or it was Bonfire Night.

CHAPTER TWENTY-SEVEN

A bit lively around the square, stragglers from the Million Masks March, the annual Vendetta protest march, were still hanging around in their black hoodies and Guy Fawkes masks, some of them still with protest banners, 'One solution, revolution'. As if revolution ever changed anything, Charlie thought. Ask the Russians.

Or the Americans.

He heard the odd firecracker, a red flare going off; a couple of uniforms in yellow jackets were wrestling with two young blokes who'd got carried away with it all. He could smell fireworks, hear police sirens over in Whitehall and the Mall.

He thought about the Guy Fawkes he and Michael had made when they were kids. They had put it on a trolley and stood outside the local Sainsbury's, asking people for their small change in their wheedling little-boy voices. On fireworks night they'd burned it in their back yard; his old man had laughed and said, 'We did that to a Tottenham supporter once.'

The Trafalgar was a Fuller's pub but never mind, it had some Sierra Nevada on draught, so he got a pint and sat in a booth by the window. It was raining, and the lights of the square were pixelated through the glass. Most of the crowd were tourists, they'd been watching the fireworks down by the Thames. They seemed to like the flags and gold chandeliers and the brass ship's bell. He'd been in here once years ago and told a group of Germans it was where Nelson used to drink and that he only ever had shandy. They believed him and took a selfie under the flag, the same one Nelson raised on the *Dreadnought* at the battle of Agincourt when he defeated Napoleon.

Heads turned as Fiona walked in. His head had turned too, first time he met her. She was a good-looking woman, no mistake. She shook out her umbrella in the doorway when she saw him. He got to his feet to greet her and got a sort of half-smile for his trouble. He considered that a result in the circumstances.

'Been waiting long?' she said as she sat down.

'I only just got here,' he said. 'Sorry I couldn't make it tonight. You know what it's like. You've seen it in the papers; I sleep, eat and dream this one.'

She took off her coat, ran her fingers through her hair. 'That's all right, Charlie. I missed your special lunch, so I suppose we're even.'

'I wasn't trying to get even,' he said.

'Of course not,' she said, but he knew by her tone that she didn't believe him. 'Wouldn't mind a drink. I'm gagging.'

He went to the bar and got her a Hendrick's and tonic. When he got back she was holding out her theatre programme. 'I got you a souvenir,' she said.

'How was it?'

'You wouldn't have liked it. It was three-and-a-half hours. You couldn't have sat still for that long.'

'Come on, I'm not that bad.'

'You have the attention span of a Jack Russell on cocaine.' She sipped her gin, and looked at him over the rim of her glass. 'It was boring as batshit. I only agreed to go because you said you wanted to see it. I'm not cultured like you.'

'Me? I'm not cultured.'

'Bollocks. Of course you are. Pretending not to be is all part of your act. The Charlie George show.'

'Well, I'm sorry you had a bad night.'

'I didn't say I had a bad night. I got talking to this bloke in the intermission. Think he was trying to pick me up.'

'Did he succeed?'

A shrug. 'I got his number. A girl never knows when she might need a spare.'

Charlie decided not to rise to the bait. He wondered if she was serious. You could never be sure with Fi. 'You stayed to the end, then?'

'Kept waiting for it to get better. Anyway, I had nothing else to do.'

'Thought you might like it. It premiered in 450 BC so that's quite a good run.'

'Not as long as *The Mousetrap*.'

'The critic in the *Guardian* said it was part *Godfather* part *Breaking Bad*.'

'There was a lot of discussion about revenge,' Fiona said, and then she added, with an unnerving smile: 'They talked about it as if it was a bad thing.'

Charlie wasn't happy he'd missed it, and not just because it hadn't gone down well with Fiona. He couldn't tell her about the note they'd found in Grimes' mouth; no one outside the incident room knew about that. Perhaps watching it would have helped with the investigation; he'd have to buy a copy and read it again now.

'I wonder if they kept to the original,' he said.

'So you already knew what it was about?' Fiona asked him.

'Well, yeah. It's about the futility of retribution. It starts with Agamemnon sacrificing his daughter to Athena, and then everyone kills everyone else, to try and even up the score. In the end, Athena steps in to prevent the three sisters, the Furies, from killing the next target on the list. Orestes, I think it is. She persuades them that mercy should take precedence over violence.'

'Why would you want to see it, if you already know how it ends?'

'Nothing is about the ending. It's about what the ending means.'

'Really? For a boy from north London, you think a lot.'

'Hard not to think about things, when you do what I do for

a living. Like, there was this couple I had to talk to this week, they lost their four-year-old girl to a drunk driver. You know who the drunk driver was?'

'The bloke on the railing. I watch the news. Enough shop talk, Charlie.' He felt something pressing against the inside of his thigh. He looked down. Fi had taken off her shoe and her stockinged foot was making its way towards his groin. She tickled his balls with her toes.

'There's people watching,' Charlie said.

'No, they're not. Even if they were, what would you care? Live a little, Charlie.'

'As long as you don't want me to get up and get you another drink in the next five minutes. I'll get thrown out for indecent exposure.'

'Five minutes? You can keep it up for a lot longer than that. I know that from personal experience.'

He slid along the banquette, out of reach. She made a face at him. *Boring.*

'How was the lunch?' she said. 'Sorry I missed your moment of glory.'

'I suppose the real moment of glory is next month at the Dorchester.'

'Now that I'm not going to miss. Will David Beckham be there?'

'It's not like the red carpet at the Oscars, Fi. You can't go wearing a dress with invisible tape over your boobs and a slit up the side.'

'Why not? The Home Secretary will. What about the Queen? Is she going?'

'Don't you start.'

'What's the matter? You deserve a fucking knighthood after what you did.'

'There's cops every day do things they deserve a medal for. Blokes who take on terrorists with their bare hands.'

'Maybe it wasn't a terrorist you were chasing, but you still could have got yourself killed. I looked it up on Google. You're mad, you are. Imagine if the cavalry had arrived a couple of minutes too late. What were you thinking, Charlie?'

'I wasn't. Just instinct, I suppose. I probably wouldn't have done it if I'd had time to think about it.'

'Well, I'm proud of you.'

'You didn't know me then.'

'I'm proud of you *in retrospect*.'

'Thanks. But it's embarrassing all this fuss. I don't mind about Lovejoy getting a gong. She deserves it more than me.'

At the mention of Lovejoy's name, the warm fuzzy atmosphere that had been growing between them suddenly frosted over. She leaned back against the banquette and folded her arms. 'How do you work that out?'

'She spent weeks in hospital, I didn't.'

'You could have spent the rest of eternity in a coffin. I think that's a bigger deal than a sore foot.'

'Bit more than a sore foot.'

'She's the one that's got your spaniel, right?'

'It's not my spaniel. I gave Charlie to her.'

'So you gave her all of Charlie,' she muttered, and there was acid in her voice. 'How is he, anyway?'

'He's got a hangover. He'll be all right.'

'Well, it's good she had someone to hold her hand during the crisis.' She toyed with the stem on her glass. 'I hope you catch this maniac soon. It's seriously interfering with our sex life.'

Charlie managed a strangled smile.

'I know you're not allowed to talk about it, but are you any closer?'

'I don't know. We have a list of suspects. We don't have enough yet to bring charges. And . . . you know.'

'No, I don't know. What?'

'Well, there's a part of me, doesn't really want to catch him. Or her. Whoever it is.'

She stared at him. 'What are you talking about?'

163

'Well, what was Grimes doing walking around, after what he did? There's something wrong with this world. Maybe that's what those protesters out there are on about. They're angry and they're frustrated because they expect a better system. This country isn't giving it to them, is it?'

'Steady on, you're a cop, Charlie. You can't be judge and jury as well. You're there to serve the law, you can't decide each time you get a murder whether it was okay or not.'

'I know. Let's drop it.'

'They slaughtered this man and stuck his head on a pole. It's *medieval*.'

'It's not black and white, is all I'm saying. What if it was your kid that he killed? It's all right talking about the law when it's all theory, but what if it happened to *you*?'

'I'd like to think I'm not a barbarian. I'd let the law run its course.'

'And after the law has run its course, and you're sitting there knowing you should be celebrating your kid's ninth birthday, and the reason you're not is walking around Kentish Town without even an ounce of remorse for what he's done, you'd go, "Oh well, fair play to him", and forget all about it?'

'You don't know he wasn't remorseful.'

'Oh, forget it.' He finished his pint and looked at his watch. 'Shall we go back to mine?'

She reached for her bag. 'Not tonight. I've got an early start and you've got a murderer to catch.' He got up to help her with her coat. He thought she might kiss him goodnight, but she didn't. She went out, struggled with her umbrella in the wind, and was gone before the door had finished closing.

CHAPTER TWENTY-EIGHT

Charlie didn't go straight to the Tube, felt like he needed to clear his head. He walked down towards the Mall; there were marchers still yelling and letting off flares, milling about in huddled groups. It looked like the aftermath of a battle. He stopped by the statue of some marble soldier, in a suitably heroic pose. War was different back when they stuck those up, he thought. It was always glorious, and England always won. If you had a bit shot off, they pinned bits of your uniform over the gaps and off you went. No harm done. Like Nelson.

That was what they had you believe, anyway.

Perhaps it was what Tom Miller had believed.

His iPhone started vibrating in his pocket. He supposed it was the Arlington. Probably Ma again, they always rang at night; either she'd lose her purse or she was having an anxiety attack and wouldn't go back to her room. Ben would be too busy shagging his sixteen-year-old to get over there.

'This is Charlie.'

'Charlie, it's Ben.'

'Ben? What's going on?'

'It's Jules. She's in hospital.'

'Hospital? Is she all right?'

'She's okay but it's the baby.'

The baby. He tried to focus, still had work going round and round in his head, then the argument with Fiona. He couldn't even remember what the baby was called, he'd only seen her once, not long after she'd been born. Fine uncle he turned out to be.

Jo, that was right. Short for Jocaster. How could he forget that name?

'Is she sick?'

'Thing is, Tel's been arrested.' Charlie felt his guts clench, as they always did when someone mentioned his sister's prick of a husband.

'He's what?'

'Apparently they were having some sort of argument, as usual, while she was holding the baby. He pushed her and she fell and the baby hit her head.'

'You are joking me. How bad is she hurt?'

'They're doing tests. I don't know much more, couldn't get much sense out of Jules on the phone.'

'I'll fucking kill him. How many times have I warned him? She should have left him years ago. He's a psycho.'

'Steady on, Charlie.'

'I don't want to steady on. You keep saying "steady on" to me, but he keeps doing this shit.'

A kid in a mask came up to him, waving a placard in his face. Moron. Charlie shoved him aside. His next thought was for his nephew, the poor little bugger who had to put up with all this crap going on around him. As if he didn't have enough problems, as it was. 'Who's looking after Rom then?'

'I'm going down to Brighton tonight. Thought I'd get him and bring him back with me.'

'And do what with him? You work during the day.'

'I've talked to Del. She's owed some sick leave, she'll look after him, her and Rom get on famous.'

'Del? Who's Del?'

'Delilah.' There was a long silence as Charlie tried to remember. 'My girlfriend.'

'Oh, her. It's been ages. You still going out with the same girl? Bugger me. Well all right, if she's willing. Does she know about his condition?'

'She's a neo-nate nurse, she knows how to look after sick kids. His bubble-itis or whatever it is, isn't going to faze her.'

'It's called immune deficiency disease.'

'You know what I mean.'

'When are you going down?'

'Soon as I can get myself ready.'

'I'll come with you.'

'Bro, are you sure? I mean, you've got enough on.'

'We'll get a few cans of Red Bull and share the driving, we'll be back by morning. My inside DS can take care of things if I'm not in for morning prayers.'

'Want me to pick you up at home or the office?'

'Neither. I'll wait for you outside Embankment.'

Charlie watched the desultory flicker of the last fireworks, listened to chanting coming from somewhere along the Strand. A car slowed, flashed his lights at him. As it got closer, he picked out Ben's red Cayenne, sleek and dangerous in the street lights. Charlie jumped in.

'Look at this bloody car,' Charlie said. 'You have too much money and too little sense.'

'And you, my brother,' Ben said, 'have the wrong job.'

'Just don't speed,' Charlie said. 'I've got enough aggravation in my life as it is.'

'I'll drive in the slow lane the whole way and give hand signals. All right?'

Ben already had two Red Bulls on the console. He took a sip out of one. 'Tastes like crap but it'll do the job. How are you, Charlie?'

'Ready to murder someone.'

'Well, let's mellow out before we get to Brighton. Murdering him isn't going to help.'

'I rang the nick in Brighton while I was waiting for you, found someone I used to know on the night shift. His old man was one of my guv'nors when I worked in CID. He told me on the QT that Tel's been released.'

'Already? How come?'

'Jules is backing his story that it was all an accident. She's refusing to press charges.'

'Christ, she does this every time.' Ben tried to ring her on the hands free. They both stared at the screen, silently willing her to pick up. She didn't. Ben tried three more times and gave up.

'Why did she call you and not me?' Charlie said.

'Why do you think?' Ben said.

Charlie fumed on that for a bit. 'I don't get why she doesn't want me to sort him out,' he said, finally.

'Because it won't help.'

'It might. Certainly help me feel better.'

'But this isn't about you, Charlie. Is it?'

They stopped at a service station on the A23 around midnight. It was cold and it was raining. While Ben filled up, Charlie went inside and got vital supplies to last them the trip, two more Red Bulls and a couple of Mars Bars. They were on special, which meant they were only three times the price of Tesco. It made him cry to think about the way they used to make them back in the day; you needed teeth like a mastodon just to get through the chocolate.

As he ran back to the car he checked out all the sorry cases in the forecourt; there was a bloke with long greasy hair, looked like he'd just buried a body in the forest, and a truck driver who hadn't had a bath since the millennium. Charlie wondered what he had in his refrigerated trailer. Please God not thirty Vietnamese.

It was Charlie's turn to drive and Ben stretched out in the passenger seat as they pulled back out onto the road. 'Sorry if I ruined your night.'

'You didn't ruin anything.'

'How's the latest? Philippa?'

168

'Fiona.'

'Right. How did you meet her again?'

'Tinder.'

'So you've finally decided to meet women the old-fashioned way. What does she do?'

'She's in hospitality.'

'What does that mean?'

'She manages a pub in the West End.'

'Tell me she doesn't have a muscle shirt and a nose ring.'

Charlie took out his phone and showed Ben a selfie they had taken in front of the London Eye. Ben shook his head. 'She's hot.'

'You sound surprised.'

'How long you been seeing her?'

'About three months.'

'How's it going?'

Charlie shrugged and put his phone away.

'What have you done now?'

'I haven't done anything. It's just, we don't agree on a lot of things.'

'You're too tired to get it up?'

'Mate, the bedroom's fine. It's everywhere else that's the issue.'

'You know your trouble?'

'Not again. Do you know how many times you say that to me?'

'Well, if you'd stop getting yourself into these messes, I wouldn't have to.'

'Who said it was a mess?'

'It was implied.'

'Was it?'

'So tell me I'm wrong.'

Charlie shrugged. 'Maybe. All right, we had a bit of an argument tonight. She'll get over it.'

'What was the argument about?'

'I don't know. She wants me to put her before work.'

'What a bitch.'

'All right, all right. I know. Thing is, I told her when we first met, I said, sometimes when there's a flap on, I can't be like, you know, normal.'

'Newsflash. You're never normal, Charlie.'

'I try to be.'

'Not quite the same thing. Let me give you a heads up. Alexis Sánchez.'

'What?'

'She sounds like Alexis Sánchez, and you, you're Manchester United.'

'Don't you call me Manchester United. That's fighting talk.'

'You remember what happened? There's Ed Woodward, going through the Premier League equivalent of Tinder, flicks right when he sees Alexis. He thinks, this is it, great player, sexy player, he's scored all these goals for the Arsenal, PFA player of the year, brilliant. Signs him up, what happens? The complete disaster. Because they bought him with their eyes, not their heads. It's so like you, Charlie. You find someone for a quick night of passion, well, good luck to you mate. No problem there. But you try and turn a Tinder date into a long-term relationship and beat yourself up when it doesn't work out.'

'We have a good time,' Charlie said.

Ben made a face. 'Of course you do. But what do you have in common?'

Charlie had to think about it. 'We both like a drink.'

'That's a unique quality. I mean, really?'

Charlie looked out of the window, gave himself time to think. This shouldn't be such a tough question. He'd liked Fiona from the moment he first saw her, and she seemed to like him. They went out on a few dates, then fell into bed, it went from there. He'd never really thought too much about whether they had anything in common.

Ben cut across his thoughts. 'Don't get me wrong,' he said.

'You're a clever bloke, Charlie. I'm sure you're top drawer at your job. And clothes, never known anyone so particular. But when it comes to women, you should be in special ed.'

'Thanks.'

'I mean it in the nicest possible way. But think about it. If you actually wanted a long-term girlfriend, you'd be a bit more particular in the girls you chose, right? Truth is, you don't want one. You just want people to think you want one because it looks good on your resume. "Poor Charlie, he tries but he never has any luck." You're not fooling me. I've known you too long.'

'Why don't I?'

'Why don't you what?'

'Come in, Sigmund Freud, why don't I want a long-term girlfriend?'

'I don't think you like people getting too close. It seems like it unnerves you.'

'I was with Nicole for five years.'

'And look what happened in the end. She was a saint, mate. You'd be a nightmare to live with.'

'Thanks.'

'You have to hear these things from someone.'

'Wait a minute. First time in your life you've got a girlfriend who's lasted more than three weeks and suddenly you're a relationship counsellor?'

'I'm just trying to help you, Charlie.'

'No, you're not. You're having a laugh here. Are you saying I'm shallow?'

'If the cap fits.'

'I'm not the one with a sixteen-year-old girlfriend called Delilah with a 42D bra size.'

'She's twenty-three, and all her attributes are God-given. Including her intelligence, which she used to get a degree in nursing.'

'Since when have you cared about a woman's intelligence?'

171

'I've changed, Charlie.'

'No you haven't. You're just in hiatus.'

'I'm in what?'

'Just shut up and let me drive,' Charlie said.

'Okay, have it your way, I'm going to shut my eyes for five minutes. Talking to you wears me out, proper. One last thing, remember, when we get there, keep your cool, all right?'

'Of course,' Charlie said. 'Couldn't be more chilled if I was in the fridge. You are looking at a Zen master.'

CHAPTER TWENTY-NINE

Empty corridors, flickering strip lights, locked doors. Charlie hated hospitals best of times; at night it was like wandering around inside a bad dream. They buzzed in at the ICU, a nurse told them she'd inform their sister that they were outside. They went to the waiting room at the end of the corridor.

Rom was sitting on his own, a surgical mask over his face. Hospitals were the worst place for someone with immune deficiencies. He was wearing his tracksuit pyjamas, and two massive green furry slippers shaped like dinosaur feet. He was playing on his iPad and he didn't even look up when they walked in. Bad sign.

'Rom, how are you doing, mate?' Ben said.

A nod. Poor sod has no idea what is going on, Charlie thought, so he's basically shut down. Probably scared to death as well.

Charlie sat on the other side and put his arm around him.

'Bad night?'

'The worst.'

A heavy door banged, Jules came out of the ICU, put her head into the waiting room. No 'thanks for coming, boys', nothing. She just looked at Charlie and said to Ben: 'I thought I told you not to bring him.'

There were mascara smudges on her cheeks and the look in her eyes, it was like she'd stepped out of a war zone.

'What happened?' Charlie said.

'It was an accident.'

'Another one,' Charlie said. 'More accidents round your place than a Qatari building site.'

'How's the baby?' Ben said.

'He didn't mean to do it,' Jules said.

'So why did you tell the police that he did?' Charlie asked her.

'I was hysterical, I didn't know what I was saying. They must have misunderstood.'

'You've got to stop protecting him, Jules.'

'Look, we were only having a row, all right? It got a bit heated and he pushed me. It wasn't hard but I tripped and fell over. Little Jo hit her head on the door as we went down.'

'He pushed you while you were holding the baby?' Ben said.

'He didn't mean to hurt her. He didn't mean to hurt either of us.'

'Sounds like a load of bollocks to me,' Charlie said.

'You shouldn't say bollocks,' Rom said.

'How's the baby?' Ben said again.

Jules slumped against the door. 'I don't know. She just went limp, you know? I couldn't wake her up.' She bent double, guilt and loss hitting her like a gut punch. Charlie went to comfort her and she held out a hand to fend him off. He backed off, sat back down next to Rom.

Ben knelt down in front of Jules. She put her arms around his neck and hugged him. 'I didn't mean for her to get hurt,' she said.

'What about social services?' Ben said.

'They said they're sending someone round. They won't take Rom away from me, will they?'

Rom looked up at Charlie, but he couldn't make out the expression in the eyes above the mask. Was it fear, or hope? You could never really tell with kids.

'How about I take Rom home with me and Del for a few days? So you can stay in here with Jo?'

Jules nodded, her face all screwed up in pain. Charlie knew

he should feel sorry for her, but there was no sorry left in him any more, just rage.

'How about that, Rom?' Ben said. 'Would you like to stay with me and Aunty Del for a few days?'

Rom nodded his head, yes.

After Jules went back into ICU, Charlie tried to imagine the skinny blonde in the tight black skirt that he had only ever seen a few times in the passenger seat of Ben's car as 'Aunty Del'. It was a stretch.

Ben nodded to Charlie and they went out into the corridor, where Rom couldn't hear them.

'What do you think?' Ben said.

'I think he'll kill her one day.'

'He's really done it this time.'

'We said that when he beat her up last time.'

'Why doesn't she learn?'

'It's like this, Ben. I had this woodwork teacher at school. He had the tips missing from two of his fingers. He lost the first one showing the class how to use a circular saw. He lost the second one demonstrating what happened the first time. There is no mistake, Ben, so dumb, so unbelievably stupid, that people won't make twice.'

'Then there's nothing we can do, is there?'

'Yes, there is. I could find him and give him a bloody good hammering. And then I could tell him that if he ever comes near my sister again, I'm going to wrap him in plastic and throw him in a reservoir with one of his ten-pound barbells jammed down his throat.'

'That's a joke, right?'

'No, I'm actually going to do it, Ben. I've had enough.'

'Calm down.'

'I am calm. Scarily so.'

'No, Charlie, we're going to do it my way for once. I'm not going to watch you lose your job over this. Now you wait there while I talk to Rom, then we can discuss this like reasonable adults.'

As soon as he'd gone back inside the waiting room, Charlie turned and headed down the corridor for the exit. He'd been a reasonable adult since he was sixteen and where had it got him? He had to go find his brother-in-law.

It was time for the nuclear option.

CHAPTER THIRTY

Still dark, getting on for morning, not as cold as you'd expect for winter at the seaside; must be the global warming, Charlie thought. He walked along the seafront with his hands deep in his pockets, the smell of salt in the air. *Calm down*, was that what Ben had said?

Calm down?

The old West Pier looked sad and desolate, like a whale that had been washed up in the shallows, only the bones left, rotting in the rain. He went down the steps to the beach, the pebbles crunching under his shoes. He saw a shape, indistinct, someone sitting in the lee of the sea wall, drinking something out of a paper bag. He could hear him muttering to himself, huddled up against the cold.

Perhaps it's better if I don't find him, feeling like this. I can feel the old man in me coming out; he wouldn't have put up with the likes of Tel, he'd have had it sorted years ago. Didn't care what he did, or what was done to him. A vicious fucker, but fearless.

Where would Tel be? Charlie thought. He had tried the apartment, there was no answer.

Terry had a brother in Hove, but they hadn't talked for years. He might have shelled out for a cheap B&B or else he spent the night on a park bench. No, Tel wasn't tough enough for that. He looked well hard, but the tosser was weak as water.

His phone buzzed in his pocket. He took it out and stared at the screen. It was Ben. He let it ring out and put it back in his pocket.

It kept ringing so finally he turned it off.

For some reason he found himself thinking about his brother Will and he wondered what time it was in Sydney. Spring over there, late afternoon. His brother would be throwing up on the beach right now, with some nice soft yellow sand between his toes. Not like this crap, all shingle and plastic bottles in the wavelets.

What a family. An alcoholic, a suicide, a priest, the other one married to a serial abuser. Only him and Ben normal, and if he found Tel before the cops did, he'd probably get the flick off the normal pile as well.

Like the old saying, right? If you didn't let go of the past, it wouldn't let go of you.

A woman went past, pushing a shopping trolley full of plastic shopping bags. She had a woollen hat, looked like one of those old tea cosies, a puffa jacket three sizes too large and odd shoes. He wondered what her story was. Perhaps she was a copper once, an inspector at a busy station who put her brother-in-law in hospital, ended up in prison and lost the lot. It was the way it happened.

'Need a cup of tea, love?' he said to her.

She stopped and looked around. 'What was that?'

'I said, do you need a cup of tea?' He fished in his pocket for change.

'No, fuck off,' she said, and kept walking.

Charlie watched her waddle off down the seafront. Well, that was nice, he thought. It sort of restored his faith in human nature. Not everyone was on the make then, not everyone wanted a handout.

There were a few B&Bs scattered along the seafront, looking drab and tired in the wind and dark. A few of them had lights on, one had a massive Union Jack hanging from a flagpole over the front door. Must have been grand down here once, all the fluted columns and white porticoes, these places were put up in more genteel days. Well, more genteel if you didn't count Jack the Ripper and World War One.

There was a telescope on a stand near the pier. For a pound you got to see a grey flat dismal sea up close. A real bargain, that. Even the touts he remembered as a kid down the markets would have a tough time selling that one.

Relics from a bygone age, piers. They were old school, from back when candy floss and a kiss-me-quick cowboy hat was everyone's idea of a good time. Then cocaine and binge drinking came along.

He got out his warrant card and went into one of the B&Bs. There was a night porter behind the reception desk, he looked old enough to remember Jack the Ripper himself. Charlie showed him his ID and he peered at him over the top of his glasses. 'You're a long way from home.'

'I'm looking for someone who can help me with my enquiries. His name's Terry Brookes. Ugly geezer with a shaved head, about this high, you can't miss him, he's got tattoos and all sorts, looks like a real knob.'

'Get a lot of real knobs in here. Can't keep track. What's he done?'

'I'm not at liberty to say. But he would have checked in last night, quite late. After eleven. He might have used a different name.'

'I'll check on the computer,' the old boy said. 'Here we go.' He clicked the mouse on the desk a couple of times and peered at his monitor. 'Better turn off me porn and get to the right page.' He peered closer at the screen. 'Only two guests checked in last night. A young couple from Norwich and a middle-aged bloke in a suit. Sales rep, my guess. Sorry.'

Charlie tried three other places along the seafront and got the same response. He couldn't cover every cheap motel and B&B in Brighton. He was about to give up.

And then he saw him. He must have been trying to sleep rough after all, else he'd been wandering the streets all night, feeling sorry for himself. That would be more like it.

He couldn't miss him, even in the dark. He was standing

under a street light, his hands in his pockets, looking cold and lost. Charlie had never wished hypothermia on anyone but there was always a first time. He followed him, saw him go into some public toilets.

He waited for him outside, leaning against a bollard.

Tel came out, still rearranging himself, checking his zipper, tucking his beanie down over his ears. *That was quick, bet you never even washed your hands you dirty bastard.*

'Hello Tel. Been shaking hands with the unemployed?'

Terry froze like a rabbit in headlights and then he turned and ran. He had a choice between the park and North Street; he chose North Street, perhaps he thought there might be someone who would stop and help him, an old lady with a Tesco trolley perhaps.

But he was a smoker, and he was pudgy, in a football hooligan sort of way, and Charlie caught him easy. Tel stopped, out of breath, turned and squared up. He must have thought that Charlie would stop and square up as well. Instead, he kept running, launched himself at him, knees up, elbows out, hit him fast and hard. They both went down but Charlie was up first, grabbed him by the throat, the red mist coming up now so he couldn't see anything except his own rage.

'No, please,' Tel said, but there wasn't going to be any more no please, it was long past that.

CHAPTER THIRTY-ONE

'No Charlie,' a voice said, and even through the mist he knew the voice and he drew back, his fist still raised, hesitated long enough for Ben to grab him by the arms and pull him away. He dragged him towards his car. 'For God's sake, get in. The cops will be here any minute.'

There was one of the early buses pulled up on the other side of the road, the driver was staring, there were people about, headed to work, they'd all have their phones out any minute, either for Facebook or 999.

Charlie let Ben bundle him into his Porsche.

Ben turned back and pointed a finger at Tel, who was sitting on the ground, his hands cupped under his nose. There was blood everywhere.

'I swear to God, Terry, you report this and I'll have someone take you out. It's dead cheap these days, only a couple of hours' wages for me.'

He got back behind the wheel and they drove off.

'How did you find me?'

'Look, Charlie. It's a Tuesday morning in the middle of winter. I see two blokes having a fight in the high street, I know one of them has to be you.'

'Not necessarily.'

'What are you going to do, fight the whole world?'

'I wasn't fighting the whole world, just the pond life that beat up my sister and has possibly left my niece with a permanent brain injury.'

'What good is it going to do? He does you for assault and then what? You want to do time for this? What happens to your career? Down the toilet, that's what.'

Charlie had never seen Ben angry before. He was shocked.

'Settle down,' he said.

'Settle down? Me, settle down? You were about to turn him into hamburger mince. I've seen that look on your face before.'

He pulled over and got out of the car.

'You can't park here, you'll get clamped,' Charlie said.

'I'll park where I like,' Ben said. 'I need a coffee.'

'I'm not going in Starbucks.'

'It's got coffee and it's open.'

Charlie followed him in. They sat at a chair by the window.

Ben came back with a flat white for Charlie and a caramel latte for himself. Dear God, Charlie thought, should be a law.

Charlie looked down. The barista had drawn a smiley face into the froth on the top. Christ. Some people made it hard to be a pacifist.

'Thanks, Ben.'

'What?' Ben said.

'I said, thanks. For the coffee.'

'And?'

'And for saving my career.'

'Don't mention it. I can't let you throw it all away for that dick-wipe. Look, Charlie, if it wasn't Tel, it would be someone else. You know what Jules is like. She's her mother's daughter.'

'I can't just stand by and watch.'

'If the alternative is going down for GBH, then yes, you can.'

'It's not in me to . . . to not do anything.'

'Charlie, you can't set the whole world to rights. Not everything is black and white and not everything can be fixed.'

'This looks pretty black and white to me, Ben.'

'Does it? Don't tell me Jules didn't know what he was like before she married him. He had form. He had an arrest for drunk and disorderly and Watford FC had banned him for racial abuse of one of their own players. Does this sound like the sort of bloke that's merely misunderstood?'

'Are you blaming her for this?'

'There's a saying, Charlie: if you invite a wolf into your house, don't blame the wolf if he eats you. You and I both know that Terry is a complete waste of oxygen. He's not going to change. So why, of all the men in the world, did she pick him? If he dropped dead tomorrow, my lips to God's ears, she'd get herself a new bloke and guess what? He'd be just like him.'

'That's a pretty bleak outlook, Ben.'

'You never know, maybe she'll surprise me.' He looked at his watch. 'Let's get back to the hospital, get Rom.'

As they walked back to the car, Charlie said: 'So are you serious about her?'

'Who?'

'Del.'

'Want the truth? Yes, I am serious, but I don't trust myself. If you want to warn anyone away from your family, then maybe you should warn *her*. Now come on, let's get out of here. We have to get you back to London to save the world.'

DAY 6

DAY 3

CHAPTER THIRTY-TWO

In Hampstead, Malcolm Barrington was getting ready to take his golden retriever, Mitzi, for a walk. He fussed with finding the lead and then had to decide whether to take an umbrella or wear his raincoat and a flat cap. The nights were drawing in, it was dark by five o'clock, London settling in for another grim and rain-slick winter.

There were comforting smells coming from the kitchen, rosemary and roasting meat. Lamb, his favourite. 'Taking Mitzi for her walk,' he shouted, put his feet in his boots and went out.

'Have a nice time!'

She always said that. It could be a raging blizzard with frost-bitten bodies piled in the yard.

The November evening was bracing but didn't have the rawness that winter would eventually bring. A light mist had settled over the goalposts on the football fields. He made his way across the parking lot towards the heath. It was dark, but low cloud blanked out the stars. A fine drizzle of rain drifted in the orange glow of the sodium lights.

There was someone standing under the trees.

As he came closer, he saw that whoever they were didn't have a dog with them. It made him uneasy, and instead of going the usual way along the path, he diverted a little across the heath, to avoid passing too close. They didn't usually have any problems with drug addicts or muggers around here, but you could never be too careful.

He looked back once. They were still standing there, had made no move to follow him.

Calm down, Malcolm, he told himself. Trouble with your job, you see troublemakers everywhere.

Mitzi moved slower these days, she was eleven years old now, kept her head down, heavy in the shoulder. He waited while she did her business, fumbled in his pocket for a doggie bag. He still felt as if someone was watching him. He looked around. Whoever had been standing under the trees had gone. He felt somewhat relieved.

Several houses backed onto the park, there were lights at a couple of the windows, it made him feel safer. Safer from what?

Come on, he told himself. Pull yourself together.

He picked up a stick and threw it. Mitzi wasn't as sharp as she used to be, but she never refused a game of fetch and went loping after it. He lost sight of her for a moment in the trees.

There was a litter of leaves along the path, the smell of mould and autumn. Mud and rain had turned the beds of oak leaves into compost where they had piled against the wire fences along the path.

'Do you remember Michael Grimes?' a voice said. The voice was cracked, a gate that needed oiling. He couldn't decide if it belonged to a woman or a man.

A figure appeared out of the trees. It was the same figure he had seen by the car park; he wondered how they had got this close without him seeing or hearing. It disoriented him. He looked around for Mitzi, couldn't see her.

He thought, I hope they haven't hurt my dog.

'What?'

'Michael Grimes. He was drunk and stoned and killed a four-year-old girl in a parked car. Remember?'

Unease turned quickly to real fear. He looked back over his shoulder. He could see someone back there in the car park, wondered whether he should call out to them and run, or try to brazen this out.

'Do I know you?' He tried to be stern, but instead he sounded strained and scared. Where was Mitzi?

'No, people like you wouldn't mix with the likes of me.'

Barrington tried to answer but his mouth was too dry, he couldn't get any words out.

'I try and picture you, standing in front of a mirror in your red robes that day, adjusting your wig, concerned for your appearance. What was going through your mind?'

Barrington shook his head. He knew what was going to happen.

'Did you ever think about Zoë Miller again? Did you?'

Suddenly there was a knife. It had a wicked curved blade and a wooden handle. He had read about people being unable to move in moments of genuine terror. He had never experienced such a phenomenon himself. His instinct was to run but for those few vital moments he couldn't move.

'I want you to remember the little girl. That's all.'

Barrington turned away, even though he knew it was hopeless. A hand went around his nose and mouth, and there were fingers in his hair, pulling his head back. 'You don't know the meaning of justice,' the voice said, 'but I do.'

There was no pain. He just had a warm feeling, flooding down his throat. He threw up his arms, heard a dog barking somewhere, and after that there was nothing.

CHAPTER THIRTY-THREE

It wasn't the quickest way to kill someone; a stiletto blade slipped into the side of the neck and up into the brain under the skull was quicker and easier, if you knew how. Holding on to the hair, sawing through the troublesome windpipe at the throat, letting gouts of blood spray onto the grass, it was messy and a bit awkward.

As he waited for him to bleed out, he tried to imagine him coming home from court that day, rubbing the dog's head, shouting hello to his wife, putting his briefcase on the hall stand. His wife calling back: *Hello dear, how was your day?* What did he say to her? Did he say, oh you know, the usual. Or did he lie awake all that night, wondering if he'd done the right thing, was he haunted by it?

The arteries and veins on both sides of the neck had been torn out with the first pass of the blade; there were puddles of blood in the grass, plenty for the CS team to work with. Footprints and such. Good luck with that.

Removing the head wasn't easy. Getting through the spine and vertebra was always tricky. The retriever came bounding back with the stick. You had to feel sorry for the dog, he'd have no one to play with.

Finally, it was done, and the head went into the green bin liner bag inside the backpack, along with the blue medical gloves. He left the headless corpse with the howling dog. Judge Malcolm Barrington was due to appear one last time at the Old Bailey.

At that moment, in the incident room at Essex Road, Charlie was in the middle of his five o'clock briefing.

It had been another fruitless day. Corporal Margaret Lennox had either been abducted by aliens or else she had been planning her disappearance for months; no one could vanish so comprehensively on a mere whim. Charlie had made her prime suspect in the case. Catlin had put her description and a recent photograph out to the media: 'Police have identified a person of interest, anyone with information of their whereabouts please contact this number.' He hoped that soon the headlines would move on to something more interesting, Brexit or Meghan Markle, and the head on the railing would just become another image search on Google.

Several times Charlie had found himself thinking: If whoever did this had left the body, all of it, in the kitchen of that grotty little flat in Kentish Town, we could have forgotten it by now. Not every murder ended up in the Crown Court in front of a jury, and he would have lost less sleep over this one than some of the other murders he hadn't solved.

If only they hadn't stuck that scrote's head on the railing.

He looked over his shoulder at the board: underneath Margaret Lennox's name were two others with question marks: Gordon Lennox and Christopher Pemberley.

'Where are we on finding this Chris Pemberley?' Charlie said.

James shook his head. 'Me and Rupe tracked down this company that hired him, DynaCorp Logistics, they work out of an office in Paddington. Two days before anyone showed up there. It was one of those places you could imagine coming back one day and it's empty. There was a desk, a filing cabinet and two chairs, that was about it. Not even a sign on the door. Tuck the mobile and the laptop under his arm, the bloke who owned it would be gone.'

'Did he have a name?'

'John Smith. Declined to produce identification. Fit looking bloke with a shaved head, dead hard. All he would say is that our boy was deployed in Abu Dhabi, but doing what and for whom, he wouldn't tell us. Said if we wanted any more, to come back with a search warrant.'

'We might just do that. I'll ask the DCI to get someone at Scotland Yard to lean on this mob. So Chris Pemberley stays on the board until proven otherwise. What else have we got?'

'Did a little more digging on our Mr Lennox,' Parminder said. 'I had the two Ds in Bolton go back to talk to Rodney Brinkley, get some background on Lennox's unit. Apparently, the squad had been engaged in tracking down a local Taliban commander in Helmand.'

'And in what way is that germane to our investigation, Parm?'

'The man's name was Mullah Amir Nafez. He had been beheading informers and putting their heads on stakes.'

Charlie heard the intake of breath around the room.

Charlie held up a hand. 'Okay, let's not get carried away. Could just be a coincidence. Anything else?'

Greene stuck his hand up. 'What does germane mean?'

'It's a female German, sarge,' Singh said, and Greene looked around the room, waiting for someone to laugh so he could laugh too. He was saved by a call on the HAT phone.

Charlie watched him pick up, heart in his mouth. Our team aren't on turn, Charlie thought, so why are they ringing us?

Greene hung up, shook his head, confirming the worst of Charlie's fears. 'There's been another one,' he said.

They weren't long into November but already the lights were up in Oxford Street; there was fake snow and gift ideas wherever you looked. The skies over Holborn were a dirty urban orange. Rain had set in over the nation's capital, and the pavements were wet and gleaming like the skin of a snake.

People hurried along High Holborn, heads down into

the wind. An ambulance siren wailed from somewhere over Chancery Lane. A motorbike weaved between the trucks and buses, jumping the lights at Giltspur Street.

The rider was wearing black leathers and the visor on his helmet was pulled down. Bystanders said later that the bike was entirely black, that there were no distinguishing marks. Hardly anyone saw anything, anyway. It was raining and most people had their heads down.

Gillian Taylor was aware of the hissing of tyres on the wet road, the roar of a motorcycle, the blast of a bus horn as the rider swerved in front towards the pavement.

Gillian was a paralegal for Huntley Fisher and was on her way home after assisting in an armed robbery case in Court 4. She was still in wig and gown when she emerged on the street just after five o'clock.

The backpack landed right at her feet. She gave a shout of surprise and took a step back. In the statement she gave later, she said she was too shocked to look around and see where the bag had come from. Another woman, a Danish tourist, walking past at the same time, screamed and backed away, thinking it was a terrorist bomb. A junior clerk came out of the Old Bailey and walked straight into Gillian's back.

'It was the bloke on the bike,' someone said, and pointed down the street. But by then the motorbike and its rider were gone, hidden by the crush of buses and taxis.

A security guard rushed out and shouted at them not to touch it and ushered them all back inside the building, speaking urgently into a handheld radio. The Old Bailey immediately went into lockdown.

Three specialist police, carrying Glock 17 handguns, were on the scene within minutes. Meanwhile, the closed-circuit cameras mounted on the front of the building were plugged directly into Scotland Yard's control room in Westminster. A short time later, the bomb disposal robot was inspecting the bag, which lay half open outside the main doors of the court, a hundred yards inside the police cordon. Everyone inside the Old Bailey had been evacuated via other exits.

The robot's cameras revealed no wires or battery terminals or plastic explosive. What it did find was not a great deal better. The backpack was placed inside a large evidence bag and removed from the scene. The media were told that no explosive device had been found and that it was all a hoax.

No other information was forthcoming.

In London Bridge Street, a journalist working late at his terminal heard his mobile buzz. He picked it up and glanced wearily at the text message. It took him a few seconds to realise what he was looking at.

It was a multimedia message, with a photograph attached. He held the phone away from him, turned it to the right, then the left. What the hell was this?

He squinted at the screen, stood up and then sat down again. 'Fuck me.'

He realised he was looking at a headless corpse lying outside, on some wet grass. It had been taken using a flash, which gave the image a lurid hue. It was a man, judging by his clothes, he was wearing a blue raincoat and brown corduroy trousers and trainers. There was a wedding ring on the left hand.

The caption read: 'You'll find judges at the Old Bailey, but you won't find justice.'

He tried to retrieve the details, scrolled over the message looking for the sender's ID. There was none. He pressed the call button to dial the number and let it ring through twice. Finally, he went back to the picture and stared at it, still uncertain if it was genuine. Could be a hoax.

But he couldn't stop thinking about Michael Grimes. He had written several pieces about it in the last week. Could this be connected?

He felt the delicious adrenaline buzz that came whenever he got an angle on a story that he thought no one else had. Had this picture gone out to every journalist in London or had the killer – if that was who the sender was – picked him, exclusively?

He stared at the caption: 'You'll find judges at the Old Bailey, but you won't find justice.' He turned back to his monitor; a few taps on the keyboard and there it was, breaking news, a bomb scare outside the Old Bailey, someone had thrown a backpack at the main entrance.

Please, please, let me be the only one who's got this, he thought. If I am, I'll have to be quick. He stood up and went into the editor's office and shut the door behind him.

CHAPTER THIRTY-FOUR

Charlie stood on the heath, feeling rain drip off the end of his nose. He could almost see his forensic evidence getting washed away, despite the duckboards that criss-crossed the crime scene. He saw the DCI talking to the government pathologist on the other side of the cordon. He had his umbrella with him, keep his coif perfect for the cameras. It was like Wembley on the other side of the tape, every news crew out there except for Nigeria Tonight. This was going to be front page tomorrow; the *Mirror* would probably do a colour supplement.

He thought he could hear a dog barking somewhere but that might be his imagination. At least they hadn't hurt the dog, that was one thing. It was Mitzi who had attracted the attention of another dog walker, though the bloke probably wished she hadn't. One of the first responders had to take him away; he was still in the Whittington being treated for shock.

He felt hot and peeled back the hood of his forensic suit. He hoped the SOCOs would be able to find a footprint, at least. This had to be someone close to the Millers; no doubt about it. He should have this put away by this time tomorrow.

But something niggled at him. This was too well planned, too well coordinated.

He still felt one step behind the game.

The DCI nodded to him, Charlie ducked under the cordon and went over.

'Want to get under the umbrella?' he said, in a rare display of concern.

Charlie wasn't sure if he was taking the piss. 'I'm all right, sir.'

'So what happened here, Charlie? Do we have any eyewitnesses?'

'Not yet. The local station house has some uniforms canvassing along the street over there, as many as they can spare. The backs of those houses edge onto the heath, someone must have seen something.'

'Time of death?'

'Apparently he left the house a few minutes after five o'clock. At a reasonable walking speed, you'd have to say he reached here between ten and quarter past.'

'We'll put out a media appeal. Anyone who was walking their dog between five and five thirty, they might have seen his assailant waiting for him or fleeing the scene.'

'His next-door neighbours say he takes the dog for a walk every night at about the same time. Whoever did this must have been watching him for a while.'

'How is his wife?'

'Not too good, as you'd imagine. Got a doctor with her; I believe he's had to sedate her.'

The pathologist's team arrived to remove the body, picking their way carefully across the duckboards with the stretcher.

'Did she see the remains?'

'Unfortunately, yes.'

'How was that allowed to happen?'

'She heard the sirens when the first responders got here. She was worried because he was late home and she came out to take a look. She recognised the dog first, obviously. And then she knew it was him by what he was wearing.'

'Not a nice thing for any wife to see.'

Charlie thought that could be a worthy entrant in Understatement of the Year.

'Didn't take you long to get to the scene.'

'When the HAT team got here, they took one look and called Sergeant Greene. They rightly assumed that there could not be two lunatics decapitating people and stealing their heads, not even in London.'

'I'm told he was the judge in the Grimes trial, am I right?'

'That is my latest intel, yes sir.'

'So, what are we thinking, Charlie?'

'We are thinking that whoever did this has close ties with the Miller family. They are taking retribution for what they see – perhaps what a lot of people see – as a palpable injustice.'

'You're wrong, Charlie. It's more than that. They've just raised the stakes. This is an attack on our entire legal system.' The rain pattered onto the umbrella. He heard a TV journalist start his talking head fifty yards away, pointing over his shoulder at the white tent and the cluster of ghostly, white-suited SOCOs. 'So, which one of them is it?'

'Well, Tom Miller uses a wheelchair. We've had him and his wife under twenty-four hour surveillance since Grimes' death, so we know neither of them was responsible for this. Jennifer Miller's sister is a weapons officer at Heathrow, she was on duty the night Grimes was killed. So we have eliminated her at this stage. Our prime suspect remains the other sister, Margaret, who has still not been located despite our best efforts and those of the army. Two of his former brothers-in-arms are also under suspicion.'

'Gordon Lennox.'

'He has been under round-the-clock surveillance, same as the Millers. But there's also a man called Christopher Pemberley. He's supposed to be in the Middle East working for a private security contractor, but we have been unable to confirm this. I was going to talk to you about it when I got the call to come here.'

The DCI's mobile rang. He listened, said thanks, and hung up.

By the look on his face, Charlie knew someone had found

the part second, as the medics liked to call it. Not the best of news either, by the looks of it. 'Don't tell me he's stuck it on the gates at Buckingham Palace.'

'The Old Bailey. Inside a backpack, tossed on the pavement outside.'

'Oh, lovely.'

'They're telling everyone it was a bomb, hoping to keep a lid on it.'

'So to speak.'

The DCI puffed out his cheeks. 'Do what you can tonight to follow this up. Meet me at Scotland Yard at seven in the morning. The deputy commissioner has asked to be updated. I think this is out of your hands now, Charlie.'

He walked away. The umbrella, the downcast look, the stoop to the shoulders, it reminded him of Steve McClaren, that night at Wembley, when was it, ten years ago now. The DCI looked just like Steve; the world turning against him, holding on to his job by his fingertips, nowhere to hide.

Yes, you can be SIO, Charlie thought, if that's what you want. Or you can hand this whole clusterfuck to Gold Group. I'm well out of it. I don't want this gig any more.

An inspector from Hampstead station came over to find him. 'There's a girl here I think you should talk to,' he said.

Charlie followed him across the grass to a patrol car that was parked on the path, well inside the cordon. He held the back door open for him. A young girl sat in the back; she looked young and excited and was wearing a lot of shocking pink.

The inspector jumped in the front. 'This is Miss Amanda Wong. She approached one of my officers about ten minutes ago and said that she thought she saw something.'

Charlie looked at her hopefully. 'What was it you saw?'

She stared at him wide-eyed. 'Has someone been murdered?'

'I'm afraid so.'

'Oh, wow,' she said. 'Cool.'

'Miss Wong,' the inspector said. 'Please tell Inspector George here what you told me.'

'Well, I was, like, walking home past the park and I saw this guy run straight in front of me. He was, like, wearing a black Lycra suit and he had this backpack.'

'Right,' Charlie said. 'Could you describe him for us?'

She shook her head. 'He was wearing a hoody. It was pulled right over his face.'

'But you're sure it was a man?'

She covered her mouth with her hand and giggled. 'Well, maybe. He *ran* like a guy. He really scared me, you know? He was moving so fast.'

'Where did this happen?'

'Over there.' It was dark, and it was raining. She could have been pointing at Mongolia.

'Come and show me.'

There was a pathway through the trees, it led to a hedge that separated the park from the road. 'He ran through the gap in the hedge,' she said.

'And you were walking which way?'

'I got off the bus about here. I live down there, in those flats.'

'And where did he go?'

She pointed to a side street that curved around between an office building and a rather expensive-looking Tudor cottage. 'And then I heard a motorbike, you know?'

'Did you see the motorbike?'

She shook her head. 'I guess it headed in the other direction.'

'Right. Thanks. Perhaps the inspector here could have one of his people take down your statement for me. Could you do that, inspector?'

'I'll get one of my boys on to it.'

'Thanks.' Charlie stood there in the dark, thinking: well, whoever you are, we've got you now. He flickered the torch over the hedge, hoping to see a footprint, some torn clothing. A bus went past, Bradley Cooper and Lady Gaga staring longingly at each other. *A Star is Born*. Wouldn't mind seeing that, he thought, one day when this bloody case is not dogging every minute of my every day.

'We'll need some of your boys down here to protect the scene,' he said. 'We'll have to extend the cordon. He might have left us some forensics when he went through that hedge.'

'I'll see to it.'

Amanda Wong was still staring at him. 'Was there something else?' Charlie said.

She pulled out her phone. 'Can I, like, get a selfie with you guys?' she said. 'My friends are going to be so green when I tell them.'

DAY 7

CHAPTER THIRTY-FIVE

It was the first time he'd been in the conference room at New Scotland Yard. He liked it. It was all very civilised, this, the highly polished furniture and clean surfaces, sitting around sipping mineral water, everyone with their iPads out, looking scrubbed and well maintained. This is what other people's lives are like, Charlie thought. Management is not a bad gig, if you can get it.

Don't think I'd last though, me.

The deputy assistant commissioner sat at the head of the table, the assistant chief constable beside him. Catlin, the media liaison officer, sat opposite the chief super. This wasn't just above his paygrade, it was another salary structure altogether.

The DCI sat next to him, fidgeting with his pen. He had on his best silk tie and he was wearing cologne.

The deputy commissioner cleared her throat and leaned forward, making eye contact with the room over the top of her glasses. 'We're here this morning to convene an internal Gold Group to oversee Operation Northfall,' she began. 'As you are all aware, there have been further developments overnight that have escalated this from a murder inquiry, albeit an unusual and rather sensational one, at least from the point of view of the media, into something quite different. Our purpose today is to provide support to and governance of the investigation so that it can be brought to a prompt conclusion.'

She checked her notes. 'Gold Group has two functions: to ensure the appropriate allocation of resources, and to oversee the work of the SIO in charge of the case.'

Charlie knew what was coming. He fixed an expression of benign equanimity on his face and waited.

'Do we have a main suspect?' Every head swivelled away from her and looked at Charlie. This is what it must be like to play at Wimbledon, he thought.

'We do, sir. We are very eager to interview one Margaret Lennox, a corporal who has been missing from her army base since 23rd October.'

'Do you have any evidence linking her to the crimes?'

'Not as yet.'

'Not as yet,' the ACC repeated. 'What evidential leads do you have?'

'A fragment of metal from the murder weapon was found at the first crime scene. We're looking into the provenance of the backpack that was left at the Old Bailey. We're hoping that might throw up another lead.'

'That's all?'

'A page from a Greek drama that was lodged in Grimes' throat. It came from a book owned by Tom and Jennifer Miller.'

'But there is nothing else putting the Millers at the murder scene involving Mr Grimes?'

Charlie shook his head, no.

'Was anything found in Malcolm Barrington's mouth?'

'We're still waiting for the results of the autopsy. It's taking place about now.' Charlie looked at his watch, to press home the point that he was busy. 'I've organised for one of my detectives and an evidence officer to attend.'

'Where were the Millers when Judge Barrington was murdered?'

The DCI saw his chance. 'I have them on twenty-four-hour surveillance,' he said. 'They were both at home.'

There were nods and frowns all around the room. Charlie thought they looked rehearsed. Everyone already knew what the result of this meeting was going to be.

The DCI leaned forward. Charlie heard the bus coming. 'DI

George has worked very hard on this case and he has my full support,' he said. The only thing he didn't add was 'and he'd like to spend more time with his family'.

'Chief inspector, I think it would be wholly appropriate if you took over the case from the inspector from this point on.' The deputy commissioner turned her somewhat chilling gaze onto Charlie. 'Inspector George, we would all like to thank you for your efforts so far. I am assured your work has been exemplary, but this case has now become too high profile to be handled in the normal way. DCI O'Neal-Callaghan will assume the role and responsibilities of SIO in this operation, effective immediately. Chief inspector, you will report twice daily to Gold Group. Questions?'

The DCI nodded. Charlie nodded along with him. Fine with me, he thought. It was like when he was eighteen and he got dumped by Angela Birch, he hadn't much liked her, but he'd stayed with her because he didn't want to hurt her feelings. It was a relief when she called it a day. This case was like that.

FONC was welcome to it. The whole thing was fucked, in his opinion. If the DCI could find some way to unfuck it, well, good luck to him. He smiled and left the room.

The incident room was packed to the rafters, or at least the strip lights. He had turned off the TV; he didn't want them all distracted by endless loops of the crime scene, it seemed like the news channels were replaying it every ten minutes. He wished there was a way of earning five quid every time a journalist said: 'come to terms with'. He could retire and get a gîte in France.

Some professional muckraker at one of the tabloids had somehow found out what had been in the backpack that had been lobbed at the Old Bailey. It had been all over the news today. Now legal experts were forming long queues outside TV stations to discuss this attack on the United Kingdom's legal system. The debates were interspersed with replays of the Millers denying all knowledge of the crimes while defending the

207

so-called vigilante's actions and giving long and impassioned speeches about what they called 'the injustice of our justice system'.

There were a lot more people in the room than there needed to be. Detectives from other teams, who should have been busy working less celebrated murders, had stopped to listen in; a few civilian staff had somehow muscled their way into the back of the room. Everyone knew this was the Big One and were hoping for a few titbits they could gossip about in the canteen.

His own team huddled closer than was usual, even Grey; any fractures in the team had been temporarily put aside because of the pressures they were all feeling from the outside. They should have been accustomed to this kind of publicity after the Lucifer killer, but nerves were getting the better of them and the strain was showing on all their faces.

New detectives had been assigned to the team from West Hampstead and Southgate. It was the biggest investigation Charlie had ever been a part of. 'No slacking on this one,' the DCI had said to him, and he realised FONC had actually believed what Grey had said; he thought he hadn't been taking the Grimes murder seriously.

Overtime had been approved for all his constables and sergeants. Even the DCI himself wasn't off the clock this time.

He'd left Charlie to run that morning's briefing. He didn't have to tell anyone to settle down. All eyes were fixed on the whiteboard behind him, the two glossy eight by tens of Malcolm Barrington, one in his wig and gown, another lying butchered and headless in the grass. There were copies in all their briefing notes if they wanted a close-up.

'I'm sure you have all heard about the latest developments,' Charlie began.

'Let's not get too despondent,' Greene said. 'They do say that two heads are better than one.'

There was an appalled silence.

'Thanks for that, DS Greene,' Charlie said.

He went through the crime scene notes from the latest victim: the time of death, the assailant's access and egress from the crime scene, the search for witnesses. They were still waiting on the report from the pathologist and the crime scene manager.

'There is an obvious connection to the Grimes murder,' Charlie said. 'I do not believe this is a copycat crime. Malcolm Barrington was the presiding judge at the trial of Michael Grimes. The news outlets, geniuses as they are, have already worked this out for themselves. We can be in no doubt about the motivation for these two murders.'

'Someone saw him,' Singh said, looking up from his notes.

'An eyewitness saw someone dressed all in black wearing running shoes, Lycra and a black hoody. She didn't see a face, but they had a backpack with them, and she said they were running very fast. That's it. Our first job will be to continue the search for eyewitnesses. We have to cover this area here.' Charlie put a hand on the map on the whiteboard. 'All CCTV, ANPR within a mile radius. We have some idea of the getaway route, but we do not know how the assailant arrived at the park, or when. We are appealing to the public on this one – our DCI is recording a media briefing on the steps of Scotland Yard as we speak.'

'This will be our finest hour,' Greene said, in a reasonable imitation of Winston Churchill. No one laughed but he was used to being ignored.

Lovejoy tapped her briefing notes. 'This eyewitness also heard a motorbike.'

'Yes, the same as the Grimes murder. That's why we need to check all the cameras in the area, see if we can find it.' Charlie turned the page in his own notes. 'Once again, we have two crime scenes. On this occasion, our assailant drove to the Old Bailey and threw a backpack containing Barrington's head outside the main entrance. That backpack is currently at Lambeth and forensics have been instructed to give analysis of the bag the utmost priority.'

Charlie threw his notes on the desk and looked around the room.

'After the murder of Michael Grimes, there was some initial debate as to whether the murder was linked with the death of Zoë Miller four years ago. I do not believe there can be any further doubt that the outcome of that trial was the motivation behind these murders.'

Someone at the back said: 'Are we bringing in the Millers for further questioning?'

'The Millers have been under twenty-four-hour surveillance since Grimes' death. Although we cannot rule them out as accessories, they are not suspects in this latest homicide.'

'But sir,' Grey said, 'they were on the TV this morning publicly thanking the vigilante – that's what they called whoever did this. They even called them a hero.'

'Whoever did this has initiated a national debate, which I suppose is what they wanted in the first place. I suspect that Tom and Jennifer Miller know the identity of the person or persons responsible. But we cannot prove complicity at this stage.'

'Barrington had a wife and family,' Grey said. 'Maybe not everyone in this room was bothered about Grimes. But this is different.'

It sounded like blame. He saw the 'fuck yous' on faces all around the room. Grey was doing himself no favours here.

Charlie decided to move things along. 'People, I'm sure I don't have to point out to you that whoever is responsible for these acts is ruthless, efficient and organised. Further, the powers that be see this latest crime as an attack on the very fabric of our legal system. We now have the eyes of the whole country on us. I'm told this has even made the news in America.

'You have been given extra resources and I am assured that whatever you ask for, you will get, with the possible exception of a pay rise. Let me stress, we are not chasing some gangbanger from the estates. Shit just got real. Questions?'

'Guv, when you were talking about extra resources, you said "you" not "us". Have you been taken off the case as SIO?'

'I've not been taken off the case, as such, but you're right, I am no longer the SIO. That onerous responsibility has been passed up the chain of command to DCI O'Neal-Callaghan. He, in turn, will be reporting directly to Gold Group at Scotland Yard.'

There were muttered comments and Charlie pretended he couldn't hear them.

'Settle down. This won't change things for most of you. DS Greene will give you your actions. Expect the hotline to get jammed up with the usual nutjobs and time wasters. Your job is to make sure a pearl doesn't get chucked out with the rotten oysters. As soon as we have something from Lambeth, the DCI will let you know.'

'Pathology?'

'Waiting for DCs Lovejoy and Sanderson to report back. I'll update you all when I have the results. That's it, people. Get to work.'

Charlie felt like he'd just dropped a backpack full of rocks. Grey was right. He'd never wanted this one from the start.

Greene had the phone to his ear, was waving him over.

'What is it, Jay?'

He held out the phone. 'It's FONC.'

Cover the mouthpiece when you call him that, Charlie mouthed at him. He took the phone. 'Sir?'

'Got a report from Amory,' the DCI said without preamble. 'His boys lost our Mr Lennox last night.'

'Lost him?'

'He was on his way home from a job out near Holloway. They lost him in traffic. Their last sighting was the corner of Holloway Road and Seven Sisters.'

'Was it deliberate?'

'We'll have to find out.'

'What time was their last trace, sir?'

'A few minutes after four o'clock.'

'Plenty of time to get to Hampstead.' Charlie thought about it. 'Do you want me to bring him in?'

'Keep your powder dry, Charlie. Let's see if we get something a bit more damning.'

A bit more damning.

That came after lunch, when James was checking CCTV from a camera in Hampstead High Street. Charlie took one look and knew they had what they were looking for. He called the DCI and within an hour he had the arrest warrant in his hand.

CHAPTER THIRTY-SIX

Charlie took a moment before he went up the path, clocked the old work van parked outside, the green bins on the path, the bay windows with shabby curtains, pulled closed. He'd been born in a house much like this, back in the day.

The bell didn't work; typical builder's house, they fixed everyone else's gaff and never fixed their own. Charlie rapped on the door with his knuckles. He heard someone cursing and stamping up the hall.

Gordon Lennox didn't look quite as large out of his work clothes. He answered the door in a pair of loose grey tracksuit bottoms and an old Chelsea shirt, which Charlie thought was a bit provocative, especially in this part of London. You'd have to be ex-SAS to get away with that round here.

There was the smell of cooking coming from inside, sausages frying in a pan; it reminded Charlie that he hadn't eaten all day. When Gordon saw Charlie, he crossed his arms and shook his head. 'What do you want now?'

Charlie heard Gordon's wife shouting something from the kitchen. 'Mormons, love. I'll deal with it.'

'Actually Mr Lennox, we'd like you to come down the station and answer a few questions.'

'Can't it wait?'

'Afraid not.'

'What sort of questions?'

'Let's not do this here. Can you tell your missus you have to step out for a while and come with us, please?'

Gordon looked over Charlie's shoulder, clocked the two uniforms standing on the pavement behind him. He'd probably come up against worse. 'No, bugger off,' Gordon said, and tried to shut the door.

And that's when it got messy. Charlie put his foot in the jamb and Gordon tried to gut punch him. The uniforms stepped in with their CS sprays and got him on the floor. Gordon's kids came out of the kitchen, saw what was going on and started screaming. The neighbours came out into the street with mobile phones, and Gordon's wife slapped one of the uniforms on the head. Lubanski had to pull her away while they dragged her husband into a waiting patrol car.

'You all right, guv?' Lubanski said.

Charlie straightened up, trying to get his breath. 'I'm all right, Lube. If he'd really wanted to hurt me, he could have. Get Mrs Lennox and these kids inside. Let's have a bit of the old decorum here.'

He went in as Lubanski hustled Patti Lennox into the house then out to the back garden, out of the way.

Charlie looked around. It was neat, no clutter like he'd supposed; there was a tiled hallway and Ikea furniture, most of it new, and the framed generic prints were all at exactly ninety degrees, like someone had been around with a set square. He caught his own reflection in the hallway mirror. Turned away, couldn't stand to look at himself right now.

The SOCOs poured in, started going through kitchen cupboards and drawers, rifling through the pockets of the coats hanging in the hall cupboard. The DCI had been absolutely crystal, this wasn't a fishing expedition, they were looking for a knife.

Charlie wandered into the kitchen. There was a child's hand-drawn picture on the door of the refrigerator; a house, a mummy, two girls with straw-coloured hair, and a daddy, separate from the others, with what looked like fire coming out of his mouth. A psychologist would have a field day with that, he reckoned.

214

He stopped to look at a photograph in the hall. It was of Tom with Gordon and the other squaddie, Joe Cole, leaning on a jeep; the same photograph that Miller had in his study.

He went out the back where Lubanski was sitting on a wooden bench with Patti Lennox. Patti had long, dirty-blonde hair tucked behind her ears and she wasn't wearing make-up. There was a hole in the sleeve of her jumper. Charlie guessed it was apathy, not because they were that hard up.

She had both daughters held in the crook of her arms, trying to light a cigarette at the same time. She was trembling so hard she kept dropping the lighter. Charlie felt sorry for her but didn't think that smoking that close to two little kids was the best idea anyone had ever had, so he didn't offer to help.

He offered her a glass of water instead. She nodded, yes. He fetched one for her. She took it, as much for something to do with her hands as anything else.

Lubanski went back inside to help with the search.

'Where have you taken him?' Patti said.

'Essex Road nick. We need to talk to him is all.'

'I told you blokes, he was here with me the night that bloke got done. What was his name?'

'Michael Grimes.'

'Why are you still bothering us about that?'

'Where was he last night, Mrs Lennox, between four o'clock and six in the afternoon?'

'Yesterday? He was here with me. He came home early. Stayed in all night.'

'Then why do we have CCTV of him walking down Hampstead High Street at 4.35 p.m.?'

'What?'

'That's why we're here, Mrs Lennox. Yesterday afternoon a judge called Malcolm Barrington was murdered on the edge of Hampstead Heath. Don't tell me you haven't seen it on the news. Around forty minutes before the fatal assault, your husband was caught on CCTV in the high street. You look surprised. We were surprised as well.'

'He was working up that way.'

'Was he?' Lovejoy said. 'Because you just said he got home early and was here with you.'

Caught out in a lie, Patti shook her head and held on tighter to her kids. One of them squirmed, said she was squeezing too hard.

'I knew this would happen,' she said.

'What was it you knew would happen, Mrs Lennox?'

'He's not been right since he's been home. He was struggling even while he was still in the army, but he didn't want to let on.'

'Let on?'

'You got a problem you keep it to yourself, that's what he said. Can't tell anyone, not Special Forces. Admit you're struggling and they give you a medical discharge and that's it. All over.'

'But that's what happened in the end, wasn't it? According to his records.'

'He wasn't always like this, my Gordie. He was so different when he came back. I don't know what happened. He's not the man I married.'

'How long have you known him, Mrs Lennox?'

'Sixteen we was, when we started going out. My old man always said he'd end up in prison. He was always getting into trouble, nicking things, stealing cars. But the army right sorted him out. Always had a heart of gold, far as me and the kids was concerned. It was only when he went over *there* that the trouble started.'

The forensics team were going in and out of the house with evidence bags; a laptop, a mobile phone, but no knives or copies of ancient Greek texts as far as Charlie could see.

'They going to leave everything like they found it?' Patti said.

'We'll do our best,' Charlie said.

'Only he's very particular is Gordie. He comes home and

one of them pictures is not absolutely exact, he'll go off his nut. What are you looking for anyway?'

'Michael Grimes and Malcolm Barrington were both murdered with a certain type of bladed instrument.'

'He couldn't do something like that.' She gave him a look, then said the magic words he'd heard a hundred times before from disbelieving girlfriends and distraught mothers and abused wives. 'He's not a bad man. You don't know him like I do.'

One of the little girls started crying. 'When can we have our tea, Mummy?'

'We won't be longer than we need to be,' Charlie said, looking over his shoulder. Lubanski came out, shook her head. Nothing. He supposed that was what he'd expected.

'I'd better ring and tell Bob he won't be at work tomorrow.'

'Bob?'

'His mate. He's the one that owns the reno business – lovely bloke, gave Gordie a job when no one else would. If it wasn't for him, I don't know where we'd be. I mean, who else would employ him? He's been in and out of hospital so many times. Not what you'd call your ideal employee.' She gave him a look of pure anguish. 'Look, he may not be right in the head any more, but he didn't do this, I'm telling you.'

As they went out to the car Lubanski said: 'So are you going to charge him?'

'What for?'

'Assaulting a police officer, resisting arrest.'

'What police officer?'

'You, guv.'

'Me? No, that was nothing. He hardly touched me.'

When he got back to the nick, Charlie went down to the locker rooms, lifted up his shirt and checked the damage in the mirror. The bruise had spread right across his three lower ribs. Lucky if they weren't broken.

And that was when 'Big Gordie' didn't have a clear shot. Imagine if there hadn't been a door between them.

Lovejoy was waiting for him in his office. She and Sanderson, the evidence officer for the Grimes and Barrington murders, had just come from the post-mortem. As Charlie walked in, Sanderson held up a clear plastic bag.

'What's that?' Charlie said.

'Middleton found it in Barrington's throat. It had been pushed much further in than with Grimes.'

Charlie took it. Inside was another page from *The Oresteia*, by the look of it. The font and layout looked the same as the one they had found on Grimes.

> *Nothing forces us to know*
> *What we do not want to know*
> *Except pain.*

'Get it over to the lab for testing,' Charlie said.

'Did you find anything at Lennox's place?' Lovejoy said.

Charlie shook his head. 'Not a sodding thing,' he said.

'So what's next?'

'FONC is all geared up to interview Mr Lennox tomorrow morning. He wants to sweat him tonight and perform his pyrotechnics with DS Grey tomorrow. That means you and I can head to the wilds of Essex and talk to Lennox's mate, Bob. I'll set it up and we'll get going first thing in the morning. Don't be late.'

DAY 8

CHAPTER THIRTY-SEVEN

Nice to get out of the city for a few hours, even if it was only Essex. He stared at a horse grazing in a field, at the clusters of housing estates nestled under the rows of electricity pylons. Must have been a great place to live once, after the plague and before the invention of the bungalow.

'How's things with the new boyfriend?' he said.

'Great.'

That wasn't what he wanted to hear, and he silently chastised himself for his double standards. Might be better to stick to talking about work, practise what he preached as his old ma used to say.

'What's your view on the investigation, Lovejoy?'

'I think we're missing something, guv. But I don't know what it might be.'

'That's what I think, too.'

'You got a theory, guv?'

'Lots of theories but none of them hold up next to the facts. What do you make of Lennox?'

'I think he's a fit. I just don't see how we're going to make it stick. And he's not acting alone.'

'Our esteemed guv'nor thinks he's going to intimidate him with his razor-sharp interrogation technique, and Big Gordie, after three tours in Afghanistan fighting the Taliban, is going to break down in tears and confess.'

'How do you think he did it?'

'Well, for a start we have to factor in that this man has

221

been rigorously trained in escape and evasion techniques. He's not your ordinary Joe Public. But with Grimes, there was no security to worry about. He breaks in, does the business, rides the motorbike into London, sprints a few hundred yards with Grimes' head in his backpack – he probably did that sort of thing every day in the army. Well, maybe not with a head. At least, not every day. The whole thing was planned like the proverbial military operation. He would have scouted the CCTV and ANPR cameras, planned his route in advance. He knew how to leave no DNA behind.'

'Where's the bike? Where's the murder weapon?'

'These are the burning questions.'

'And what about Barrington? If Lennox knew where the CCTV cameras were, how is he walking down the high street, a few minutes from the crime scene, in full view, half an hour before the murder? He made no attempt at disguise.'

'And there's our eyewitness. She says she saw a bloke in trainers and black Lycra running from the scene. She said he was lean and fit. Lennox has ballooned out since he left the army. There's no way he fits the description.'

'Perhaps there's two of them,' Lovejoy said. 'One to kill, one to carry.'

'Perhaps.'

Lennox had been in Hampstead, no question, at the exact time Barrington was murdered. But no one had seen him enter the park, and there was nothing in the forensics report that linked him to the murder. There was a partial footprint, size 40, the same shoe size as Lennox, but the search and seizure had not found any matching footwear at his home.

The ANPR and security cameras around the Old Bailey had not really advanced the investigation: a motorbike, similar to the one caught on camera near the Royal Courts, but no plates. The rider was dressed all in black, a full-face helmet.

They were tantalisingly close to solving this, Charlie thought; at the same time, they were a million miles away.

'And who texted the photograph to that journalist?' Lovejoy said. 'Was it him or the same person that posted on Facebook the picture of Grimes' head on the railings outside the Royal Courts?'

'Meg Lennox?' Charlie said.

'Who has vanished off the face of the earth.'

'Well, not my problem any more,' Charlie said. 'It's the boss's problem. I'm only a foot soldier now, same as you.'

Bob McDonald lived outside a little village not far from Harlow, forty minutes up the M11. Wouldn't have found it without the GPS. They pulled into a gravel drive between the hedges, and Charlie took a deep lungful of fresh air as he got out of the car. Hadn't had one of those in a good while. A bungalow with pebbledash walls looked out over woodlands; even in the grey of November it looked a hundred times less desperate than Islington. Out the back there was a chicken shed with a corrugated roof, a gazebo and some old raspberry cages.

'Lush,' Lovejoy said as she got out.

'Sort of place Wordsworth wrote poems about. We're in the wrong business, Lovejoy.'

They'd rung ahead to let the McDonalds know they were coming, and Bob met them at the door. He led them through the house to the living room. There was a nice timber fireplace with black leather sofas; French windows looked over a lawn and a willow tree.

It was one of those traditional households where the wife made the tea and the man of the house sat in his armchair and told his guests what a wonderful wife he had. Charlie could see Lovejoy bristling and gave her a warning glance.

They exchanged pleasantries and the tea arrived on a tray with some Jaffa Cakes. Get in, Charlie thought. Love Jaffa Cakes. But he could take or leave another bloody cup of tea.

Bob looked ex-military himself, with his tattoos and the way he sat to attention. What hair he had left was shaved short. He had on chinos, loafers and a pinstriped shirt, dressed more like a banker than Bob the builder.

'So you said on the phone that Gordie's got himself into a bit of trouble?' Bob said, when they were settled.

'He's a suspect in a murder inquiry.'

'Murder? Did he get in a fight down the pub?'

'We're investigating the murders of Michael Grimes and Malcolm Barrington, QC.'

'The ones that have been all over the news? You think it's him?'

'We're hoping you can provide us with a bit of background.'

'Gordie wouldn't do something like that! Not his style.'

'I wouldn't have thought you could say that about someone who was in the SAS, Mr McDonald. Those lads are trained to kill, know what I mean?'

Bob shrugged, conceding the point. He held out the plate of Jaffa Cakes. Lovejoy shook her head, but Charlie couldn't help himself. Couldn't ever knock back a Jaffa Cake. Be like saying no to a beer.

'Mrs Lennox tells us that you employed her husband, Gordon, when he got out of the army. Said he couldn't get a job anywhere else.'

'Just wanted to help out. We go back a long way. He's always had my back, when we were younger, I couldn't watch him go downhill like that. Bloody army never did anything for him when he got out. Someone had to do something.'

'What's the arrangement?'

'I was about to give the whole thing away. I was sick of people moaning about how the power sockets were in the wrong place, that sort of nonsense. Gordon's always been pretty handy so I let him take over. My licence, I do the quotes, look after the books, keep an eye on his work, he gets a good percentage.'

'Mrs Lennox says she wouldn't know where he'd be without you.'

Bob dropped the country squire bit and sat forward. 'Look,

mates are mates. I was in a position to do him a good turn. Why not? He was a right mess after they discharged him.'

'Why did they discharge him?' Lovejoy said.

'They didn't tell you?'

'They were . . .' She looked at Charlie, searching for the right word.

'Reticent,' Charlie said.

'The army's never bloody reticent about anything. If they don't want to tell you something, they'll say so.'

'What was it they weren't telling us?' Charlie asked him.

'He had mental health issues. Long and short of it, he was a bloody mess.'

'And leaving the army didn't help?'

'What do you think? It was the only life he knew. He started taking it out on her. I told him, "You keep treating Patti like that, she'll leave you, don't think she won't. And she'll take the girls with her." I made him go and get help.'

'What sort of help?'

'You know, counsellors. Shrinks. The army doesn't care fuck all once you're out, but there's groups you can go to, people you can see. I don't know, maybe it's all bollocks, but it seemed to calm him down a bit. If he lost Patti and the girls, I don't know what he'd do. He idolises her and those kids.'

'Must have hit him pretty hard, what happened to his sister's kid.'

'Fuck, of course. It just about did his head in.'

'Right. And what do you do these days, don't mind me asking?'

'I play the stock market, online. Been doing it for years. Pays better and I don't get splinters.'

'One other thing,' Lovejoy said. 'I'm afraid we have to ask.'

He gave her a twisted smile. He knew what they had been leading up to, he wasn't stupid. 'What was I doing the night your Mr Barrington was killed?' He took out his phone, scrolled through his calendar and handed it to Charlie. 'Every Tuesday

225

night me and Annette go to line dancing classes at the church hall. Starts at 4.30, goes on for an hour. Keeps me fit. I'll get the instructor to send you the class list and you can check for yourselves. That be all?'

When he got back, Charlie found the DCI leaning on the vending machine in the corridor outside the interview rooms.

'How's it going?' Charlie said.

He grunted something and shook his head. He looked like a man who had had all the vitality drained out of him through a plug in his feet. He'd even undone the top button of his shirt and loosened his tie.

Gold Group must be giving him a proper roasting, Charlie thought.

The DCI ran his fingers up and down the hot beverage options. Charlie waited, wondered if he was going to buy him a coffee. It posed a dilemma; Charlie would rather drink rat poison than coffee out of a vending machine, but if the DCI bought him anything out of his own coin, he'd down it for the novelty and light relief.

'Want something, Charlie? Cappuccino or a hot chocolate?'

'I'll have a hot chocolate please, sir.'

The DCI felt around in his pockets. 'Got any change? I've only got a twenty-pound note.' He held out his hand.

'Oh, well played,' Charlie said, under his breath.

'What was that?'

'Nothing,' Charlie said and handed over a few pound coins.

'How are we going with the phone companies?' FONC asked.

Charlie thought it was a desperate move, trying to track whoever sent the image of Barrington's corpse to the press. You would have to be a complete idiot to leave an electronic footprint, and whoever killed Grimes and Barrington wasn't stupid. Still, it had to be done or questions would get asked later.

'Sorry, sir. No cheese down that tunnel, I'm afraid. Whoever sent the photograph would have dumped the bloody thing as soon as they sent it. Telephone unit at Lambeth reckon it was from a Carphone Warehouse.'

'Is that good?'

'No. The closest trace you can get on one of those is the warehouse it was shipped out from.'

'So they even got lucky on where they bought the phone.'

'Hardly lucky. Not if you're expert at comms like Margaret Lennox.'

'Well, the clock's ticking,' he said. 'We've had him . . .' He checked his watch. 'Twenty hours and ten minutes.'

'And getting nowhere, sir?'

'Says he went to Hampstead to take a look at a job, the people weren't there so he felt like a walk and went to visit Keats' house.'

'Can Keats verify that?'

'Very funny.'

Grey came out of the video room with a cup of coffee. Charlie wondered if he'd got it himself or if the DCI had bought it for him. He nodded at Charlie. 'Sir.'

'Sergeant. He hasn't broken down yet, then?'

'Nothing seems to faze him. I thought he'd hide behind "no comment" but you can't shut him up.'

'Well, he was part of an elite military unit,' Charlie said. 'I imagine that saying nasty things to him to try and hurt his feelings might not work.'

'Have you seen the results of the search and seizure?' the DCI said.

Charlie nodded, Jack had broken protocol and rung him first thing that morning, as if he was still SIO. 'Nothing on his laptop or his iPad, no Greek dramatists on his bookshelf; the closest thing he had to highbrow was a Salman Rushdie novel, and he used that as a doorstop in the kitchen. They pulled his work van apart, none of the sharp-edged tools were positive for blood. They even tested the power saw, I believe, though that would be hard to carry around on the back of a motorbike.' He saw the look the DCI gave him. 'That was a joke, sir.'

'I know what it was.' He shook his head. 'His solicitor is threatening to lodge a complaint for wrongful arrest.'

'That's his job. The evidence must seem pretty thin when you're on his side of the red line.'

The DCI lowered his voice. 'We could charge him with assaulting a police officer.'

'Really? Who?'

'One of the uniforms saw him hit you.'

'Took a bit of a half-hearted swing, sir. Missed by a country mile.'

'Does it matter if he missed or not? It would help me out.'

Charlie shook his head. 'Sorry. I'm not laying a charge.'

'Take one for the team.'

'No. Wouldn't sit right with me.'

The DCI tried to stare him down but Charlie wasn't having it; he was good at that game. He'd stared down his old man when he was sixteen, and there was no one in the whole of north London harder than him.

The DCI turned away after a few seconds, as he knew he would. 'We'll give it one more go,' he said to Grey. He made a face. 'This coffee's rubbish, Charlie, I don't know how you can drink it. Waste of money.' And he tossed his, still three-quarters full, into the bin.

Charlie went into the video room to watch the rest of the interview. Gordon looked utterly relaxed as Grey and the DCI walked back in. Charlie had never seen him so Zen; no trucks backfiring in the street, no ghosts chasing him through his dreams. This set-up was made for him. Home turf.

Charlie didn't subscribe to the belief that you could crack suspects with a brilliant interview technique. In his world you just piled up the admissible evidence and presented your suspect with it, gave them the chance to produce a reasonable explanation as to why the knife that was sticking in Taz Boy's back had his fingerprints all over it and why Taz Boy's blood was all over the pair of Nikes they found under his bed. *Want to tell me what happened or hide behind 'no comment' and take your chances in court?*

Charlie never went much further than that with his subtle interrogation techniques. He didn't suppose he'd ever make profiler for the National Crime Authority.

He watched as the DCI ran through it all again; why were you in Hampstead, what was the name of the people you had come to quote for renovations, what made you go to Keats' house instead of going home?

He was looking for discrepancies, that was one thing he did know about interviews. If someone was telling the truth, their story never varied; when they'd had to rehearse it, no one ever got it right three times in a row. People were never as good at lying as they thought they were.

Gordon Lennox was an exception. Or perhaps he was telling the truth, perhaps he did like Keats that much.

'Tom said it was you and Joe Cole that saved his life,' the DCI said to him.

Gordon shrugged. 'If that's what he says.'

'It's not true?'

'It was like this. He was up front with this bloke, Ferguson. Suddenly I felt this blast of heat, it was like standing behind the afterburners on a jet fighter. This pressure wave hits you, and the noise, man, you go deaf for about ten seconds. The first thing you think is: oh fuck, is it me, am I hit? And then you get up and dust yourself off and you realise, shit, it's not me, it's my mate.

'We went up forward, first thing I saw was Ferguson, what was left of him. It was like he'd been put through a meat grinder. Only way I could tell it was him was some bits of ginger hair and a tattoo. Then I saw Tom. He was fucking screaming his head off. And the captain, he says to us, "Stay down!" I looked at Joe and we both thought the same thing at the same time.'

'Which was what?'

'Which was: Fuck you, captain. We got up and started to run. The rest of the boys laid down a covering fire for us and we grabbed Tom and ran fast as we could. I don't know how we didn't get hit. The fucking Taliban we were up against, they couldn't shoot any better than them white robots on *Star Wars*, must have been off their heads on hash or something. I got a commendation for bravery, so did Joe, but to be honest, I don't remember much about it. When we got back and jumped behind the wall again, there was this smell. I realised I'd soiled myself. So that's what a hero I was.'

'What happened to Tom?'

'You know what happened to him. The IED blew his fucking legs off.'

Gordon leaned forward. 'Barely rates a mention on the TV, does it? No one really cares. They'd rather not know. They don't know anything about the war we were fighting until someone gets knifed on London Bridge – it's something that happens to someone somewhere else.'

'That must have made you very angry,' the DCI said.

'I went to see him when I got back, and Jen answered the door. You know what she said? She said: "You promised me you'd look after him." And she slapped me round the face. I was standing there on the doorstep, crying my fucking eyes out, and she wouldn't even let me in the house to see him. My own sister.'

'I suppose there's times you wished the Taliban could shoot straight,' Grey said.

A strangled smile. 'Every. Fucking. Day.'

The DCI leaned in. 'You'd do anything for a mate, wouldn't you?'

'Yeah, I would.'

'You'd kill for him and you'd die for him.'

'That's right.'

'Is that what you did that night? Did you kill Barrington for Tom? Some people wouldn't blame you, you know. After all you'd been through, the two of you. And then what happened to Zoë.'

'Thought about it,' Gordon said. 'What shall I do with my afternoon? I know, I'll go round that judge's place and whip his head off with my putty knife.' He grinned. 'But then I thought, no. And I went to Keats' house instead.'

'The thing is, Mr Lennox, Keats' house is closed on a Tuesday.'

'Yeah, I know. A right bugger, eh? All that way for nothing.'

Charlie was still there when Gordon Lennox came out of the interview room with his solicitor. They didn't have enough to charge him, so the DCI was letting him go. As he came out he saw Charlie and came over. He wondered if he was going to have another go. Even his brief looked worried.

'Sorry about what happened,' Gordon said. 'I appreciate you not taking it any further.'

Charlie nodded.

'I know what it's like,' he whispered, 'having to do a job you don't think is right.'

Charlie didn't know how to answer him, and by the time he thought of an answer Gordon had moved on and was headed towards the lifts with his solicitor.

CHAPTER THIRTY-EIGHT

Charlie had bought a copy of *The Oresteia* in the local Waterstones. He went down to the evidence room, signed himself in, and found the bagged copy taken from the Millers' house. He checked the two quotes against the missing pages.

He went through the rest of the book. There were a number of other loose pages but only three missing in total. He compared the book with his own copy; it confirmed what he had suspected ever since they found Barrington's body.

There was going to be at least one more victim. And now he had a pretty good idea who that was going to be.

The DCI looked harassed. Having to do some real work for a change, Charlie thought. Being SIO on a big case isn't a ticker-tape parade if you don't catch the villains; all you get is endless bollockings from your bosses and late nights wading through more paperwork than the VAT office.

It wasn't often he saw his boss in his shirtsleeves, and the papers on his desk were always arranged in neat piles. Not today. Even the plants on the windowsill were dying.

'Sit down, Charlie,' the DCI said. 'Have you got something for me?'

'I think so, sir. We may not yet be able to prove who did for Grimes and Judge Barrington, but I think I know who the next target is.'

'I'm listening.'

'The page shoved down Barrington's throat matched another

missing page in the book we seized from the Millers' house. There's still one more we haven't yet found. So I checked their version against a copy of my own.' He passed the book he had bought at Waterstones across the desk. 'The missing page has this quote.'

The DCI peered at the section Charlie had highlighted and he nodded slowly:

> You wish to be called righteous rather than act right.
> I say, wrong must not win by technicalities.

'Who does that sound like to you?' Charlie said.

'All right, Charlie, you know what to do. I'll authorise protective surveillance.'

'Seems a shame, though. More taxpayer money down the drain.'

'That's life in Britain in the twenty-first century, Charlie. You can't fight it. Don't even try.'

Lovejoy knocked on Charlie's door, put her head around the corner. 'Guv?'

'Lovejoy. What have you got for me?'

'I checked Lennox's alibi, like you asked. The address he gave us, the couple who wanted a quote on some reno work in Hampstead?'

'What did they say?'

'Went around there, but there's no answer. Neighbours say they've gone away on holiday.'

'Right.'

'Who goes on holiday in November?'

'Rich people,' Charlie said. 'Keep trying.'

'You all right, guv? You look like Arsenal just got relegated.'

'I'm about to go and see a QC called Mark Williams. I have been told to offer him round-the-clock security.'

'You think he's the next target?'

'I'm convinced of it. He was the defending counsel for Michael Grimes at his trial. Not that he did a lot. I've read through the transcript and it wasn't exactly O. J. Simpson. He kept Grimes' previous from the jury and it was basically the 'poor him' defence: deprived childhood, father was a drug addict, pass the tissues round the court, the usual bollocks. Nothing anyone hasn't heard a hundred times before. The so-called lenient sentence was as much down to the sentencing guidelines as it was Barrington or Williams.'

'So why the long face, as the barman said to the horse?'

'It's a long story.'

'As long as it's got a good punchline.'

'All right, if that's what you want. Sit down, Lovejoy.'

She came in, sat down. He noticed she still had a bit of a limp. He promised himself he would never again let one of his team get injured on his watch.

'Okay, it's like this. There was this big case, probably happened before you joined the Met, I was only a sergeant myself at the time. My DI, he thought he was a bit clever, a bit of a maverick, his heart was in the right place but he thought he could make his own rules.

'So there was this little girl went missing, and we had this bloke bang to rights; we had CCTV putting him right there at the time she disappeared, and he had previous, lots of previous. So my boss, he put a surveillance team on him, and we followed him, drove all the way out to Rainham Marshes, and while he was sat there in his car, surveillance said to him, "So what do we do now?" Because there was hope, see, that she was still alive, that he had her somewhere.

'And we waited, and we waited. But we couldn't get too close, right? There were three cars, covering all the exits, but this scrote had gone in and he still hadn't come out. Every few minutes on the radio, it was like: "What shall we do, what shall we do?" And I was there, I was sitting in the car with my DI, you could have cut the air with a knife. What if this prick topped himself? What if he was destroying evidence? What if he had the girl with him, in the back of the van, and he was finishing her off?

'Finally, my boss picked up the radio and told the surveillance team to collar him. And when we got there, they had him cuffed and on the ground in the car park, and there was pills everywhere, he'd taken a whole cocktail of stuff. They'd called for an ambulance, but he was still conscious. We didn't know if he was going to die, if he was going to be in a coma, whatever.

'And my boss said, straight out, "Where is she, what did you do with her?"

'And he said: "I didn't mean to kill her. It was an accident. I was only trying to shut her up."

'So my boss said, "Where is she?" And he told us, he said "I buried her." He told us where, it was off the A40 near Denham. Marsh Lane, he said, near the dead oak. Kept saying: "It was an accident." They were his words. We all heard him, clear as day.

'And you know what? We sent a team up there, they found a dead tree and some freshly moved earth about fifty yards away, in the woods. And that's where she was. Seven years old, and he'd throttled her, only he'd buggered her first. I was at the PM with my boss. Only time I ever saw him angry. Only time.'

Charlie put his hands under the desk so Lovejoy couldn't see that he was shaking.

'That was it, right? Good bit of police work. Couldn't bring her back but at least we found her so she could get a decent burial, not rot in some field in a shallow grave. And we collared the scum that did it.

'When we got back to the nick there was this absolute media scrum, the case had been on the TV for days.'

'I think I remember this.'

'Yeah, it was everywhere. Anyway, the media team approved a press release which my boss read to them on the steps right outside our station. It said a thirty-five-year-old man had been arrested on suspicion of murder, and that he had led us to the location of the girl's body, near Uxbridge. We all thought that was that. There was no celebration exactly, the poor little mite was dead, but at least we'd done our job. The bloke that did it, they pumped his stomach, he recovered, made a full confession.'

Lovejoy looked at him, bewildered. 'So?'

'So then he got this defence solicitor, Raymond Merrick, who persuaded him to retract his confession.'

'How could he do that?'

'Well, it was like this. The defence barrister got my boss on the stand. And he said to him, "Did you caution my client, as the PACE laws demand?" My boss tried to argue with him. He said that his first concern was finding the little girl alive. But this barrister wasn't having any of it. He said, "So the end justifies the means, does it? You decide when and where to breach PACE regulations?" My boss gave him some answer, said that if he hadn't done what he did, we might never have found the little girl.

'Then the barrister turned to the judge and said that the police had not followed the PACE laws in obtaining the confession, and that it was therefore inadmissible in court. But he wasn't satisfied with that. He also said the police had precluded his client's right to a fair trial by their media strategy, by putting certain information in the public domain.'

'That's bollocks.'

'No, Lovejoy, even when it's bollocks, it's still the law. That is precisely the problem with it. We had an open and shut case; this fucking monster had said he'd done it, he'd even told us where the little girl's body was. That was what happened so that should have been that. But the barrister argued that whatever his client had said, even a full confession, should have been *sub judice*. My boss, I thought he was going to have a seizure. He was always so calm in the witness box, but he was practically frothing. He shouted at this bloke: "How can the truth be prejudicial?"

'Me, I couldn't believe what I was hearing. And you know

what this barrister said, to the judge? He said: "This isn't about truth or justice, it's not about guilt or innocence, it's about whether the evidence is admissible or not."

'He did to my boss the same thing they did to that other poor bastard, Fulcher. And in the end it all came down to the judge, whether he would allow the confession to stand. And when he gave his ruling, I can't remember exactly what he said, he rambled on and on about points of law, and all in this bloody monotone, like it was a mathematics problem, not about a little girl getting sodomised and strangled. He said the confession would have an adverse effect on the fairness of the trial. They were his very words. He was prepared to let this bastard get away with murder on a point of law. That's when I lost all my respect for the so-called justice system and the courts, which isn't a good thing for a cop, is it? I suppose I've struggled ever since.'

'Who was the judge?'

'As it happens, it was Sir Malcolm Barrington, CBE, QC. Question for you, Lovejoy: If we find the bloke that beheaded him, do you reckon his wife, his kids, will want us to follow the PACE laws to the letter? It would be an interesting question to ask but I suppose we'll never know.'

'What happened to your boss?' Lovejoy said.

'He resigned a month later. Took early retirement. He was basically hounded out of the force, same as Fulcher was. I have no idea where he is these days. He dropped off the radar, wouldn't answer my calls or emails.'

'The defence team must have been laughing their socks off,' Lovejoy said.

'Well Merrick made the most of the acquittal. He dined out on that for years and went from some seedy office up by Euston station to his own practice over in Holborn.'

'And the barrister?'

'He's got chambers at Lincoln's Inn. Specialises in criminal law, and not too fussy where the work comes from by all

237

accounts. Still gets a lot from Merrick, as it happens. He's doing very nicely thank you very much.'

'What was his name?' Lovejoy said.

'It was Williams. Mark Williams.'

CHAPTER THIRTY-NINE

Lincoln's Inn reminded Charlie of Hogwarts, all Gothic halls and chapels around a snug little green, within a siren's call of High Holborn with its tourists and desperados and bicycle couriers and buses.

He was shown into a conference room and invited to wait at a large antique table that looked as if the Magna Carta was signed on it. He was given Assam tea in a bone china cup which he enjoyed smelling and looking at but didn't drink. He wondered what would happen if he followed his juvenile impulse to steal the spoon.

Mark Williams came in wearing a dark blue single-breasted suit with Milanese buttonholes and pic stitching, and a silver and black basketweave tie. He looked as if you'd get a paper cut if you touched him. He had hair dark and flat as unpolished silver and looked at Charlie as if he was a stain on the carpet.

'Inspector George.' His handshake was brief, and hard. 'Is that your first name or last name?'

'Which? Inspector or George?'

Williams sat down and crossed his legs. 'I like a man with a sense of humour.'

'I think integrity's more important myself, but I'll take humour. You're Mark Williams?'

'Do I know you?' There was a faint Irish brogue in there somewhere. Your grandies and mine would have shared a lease on a potato field back in the day, Charlie thought. Now look at us.

'We've never met,' Charlie said.

'You look vaguely familiar. What can I do for you, inspector? Have you murdered one of your suspects in the custody suite? Don't worry, I'll get you off. Any CCTV?'

'You know we never abuse a prisoner if there's cameras about. That would be unprofessional.' Charlie looked around. 'Nice offices.'

'Thank you. But that's not why you're here. Is this about Malcolm? Poor man.'

'Partly about him. Also about a Michael Grimes, who we believe fell victim to the same assailant. Do you remember Mr Grimes?'

'Should I?'

'You represented him once in court.'

'The name escapes me.'

'Really? His name's been all over the papers. And he was one of your high-profile cases a few years ago. I imagine you got the brief from Merrick, White and Fisher. It wouldn't have been much of an earner.'

A theatrical sigh. 'Do you have a point?'

'His Right Honourable presided over that case as well.'

'Malcolm? He was the judge who sent Grimes down?'

'Not for very long, in some people's minds.'

'Wait a minute. What are you saying here?'

'You're a smart man. I'm sure you can work it out.'

'You think I'm next on the list?'

'If there is a list. But yes, we have reason to believe your life could be in danger.'

'I thought I heard on the news that you have someone in custody?'

'They were helping us with our enquiries. They have since been released without charge.'

'Because you don't think they did it or because you don't have proof that they did it?'

'I'm not at liberty to discuss the details of an ongoing inquiry with you, I'm afraid. But in the end, it's all about the evidence, isn't it?'

'Did this person say anything to you to indicate that I was a target?'

'You were Grimes' QC during the trial.'

'But I lost. It was hardly an important case. I did what I could, but . . . I hardly remember the man.'

'Yeah, I know,' Charlie said, and grinned. 'Seems a bit unfair.'

'So now, for just doing my job, some maniac is going to come after me and try and cut my head off. Is that what you're saying?'

'Barrington was only doing his job. Someone took exception anyway.'

'So how many good people have to die before you catch this person or persons?'

'Well, I wouldn't describe Michael Grimes as a good person. That would be a bit of a stretch. But I can assure you, Mr Williams, we are throwing all our resources into finding and detaining the person responsible. But we can't go and grab anyone we like off the street, or their defending barrister will tear us apart in court. Won't they?'

'What exactly do you want?'

'I don't want anything. We would like to provide you with protective measures. Special Branch can have someone come to your residence and assess the security arrangements you have in place, see if they need to be improved or updated. Also, we'll have two members of the Protection Command assigned to you at all times until the threat has passed.'

'What do you mean "at all times"?'

'I mean, "at all times".'

'I assume I'll be allowed to go to the bathroom on my own?'

'You can hold their hand through the door.'

'Is that meant to be funny?'

'You said you liked a man with a sense of humour.'

'This individual that you have just released, does he have an alibi? Are you satisfied that he has nothing to do with this?'

'No comment, as they say.'

Williams stood up and went to the window. He seemed to have lost his hubris; now he just looked agitated. Perhaps he was imagining his head on a railing at Lincoln's Inn Fields.

'He couldn't remember a thing, you know?'

'Who?'

'Grimes. I remember now, talking to him in his cell, before sentencing. A wreck of a man. He stank, more than most. Sweat and fear. All he kept saying was he didn't remember anything. He'd had a tragic life. Been on hard drugs since he was fourteen. His father used to buy them for him. He was an addict as well.'

'Mr Williams, you have to pick your audience. I'm not a jury. None of that washes with me. Grimes had a life at least. Zoë Miller didn't ever have the chance to do anything with hers, good or bad. She's the one I feel sorry for.'

'Well, I hope your personal feelings won't stand in the way of you doing your job.'

'They won't,' Charlie said, and he stood up. 'You'll get a call within the hour. Someone will walk you through it. Hopefully this will all be cleared up in a couple of days and you can get back to your normal life.'

'Are you sure I don't know you?'

'Like I said, we've never met.'

'But I've been the defending QC in one of your prosecutions. Am I right?'

'Just one.'

'I thought so. That's where I know you from? Which one was it?'

'Long time ago now. You had longer hair in those days.'

'I took whatever cases I could get back then.'

'Kelsey Duffy.'

'Ah, that one.'

'You were proper on fire that day.'

'Can't blame me for that. Your boss didn't follow the PACE laws.'

'Well, I got over it. But I wasn't the one that was sodomised and strangled. Like I said, really nice office. Well done.'

He left.

CHAPTER FORTY

He stood in the shower, turned on the cold tap, held his breath as the water sliced across his scalp and down his shoulders. There was plenty of hot water in the tank, but he guarded against anything that might take away the edge.

Couldn't afford to get soft, not now. Too much at stake. He had one ear to the breakfast news on the television. Another marine had been killed by an Afghan commando in Kabul. The whole thing had been pointless. So many good men gone, and nothing had changed.

He put on a pair of shorts, did one hundred press-ups with one arm, another hundred with the other. He rolled onto his back and counted two hundred sit-ups. He stood up, put on running shorts, studied his torso in the mirror. It wasn't vanity that made him do it; it was more like cleaning and oiling your weapon when you were in country. He was making sure everything was in proper condition. If you didn't look after your gear, it would let you down when you needed it. He couldn't afford his body to let him down, not now.

The regimen was taped to the mirror above the vanity.

200 push-ups
200 sit-ups
50 pull-ups
50 four-count flutter kicks
6-mile run: 42 minutes

He hammered his fist into his belly, his muscles were hard as a brick, like they were when he was with the regiment. Satisfied, he put on a t-shirt and went downstairs to get breakfast.

They were sitting at the table, not speaking. He stood by the sink, cracked two raw eggs into a glass of milk and swallowed it down, then went over to the table and picked up one of the bowls of cereal he'd poured for them.

'You haven't touched it,' he said. 'You can't not eat.'

He hated the way they looked at him. They looked shit scared. He'd never hurt them, didn't they get that?

But he had hurt them, hadn't he? During one of those blinding rages he got that he couldn't control.

He'd come back different, that was what she'd said. 'I don't know you any more.' Maybe she was right, he couldn't tell. He only had her word for it, he couldn't remember what he was like before. Over there you did certain things to stay alive, so you could get back to your life again, but people said you were dead anyway. You tried to do your best for them and all you got were these looks.

He had tried to pretend he was normal again. He thought he was making a decent fist of it and then she'd say something and he'd realise, it's not working, they all think I'm crazy.

That was the worst thing, feeling like you were going mad. Like other people saw things in you that you couldn't see. It was frightening in ways that being in combat never was.

'Why won't you eat?'

They all kept their heads down, wouldn't look at him.

A newsreader was still gabbling about something on the television. 'What did I tell you about leaving this crap on?' he said. 'I don't want the kids' heads filled with this junk. They shouldn't have to look at this shit.'

There were pictures of some bus attack in Egypt, bloody clothes lying on the ground, a bus riddled with bullets through the coachwork and the glass. A fifteen-second grab of a white coffin coming out of a church, a woman screaming in a hospital.

He turned it off and went into his study. His desk was covered with a litter of papers and printouts and newspaper cuttings and manila folders. The next operation was on the pin-board; maps of the area, times, escape routes, location maps of CCTV cameras and ANPR, a schedule of the operation worked out to minutes and seconds.

What was it they always taught you in training? PPP = PPP. Poor Planning and Preparation leads to Piss Poor Performance. But you also had to watch out for Sod's Law, no matter how precisely you planned. Sod's Law said that if something could go wrong, it would. You had to always be ready to adapt.

'Soon be over,' he said. When it was done, he could relax and be himself again.

He ran his finger across the glossy ten by eight at the centre of the noticeboard. 'You low-life dick-wipe,' he murmured. 'Your turn now.'

He went outside, put on a pair of trainers and set off for his run, as he did every morning. There was sleet in the rain; it stung his face, felt good, cleared his head. He liked the smell of wet grass, stopped to hold a handful of leaves to his face. Sometimes his brain tricked him, and the smell was like holding a clump of burned flesh. Not today. Today it smelled like earth and mulch, good smells.

But then he ran around the corner and saw someone had left a jumper lying there in the grass, all wet and sodden. Perhaps some kid had forgotten it, left it behind. He picked it up, and he remembered how once he'd had to pick up body parts, they were heavy and sodden too. Pulpy. He dropped it and kept going, tried to run off the memory.

No good.

They were in country, some dusty shithole in the mountains, this little boy, couldn't have been more than six or seven, used to bring them bread and goat's milk. They played football with him in the square. One day he didn't show up; they found him floating in pieces in their water supply.

It was their fault. The Taliban had killed him but, in a way, so had they.

He'd wanted to find the bastards who did it but how did you know who were the good guys and who were the bad guys? This time, at least you knew who the killers were, and who was helping them. He finally felt like he wasn't helpless any more.

When he got back, he reset the tripwire, made sure the tension was right. The kids knew not to leave the house. He didn't want any accidents.

Then he went back inside and hunkered down, waiting for the night.

CHAPTER FORTY-ONE

Mark Williams escorted his date through to the bar for pre-dinner cocktails. He ordered a single malt and handed her the menu, which was inside an antique leather book jacket. She said, 'I've got a big day tomorrow' and asked for mineral water with a slice of lemon.

The place was cosy and intimate, a blazing fire, antique books, comfortable leather chairs. The type of place he liked, a place you went to when you wanted to congratulate yourself on how well you were doing.

And he was doing very well indeed.

Paula had danced around his light for a while now, trying to absorb some of the magic. She was perhaps a little too young and a little too easy to get, but it was only a weeknight so why not?

'Are you enjoying your first year in chambers?' he asked her.

'I enjoy the intellectual challenge.'

'But?'

'Was there a "but" in there?'

'It was in the tone of your voice.'

She smiled. 'Never try and fool a Queen's Counsel.'

'Exactly.'

'I was out at dinner last night. Someone asked me how I got into law, how I can do this job. You know, defend someone I know is guilty.'

'But we don't do that. If someone tells us they're guilty we have to retire as their legal team or we'd be disbarred.'

'Yes, but like the case we're trying now. Neither of us really believe his story.'

'Personal opinions don't come into it. So anyway, how did you answer the question? You must be used to that sort of thing by now.'

'I mumbled something. I don't know. How the system can't work without good lawyers on both sides. Have to keep the bastards honest. That sort of thing.'

'Well, it's all true.'

'What do *you* say?'

'I used to trot out that old line about everybody deserving a right to a fair trial. But to be honest, that isn't the whole truth.'

'And what is the whole truth?'

'The fact is, I like guilty people. They're flawed and they're complicated and they're interesting. I am interested in the causes of human conduct, I like dealing with life, with its hopes and fears . . .'

'Its aspirations and despairs,' Paula said, finishing his sentence for him. 'That was Clarence Darrow. It's a good quote. I'm sure he won't mind you borrowing it.'

Bitch, Williams thought. 'Look, I'm happy to lose a case, any case, if the prosecution does their job and proves theirs. No matter what a defendant has done, he's not legally guilty of anything until a prosecutor offers up enough evidence. That's our job, to make sure that happens. It may not be popular with everyone, but it ensures all our liberties. I sleep easy.'

'But do you really believe that?' she said.

The drinks arrived. He sipped his malt and considered. So earnest, this one. A brilliant mind but she was too conflicted ever to make a good living out of the law. Such a waste.

'The adversarial legal system is the very foundation of British law and without good defence counsel that system would collapse. The first principle is this: it is not up to the barrister to judge guilt or innocence. Nothing, absolutely nothing, can cloud your cold professional judgement. You are not entitled to the luxury of a personal point of view. You are there solely to promote your client's cause, without fear or favour.'

Paula bit her lip. She's watched too many television shows growing up, he thought, where the heroic defence lawyer saves the wrongly accused. She wants to be on the side of the angels every time.

Poor girl.

I hope, at least, that she's good in bed later.

'But what about Barry?' she said.

Barry Adams, accused of the sexual abuse of his daughter between the ages of thirteen and seventeen. Williams had made his final address to the jury that afternoon and they had retired for their verdict.

'What about him?'

'He's a pig.'

'Sustained,' he said, and smiled.

'I mean, when he came to chambers that first time, he made my skin crawl. The way he looked at me. His whole demeanour. If someone had accused me of doing that to my daughter, I wouldn't be smirking about it.'

'It doesn't mean he did it.'

'I went through his social services records, remember? I found the case notes from when his daughter was fourteen. She was saying ten years ago that he was doing things to her. No one followed it up.'

'Unfortunately, it's a pattern in her life. No one from the prosecution found those notes either. It shows that I employ better people than they do.' He leaned forward, touched her knee. She didn't flinch away, so that was promising. 'It's just a game, Paula.'

She shook her head, wanting to be persuaded. 'Sometimes I struggle with this.'

'If we secure the acquittal of someone who is guilty, or the conviction of someone who is innocent, that is not our professional concern. We present our evidence, the prosecution presents theirs. The members of the jury are the ones commissioned with the final decision.'

'But what you did to that girl today. I don't know that I could do that.'

'Did it upset you?'

'You crucified her. She's never been in a courtroom before, she has no education, she was totally intimidated. She was no match for you.'

'I would hope not. I was head of the debating team at university. Our job in cross-examination, as you would have learned at law school, is to make the witness say what we want them to say.'

'But what you did to her was cruel. After all she's been through.'

'We don't know for certain that she's been through anything. Let's be honest. The purpose of a defence lawyer is to destroy. If her father really did what she said he did, there is not the possibility of eyewitnesses to gainsay it, and he can't provide an alibi to say he wasn't there when it happened. It supposedly occurred in the family home, so our only defence is to destroy her credibility. You have to admit, she provided me with plenty of ammunition.'

'Yes, she was no angel. Neither was I when I was that age. All teenagers tell fibs, or defy their parents, or do things they shouldn't do.'

'Yes, and my job was to weaponise those things.'

'But a lot of the drinking and the psychiatric episodes you brought up could have been brought on by the abuse.'

'I agree, they could have. But it's not my job to speculate, nor yours. My duty is to my client. And let's not forget, the daughter is on record as telling her counsellor that she was going to make her father pay one day.'

'Well, if I was her and I was with someone I thought I could trust, I'd probably say that too. It's human nature.'

'She made it a lot worse for herself by trying to deny it.'

Paula finished her drink. That was quick. Fortunately it was only mineral water or she'd be falling over drunk by the time they finished dinner. Then where would they be?

'Enough about work,' he said. 'Let's have dinner.'

The maître d' escorted them through a long corridor, shimmering with diffused bronze lighting under an intricate mirrored ceiling. In the centre was the largest vase of flowers he'd ever seen. The room itself looked like it had been lifted from some private banquet hall in thirties Shanghai, with its glossy black lacquer and grand sofas and chairs. Only the huge blazing fire broke the illusion.

He heard Paula murmur: 'Wow.'

Good. He had wanted to impress her. If his prowess in front of a jury had made her uncomfortable, he felt he had more than swayed her with this. *This is what your life could be like*, he wanted to tell her, *if only you weren't so squeamish.*

It was midweek and there were few other diners. He idly wondered where his minders were. Still, never mind. All these mirrors, he should be able to see someone coming up behind him.

'This is amazing,' Paula said.

'Do you like it?'

'I've heard them talking about it, in chambers, but I've never been here.'

'In chambers?'

'They say it's your favourite restaurant because you can see yourself from a hundred different angles.'

She laughed, and he wasn't sure whether he should laugh along with her. He didn't like the idea that people talked about him that way.

He got her talking about her life, not that there was much to tell, there hadn't been enough of it yet. She had grown up in Oxfordshire, her father had made his money in the City and now liked to dine out on the fact that the kitchen in their rambling five bedroom house had once been a cottage so old it had been recorded in the Domesday Book.

He asked her about boyfriends and got a coy response, as if she thought he might be jealous. She told him about her ambitions, grandiose plans that had a lot to do with the accumulation of money but were sparse when it came to the means of acquiring it.

She had no idea.

Listening to her only increased his unease. He liked his life and had worked hard to get where he was, after years and years of excruciatingly long hours. He had taken his opportunities, and finally had his life how he wanted it.

He didn't like the thought that there was someone out there who might take it all away from him.

He couldn't stop thinking about the copper who had come to see him. He looked like a reject from an Albanian boxing school, sitting there in his fancy shoes, telling him he believed he was in imminent danger and smiling when he said it.

After he'd gone, he'd checked the file, but he still couldn't remember much about this Michael Grimes. The truth was, the case hadn't mattered to him that much. Merrick had only sent him the briefing notes the day of the trial, it wasn't his fault Grimes received what even he thought was a ridiculously light sentence. He'd left most of the work to his junior advocate. Luckily for Grimes, the judge was one of those bleeding hearts who genuinely thought some people were redeemable.

He ordered the crispy Dover sole, hand cut chips and truffle mayonnaise. When it came, he wished his mum could see him, the cow. Tempura batter, not the floury crap that stuck to the newspaper, like the stuff she used to buy from the chippie in the high street. Even the chips were different, stacked in a square-cut pile like a Jenga game.

He smiled. He'd come a long way from those days.

Paula had ordered an off-menu selection of steamed vegetables. They came prettily arranged, like a piece of modern art.

'So what did that murder squad detective want to see you about?'

'How did you know about that?'

'Nothing goes on in chambers I don't know. Jamie said he looked like that actor in the *Fast and Furious* movies, what was his name? Statham. The sexy one with the shaved head.'

'Did Jamie fancy him?'

'He said he was all right. But you know Jamie. He's a bit of a tart. So, are you going to tell me?'

'It was nothing. It was about an old case.'

'Anything to do with the goons who followed us here tonight?'

'You saw them?'

'I'd have to be legally blind not to. Not exactly subtle, are they. Are they carrying?'

'I hope so.'

'Are you in danger?' she said, and he could see that the thought excited her. Her knee touched his under the table.

'Possibly,' he said, going along with it.

'Bothered?'

'Not really. Are you?'

'Only makes you sexier.' She looked at him over the rim of her glass. 'Do they follow you everywhere?'

'They stand outside the door of my bedroom. If they hear screams, they have orders to break in.'

'I'd better gag you then.'

When they left the two cops were waiting in the grand Edwardian forecourt, talking to the concierge, who clearly knew who they were. Paula raised her eyebrows and smiled. 'This is great,' she whispered. 'Like the movies.'

His mobile rang. He glanced at the screen. It was Merrick. 'Sorry, I have to take this,' he said to her, and turned away.

'Mark, bad time?' Merrick said.

'Tell me what you've found out.'

'I did what you said, I rang around. Wasn't one of my solicitors who got called in for the interview.'

'Fuck.'

'Steady on. I made a few calls, found out who it was, and he was happy to oblige. Wasn't cheap.'

'Bill me.'

'The bloke's name was Gordon Lennox. Seriously hard. Ex-SAS, the dead girl was his niece. He was seen in Hampstead about a hundred yards from where Barrington was murdered. They got him on CCTV, but they can't put him at the crime scene.'

'Christ. And they've let him go?'

'Had no choice.'

'They've got two of their goons following me everywhere. It's bloody nerve-wracking.'

'You want help with this?'

'Such as?'

'I have a friend, a Mr Spirelli, who might be able to help on the QT. All it would take, the promise of future services, in exchange.'

'Like *The Godfather*, you mean?'

'If you like.'

'I'll let you know.'

'Have a good night,' Merrick said and hung up.

Williams turned around and smiled at Paula. 'Sorry, work again. It never stops.' He was about to put an arm around her when there was a loud bang. He flinched before he could stop himself. Even the two cops turned to look, one of them already had a hand inside his jacket.

Just a motorcycle backfiring on High Holborn. 'Are you all right?' Paula said.

'I'm fine,' he said, annoyed that she had seen him react. She squeezed his hand as they waited for the taxi.

She nestled close to him in the back of the cab but he couldn't relax, found himself glancing at every motorcycle that came up beside them in the traffic. He'd read about it in the papers, it was one of these black-clad bikers that had thrown Barrington's head at the Old Bailey steps, got in and got out fast, before anyone could react.

He looked around once, for his protection, saw the BMW X5 just behind them. Relax, he told himself, there's nothing to worry about.

Paula nudged him with her arm. He looked down. She slid two fingers under her dress and then put them in his mouth.

'A taste of what's to come,' she whispered.

He grinned.

When they reached her place he jumped out, threw a handful of notes at the driver. 'Keep the change,' he said. He just wanted to get inside. The driver thought he was in a hurry for the sex. Only knew the half of it.

'Going to bring your boys up and make it a foursome?' Paula said.

'They've already got a job to do,' he said.

She keyed them in. When they got in the lift, she didn't say anything until they reached her apartment. As soon as they were inside, she turned around and kissed him on the mouth. 'Don't worry,' she whispered. 'I'll take care of you from here.'

He slipped out of bed. She was asleep or pretending to be, her hair loose and fanned over the pillow. His jacket was neatly folded over the chair; he took his mobile out of the pocket, put on his underwear and slipped out of the room.

Fuck this.

He peered through the curtains, he could see the silhouette of the X5 a few yards down the street. The two goons were in the front, they were probably asleep.

Being inconvenienced by this lunatic was one thing, but when he couldn't get it up he took exception. It would be all over chambers by tomorrow. He imagined trying to tell her that it had never happened to him before. That would go down well. Wasn't he the one always telling her and the other juniors:

'The truth doesn't matter, the only thing that matters is the evidence.'

He hesitated, his finger hovering over the keypad. Desperate times called for desperate measures.

He heard Merrick's voice, he sounded amped. Must have scored some Bolivian marching powder.

'It's me,' he said.

'What's up?'

'I was thinking about your Mr Spirelli.'

'You want to do it?'

'Absolutely.'

'When?'

'As soon as possible.'

'I'll get back to you.'

He went back into the bedroom and got dressed. Paula didn't wake up, or she was awake the whole time and didn't want to go through the whole 'it's not you, it's me' thing. He sat on the stairs in the dark and waited for Merrick to ring him back. He didn't have to wait that long.

Merrick gave him a name and an address and hung up. He called an Uber, waited in the entrance until it pulled up outside, and then went out and jumped in.

Williams got out at the Langham and walked through reception to the Artesian. He nodded to Damiano behind the bar. 'Long time no see,' he said and shook his hand, leaving a twenty quid note in his palm.

Damiano slipped it into his pocket.

'Is there a back way out, mate?'

Damiano nodded to a door that said Staff Only.

'You never saw me.'

The door led to a staff toilet, a storage room and a fire exit. He pushed open the door, went down the alley and hailed a taxi off the street. If it was that easy to get around his security, they were going to be fuck all good if Lennox came along.

He wondered if they'd try to follow him into the hotel. He doubted it. They probably thought he had another woman – or a man – on the go.

He hoped so.

CHAPTER FORTY-TWO

The cabbie dropped him at a roundabout in Sutton; the pub was on the north side, one of those big red brick places from the fifties with a massive car park for the coaches to pull in with day trippers and football fans. Williams stepped over a puddle of vomit by a bench on the way in; the place had seen better days than this.

He got looks as soon as he walked in. Not the sort of place where the customers wore suit jackets, this was the Harringtons and Doc Martens set. He made his way to the bar, gaps quickly closed, blokes eager for him to give them a shove so they could start something.

Some loudmouth in a leather jacket was giving his mates his world view. 'We need another fucking war to teach those fucking ragheads a fucking lesson.'

He tried to catch the eye of one of the staff, edged nearer the bar. Someone shoved him hard in the chest.

'Oi. You fucking spilled my beer. Never mind you're fucking sorry. What about my fucking shirt?'

Suddenly there was another bloke, waving him away. 'Leave it, Gaz. He's all right. Are you Williams?'

He was gnarly looking with crooked teeth and a bad haircut; Williams thought he was one of the ugliest people he'd ever seen. But the tattooed bruiser who had snarled at him about his beer just nodded and turned away, which told you something.

'Yeah, I'm Williams.'

'This way.'

He led him towards a banquette in the corner. 'I'm Geoffrey. Don't call me Geoff, I hate fucking Geoff. This is Tyrone.' Tyrone was the business. He was the size of an outhouse, with blond hair shaved close, a swastika tattooed on his forehead. He was fit, too. It looked like he had a sack of potatoes under his shirt.

He didn't look over, didn't take his eyes off the football on the Sky TV above the bar. Geoffrey sat down, put his trainers on the salmon-pink upholstery and started rolling a cigarette. Williams hadn't seen anyone smoking inside a pub for years.

'You like football?' Tyrone said, his eyes still on the game.

'Who's playing?'

Tyrone turned his head for a moment, to register his disdain. Then he flipped him off and returned his attention to the screen.

'It's your round,' Geoffrey said. 'We're drinking Jimmy and Cokes. Make them doubles.'

Williams made his way back to the bar. This time no one moved to stand in his way. He came back with the drinks. He'd ordered a pint of something, no intention of drinking it.

'Where's the CCTV in here?'

'It's broken.'

'You're sure?'

'We're regulars, Mr Williams. And Mr Spirelli owns the place. If he says the CCTV is down, it's down.'

'Okay, if you say so.'

'I do say so.'

Williams leaned in and lowered his voice anyway. 'I've got a job for you,' he said to Geoffrey.

'A job? You need a builder?'

'A contract. Mr Spirelli sent me. I have come to the right guys?'

Tyrone shook his head. 'You never done this before, right?'

'Do I look like I've done this before?'

'You want the house redecorated, or completely demolished?' Geoffrey said.

'Demolished.'

'That could be expensive, demolition.'

'You need a permit?'

Geoffrey turned to Tyrone. 'He's a funny guy.'

'This house,' Tyrone said. 'Is it well built?'

Williams thought about it. Like a jury, in a way. There are some things it's better for people not to know. 'Not particularly,' he said.

'Do we have to take away the building materials as well?' Geoffrey said. 'Because, you know, that's extra.'

'No, you can leave the site as it is. I just want it down.'

'Fuck me!' Tyrone shouted, and pointed at the screen. There were cheers from the crowd standing around it. 'I could do better. They should give me a shirt.'

'We were told you were in a bit of a fix,' Geoffrey said.

'It's like this. I'm afraid if I don't get it demolished in a hurry, it's going to collapse on top of me.'

'Mr Spirelli says we should do this for you. You a friend of his?'

'A friend of a friend.'

Geoffrey swallowed half the Jim Beam and Coke in one pull, wiped his mouth with the back of his hand.

'There's one problem,' Williams said.

'I guessed that.'

'This house. It has two night watchmen.'

Tyrone and Geoffrey exchanged a glance.

'Whose night watchmen are they?'

'They belong to the local authorities.'

'What the fuck they doing there?'

'Keeping watch.'

'You should do stand-up. Okay, well we'll deal with it. But that will be extra.'

'Great. What's the going rate?'

Tyrone looked at Geoffrey. 'The. Going. Rate?'

'We'll send you an invoice,' Geoffrey said.

'I need to know that I can afford it.'

'Nothing as grubby as money, pal. Like you said, you and Mr Spirelli are friends, now. All right?'

'When will I know when . . . we're even?'

'You let Mr Spirelli worry about that.'

Some chav in a baseball cap and bling, looked as if he was dressed to get on a plane to Ibiza, broke away from the crowd watching the football and headed towards the toilets at the back. Williams moved his shoulder to let him past. He was staggering, clearly had too many Stellas. He knocked the table as he went past, spilling Tyrone's drink.

Geoffrey grabbed him from behind by his collar and the back of his jeans and ran him into a wooden pillar. He sat down again. There was a hush for a moment and then everyone turned back to the game. Two of the bar staff carried the guy outside. His nose was all over his face.

Geoffrey sat down again. 'I cannot stand bad manners,' he said.

'I can pay you ten,' Williams said.

'What? Are you *bargaining* with us?'

'I think that's the going rate.'

'What did you do? *Google* it?'

'I was told you could help me.'

'We will help you. We've told you how this works, Mr Williams. Take it or leave it.'

It had been a long time since Williams had found himself on the back foot in a negotiation. He thought about walking out. And then what? Go to Plan B.

Plan B: trust the cops to arrest Lennox before he did to him what he did to Grimes and Barrington.

'Okay, let's do it,' he said.

'Good. Write the name of the premises and the owner on here.'

Williams wrote Lennox's name, and the address Merrick had given him, on the back of a beer coaster. Geoffrey pulled it towards him, looked at it like it was the last draw in a poker hand.

Suddenly the whole place was in uproar. Tyrone stood up, hands in the air, spilling his drink. Someone must have scored.

'Fucking Watford,' Geoffrey said. 'Elton John's fucking poofter club. I had a tenner with Tyrone that Norwich would win.'

'You can do this, right?'

'Fuck off,' Tyrone said, and jerked his thumb towards the exit.

He didn't feel as relieved as he thought he would as he walked across the car park. It had started raining again. He heard Tyrone singing inside the pub, one of those moronic chants you hear at all football games. He felt frightened. He suddenly wanted to be back in London, his London.

It took ten minutes to hail down a cab, he couldn't call an Uber, he had switched off his phone when he left the Langham. He replayed the scene in his mind on the trip back into the city. What would happen if those clowns were caught? He was putting a lot of faith in Merrick and this Spirelli. He assumed Merrick had had the sense to call him on a burner.

He got out of the cab on the corner of Langham Place and Riding House Street, made it look like he was coming out of the front entrance, saw the two Special Branch guys still parked on the double yellow lines across the road. He walked over, tapped on the driver's side window.

'Hi guys,' he said, as the window came down. 'Want to give me a ride home?'

DAY 9

CHAPTER FORTY-THREE

Charlie parked the Sierra inside the cordon, turned off the engine, then just sat there. He was in no hurry for this. There were police posted outside the house to keep away the journalists, two television reporters were doing talking heads at the end of the street. Crime: it was like a moveable circus.

'This is the part of the job I hate,' Charlie said to Grey. 'Let's get in and out as quick as we can.'

The calls had been pouring in; it wasn't that they didn't have enough information, they had too much. The hardest part wasn't getting it, it was sifting through it all and weeding out the lunatics and the people trying to cause trouble for someone they didn't like. Some people thought they saw serial killers the same way people thought they saw UFOs and visions of the Virgin Mary and Tupac.

One bloke had rung in claiming to be the Antichrist. DS Greene had written him down as Nigel Farage.

They got out and crossed the road. Leaves skittered across the pavement, there was a thick glue of mulch in the gutters.

It was a double-fronted Edwardian house, set back from the road, with security gates, CCTV, the business. A uniform spoke into the intercom and they were buzzed in. As they walked up the gravel drive, Charlie heard a dog barking in the Barringtons' window. That would be Mitzi, he thought. *She's had a tough week as well.*

They were met at the door by a young man who said he was Malcolm Barrington's son. He shook their hands formally and

Charlie told him he was sorry for his loss, a well-worn phrase that tripped off his tongue all too easily these days. He led him through the hall to the front room.

Charlie was expecting something stuffy and Victorian, but the inside of the house was surprisingly bright, with modular furniture and lots of glass and stainless steel. The house seemed to be full of people, friends and family he supposed, all hovering and looking appalled and embarrassed at the same time.

There were pictures of Barrington everywhere. The centrepiece of the dining room wall was a framed photograph of the judge and his family, a posed studio portrait. They were all smiling, even Mitzi.

There were more photographs dotted around the house: sons and daughters in mortarboards and gowns, holding degrees; grandchildren in school uniforms, others still in nappies. It was a lot to leave behind.

This was the hard part, when the corpses came back to life in photographs and video clips. Then they became more than just a puzzle to solve; he couldn't let himself think about it too much if he was going to be effective at his job.

Mrs Barrington sat by the window in a high-backed Chesterfield, an island of desolation among the hushed conversations. She was wearing a simple black dress. She stared out of the window at the landscaped garden, oblivious to Mitzi's barking, the people bringing flowers, the phone ringing. Not even a flicker of the eyes.

She was younger than he thought she'd be, with long chestnut hair tied back in a ponytail. She looked awful, which he supposed was how she should look in the circumstances. She was not wearing make-up and there were deep rings under her eyes.

Charlie introduced himself and DS Grey. 'I'm very sorry for your loss,' he added.

She nodded and went back to looking out of the window. Charlie and Grey perched themselves on the end of the sofa.

'We'll get the persons responsible for this,' Grey said, and Charlie gave him a look to shut him up. That was something he never ever promised, because you never knew if you would or you wouldn't. It wasn't what they were here for, to jolly along the bereaved. Nothing was going to make Mrs Barrington feel better.

'I'm sorry to intrude at this time,' Charlie said. 'I can't begin to imagine what you're going through. But we do need to ask you some questions. It may help us in our enquiries.'

She nodded her assent.

'Had you noticed anything unusual in the weeks leading up to the attack on your husband? Had he received any threatening phone calls or emails or anything?'

She shook her head. 'If he did, he never told me about it. Don't you know? Didn't you people take his computer?'

'Our forensics team are going through everything. But we need to make sure there's nothing we missed. There were no letters, nothing like that?'

Another shake of the head.

'In the past few weeks, have you seen anyone following you or your husband, or seen anyone loitering outside the house?'

'Nothing at all.'

'Does he take the dog to the park every night at the same time?'

'Usually. He said it helped him wind down. He found his work very stressful. It gave him time to think about things. He worried a lot.' She turned away from the window and it was as if she was seeing them for the first time. 'Has someone offered you a cup of tea?'

'We're fine,' Charlie said. 'We'll be on our way now. I just wanted to make sure we haven't missed anything.' He handed her his card. 'If you think of anything, anything at all you think might help, give me a call.'

She took it, without looking at it. 'Why would someone do this?' she said.

It seemed a genuine question; she hadn't been reading the papers or watching the news, clearly. DC Khan, his FLO, had told him she had spent most of the last three days heavily sedated.

'He was a kind man. He would do anything for anyone. I don't understand.'

'We believe it is in connection with a trial he presided over at the Old Bailey.'

'I knew that sort of thing happened in the Family Court. Judges there get threatened all the time, don't they? But I never thought anyone would do something like this . . . to us. We only recently had a security upgrade on this house because of police advice. He never took it seriously. I suppose I thought that . . .' She drifted off.

Charlie waited. 'You thought what, Mrs Barrington?'

'I suppose I thought we were safe here. It's . . . unimaginable.' She turned back to the window. 'He had so much to live for. It's just not . . . fair.'

Charlie started the car and they drove for a long time in silence.

Finally, Charlie said: 'Don't ever do that again.'

'What, sir?'

'Don't ever say: "We're going to find who did this." They never found Lord Lucan. They never found Madeleine McCann. Don't make promises you can't keep.'

'But we have to find him. This is a direct attack on the laws of this country. Even if you don't like them.'

'Knock it off, DS Grey.'

'I know you think the people who did this have a point, but Barrington didn't make the sentencing guidelines. If we want to bring back the rack and the death penalty, we need a plebiscite.'

'Or maybe you need stress leave,' Charlie said.

'Sorry, sir,' Grey said. He put on his seat belt and wiped the condensation on his window. There was a long silence while he gathered himself, a gulp as he swallowed his pride. 'I was out of order.'

'There's a "but" in there.'

'*But* I believe in the law. That's why I quit that dodgy solicitors and joined the Met.'

'I'm not defending murder, all right? But this isn't a senseless crime like the others we see, day in, day out. I get the point of this one. I may not agree with the point, but this isn't some gangbanger stabbing someone because they want their Nikes or their iPhone. It's not shooting someone because of a fifty-pound drug debt. The people who did this, they may not be right, but they're not brainless, immoral shits like the scrotes we bang up every week on the estates.'

'Barrington didn't deserve what happened to him.'

They reached Essex Road and Charlie turned into the yard. 'Maybe not. Just don't tell me he was blameless, sergeant. Now come on, let's get this sorted.'

CHAPTER FORTY-FOUR

Constable Steven Mazzini had come straight from his nick in west London. He was wearing gym gear and trainers; said he normally went to the gym after a shift. He sat in the interview room, toying with his coffee cup, his foot tapping on the floor. He was a big lad with rosy cheeks, and not long out of his teens, Charlie reckoned.

Mazzini had asked to speak to whoever was leading the inquiry into Barrington's murder, said he had information. The DCI had phoned down to Charlie. 'See what it's about, Charlie. I'm due over at Scotland Yard in half an hour.'

Charlie powered up his iPad for his notes and sat down.

'I shouldn't be here, you know,' Mazzini said, after Charlie had taken his details.

'Why are you here, constable?'

'What did she say to you? Tracy?'

'Tracy who?' Charlie asked him, although he already supposed, hoped, that Mazzini was talking about Tracy Lennox.

'I should have come in here before this. I knew, didn't I, soon as I heard what had happened.'

'You've lost me,' Charlie said.

'I can't have this on my conscience any more. I read in the papers about what happened to that judge.'

'Which judge?'

'Barrington. Are you the SIO?'

'No, that would be Detective Chief Inspector O'Neal-Callaghan. I'm his deputy. Now can we be a little more specific? You have information about the murder of Malcolm Barrington?'

But Mazzini was too agitated to follow direction. 'If she finds out I've been here, it'll be all over between us.'

'But you are here,' Charlie said.

Mazzini hung his head. 'When I heard she hadn't shown up for duty, that's when I knew something was wrong.'

'Suppose we start at the beginning,' Charlie said.

Torturously, over the next few minutes, Charlie established that Tracy Lennox was Mazzini's girlfriend. They hadn't been going out long, he said, a couple of months. He wasn't living with her, but it was starting to get serious. He had been hopeful that it would lead somewhere, despite the difference in their ages.

'How did you meet?' Charlie asked him.

'It was one night after work. One of the sergeants was having a birthday, she'd been through the academy with him. We got talking, you know? I mean, she's a bit older than me but she's pretty fit, right? I'm not one for the chat but she seemed to like that.'

'What has this to do with the murder of Malcolm Barrington?'

'We were supposed to be going out that night. I went around her place about half seven, and she wasn't there. I mean, her car was outside, but she wasn't in. Look, I'm not the first bloke that's had someone cheat on him, right, but I was pretty pissed off. Next day, on the way to my shift, I called round, wanted to give her a piece of my mind. I mean, there's ways of breaking up, isn't there? At least a phone call.'

'What time did you go around?'

'About half past six.'

'And what happened?'

'The way she looked, it shocked me. She looked like she hadn't slept, her hair was all over the place, and she was acting guilty, like. I thought she had a bloke in there with her, so I told her what I thought of her. She said she was sorry, and it wasn't

273

what I thought. That she still wanted to see me. She just needed some space.'

'Did you ask her where she'd been the night before?'

'Southend.'

'Excuse me?'

'She said she has a brother in Southend.'

'She doesn't have a brother in Southend.'

'Well, it's what she told me.'

'And what has all of this got to do with our investigation?'

'Well when I heard about what had happened to Judge Barrington, I put two and two together, didn't I?'

'Why the sudden need to start doing sums?' Charlie asked him.

'Well it all started when that bloke got beheaded. She's been acting weird ever since then. She told me you lot had interviewed her about it. She said it brought it all up again for her.'

'About her niece's death.'

'Yeah. She kept saying to me, "I don't care about Grimes – it's that judge, he was the real criminal."'

Charlie sat back in his chair. Southend. If someone was struggling with stress, why in God's name would they go to Southend? Had to be the last place you'd choose.

'There's one other thing,' Mazzini said. 'It might be nothing. I don't even know why I'm telling you.'

'Tell me anyway,' Charlie said.

'As I was walking away, I saw a car parked right outside, I'd never seen it there before. It had a rental sticker on the back. I took notice because I figured it must be this new bloke she was seeing. I thought about keying it, you know, I was right pissed off, but then I remembered I wasn't a teenager any more.'

'Good for you. This sticker, was it Hertz, Avis?'

'Some company I'd never heard of. It was an odd sort of logo.'

'Do you think you might be able to recognise it if we show you some pictures?' Charlie said.

'I'll try.'

'We'll get a formal statement from you, then if you wouldn't mind waiting, we'll see if we can track down the rental company. All right?'

He nodded, looking utterly miserable.

'One other thing,' Charlie said. 'Does she own a motorbike?'

'Not that I know of. She's got some sort of Land Rover. Racing green. Kind of what you'd expect.'

'Never mind.'

Mazzini pressed his knuckles into his forehead. 'I suppose I hoped this would all work out, that she hadn't been lying to me. This is it, though, isn't it? It's worse than her having another bloke.'

'Put it this way,' Charlie said, 'I wouldn't take down your Tinder profile.'

Charlie found Grey, told him to go in and write up a formal statement. He rang his boss, told him about Mazzini. The DCI was in traffic, on his way to another Gold Group meeting.

'What do you make of it, Charlie?'

'Leading us a right dance, isn't she? She definitely didn't do the first one, but this is strange.'

'You'll have to get her in and question her again.'

'This doesn't make sense.'

'Just get her in, light a fire under her, Charlie. This case is giving me ulcers.' He hung up.

Finding the car hire company from a logo wasn't as easy as Charlie thought; Mazzini finally identified a company they traced to a second-hand car dealership and repair garage in Westcliff, a few miles from Southend, that rented cars as a sideline. It was called California Cars.

Charlie rang them. They said a Tracy Lennox had used her Visa card to rent a second-hand Isuzu from them at one o'clock in the afternoon on the day Barrington had been murdered. They gave Charlie the registration plates and he had Lovejoy check them against ANPR and CCTV from the high street.

275

After several hours of checking, James spotted her on CCTV footage from a council camera outside Joe the Juice on Hampstead High Street. It showed her getting out of the rental car at 5.03 p.m. and driving away again at 5.31.

Charlie wrote the paperwork for a search and seizure warrant of Tracy Lennox's house in Hounslow and told DCs James and Singh to get themselves some armed police officers and bring her in for questioning. They called him back an hour later. They'd had to use the big red key. She wasn't there.

Almost midnight and there was still a couple of the team left, James and Lovejoy, hunched over their screens in the semi-dark office. The desks were a litter of takeaway boxes and empty coffee cups. The cleaner hadn't been in yet.

Charlie could hear the background hum of the city, a siren wailing somewhere.

He promised himself that once he'd finished filling in the overtime forms he'd go home. He glanced at his phone. There were messages from someone at the CPS about a missing witness statement and another from Ben – Jo was out of danger but there was no word on whether there might be any long-term damage. Social services were involved now so it didn't matter what Jules said about Tel, the decision about Jo's future could be taken out of her hands.

The phone buzzed while he was scrolling through; it startled him and he nearly dropped it on the carpet. It was Fiona.

He picked up. 'Fi. You still up?'

'When are you getting home?'

'Soon. Sorry. Things won't get back to normal until after we've caught this bloke.' There was a long wait on the end of the phone and he thought he'd lost his connection. 'Fi?'

'What's normal, Charlie?'

Charlie knew the cue for a fight when he heard one. He decided to cut it short. 'I'll be home soon as I can.'

She hung up.

It was a cold night, clear. He parked in the street and sat for a few minutes, listening to the engine tick as it cooled. Someone went past, walking their dog. This time of the morning. It was a German shepherd, so no mugger was going to bother him, he supposed.

He slipped the key in the lock, used the light on his phone to find his way into the living room. He undressed in the dark. He told himself it was because he didn't want to wake her, but he supposed the real reason was, he was too tired for another fight.

He crept up the stairs, checked his phone, made sure the alarm was on for six. With any luck he'd get four-and-a-half hours sleep, and in his own bed, too.

He slipped between the sheets as quietly as he could. He slid a hand across the bed to her side. It was cold. She wasn't there.

He wasn't sure what it was he felt; was it relief or disappointment? There were a lot of nights before they met when he had wished for someone to spoon with when he got home from a long shift, but tonight the Arctic expanse of his double bed felt luxurious.

What was wrong with him? *A constant and desperate search for whatever it is you don't have,* Ben had said to him once. And when you've got it, an urgent need to get rid of it.

On the way back from the nick he'd hardly been able to keep his eyes on the road, but now he lay there staring wide eyed into the darkness, seeing witness statements and CCTV images and jpeg attachments from Lambeth of the notes they had found in the mouths of their two decapitated heads. The one they had found in Grimes' throat echoed around his brain.

> *This is the reason that you see this man fallen here.*
> *I am he who planned this murder and with justice.*

It was planned, all right. Very well planned indeed.

CHAPTER FORTY-FIVE

Gordon Lennox woke up to noises in the house. In his dream someone was coming up the stairs with a knife. He sat upright, muscles bunched, sweating, straining to the dark. His heart was pounding, drowning out the silence he needed.

He listened for the hum of the refrigerator motor, footfall on the stairs, the squeak of tongue and groove. Nothing. Sometimes – over there – you could sense if something was wrong, if there was quiet when there should be voices, or something that smelled different in the air.

He'd had that same nightmare again. Patti woke and reached for him, he shrugged her off roughly and his elbow caught her in the mouth. 'Shut up, shut up,' he said. Christ, he'd hurt her, and he hadn't meant to.

He slowed his breathing, tried to focus. Rain lashed against the window, the wind moaned around the eaves. A storm had blown in during the night.

The noises he'd heard. It was only the storm.

But he had to be sure. He got out of bed, moving slowly, softly, and edged open the door.

No shadows on the stairs, and the hallway was empty. His hand edged around the door and he flicked the light switch.

'Gordie?'

'There's someone outside.' He looked over his shoulder; she was sitting up, there was blood on her lip from where he'd caught her with his arm. He couldn't worry about that now. He went to the window. Nothing out there, just the trees bending in the wind.

He put on tracksuit bottoms and a t-shirt, went back to the landing, inched open the door to the girls' room. He was ready, on the balls of his feet, balanced. He looked in, the night light was on, he counted two heads, soft toys piled up either side, a *Frozen* poster on the wall. He pulled back the edge of the covers, stroked a cheek, then the other. Anyone ever hurt his girls, he'd tear their fucking hearts out.

He thought about Zoë, about Tom. How did they stand it? If it had been him, he would have topped himself by now.

He checked the bathroom, flicked on the light, pushed aside the bathroom curtain. All clear. He crept down the stairs. He went in the kitchen first, got a knife from the drawer, held it ready, blade cold and snug against his arm. He swung open the door to the living room.

Nothing. He checked all the windows. Looked outside for shadows where there shouldn't be any.

The back door rattled in the wind.

Come on, Gordie, what are you worried about? No one could get in the house unannounced, you've made sure of that.

He sat down on the stairs, put his head in his hands. These dreams he was having were driving him crazy.

Patti. He should go upstairs and see to her. He'd cut her lip. But she shouldn't grab him like that, not when he was having one of his nightmares, he'd told her that.

He couldn't face her right now. He went back to the kitchen, boiled the kettle, made himself a coffee. Then he turned off the light and sat there in the dark. There was no sniper with a telescopic lens round here, but old habits died hard.

Before he went over there, nothing seemed to bother him. Even when they lost Johnno in training, when his chute didn't open, yes it was fucking terrible, but he dealt with it, they all dealt with it as a team. This was something else.

A man shouldn't be scared to go to sleep. Even through the worst of it, sleep used to be a way to press the reset button. Now he was terrified of letting go, letting sleep take over. Losing control.

In the Stan you could be amped twenty-four/seven, constantly alert to danger, and no one thought you were crazy. You let your guard down for a moment and an officer would kick your arse. The constant adrenaline was the normal.

He felt so naked now without his C8. He should have got himself a gun when he had the chance, Tom had given him a bloke's name and the pub where he could find him, but the truth was, he didn't trust himself. What if he had one of his episodes when he was home alone with the girls?

He didn't belong here. The only place he belonged was back with his squad, but those days were over. What was he going to do? He hated being a civilian, hated dealing with other civilians, doing things that didn't really matter.

That was the hell of it. The problem was, once you weren't fit for duty any more, you weren't fit for anything else.

DAY 10

CHAPTER FORTY-SIX

Charlie didn't remember falling asleep. He woke to the sound of the alarm, startled and disoriented. He jumped out of bed and stood in the middle of his bedroom, trying to remember where he was. His head ached and his eyes were stinging from too many hours in front of a computer. He went into the bathroom and stood under a cold shower until he was awake.

It wasn't until he was standing in front of the mirror, brushing his teeth, that he realised all Fi's stuff was missing. Most mornings his washbasin vanity was a litter of foundation and eyeliner and cotton buds and face wipes, but this morning there was just a glass beaker with one toothbrush and a half-squeezed tube of toothpaste.

He opened the bathroom cabinet. She'd cleared it out.

He went to the walk-in, clocked that her stuff was gone; she always kept some spare outfits for the nights she stayed over. The drawer he'd given her for underwear was empty.

Well, that's pretty final, he thought.

I wish I had a dog. A weird thing to pop into his head like that when his girlfriend had cleared off. But it would have been nice. He could see the value now. Sometimes he saw tradesmen head off to work in the mornings with their Staffies and Border collies, now he got why. The dogs went with them everywhere; they always had back up.

Perhaps I could ask FONC if I can bring in an emotional support dog? Just for a laugh, of course. But if I could, I'd have a dog like Charlie. He could just imagine him at crime scenes, pissing on the evidence and licking up the unsavoury spills.

He dressed and went downstairs to the kitchen. There was a note on the table.

   Dear Charlie,

He read it through a couple of times, but it didn't tell him anything he didn't already know. Fi was gone. No hard feelings. It had been great, but it was time for the next adventure. Words to that effect.

He felt curiously empty. He wasn't sure what he needed right now.

A double espresso. That would be a start.

The DCI led the briefing. Amory, the head of surveillance, was there too. Charlie joined him and the rest of the team in a semi-circle around the whiteboard. There were four names written at the top in red marker: Christopher Pemberley, Margaret Lennox, Tracy Lennox, Gordon Lennox.

His boss looked harassed. The media was full of it, the sensational aspects of the two murders were absolute clickbait. A few of the tabloids were trawling with 'exclusives' to bulk up their online subscriptions. The timing of Barrington's death couldn't have been scripted better; Grimes was the teaser, but in the Age of Outrage hacking off a judge's head in broad twilight had lit up the TV chat shows. No one wanted to talk about anything else on the radio phone-ins. There were even memes.

'I have the crime scene report on the Barrington homicide,' the DCI said. 'It's all there in your briefing notes. The canvass of the local area gave us several eyewitness reports of someone who was seen running from the scene; they were dressed all in black, wearing either a hoody or a ski mask, no one seems very clear on that. There were also reports of hearing a motorbike drive away from the scene, but because it was a residential area we've been unable to capture any CCTV.

'In your notes you'll see there are several eyewitness reports of the motorbike involved in the incident outside the Old Bailey, a black BMW S1000R. It didn't have plates and we have so far been unable to locate it. At this stage, there isn't much in the way of forensics. Questions?'

'The piece of paper in Barrington's throat,' Lovejoy said. 'It was from the same book?'

'It was. Tom Miller still maintains that it had a number of pages missing when it was given to him in the army, and, to date, we still have no way to disprove that.'

Several of the team shook their heads. This made no kind of sense.

'Let's start with Christopher Pemberley,' the DCI said. 'What do we have?'

'The AC leaned on someone at the Ministry of Defence,' Lubanski said. 'DynaCorp have finally released their records to us. According to them Pemberley has been in Baghdad from 23 September to the present. He's not due to return to the UK until the end of his six-month contract in March.'

'Can we trust this information?'

'There's no other way of checking,' she said.

'What if he's going in and out on a false passport?' James said.

'No,' Charlie said. 'Whoever's doing this has spent weeks, if not months, here in London, planning and organising this.'

'What about the Millers?'

'Here's my team's report,' Amory said, and dropped it on the desk in front of the DCI. 'When Barrington was murdered, Tom and Jennifer Miller were in the local Tesco supermarket. They went together, their Toyota Landcruiser has been modified to accommodate Mr Miller's wheelchair. They were nowhere near Hampstead.'

'Still no luck on Margaret Lennox?'

James and Singh had been tasked with finding her. They both shook their heads. 'She has literally disappeared.'

'Not literally,' Charlie said. 'Apparently.'

'Thanks Charlie,' the DCI said. 'I think we know what they mean.'

'Maybe she's topped herself,' Grey said.

'Maybe,' Charlie said. 'Maybe she joined ISIS or went through a warp in the space-time continuum, but all we can do is keep looking. When we find her, we'll know.'

'How are we supposed to get through this space-time whatsit, guv?' James said.

'Ask Jay,' Charlie said. 'He's the proper expert on quantum physics.'

'Where are we with Gordon Lennox?' Grey said. 'We know he was in Hampstead when Barrington was murdered.'

'We don't have enough to charge him,' the DCI said. 'We found nothing incriminating at his house or in his vehicles. There's nothing suspicious on his phone or his computer either. We had to let him go but we're continuing with round-the-clock surveillance.'

Amory reached in his briefcase for another manila folder. 'We've had eyes on him the whole time. Yesterday he left for work at 6.53 a.m., worked at a house in Stratford until 4 p.m., went home, left the house at 5.04 p.m. in his running gear, ran six miles, didn't return until three minutes before six.'

'Your blokes must be fit,' James said.

Amory smiled. 'It was a team of twelve, working tandem.'

'And he was in all night?' Singh asked him.

A nod.

'What about Tracy Lennox, then?'

The DCI looked at Charlie.

'Her mobile phone is switched off. She hasn't used her credit card since she hired the rental in Westcliff. No contact with her line manager at Heathrow, nothing on her social media accounts. I've called her family – as usual Jennifer Miller and Gordon Lennox aren't talking. She hasn't returned the rental car, which is still parked outside her residence in Hounslow.'

'So, where is she?'

'That is the burning question. We've checked with the cab companies and Uber, we've looked at the CCTV from the local underground stations. Nada.'

'She could have caught a bus somewhere,' Greene said.

'Could have. But unless we know when exactly she left the house, sifting through CCTV on all the local bus routes is almost impossible. And if she's wearing a disguise, it will be *literally* impossible.'

'I'll give her photograph to the TV and the press – get it circulated. We have to find her.'

'What about her house? Did Crime Scene find anything?'

'There was a knife, looked like it had come from the Orient somewhere. The SOCOs found blood traces on the blade. We're waiting on lab results.'

There was dead silence.

'And we have CCTV of her in Hampstead at the time Barrington was killed, sir,' James said, finally.

The DCI reached for his iPad and found the file he was looking for. They all looked up at the screen behind him. After a few moments, there were some flickering black and white images from a council camera of Tracy Lennox getting out of her rental car in Hampstead High Street. It was like watching an old newsreel on YouTube. There were two more short clips, in colour, from commercial premises, then back to the council footage of her returning to her car. Then the media file went black.

'So she was in Hampstead for almost an hour either side of when Barrington was murdered,' Lovejoy said.

'Do we have a theory around what happened?' James said.

'Perhaps there's not one killer, but two,' Lovejoy said. 'They're working in tandem. Gordon does the first one, Tracy does the second. With Margaret helping them.'

'It's possible.'

'The question is,' James said, 'are they done, or will there be more?'

'That's what I thought,' the DCI said. Charlie raised an eyebrow. That wasn't quite how he remembered it, but never mind. 'It struck me that Grimes' barrister at the trial could be considered a target. I've organised for Special Branch to afford him protection. We still can't be sure what we're up against here. These murders demonstrate a high level of planning as well as ruthless execution. The access and egress from both crime scenes show a great awareness of the positioning of CCTV and ANPR cameras, and the lack of forensics is telling. Charlie?'

'I agree. Killing two people in this manner is not something you could imagine from an amateur.'

'Tracy Lennox and her brother,' Grey said. 'Has to be.'

The DCI went to the whiteboard, stared at it, then rubbed out Pemberley's name. That left three. 'We have eyes on Gordon Lennox. We now have to find the other two. Let's hope the public can give us a lead on this. Okay everyone, back to work. DS Greene will action the jobs. Let's make things happen today.' He clapped his hands together like he was sending his Sunday football team out to play the league leaders.

As the others drifted away, he put an arm around Charlie's shoulder and steered him out of the room into the corridor.

'Are we sure about all this, Charlie? I've got a Gold Group meeting at nine this morning and I'd like to feel a bit more confident before I go in the lion's den.'

'I have some reservations.'

'Will you still be so gloomy if that fancy knife we found at Tracy Lennox's flat comes back a positive for Barrington's DNA?'

'It won't.'

'Don't be so bloody negative. Why would you say that?'

'Just a feeling in my water.'

'You keep your water to yourself. I'm going to tell Gold Group that Lennox and his sister are our prime suspects and we expect to lay charges in the next twenty-four hours.' He turned away.

'That's premature,' Charlie said.

The DCI turned back on his way to the lifts. 'You have no idea the pressure they've got me under,' he said. Charlie almost felt sorry for him. Well, first time for everything.

At 9.30 that morning, after his Gold Group meeting, the DCI held a press conference on the steps of Scotland Yard and announced that the Metropolitan Police were anxious to interview a fellow officer, Constable Tracy Lennox, in connection with the murder of Malcolm Barrington. Her photograph was flashed up on the screen. He warned members of the public not to approach her, but if they saw her to get in touch with police immediately. The hotline number, Incident Room Twitter handle and email address scrolled across the bottom of the screen. He followed up with another appeal, this time for Corporal Margaret Lennox.

While Greene, Grey and Lovejoy fielded the avalanche of calls that followed, Charlie went through the interviews with her friends and colleagues that had been logged on to the HOLMES system, looking for any leads they had not yet followed up. He sent Lubanski and McCullough to reinterview other members of her armed response team at Heathrow; called detectives in Leicester, Northumberland and Ipswich and asked them to talk to cousins and uncles who might have been in contact with her.

And then, not long after lunch, he got a message from the sergeant downstairs at the reception that Constable Tracy Lennox was at the counter with her union lawyer and had surrendered herself for interview.

CHAPTER FORTY-SEVEN

The interview table was empty, except for four cups of water, a box of tissues and a ballpoint pen. The pen had been positioned so that it sat halfway between himself and Tracy Lennox. Charlie had a theory: the first person to pick up the pen and fiddle with it, loses.

He pressed the record button and went through the formalities. He advised her that she was under suspicion for the murder of Malcolm Barrington, QC, as required by the PACE laws.

After he was done, her union lawyer leaned over and whispered something in her ear. She nodded.

Charlie wondered what was going on here. She looked different to when she had first sat here a few days ago. For a start, she was bottle blonde and seemed to have got her civvies from a charity shop, not that there was anything wrong with that, of course, if you were looking for a cut price Corneliani. She had on cheap jeans that didn't fit and a Manchester United shirt which looked like it dated from the Alex Ferguson era. Was she doing it just to wind him up?

She looked thinner and fragile, which was at odds with the snarl on her face.

'Been to the hairdresser's?'

'Is that why I'm here? Because when I went through training at Hendon, they never mentioned getting your hair done was illegal. But it was a long time ago. Maybe I missed something.'

So that's the way it's going to be, Charlie thought. He supposed he'd get more attitude if he asked her about her new wardrobe. Had she been trying to disguise herself, or just pretending to?

At times, it seemed to him like everything in this investigation was a double-feint.

Charlie reached into his file and passed a sheet across the desk. 'This was provided to us by your line manager at Heathrow. It's the duty roster for the night of the sixth. You were supposed to be at work. But apparently you did not show up for your shift, or either of your two shifts since. This has caused him some consternation, especially as he tells me you have a previously unblemished record.'

'I was feeling under stress. I had to get away.'

'If you were under stress, you only needed to ask for leave. You are handling firearms every day. That branch of the service takes stress concerns very seriously.'

'No comment.'

'Your commanding officer didn't know where you were. In fact, no one knew where you were, did they?'

A shake of the head.

'For the tape.'

'No.'

'We expended considerable time and trouble trying to find you, you realise that?'

'Why?'

'Because we need to eliminate you from our enquiries into the death of Malcolm Barrington. He was the judge in your niece's manslaughter case.'

'That arsehole.'

Charlie glanced at the brief, wondering if she was going to intervene. She didn't, but it must be getting close.

'Where were you between five p.m. and five thirty p.m. on the afternoon of the sixth?'

'I don't remember.'

'Well, can you give it a bit of a think, then. It's important.'

'At home, I suppose.'

Charlie reached into his file, passed over a faxed copy of the rental agreement for the hire car she had obtained in Westcliff. 'Is that your signature?'

'It looks like it.'

'What were you doing in Westcliff?'

'No comment.'

He reached into his file and produced a series of photostat copies, CCTV images of Tracy in Hampstead High Street. He pointed out to her the times that the images had been recorded.

'Around the time that Malcolm Barrington was murdered, CCTV cameras recorded images of you in Hampstead. What were you doing there?'

She looked closer. He thought he saw a flicker of expression on her face. What was it? Surprise? Anger? It looked like something else to him; was she smirking? She looked at the photostats for a long time, then sat back.

'No comment.'

'Were you aware that your brother was in Hampstead at the very same time?'

'Really? I didn't see him.'

'He said he went to Keats' house.'

'I don't like Keats, I prefer Wordsworth.'

'Some coincidence, this. You were both in Hampstead; Malcolm Barrington was assaulted and murdered.'

Tracy shrugged. Her brief leaned in. 'Do you have a question to ask my client, inspector?'

'Can you tell me your movements since you finished your last shift with Armed Response at Heathrow on 5 November?'

'No comment.'

'During a search of your home, this was found, hidden behind a false panel in the wall.' Charlie put a clear plastic cylinder on the table, an evidence tag attached. Inside was a knife with a curved blade; it had a wooden handle and an inscription in Arabic.

'It's called a *pesh kabz*,' she said.

'Your brother-in-law has one very much like it.'

'I asked him to bring me one back from Afghanistan.'

'Our technicians detected traces of blood on the blade.'

'No comment.'

'Will it return a positive match for Malcolm Barrington's DNA?'

'You're hoping it will, but it won't.'

Charlie leaned back, gave himself time to gather his thoughts. Grey sat forward, eager to get at her. Good luck, son, Charlie thought. I've got a feeling it won't do any good.

'You're putting your whole career at stake here,' Grey said. 'Why won't you cooperate?'

'Are you threatening me with dismissal in front of a union lawyer?'

'I'm saying that you're a fellow officer and you are being blatantly obstructive.'

The brief shook his head, like he was remonstrating with an errant schoolboy. 'My client presented herself here this afternoon voluntarily. That is hardly being obstructive.'

'Why were you in Hampstead that afternoon?'

Tracy leaned forward, stared at Grey, their faces a few inches apart. The seconds ticked by. 'No comment,' she said.

Charlie had had enough. 'Interview suspended at . . .' He looked up at the clock. 'Fifteen thirty-three. Anyone like a coffee? My shout.'

The DCI was waiting in the corridor when Charlie came out. He was in his shirtsleeves, his collar open at the first button. Any day now he's going to start looking like one of us, Charlie thought.

'Anyone else want to have a crack at her?' Charlie said.

'What's her game? It's almost like she's baiting us.'

'Do we have the results back on the knife?'

'The AC has fast tracked it, but it could still be another twenty-four hours.'

'We have nothing to tie either her or her brother to the

murder scene. Their actions are monumentally suspicious, but they don't amount to solid evidence.'

'That knife was well hidden.'

'Not so well hidden that our CS team couldn't find it.'

'It's got to be her.'

'We could charge her with going to Southend,' Charlie said. 'There must be something in the statute books about that. If it isn't illegal, it probably should be.'

The DCI seemed to be in pain. Perhaps he wasn't joking about the ulcer, Charlie thought.

'I think the superintendent is going to take over as SIO. Gold Group are not happy, Charlie. I can see I'll have to brush up on my golf game. I may have a lot of time on my hands soon.'

You and me both, Charlie thought. Only I don't play golf.

But getting shot down this far into his career wasn't what was bothering him. He had never seen himself as one of those blokes in a dress uniform and an apron in the cupboard for his Freemasons' meetings. That wasn't why he'd joined.

All he could think of was Mrs Barrington sitting by the window, numb to the world; and Jennifer Miller, looking across the interview desk at him, her face ugly with bitterness.

He felt like it was somehow on him to make it all right, but right now there didn't seem any way that he could.

CHAPTER FORTY-EIGHT

The Ford Transit was parked five doors down from Gordon Lennox's house. It looked from the outside like another builder's van, not that much different from Gordon's own rust heap, parked in his driveway. The Transit had a bad paint job and a few dents on the back fender. It looked legit, as it was meant to.

It was the inside of the van that was different to Gordon's. There was a workstation, video recording equipment, a mounted video camera, two monitor screens and a bunk bed. Two officers from the Covert Surveillance unit had been there since six the previous evening, over halfway through a twelve-hour shift. One of them, Spencer, lay on the bunk asleep, the other – Robson – was watching the monitor screens and tapping a pencil on the edge of the desk. He wore earphones.

He saw car headlights swing into the street, but the vehicle showed no sign of stopping outside the target house. It was only at the last moment that Robson realised there was a threat, as the headlights veered across the road towards him.

The car slammed into the right front of the van. Robson was thrown against the padded bulkhead while his partner ended up on the floor, his head slamming against one of the stanchions supporting the workstation. He woke up long enough to realise he was bleeding heavily from a scalp wound, then passed out again.

Brian Barnes got out from behind the wheel of his battered Nexus and inspected the damage. His own car wasn't too bad, the right front headlight was out, and the bonnet was crumpled, but the way they built cars these days, that wasn't surprising. He bent down to check underneath, there was no radiator fluid leaking, it could have been a lot worse.

He got back to his feet and shrieked when he saw a man coming towards him holding a pair of speedcuffs, screaming at him to get on the floor.

He got on the floor.

He was saying something about the police. 'It's only a car, man,' Barnes shouted back. 'It's only a fucking car.'

Geoffrey and Tyrone had started running towards Gordon's house as soon as the Nexus took the corner. They were wearing black jeans, black Lycra sweats and ski masks, and were both carrying Glock silenced pistols. By the time Barnes hit the van they were already vaulting the low brick wall at the front of the house and over the wooden fence at the side.

They had allowed two minutes for the kill.

They were not new to this. They had done maybe half a dozen hits like this over the years, two of them in Ireland. The key was preparation; you had to scope your scene first, check for security, disable it before you went in. In this case, the security was a little different to anything they'd had to deal with before, but when you had Tony Spirelli providing the auxiliaries, even that wasn't hard to take care of.

They always went in at three in the morning. People were at their lowest ebb then, it was biorhythms and that shit. Hardly anyone had proper locks on their doors, most of them you could pick in ten or twenty seconds, or else you just used a crowbar and wrenched the fucking thing open.

Then up the stairs to the bedroom, pop-pop, mind the wife and kids, apologise for the interruption, get the fuck out. Easy as.

They could hear the commotion as one of the surveillance agents arrested Barnes; there would be lights flicking on up and down the street soon, but eyes would all be on the shunt between the Nexus and the Transit, not them.

Geoffrey was in front; didn't even feel the tripwire. He heard a bang that near enough broke his eardrums, and a wave of heat knocked him off his feet and sent him crashing backwards into the fence.

There was no pain at first, only a sort of dull surprise. What the actual fuck? He couldn't get his breath. He was aware of Tyrone kneeling over him. He raised his head and looked down, couldn't make out where his feet were.

'Oh fuck, oh fuck,' Tyrone was saying over and over. '*Your legs.*'

Geoffrey tried to say, *What about my legs?* But his tongue seemed too big for his mouth and he couldn't get his words out. There was buzzing in his ears. He felt faint.

'He's booby-trapped the place,' Tyrone said. 'Who the fuck does he think he is?'

Gordon Lennox was enjoying his first peaceful sleep in months, but the sound of the explosion catapulted him out of bed. The windows cracked and blew in, and his wife sat up and screamed. Gordon was already on his feet, wide awake in an instant and running. 'Get the kids, get the kids!' He grabbed Patti by the arm and almost carried her to the girls' bedroom. 'Get in there with the kids and lock the door.'

He just had on a pair of shorts; he never slept naked, not since he joined the army, you always had to be ready for situations like this. He'd put a combat knife under his pillow and now he vaulted down the stairs with it in his left hand, was in the kitchen in three jumps; whoever was out there, he didn't plan to leave them alive to come back for a second go.

Apart from the combat knife, the other bit of gear he'd resurrected were his night-vision goggles; they'd gone missing from the quartermaster's store when he left the SAS and he had no intention of giving them back.

He slipped them on and threw open the back door; speed and aggression was what won you a fight, any fight. There was something on the patio, he kicked it aside; looked like a bit of flesh, could have been a foot. He recognised a familiar smell, a bit like a barbecue on fireworks night, burned meat and gunpowder. He heard noises round the side path, one of them was lying there twitching and moaning, the other one was leaning over him.

The bloke got to his feet as Gordon came at him, but he was too slow. Gordon slashed with his knife at the hand holding the gun, heard a scream, then he was behind him, one hand across the bastard's face, fingers in his eye sockets. He sawed the knife across the throat, never mind the gristly bits, make sure you get the veins and the arteries, then dropped him, left him on the path to gurgle and die.

When he was done, he looked down at the other one. His feet were gone but he wasn't even yelling. The pain couldn't have hit him yet, must still be in shock. He was scrambling on the ground for something, his gun. There was a blossoming of bright green in Gordon's night vision glasses and something hit him hard in the chest. He threw the knife in the shooter's direction, like he'd done a hundred times in training, then turned and went back inside the house.

He turned on the kitchen light and took off the night-vision goggles. He collapsed to one knee, knew he was bleeding out. He'd seen blokes die like this, knew it wouldn't take long. It didn't trouble him too much; fact was, it seemed like the logical way out of the situation.

DAY 11

DAY II

CHAPTER FORTY-NINE

The DCI stood outside the house, among the chaos of police cars and paramedics and CS vans and the SOCOs in white suits. The look on his face. Charlie imagined it was how Napoleon must have looked on the way back from Moscow.

He saw Charlie but didn't say anything at first. They stood there for a moment in almost companionable silence.

Finally: 'Why always you, Charlie? That's what I ask myself. Had to be one of your cases this happens. You're like a four-leaf clover, only in reverse. I don't blame you for all this. But there's something about you, isn't there? That case last year, one murdered little girl and what was the body count on that one? Four, five? And that woman that went missing. Started off with one body and ended up with a death toll like the Battle of the Somme.'

'This is really none of my fault.'

'So you say.'

'What happened here, sir?'

'Your Mr Lennox had booby-trapped the place. Lucky for us we didn't try to put any surveillance gear inside the house or right now we could be mourning two of our own. Apparently, there was a tripwire; forensics can't be sure if there's more, so this is going to take some time until the bomb squad give us the all clear to go in.'

'Any witnesses?'

'His wife and kids perhaps. They're safe, that's one thing, but I don't think his missus can tell us much. She's in shock.

She didn't see much, heard the whizz bangs going off and some screaming and hid in the bedroom with the little ones. Mr Lennox died on his way to hospital, bullet wound to the chest. There are two as yet unidentified individuals on the side path, one minus his lower limbs and a combat knife in the middle of his chest and the other almost decapitated. Have to wait for pathology and forensics to tell us how it played out, but I'd hazard a guess that someone decided to retaliate. A pre-emptive strike, as it were.'

'But we're not certain that Lennox was responsible for either of the homicides. He was only a suspect.'

'Well someone thought he was enough of a threat to go after him. You didn't mention names to Mr Williams, did you?'

'Of course not, sir.'

He could see it on the DCI's face. He didn't believe him.

'What about our surveillance team?'

'At the time the home invasion was underway, a car travelling west along the street front-ended their van, injuring one of Amory's men and distracting the other sufficiently that he was unaware of what was happening until it was too late to intervene. A surveillance officer was putting cuffs on the driver and reading him his rights when he heard the explosions behind him. He ran through what was left of the fence and found Mr Lennox expiring in the kitchen. In the circumstances, it was lucky he wasn't hurt as well.'

'What about the driver of the car?'

'He's been detained of course, but he steadfastly maintains his innocence of anything but a moment's inattention at the wheel.'

'So, what now, sir?'

'Well, if Lennox was the killer, according to your theory, the threat could be past. One of the two main suspects is now deceased, the other is in custody.'

'Or the wrong man is dead.'

'That is what we now have to ascertain.'

'This could start off yet another vendetta.'

'I had considered that, but I have discounted the possibility for the time being.'

'Why is that, sir?'

'Because it was making my head ache.' The DCI turned away. 'Be at Scotland Yard at eight. We'll have to bring Gold Group up to speed. I'm not going into that bear pit on my own, thank you very much.' And he left.

Charlie watched the mortuary team wheel one of the body bags out to the van. He suited up and went in. Jack was standing on the path writing notes on a clipboard.

'Morning Charlie.'

'Come to take a look at the crime scene,' Charlie said.

'Reckon it's a crime scene, do you? Would you have called Stalingrad a crime scene?'

Bomb Disposal had swept the exterior of the house and had declared it safe. It had now started raining again, hard, and Jack had laid down duckboards to protect evidence. He walked Charlie through the scene. There were yellow markers everywhere: spent cartridges, a combat knife, a bloody trainer, body parts.

'The tripwire had been set right here,' Jack said, 'and the explosive device was placed here.'

'What kind of explosive?' Grey said.

'Too early to tell. I'll get the report to you as soon as we can. We've had a bit of a hurry up on this one from on high.'

Charlie clocked the tool shed and the child's play swing set. It looked like a normal suburban back garden if you looked left; look right and, as Jack had said, it looked like a battlefield; a mutilated body covered in a sheet, bits of human tissue hanging off what was left of a timber fence, which was mostly just matchwood.

'How many is this now?' Jack said. 'You get a commission from the morgue, Charlie?'

'Five.'

'I'm running a sweep among the team. I'm down for seven by the time you're done with it. Still fancy my chances.'

Charlie went back to his car, stripped off the suit and foot protectors and threw them in the boot. He looked up in time to see Gordon's wife and two kids driving away in the back of a patrol car. Their eyes met for a moment and Charlie knew what she was thinking. *You're that copper who came to see Gordon. You brought this on us. This is all your fault.*

CHAPTER FIFTY

No fizzy water this time, not even a cup of tea or a bourbon biscuit in sight.

The assistant commissioner looked down the table at Charlie, lowering his head a little so he could peer at him over the top of his glasses. 'How did Gordon Lennox obtain the explosives?'

'I had a phone call before I came into the meeting,' Charlie said, 'from Jack Reid, the crime scene manager. He said it was TATP, triacetone triperoxide, the same gear that was used in the Manchester bombing in May 2017 and the Tube bombing in Parson Green the same year. Most of the chemicals, like hydrogen peroxide, are common household products so they're quite easy to get if you know what you're doing. He packed the bomb with nails and ball bearings. The tripwire was a bit of fishing line.'

The superintendent flicked through the briefing notes the DCI had prepared. 'It's chilling that explosives like this could be deployed in the suburbs. Was this individual on any sort of official watchlist?'

'He was receiving counselling for post-traumatic stress since leaving the army,' the DCI said. 'He had been diagnosed with paranoid delusions. In the event, he wasn't paranoid and he wasn't deluded. It appears the two other men who died at the scene had been sent there to kill him.'

The rustling of paper as the brass read their briefing notes. 'You believe the person you have named here in your notes was responsible for ordering Gordon Lennox's murder?'

'On the balance of probability.'

'But you have no evidence.'

The DCI shook his head.

'Then your conclusions cannot leave this room. Mark Williams is an upstanding member of the legal profession.'

'Well, he is a *member* of the legal profession,' Charlie said, and got an angry look from the DCI.

'Has Mrs Lennox been able to give you a statement?'

'Yes, sir. She wasn't able to help us much, apart from establishing that Mr Lennox's mental state before this horrific incident was . . . fragile.'

'You still have suspicions that he was responsible for the homicide of Michael Grimes and Malcolm Barrington?'

'We think he may have been involved in one or both, but we have no evidence to support that theory as yet.'

The superintendent sat forward and the DCI put on his glasses and looked down at his own notes. It seemed to be the signal that Charlie had performed well enough but now he was taking over.

Charlie realised he was the only one in the room who wasn't wearing glasses. And probably the only one who wasn't a Mason either. Both put him at a disadvantage in this company.

'We are still looking for Lennox's sister, Margaret,' the DCI said. 'She went missing from her army base on 23 October and still cannot be traced. She also has motive, and army training, of course. We believe a motorcycle was the getaway vehicle used in both homicides and she obtained her motorcycle licence in May of this year.'

'She works in IT,' Charlie heard himself say.

Every head turned towards him. The DCI gave him a look that made him wish he'd kept his mouth shut.

'Yes, she's in the army, but she's a geek,' Charlie said. 'She's in communications and technology. It is highly suspicious that she has gone missing, but her army specialisation is in digital technology. Ripping the hard drive out of a laptop is not the same as ripping the head off a Crown Court judge. She might be an accomplice, but that's all.'

The superintendent leaned forward and said, patiently, putting her hands very carefully on the desk in front of her, as if they were a pair of gloves, 'And do you agree with Detective Chief Inspector O'Neal-Callaghan's theory, that Lennox and his sisters may have planned and executed these murders together?'

Well, I should, Charlie thought. It was my theory to start with.

Instead, he heard himself saying: 'To a point.'

'Meaning?'

'Ma'am, I think there's something we are all missing, and I don't think that taking the path of least resistance is necessarily going to lead us to the right answer.'

The assistant commissioner finally took off his glasses. 'You're the one who nearly got savaged to death by a wild animal recently, aren't you?'

'Yes, sir.'

He nodded towards the DCI, who was glaring at Charlie with a vein bulging in his temple. 'It would seem that you like to live dangerously.'

As he and the DCI got in the lift later, Charlie said: 'There's CCTV in this elevator, sir. If you strangle me, it will all be on film.'

'Strangling is too good for you, Charlie. I'm devising something slower and infinitely more painful.'

'We're rushing to conclusions.'

'You have to learn to keep your mouth shut.'

'I try. But there's like a genie in me that takes over. Sir, we can't take the investigation down a single path too soon.'

'Too soon!' The lift doors opened. Some startled clerks and three senior policemen almost took a step back. The DCI barged through the middle of them.

He waited until they were inside the car before he let him have both barrels. 'We have been chasing our tails for almost

307

two weeks on this fucking case, Charlie.' It was the first time Charlie had heard him swear. There was even a fleck of spittle at the corner of his mouth. 'Two weeks! Every day of those two weeks the press has been on our case. This is not too soon to direct the investigation. You're dragging your feet, Charlie! It's precisely the reason why I told Gold Group that I should take over.'

'I thought it was *them* that told you to take over, sir.'

There was a moment. He watched a whole gamut of emotions flicker across his boss's face. He'd been caught in a lie. 'The Met doesn't like mavericks, Charlie. Just do as you're told.'

They drove back to Essex Street through the traffic in silence.

Charlie had never seen the incident room so full. The DCI was parading up and down at the front as if he was about to give the Gettysburg Address. After the previous night's debacle, more officers had been moved over from other cases to bulk up the numbers. The rest of London could chop each other up as much as they liked for the next few days, right now they had to get crime off the front pages and back on page seven, safely out of sight.

The whiteboard looked like a goth teen's mood board; there were names scribbled everywhere in different coloured marker, and portrait photographs of both deceased and suspects, with TODs overlain with morgue photographs of decapitated bodies.

Anyone walking in here would think we were all mental, Charlie thought; and perhaps we are, staring at headless corpses in between endless cups of coffee and loops of CCTV. By the time we're fifty, boxers will have better brains.

You'd have to wonder sometimes why we do this. It comes at a cost, and no one loves us when the fuss dies down. When a passing scooter grabs their handbag or someone tries to martyr themselves outside a tourist attraction, they want us then. The rest of the time, we're the enemy.

And this operation was taking its toll. They now had two dead innocents – if you could call a bloke like Grimes innocent

– one dead suspect and two collaterals. Five corpses. That was a lot for one operation, outside of D-Day.

And still no charges laid.

Someone had put a red cross through Gordon Lennox's photograph on the whiteboard. There was a question mark next to Tracy Lennox's name and they hadn't yet found Margaret Lennox. But what if the killer was still out there, and their name wasn't on the list?

Not his problem any more. That was for the DCI and Gold Group to decide.

As for Lennox, as they'd advised Gold Group, he was pretty sure who had ordered the murder, but proving it was going to be almost impossible. The only two blokes who could tell them something like the truth were both stuck in drawers at Lambeth mortuary.

Chairs were dragged from the windows or from under desks and everyone crammed in around the long table, which was a chaos of coffee cups and witness statements. Detectives flicked through briefing notes, trying to focus, rubbing tired faces. Charlie had never seen so many plain clothes and uniforms at one briefing, not since the Lucifer case.

The DCI threw his jacket on the back of a chair and the room grew quiet. FONC in his shirtsleeves. Christ, he must mean business.

'Okay boys,' he said, 'we've all put in long shifts this last week, and I know most of you are dead on your feet. I'll arrange leave for some of you when this is all over with. But for now, we've got some work to do.

'Hopefully you've had a chance to look at the crime scene brief. This is just the initial report, we're still waiting on a lot of the forensics, but it seems that last night, at 2.54, two men tried to gain entrance to the home of Gordon Lennox by jumping over the side fence. Unbeknown to them, the side path had been booby-trapped. One of the men lost the lower part of his legs in the initial explosion.'

There were mutterings around the room. That's what they'd all heard but having it confirmed didn't make it any less astounding. This was shocking, even for the East End.

'Didn't this bloke have a wife and two kids?' someone said.

'Correct. We can only assume that he disarmed the IED every morning and re-armed it again at night. It was a simple tripwire device.'

'Where did he get the explosives?'

'They were mostly home made. It's in the report, son.' He's starting to get testy already, Charlie thought. Detectives never read briefing notes, not when they can rely on you to shorthand it for them. Welcome to my world, boss.

'After the initial explosion, it appears that Lennox rushed out into the garden, armed with a combat knife, probably a souvenir from his army days. We'll have to wait for the crime scene report for a more accurate timeline of events, but both men died at the scene from knife wounds and Lennox himself expired later at the hospital from a bullet wound to the chest.'

'It says here,' DC James said, 'that one of the blokes had his throat cut. Are we inferring from this that he is the same individual that murdered Grimes and Barrington?'

'No, we are not inferring anything at this stage. Now look everyone, and this is important: our primary focus is to remain on identifying the killer of Michael Grimes and Malcolm Barrington. To that end, Tracy Lennox remains in custody, and will be reinterviewed later this morning.'

'Does she know about her brother?' Lubanski asked him.

'She has been informed.'

'And?'

'Well, what do you think, constable? She's devastated. She's been put on suicide watch, as a precaution. No doubt her lawyer will be pressuring for us to release her from custody on compassionate grounds.'

'Will you, sir?'

'What I'm thinking is that her brother's death could be a game changer. She may now be willing to cooperate with us.'

'That's what I don't get,' James said. 'She works for armed response. She's supposed to be on our side.'

'So what about the battle of East Ham last night?' Greene said. 'Who were the two hit men?'

'They have been identified from fingerprints on the NPC database as Geoffrey May and Tyrone Marius Jorkovic. They both have significant form. It's all there in your notes. Intelligence say they were used as enforcers in the Spirelli crime organisation and were currently under investigation by the NCA for the murder of one of their informants.'

'And the driver who took out our surveillance team?' Singh asked him.

'Brian Barnes is presently in custody and DI George and DC Lovejoy will be interviewing him shortly. Blood tests show zero alcohol in his blood system and he was also negative for narcotic substances. He claims he fell asleep at the wheel and that it was all a terrible accident. His solicitor tells us that he is prepared to plead guilty to driving without due care and attention.'

'And his solicitor is?' Grey asked.

The DCI made a great play of checking his notes, for dramatic effect. 'Raymond Merrick.'

'Merrick,' Charlie said. 'God give me strength.'

'DS Greene will give you all your actions. Inspector George will handpick a separate task group to look into the killing of Gordon Lennox which will liaise with the overall operation. The main thrust at this stage remains in finding Margaret Lennox. Meanwhile we will continue with the current twenty-four-hour surveillance on the Millers. Okay, let's get to work. I don't need to tell you, the media is out there and watching every move we make. Let's get this sorted.'

Everyone nodded and went back to their phones and their computers, trying to look a lot more confident than they felt. If

311

Meg Lennox was there to be found, they would have done it by now. They needed a break.

Their best hope now was the hotline. Her picture had been in the newspapers and on the internet for over a week. Someone must have seen her. She couldn't have just disappeared.

The DCI drew Charlie aside. 'I'm tasking you with finding whoever contracted May and Jorkovic.'

'You know it's just going through the motions? Whoever it was will have used burner phones to set this up.'

'It has to be done. Whatever resources you need, I'll give them to you.'

'But we know it was Mark Williams.'

'But we have to prove it. Perhaps Mr Barnes will give us a lead.'

'Yeah and the Arsenal will win the treble this year,' Charlie said.

The DCI nodded at Grey and they made their way to the lifts, headed for the custody suite to have another crack at Tracy Lennox. Charlie went back to his office to prepare for the interview with Barnes. 'Let's get this sorted,' the boss had said. Charlie's greatest fear was that they would never get it sorted, that it would end up as the one case that would niggle at him for the rest of his life, not actually sorted at all. What they needed was hard evidence, not supposition and theories.

And no more heads impaled on railings.

CHAPTER FIFTY-ONE

Finally, all the paperwork had been done, blood and urine samples taken, and Barnes had been declared medically fit for interview. It was midday and he had been in custody almost nine hours.

Charlie waited for Lovejoy in the recording room next to interview room 2. He stared at the monitor; the two men waited side by side, one staring blankly at the wall, rigid, briefcase on his knee, the other sprawled like a life-size marionette with its strings cut, mouth open, staring at the ceiling.

Charlie shook his head. 'Well, we are honoured. Mr Merrick himself.'

Lovejoy looked over his shoulder. 'Who is he?'

'Mr Barnes' brief? That is Raymond Merrick, as in Merrick, White and Fisher.'

'Barnes gets the top man on legal aid?'

'That shows what a proper fair system we have.'

'Or that the fix is in.'

'That's a very cynical viewpoint, Lovejoy.'

'I heard this joke the other day. What's the difference between a lawyer and a catfish? One is a scum-sucking, bottom-feeding shark. And a catfish . . . well, is just a catfish.'

'Not all solicitors are like that. There's a lot of good ones. But not here. Not today.'

Made Charlie sick, this. When the government, in its wisdom, had decided to slash the legal aid budget, men like Merrick had made sure they kept their fat share of the pie. He had turned it into a volume business, had his team of solicitors treat legal aid as a loss leader. Once his clients were charged, his firm cashed in the legal aid certificate, and promised their new client a guaranteed acquittal. But after they were signed up, he persuaded them to plead guilty or else he sent one of his junior barristers into court with a brief scribbled on the back of an envelope. He took the court fees, and waved goodbye as the prison van headed to whatever walled facility their client had been invited to attend.

Done right, it was a nice little earner. And the punters kept signing up because Merrick, White and Fisher had a handful of high-profile clients, people with money, like Tony Spirelli. They were the ones who got all the man hours, the best QCs and all the headlines. They were used as bait. The punters thought Merrick would perform the same miracles for them in the Old Bailey as he did for the Spirellis of the world.

'So, what is Merrick doing in here this morning?' Lovejoy said. 'This isn't a multi-million-pound drug bust. This Barnes geezer doesn't look like he's got two pennies to rub together.'

'Well, that is the telling thing, isn't it? Are we ready, Lovejoy? Let's go and listen to another pack of lies.'

Charlie sat down, got himself settled. He looked at Merrick. Merrick looked back. He was sharp, Merrick, suave, like you could get a paper cut if you touched his suit or his hair. He sat with his briefcase on his knee, his face blank. Charlie imagined the strain he must be under, but he wasn't letting it show.

'A bit lower league for you, this, isn't it?' Charlie said to him.

'I don't know what you mean.'

'Thought you'd send one of your minions.'

'The law is for everyone.'

Charlie laughed. 'No, it isn't. The law is for rich people, like Mr Spirelli, for instance. Now if it was him sitting here, I'd expect to see you tugging your forelock, but not for someone as dopey as this. No offence, Mr Barnes.'

'Can we get on, please?'

Charlie turned on the digital recorder. He read Barnes the caution and for the tape he declared the attendance in the room of himself, DI Charlie George, DC Lesley Lovejoy and Raymond Merrick, the duty solicitor. Barnes announced himself along with his date of birth. He was dressed in a greasy woollen jumper and brown corduroy trousers, what hair he had left was all over the place and he needed a good dentist. Even looking at him made Charlie feel queasy, like he was eating a greasy breakfast after a hangover.

He opened his file, even though he already knew it almost by heart, and spent a few moments reading it, making a point of sighing at all the appropriate places.

'Well, Mr Barnes, you have lived a colourful life.'

Merrick leaned forward.

'Mr Barnes' legal history has nothing to do with the charges he is facing. His blood and urine samples are all clear, he was unaffected by alcohol or any other chemical substances, prohibited or otherwise, while behind the wheel. Once you are finished examining his mobile phone you will also be advised that he was not using it at the time of the incident. He has pleaded guilty to a charge of driving without due care and attention and we have provided you with a statement to that effect.'

Charlie leaned back, sucked his teeth with his tongue, looking pained. 'Mr Barnes, this must have been your first sober day in quite some time.'

Merrick tapped the desktop with an index finger. 'Do you have a question, inspector, or are these your random musings?'

'Where had you been last night, Mr Barnes?' Charlie asked him.

'At home.'

'So where were you going at the time of the accident?'

'Oh, nowhere.'

'You were in your car. You must have been going somewhere.'

'No, I couldn't sleep, see? But driving, it makes me tired,

like. So, I thought I'd go for a drive, relax myself. It worked, didn't it?' He grinned.

'Do you often go for a drive at three o'clock in the morning?'

'Only when I can't sleep. It's your fault, really.'

'Me personally?' Charlie said.

'No, you people, all of you. Cops. Judges. You won't let me take drugs so now I can't sleep.'

'How about you explain, in your own words, what happened.'

'Well,' Barnes said, and appeared pleased that his moment had arrived. 'It was like this. I remember turning into Fernway Crescent, I was heading for Balls Pond Road. I was going to head home along Archway Road.'

'Why Fernway Crescent?' Grey asked him.

A shrug. 'I don't know. Just driving aimlessly, know what I mean?'

'Go on,' Charlie said.

'I was driving carefully, obeying all the road rules. I wasn't doing more than thirty miles an hour.'

Merrick leaned forward. 'Your crime scene technicians will be able to verify his speed.'

'Thanks for that insight, Mr Merrick. Go on, Mr Barnes.'

'That's all I remember. I must have had one of those micro-sleeps. That's when you go to sleep for a split second.'

'Right. Thanks. Something else I've learned.'

'I remember a loud crash and being thrown forward. Fortunately, I was wearing my seat belt, as required by law. I realised I had driven into a Ford Transit van parked on the other side of the road. I got out to inspect the damage. It didn't seem too bad. I mean, mine was still driveable. I wasn't sure what to do, I was about to go back to my car, look in the glovebox to find a piece of paper and a pen, so that I could leave my name and phone number under the windscreen wiper for the owner of the van, and that was when it happened.'

'When what happened?' Charlie said.

'All hell broke loose.'

'Describe that for me.'

'Well, all of a sudden there was this sort of James Bond geezer coming at me. I near shat myself, I did. He was shouting at me and telling me to lie face down on the ground. It was only a bent fender and maybe a cracked radiator, I thought it was all a bit extreme. And then there was this other loud bang, I couldn't see anything because this crazy bloke was kneeling on my back, cuffing me up. Then he started swearing and left me there, lying in the road, handcuffed. That was dangerous, that was. I could of got injured. And all these people came out their houses in dressing gowns and shone torches in my face and made sarky remarks. It was egregious to my reputation. I could make a complaint.'

Charlie listened to all this rubbish in silence. When Barnes had finished his monologue – which was almost verbatim to the statement, apart from mixing up 'egregious' and 'injurious' – Charlie leaned in. 'Do you know someone called Geoffrey May?'

A shake of the head.

'What about Tyrone Jorkovic?'

'No, who is he?'

'You would remember Mr Jorkovic. He has a lot of tattoos, especially on his face. He's very violent. If you'd met him, I'm sure you'd remember.'

'What has he got to do with this? Did he own the van?'

'Has Mr Merrick told you that one of our policemen was injured when you rammed our vehicle?'

'Ram it? It was an accident.'

'Let me be clear. If we discover that you have had any communication whatever with Mr May and Mr Jorkovic, it will lead to a charge of conspiracy to murder. Has your solicitor told you that?'

There was a moment when he thought Barnes might crack. He looked at Merrick, and then back at Charlie, and he hesitated. Merrick cleared his throat and tapped Barnes on the knee.

'I'm sorry about the van,' Barnes said.

'If my client is a suspect in a murder investigation,' Merrick said, 'then you should proceed under caution from here, inspector. May I remind you that my client has surrendered his phone, and, as you will therefore be able to confirm, he has had no communication with either of the gentlemen you mentioned. Now can we proceed with the charges as they stand, or are we going down the rabbit hole into Cloud Cuckoo Land.'

Charlie ignored him.

'Do you know someone called Tony Spirelli?'

'Does he make tyres?'

'No, that's Pirelli,' Lovejoy said.

'Interview suspended 9.37 a.m.' Charlie turned off the tape. 'Mr Barnes, contrary to what you have been told by Mr Merrick here, Mr Spirelli is going to be quite upset about all this. He does your brief a favour, and two of his best lads end up on a slab in Lambeth, their bits lying in kidney dishes on the bench. Not very nice, is it? Are you sure you're playing for the winning team?'

'Don't say anything,' Merrick said to Barnes. Then he turned to Charlie. 'I believe the interview is over. You have my client's statement. I shall be advising him that from this point on he is to refuse to answer any further questions, as is his legal right under the Police and Criminal Evidence Act 1984.'

'What did Williams say about all this, Merrick? He's proper over a barrel now. He'll be doing all his Crown Court cases for free now till the day he joins Tyrone and Geoffrey in eternal rest.'

'I don't know what you're talking about.'

'I've had enough of all this bollocks. Mr Barnes, you will be charged with dangerous driving, which carries a minimum twelve-month suspension from driving and a maximum sentence of two years in jail.'

'Seems a bit harsh.'

'You were driving when knowingly deprived of adequate

sleep or rest. You can discuss it with your lawyer. I need a coffee.'

He and Lovejoy joined Greene in the viewing room. 'What do you think?' Charlie said to him.

'Nice performance. He should get an Oscar.'

'Merrick has got him well coached. He's not going to put his hands up to conspiracy to murder.'

'Besides,' Lovejoy said, 'does Scotland Yard want details of our covert operations read out in the Old Bailey and splashed all over the tabloids.'

They stared at the relay, Barnes and Merrick sitting side by side in the interview room, saying not a word to each other.

'What do you think the story is?' Greene said.

'Well, looking at Mr Barnes' file, and his various drug issues, I'd say he's probably run up some sort of debt to one of Mr Spirelli's dealers, and was given a choice between having his legs broken or taking the rap for a dangerous driving charge. I wouldn't think that even he had to think very long and hard about that one.'

'So what are we going to do?'

'Do?' Charlie gave him a long, hard stare. 'We do what the DCI says. Do search and seizure on May and Jorkovic and then hope and pray that this all ends with Gordon Lennox.'

CHAPTER FIFTY-TWO

There came a time, Charlie thought, when you got so behind with all the paperwork you had to contemplate either early retirement or arson. Burn the whole nick down then you'd have a ready excuse why you weren't up to date. He still had to write up his daily reports and his policy books, and the best way he could think of getting on top of it was taking the whole lot home and dictating it onto his iPhone, and then slipping a few quid to one of the trainees to type it all up. His own computer skills had never got past two fingers. The skipper had said watching him at a laptop was like watching a chicken picking sunflower seeds through a tennis racquet.

He looked up and saw the DCI standing at the door, his hands in his pockets. He was twirling the keys to his Beemer around the index finger of his left hand. Charlie hoped he didn't want him to hold his hand at another Gold Group meeting.

'So, Williams has pulled the pin.'

'Sir?'

'He's called off his bodyguards. Says he doesn't want personal security any more. He seems to think the danger has passed.'

'Really,' Charlie said.

'Yes. Really.'

'Hubris in the face of the gods is always a fatal mistake.'

'What does that mean, in English?'

'It means he could be sorry.'

'Why couldn't you just say that?' the DCI said and walked

out. Poor bastard, he sounds peevish, Charlie thought. Probably not getting enough sleep.

After he'd gone, he read through the intel report Parm had put together for him on May and Jorkovic. His finger hovered around the section on known haunts and KAs. He grabbed his jacket off the back of his chair and went out to the squad room. Grey was doing a search and seizure on Jorkovic's property out by Carshalton somewhere. Lovejoy was at her desk, skimming through CCTV on her monitor.

'Lovejoy,' he said. 'Leave it. We're going to a pub in Sutton.'

'Great. Mine's a G&T.'

'Forget it. Best you can hope for is a lemonade and a bag of crisps in the car park.'

The Coachman had a tall brick chimney and dormer windows set in the tiled roof. There were wooden picnic benches out front so that the regulars could sit outside in the summer and admire the traffic heading in and out of the local industrial estate.

Lovejoy followed him across the car park. There was a broken glass in the forecourt next to a litter of fag ends. England, my England, Charlie thought.

'What are we doing here, guv?'

'According to intel, this was where Tyrone and May spent most of their evenings. I want to ask if anyone saw Mark Williams drinking here in the last few days.'

'No one's going to talk to us, guv.'

'Don't know unless you try, Lovejoy.'

It was dead, for a lunchtime, just a couple of plastic gangsters in the corner, a fat boy behind the bar with a shaved head and enough ink to make a Premier League footballer look underdone. He was wearing a red and white striped Brentford shirt. There was moronic noise coming from a betting machine in the corner. The TV was on, tuned to a music channel that didn't synch with the bar manager's playlist. The usual crap.

Fat Boy looked them up and down. 'Yeah?'

'I hear tone,' Charlie said. 'Did you get that Lovejoy? He was definitely using tone.' He leaned on the bar and showed Fat Boy his warrant card. 'Detective Inspector Charlie George. Essex Road Murder Squad. When was the last time you performed a fire risk assessment?'

'Do what?'

'The Regulatory Reform Order 2005 tends not to be widely understood in the hospitality industry. It requires business owners to carry out fire risk assessments and act promptly upon the results. Now one phone call to the pertinent authorities and there could be a senior member of the fire brigade around here this afternoon to check your compliance and if it's not in order he will slap a prohibition order on you faster than you can say "last orders" and you will be closed until further notice. Or –' Charlie reached into his coat pocket and produced a six by four glossy of Mark Williams and slapped it on the counter, '– or, you can tell me if you've seen this bloke.'

'I'll have to ask the owner.'

'You mean Mr Spirelli? Do you need to ask him if you're compliant with fire regulations or ask him if you've seen this bloke?'

'What?'

'You didn't even look,' Charlie said and held up the photograph so that it was in Fat Boy's line of sight. 'Ring any bells for you, sunshine?'

'I said, I'll have to ask the owner.'

'You do that. Is the kitchen open?'

'Why, you want fish and chips?'

'No, because I'm sending someone round from the Department of Health as well. Unless you can tell me if you've seen this gentleman.'

'I'll have to ask—'

'The owner. Got you. Have a nice day. Love your shirt. Brentford. Is that a real football club or is it your pub team?'

He went back to the car.

'Told you, guv,' Lovejoy said.

Greene looked up as soon as Charlie walked back into the nick and held out a scrap of paper. There was a name and address on it. 'This bloke's been looking for you,' he said.

'Who is he?' Charlie said, and tried to decipher the scribble. 'Jay, you've got to do something about your handwriting. What alphabet do you use? Is this Cyrillic script?'

'No, not Cyril. Anthony. Anthony Grover. That's the address. It's . . .'

'Okay I can read that bit. Did this come in on the hotline?'

'No, it came through the front desk. He said he saw you an hour ago out at a boozer near the airport. Have a nice lunch did you, guv?'

'Yes thanks, Jay. Lovejoy and I had grilled lobster and a very cheeky bottle of Pinot Grigio.'

'Bottle of what?'

'Never mind.' Charlie took another look at the address. 'Is that a twenty-one or a twenty-seven, Jay?'

'Twenty-seven. It's obvious.'

'Only to you. Lovejoy, don't get too comfortable. We're headed back to the colonies.'

The GPS took them to some flats out by the airport, the sort of concrete ghetto that developers had thrown up anywhere they could back in the sixties. Someone had dumped a Tesco's trolley in the middle of the kids' playground. Charlie couldn't imagine that any halfway responsible mother would let her kids play in the sand under the swing set, it had to be full of used needles.

As they went in, a Boeing 747 went overhead, it was so low he heard the glass door rattle. The strip lights were on inside, even though it was the middle of the afternoon, and they made an incessant buzz and flicker. 'Great place if you're epileptic,' Lovejoy said.

323

The lift wasn't working, and they had to use the concrete stairs; they reeked like a urinal. They went along a walkway, protected by metal grilles. The place was like a World War Two fortress, a maze of cement walkways and bunkers, perfect for drug deals and the odd recreational stabbing. They stopped outside number twenty-seven and Charlie rapped on the door with his knuckles.

He recognised Anthony Grover straight away as one of the hard men he'd seen at The Coachman. He hurried them inside. It wasn't half as bad as he was expecting, Grover was clearly a fan of both Scandinavian furnishings and Japanese technological innovation.

He sat them down at an Ikea table in the kitchen and leaned in close, his voice low, like the three of them were going to work out the finer details of a drug deal in the middle of Leicester Square. 'Who's this?' he said, nodding at Lovejoy.

Lovejoy showed him her warrant card. He seemed satisfied.

'All right. Let's be quick about this and you never heard this from me.'

'Straight down to business then, is it?'

'Look, I want you in and out of here. Anyone sees me talking to the Filth, I'm in proper shite, right? This is a one-off.'

'You have information,' Lovejoy asked him.

'That photo you were waving around down the boozer,' Grover said. 'Who is he?'

'You know him?'

'Not from a bar of soap. But he was in the boozer talking to Tyrone the other night.'

'You saw him?' Lovejoy said.

'Yeah, I saw him. And I know to keep my mouth shut, right? But after what happened, all bets are off.'

'Were you a friend of Tyrone Jorkovic?'

'I was, yeah. We've been mates for years. He was all right until him and that May prick got caught up in shite, but he was still a mate.'

Charlie pulled out Mark Williams' photograph. 'This was the man he was talking to?'

'Yeah, it was him.'

'Do you know what was discussed?'

'Tyrone said he asked him to put the frighteners on some geezer.'

'Not just the frighteners. It was a contract, Mr Grover. A hit.'

'I don't know anything about that. All I know is, it was a proper set-up. When I read about it in the paper, I couldn't believe it. He never told Tyrone that this bloke was ex-SAS. He wouldn't have taken the job if he'd known. Fucker!'

'Do you know how much money changed hands?'

'I don't know any of the details. Tyrone was laughing about it with me is all, thought this geezer was a bit of a joke. Look, that's all I got. Like I said, you never heard it from me, I'm not giving you a statement and I'm not going to court. I don't care what you do with the information. I'm giving you the heads up because this whole deal pisses me off.'

'Have you thought about . . . contacting this man yourself?' Lovejoy said.

'Even if I knew who he was, no.'

'Why not?'

'Why do you think?'

'Spirelli,' Charlie said.

'Yes, Spirelli. Like I said, you've never been here.' He got up and went to the kitchen, peered out of the window. 'Now, piss off. Don't let anyone see you.'

'Thanks,' Charlie said and got to his feet. He would have liked to ask Grover some more questions, but there hardly seemed any point.

By the time they were headed back to Islington it was already getting on for late afternoon. They still had plenty of time.

'Back to the nick, guv?' Lovejoy said.

'No, it's time to pay a call on Mr Williams. I think we should ask him to accompany us to the station, as the saying goes.

***

There was a time, Williams thought, when a visible air-conditioning duct was like, well it meant you were poor. So did bare brick walls and metal lamps hanging from the ceiling on long bits of flex. These days he reckoned the ducts were used for sending lots of money to the bank and the bare brick meant you could charge twice as much for cocktails. Not that he minded. Paying over the odds for cocktails was why he came to places like this. It filtered out the hoi polloi. It also meant he *belonged*. Not like the old days.

Couldn't pull chicks like Paula when he first started out, but these days, he had them lining up. She sat on one of the battered metal stools at the bar, sipping suggestively from a long metal straw. There were dimples in her cheeks and in her eyes a promise of more later.

If only he could relax a little bit. The whole Lennox thing had turned into a proper cock-up. Even Merrick wasn't returning his calls. Perhaps he'd been too eager calling off the dogs from Special Branch.

But first things first. He had a point to prove with Paula, make sure she experienced the real Mark Williams. He couldn't let her go gossiping around the office that he couldn't get it up.

'Congratulations,' she said, touching her glass to his. 'A big win.'

'Was there ever any doubt?'

'I honestly thought the jury was against us. I was watching them during your close. I thought that black woman at the front, the one with the big glasses, she looked like she wanted to hit you.'

'You can never tell with a jury. You think: that one's for us, that one's going for the prosecution, but you're nearly always wrong.' He leaned close to her ear. Her fragrance had to be very expensive. He liked to tell himself she bought it just for him. 'Why don't we get out of here?' he said.

She finished her drink. 'No objection, your honour.'

He squinted in the glare, even the overcast of a grey November afternoon seemed bright after the dimly lit bar. There was a pair of Japanese tourists wandering down High Holborn, they were probably looking for the British Museum, trying to make sense out of a map. Why weren't they using their phones, didn't those people invent technology? They looked hopefully in his direction and he ignored them, hailed a cab and guided Paula towards it.

There was a moment when he heard the roar of a motorbike, looked up and saw a rider all in black pass by very close, the roar of the engine echoing off the walls of the tower blocks either side, and then it was gone. He laughed off his own apprehension. Didn't have to worry about that any more.

CHAPTER FIFTY-THREE

It was a nice little fare for the cabbie, Williams thought, all the way out to Guildford, but he had a feeling of, what was the word? Largesse. That sounded about right. He might even give the driver a tip on top of the fare. He'd won a big case, got himself a decent bit of squeeze for the night.

Life was good.

They were heading past The Weyside on the Godalming road when a black motorbike roared past, the rider came so close he nearly took off the cab's wing mirror, and the cabbie leaned out of his window and gave him some well-chosen words. The rider turned around on his seat and flipped him the bird, then weaved through the incoming traffic and was gone, revving his motor as he overtook the van in front on a tight bend.

'Never a bloody copper when you need one,' the cabbie said.

They turned off the A281 and left the twentieth century behind. Williams directed the cabbie down a no through road; he couldn't wait to see Paula's face when she saw the house. He'd bought it three years ago and had it redesigned by a local architect, it looked like something one of Henry VIII's wives might have owned, if they'd needed a double garage for their Porsche and an X5. The place was a hundred years old, had cost him a small fortune to make it look three hundred years older.

The cabbie turned off the laneway onto a long gravel drive-way. 'This your place?'

He sounded suitably awed. That was worth a tip.

'Wow,' Paula said, staring at the gardens and immaculately trimmed hedging. If she thought this was something, she should see it in the daylight; there was a sun terrace and a grass tennis court, and views over the Merrow Downs. He even had direct access to Guildford Golf Course.

Not bad for a boy from the wrong side of London.

Paula got out, waited on the steps, stamping her feet in the cold. She had her hands deep in her pockets, looking up at the lattice windows, the gabled roofs.

As the cab drove off, he put an arm around her and led her up the steps to the studded oak door. 'This is amazing,' she murmured.

He opened the door for her. She turned around, perhaps to kiss him, but then stepped quickly back; her eyes went wide, and her hand went to her mouth. He realised there was someone behind him.

He felt a quick icy fear and started to turn around. He didn't have time. An arm went around his throat, choking him and jerking his head back. He didn't even feel the knife as it went in.

Charlie phoned Parm to get Mark Williams' home address. Lovejoy punched it in to the GPS. 'Guildford,' she said. 'That's miles away.'

'Nice drive out to the country,' Charlie said. 'Lovely.'

As Lovejoy picked her way through the traffic on High Holborn, Charlie's Nokia buzzed in his pocket. It was the DCI.

'Charlie. We have the results on the knife we found at Tracy Lennox's flat.'

'You don't sound overjoyed.'

'The blood traces were so degraded they couldn't extract any DNA. Which means they couldn't be Barrington's, because he was only murdered three days ago.'

'So why did she hide the knife?'

'I don't know.'

'So what now?'

'We'll keep her under surveillance, overt and covert, see where she goes, who she sees. I am going to ask for a mobile phone intercept.' Charlie knew what was coming. It would be payback for disagreeing with him at the Gold Group meeting. 'Charlie, you organise that, will you?'

That's why they call him FONC, he thought. The warrant for a phone intercept was subject to RIPA rules and would have to be signed by the Home Secretary. It would tie him up for hours, all of it unpaid overtime, filling in the forms. And even if they did get any evidence, it wouldn't be admissible in court.

'Where are you?'

'We're on our way to talk to Mark Williams. I'm bringing him in for questioning.'

'I didn't authorise that.'

'I got a tip-off. He met with May and Jorkovic two nights before they tried to hit Gordon Lennox.'

'Great work. You have a written statement from an eyewitness?'

'Not exactly, sir.'

'What do you have?'

'A tip-off.'

'No, Charlie, no, you're not opening that can of worms. He won't answer questions, and if you arrest him you'll kick over a right hornets' nest. You're not going on a fishing expedition. Leave it alone.'

'There's a lot of mixed metaphors there, sir.'

'Charlie, back to the nick, now.'

'Sorry, you're breaking up. This is a bad line. Can you repeat?' He nodded to Lovejoy, indicated that she should put her foot down.

'I said back to Essex Street, now.'

'Can't hear you. I'll have to call you back.' He powered off the phone. 'Batteries on these old phones,' he said to Lovejoy. 'They don't last five minutes, do they?'

CHAPTER FIFTY-FOUR

It took an hour to get out there. Charlie fidgeted the whole way, his fingers tapping the dashboard, opening and shutting the glove-box, fiddling with the radio. 'You all right, guv?' Lovejoy said.

'Got a bad feeling.'

'About Williams? We know what he's going to say. He'll deny everything. We don't have evidence and he knows it.'

'It's not just about Williams. It's like I got this . . . don't know what you'd call it. Premonition.'

'Didn't think you believed in that stuff.'

'I don't. That's why I'm not all right. Watch out for that cyclist.'

There were roadworks past Wandsworth Common, which cost them another quarter of an hour. Charlie tapped his foot, muttered under his breath.

'Look at that wet wipe with the Stop sign,' Charlie said. 'Who does he think he is? He's enjoying this. Holding everyone up.'

'Settle down, guv.'

She gave him a look. 'Is this about your girlfriend?'

'What are you talking about?'

'Your bad moods lately.'

'There is a degree of stress at work this last couple of weeks, if you haven't noticed.'

'I don't buy that. When you've got a misery on, it's either your love life or the football.' When he didn't answer, she said, 'Not going too well, then?'

'Arsenal are doing all right.' When she didn't laugh, he said, 'She cleared out.'

'Sorry to hear that, guv.'

'Well, I don't know, Lovejoy. Part of me is relieved. I mean, it's not like she was the love of my life. But, you know.'

'Yeah, I know. A bloke likes to have something in reserve, till he finds what he's looking for.'

'It wasn't like that.'

'Nothing wrong with it. She was probably the same. Only she got a better offer before you did.'

Charlie stewed on that all the way down the A3. She knew him too well; in some ways, she sounded like Ben. The only difference was, she couldn't say 'you know your problem?' Not if she wanted to stay in the squad.

'Into the Tory heartlands,' Lovejoy said, as they followed the crawl of traffic over the river. 'I thought it would all be cobbled streets and cathedrals.'

'Used to be,' Charlie said. 'Since Brexit the Tory heartland has moved to Stoke. Trouble with Guildford, everyone over the age of five drives a car.'

'Why would Williams want to live down here?'

'It gets better when you get off the main drag. Turn left here. We want the Godalming road.'

They turned off the main road on the other side of town and drove through a cluster of suburban bungalows and semis. They reached the end of a cul-de-sac, a hedge and empty green fields. Charlie saw a sign for the golf course.

'Where to?' Lovejoy said.

A black London cab pulled out of a narrow lane, drove past them, headed back towards town. There was a sign that said: 'Private Road, Keep Out.'

'Up there,' Charlie said.

They drove about fifty yards; it was right on dusk, Charlie could just make out the gables of a house through the trees. 'In here.' Lovejoy pulled onto a long gravel drive. 'Christ, watch out!'

The motorbike almost hit the driver's door. Lovejoy pulled the wheel hard to the left and skidded onto the lawn. The rider braked and slid, almost came off, but didn't stop, roared out of the gates behind them. 'Fuck was that?' Charlie said.

Lovejoy swung off the lawn; there was a mock Tudor house illuminated in the headlights, all red brick and gables. It would have looked like something out of *Horse and Hound* if it wasn't for the headless body sprawled over the front steps and the woman standing over it, screaming hysterically. Lovejoy jumped out and was straight on the phone, calling for back up. Charlie ran round to the driver's side. 'You go,' he said and pointed to the house. He jumped behind the wheel, threw the car around, spitting gravel from the back wheels. He reached under the seat, found the blue light and plugged it in, put it on the roof as he sped back down the lane.

He called it in on the Airwave. He had to find whoever it was on that bike.

He caught up with it just before he reached the main road. He wasn't close enough to see the plates, if it had any. He knew that once he lost sight of it, that would be it. He had to get a chopper in the air, organise a roadblock, something, before the bastard got away.

The bike weaved down the centre of the road, through the press of traffic, and Charlie followed, his fist on the horn. Oncoming cars pulled over to the side; there was at least one shunt, a bit of paperwork there, he'd better make this worth it.

Charlie kept sight of the bike past the car park and almost to the old Debenhams, got stuck behind a laundry van. He kept his hand on the horn, but the bastard wouldn't pull over. 'Come on, son, come on!'

He veered to the other side of the road, there was a fancy SUV coming the other way, flashing their lights, the driver panicked and stopped dead in the middle of the road. That was it, then, he was going to lose them.

He swerved around it, got to the corner in time to see the lights at the end of the high street turn red. Whoever was on the bike pulled out to overtake the Honda in front, narrowly missed a woman in a *hijab* wheeling a child in a buggy, crossed to the wrong side of the road and lost control. The rider dropped the bike and it skidded into the railings. He heard people screaming. He thought that was it, over, then he saw the rider pick themselves up and limp off towards the church on the other side of the river. The leathers they were wearing had saved them from the worst of it.

Charlie stopped the car, jumped out, and headed after them. Where was the cavalry? He heard sirens on the other side of the river. Come on boys. Look lively.

The rider was headed down Riverside Walk, sent a woman tumbling onto her knees as they ran past, then disappeared out of sight. Charlie followed. He had a stitch in his side already; he was definitely not SAS material. He was vaguely aware of a weird-looking metal statue and a timber shed in the half-light. As he ran around the corner, the biker was waiting for him on the other side of a waist-high metal fence.

Charlie stopped, thinking they must have a weapon. He stared at the helmet's black visor and then looked down at the black leather gloves. But they weren't holding a weapon. It was a backpack.

The biker reached inside, took out a thick green bin liner and tossed it at him. He caught it, pure instinct. He felt something warm and liquid oozing down his fingers. A head rolled out of the plastic and dropped onto the paving.

He heard someone screaming. A shopper, or someone just come down for a nice walk by the river. He turned around, it was a young woman, halfway to lighting a cigarette. She fainted, hitting her head on the concrete as she went down.

He put the head back in the bin liner. There were people standing up on the bridge, staring. 'Someone come and look after her,' he shouted at them, and vaulted the fence.

What had made him stop? Shock, perhaps, even after all these years of doing the job. You can't afford moments like that, old son, he thought. Maybe you're losing your touch. He hesitated by Friary Passage. Had the biker gone down the underpass? He kept going, went under the bridge, caught a glimpse of a figure in black running up the steps towards the road. They vaulted the railings.

There was a squeal of brakes and a loud bang. Charlie sprinted up the steps, saw the biker lying in front of a yellow and blue Arriva bus. The driver clambered out of his cab and stood there, too horrified to go near. He kept saying over and over: 'There was nothing I could do.' Some of the drivers on the bridge had got out of their cars; a passer-by had stopped to help, was vomiting noisily into the gutter.

Charlie knelt down, pulled up the biker's face guard, got sprayed with a mist of blood for his trouble. 'She's choking,' he said. A woman came over, she was wearing green hospital scrubs. 'My name's Jammai. I'm a nurse.'

'Great,' Charlie said. 'We have to get this helmet off. Can you hold her head?'

'You know how to do this?'

'Yeah, I'm a brain surgeon,' Charlie said. He undid the chin strap and waited while Jammai held the biker's jaw and worked her other hand under the helmet as far as she could, to stabilise the head. He splayed the edges of the helmet outwards and rocked it towards him. With every few inches he let Jammai work her hands further up until she had a firm grasp of the skull.

'We've got to hurry,' Jammai said. More froth sprayed into the air. The rider's cheeks were turning blue.

'It's off,' Charlie said and hurled the helmet aside. 'Come here,' he yelled at the bus driver who was just standing there with his mouth open; poor bastard. Charlie grabbed him by the jacket and dragged him over.

'We've got to roll her over,' he said.

'But what about her spine?'

'Do as I say,' Charlie said. 'Show him, will you?' he said to the nurse.

Jammai crossed the injured woman's legs, then took the bus driver's hands, showed him what to do. She put her own hands on the shoulder and the hip. 'Ready,' she said.

Charlie took off his Stone Island. Say goodbye to another nice piece of gear, he thought. He put his hands either side of the biker's head. 'Roll on the count of three, Jammai. Really slow.' The bus driver looked like he was going to faint. 'We have to keep her neck and spine in a straight line. Now one, two, three and . . . roll.'

As soon as the rider was on her side, she coughed up another gout of blood. Jammai scooped two fingers into the woman's mouth, swept out some broken teeth and another gush of blood and saliva came with them. The woman gasped and drew in a deep, gurgling breath.

'That sounds better,' Charlie said.

Jammai took Charlie's jacket, folded it tight and placed it under Charlie's hands to help keep her head straight. Then she took a bright coloured scarf from her bag and wrapped it round and around the unconscious woman's neck as a makeshift collar. The bus driver started to shake; not just his hands, his whole body. Charlie was aware of someone standing over him, peering over his right shoulder. 'I'm a doctor. Do you people need a hand?'

'You any good at driving buses?' Charlie said to him. 'I think that bloke there would definitely like a break.'

The paramedics loaded the stretcher into the ambulance, Charlie jumped in the back, strapped himself in the spare seat. He was there for the dying declaration, admissible in a court of law, though there looked to Charlie to be very little chance of that.

He figured the woman lying there on the gurney, under the

oxygen mask and neck brace, was Meg Lennox. She was the only one who could tell them what had happened to Michael Grimes, Malcolm Barrington and Mark Williams.

Don't die on me, Meg.

He was covered in blood and muck. He thought about the shocked faces of the people on the footpath just before they shut the doors, the bus driver doubled over spitting bile into the gutter, Jammai and the doctor staring after him, wondering who he was and what had happened.

The senior paramedic was working with the suction, trying to keep Meg Lennox's airway clear, as the ambulance lurched through the traffic, on blues and twos, the siren deafening; occasionally the driver had to use the horns as well at someone too slow to move over.

Charlie glanced at the ECG. It didn't look that flash to his untrained eye. Hard to tell with the lurching in the back of the van, but the look on the paramedic's face told its own story. The constant braking and accelerating, the smell of plastic from the oxygen mask and the reek of coppery blood made Charlie feel nauseous.

He looked down at the green bin liner, lying on the floor next to him. He parted the blood-smeared folds of plastic and a pair of eyes, half-lidded and glassy in death, stared up at him. He grimaced and twisted the plastic shut again.

He followed the medics as they raced the stretcher into the Emergency Department at the Royal Surrey. He pulled out his warrant card, but a nursing sister shook her head and steered him back out into the corridor. A specialist team swooped on the injured woman as the paramedics shouted the handover, and then they were gone, back out to the doors with their stretcher.

Charlie sat down on a plastic chair, the bin liner between his feet. At least it wasn't leaking. He looked down the hall and saw a coffee machine. He thought about grabbing one and then thought: No, Charlie son, bit of decorum please. That's Mark Williams' head you've got there in the bag.

He fished in his pocket for his phone, rang the nick, and told Greene that he'd left a Met vehicle in the middle of Guildford with the door open and the keys still in the ignition. It would need to be retrieved. He also told him to send someone to the hospital right away to transport a body part to the mortuary at Lambeth, and to find Meg's sisters, get them down here.

'Guv. You all right?' He looked up. It was Lovejoy. It looked like half the Met was with her. She sat down on the plastic chair next to him.

'Well, that was unexpected. You get everything sorted, Lovejoy?'

'I hear they've sealed off half of Guildford. I think we're back on the front page tomorrow.'

'Pity we don't get appearance money.'

'What's in the bag, guv?'

'I'll give you three guesses.'

Lovejoy nodded and put her hands in the pockets of her coat.

'Who was on the bike?'

'Hard to be sure in the circumstances but it looks like Meg Lennox.'

'Is she going to be okay?'

'God knows. I've told Jay to get someone to pick up Tom and Jennifer Miller and bring them over here quick smart. Tracy as well, if she's still at the nick.'

'It was her then, all along?'

Charlie didn't say anything.

She put a hand on his arm, withdrew it almost straight away. 'Sorry. But you look like crap.'

'Don't mind dead people, it's the ones that are only halfway there that shake me up. You should be getting back. There's going to be a lot of paperwork. Jay will need all the help he can get.'

'You sure you don't want me to stay here for a bit?'

'You'll be more use at the nick, Lovejoy.'

'Guv,' she said. She got up and left.

An hour later the registrar came out of the emergency room. Charlie stood up, prepared for the worst. If Meg Lennox died, they might never make sense of all of this.

The doctor was still wearing his scrubs. He had his mask pulled down, and he looked grim. 'How is she?' Charlie said.

'Do we have a name?'

'We think we do. It's Lennox. Margaret Lennox. Her family is on their way. We've called them.'

'Are they far away?'

'You think she might not make it?'

'She has a haemothorax, that's blood leaking into her right lung, as well as a crushed pelvis and severe chest trauma. A number of her ribs are broken, we've sent her into surgery for a splenectomy. She's lost a lot of blood internally. She went into arrest ten minutes after she was brought in, but we were able to resuscitate her.'

'That doesn't sound too good.'

'That's because it isn't. I have to get back in. Let the nurse know as soon as the family arrive.' He turned to go back into the emergency room, then hesitated. 'The paramedics said you treated her at the scene.'

'Just rolled her on her side, like they showed us in first aid class. She was choking on her own blood.'

'Well. Good job.'

After he'd gone, Charlie sat back down. He knew he should be getting back to the squad, but the release of adrenaline had left him feeling completely drained. If anyone needed him, they knew where he was.

CHAPTER FIFTY-FIVE

Charlie saw the Millers coming towards him down corridor. It shocked him, seeing Tom Miller upright. He'd never seen him wearing his prosthetics before, and it surprised him how easily – and how quickly – he could move in them. It gave him the look of a soldier again. He could imagine him now with a C8 in his desert kit and boots. Must have been a fearsome sight.

Jennifer clung to his arm. If he looked stronger, she looked diminished by the events of the last week. Her face was grey, and she didn't look like she'd been sleeping or eating.

'Where is she?' she said.

'We don't know a hundred per cent if it's her,' Charlie said. 'We need you to ID her for us.'

Neither of them looked surprised to be there. How much have they not been telling me? Charlie wondered. He called for the nurse and she took them up to the ICU. This time Charlie was allowed to follow, and he watched through the glass as they went in.

Meg Lennox lay in the bed, a wreck of a human being lying in the semi dark, lit by the green screens of all the machines that were keeping her alive. She'd been intubated, and there was a tangle of IV lines and catheters and drainage tubes and ECG wires.

Jennifer howled and collapsed to her knees. So, I was right, Charlie thought. It is Meg.

Tom and the nurse helped Jennifer to a chair. Tom turned and looked over his shoulder. Charlie was glad he didn't have his C8 or he would have been spread all over the wall behind him.

He left a uniform outside the door and told him that he was to be called if and when their prisoner regained consciousness.

Perhaps it ends here, he thought. Perhaps it's finally over.

It was well into the evening and Williams' house and front lawn were lit up with halogen lights; it looked like a film set. Charlie signed in with the officer at the cordon outside the gates. He looked for the DCI but couldn't spot him in the crowd. Last time he'd seen this many brother officers was at a Met charity ball. There were SOCOs everywhere, and brass from the local headquarters as well as Scotland Yard and Essex Road. He felt like he'd been invited to a party where he didn't know anyone. Finally he spotted Grey with DCs James and Singh, talking to the crime scene manager. James raised a hand.

'You all right, guv?' James said.

'I'm all right, Wes. Think I need to get back to the gym. All that running, I'm feeling it in the hamstrings.'

'We heard what happened,' Singh said. 'Is it Meg Lennox?'

Charlie nodded.

'Question is,' Grey said, 'where has she been hiding out this last two weeks and did she have an accomplice?'

All the lights were on inside the house; he could make out the SOCOs moving about up there as part of the search. He was hoping they would find something on Mark Williams' laptop or on his phone that would link him to Tyrone and May, then perhaps they could put the whole sorry business to bed.

'Have the local boys organised a thorough search of the area?' Charlie said.

'Too dark, sir,' Grey said. 'They thought perhaps in the morning.'

'No, not in the morning. This is urgent.'

Charlie's Nokia buzzed in his pocket. It was the DCI, he

said he was with Gold Group and he needed an update and he needed it *now*.

'Are you at the scene, Charlie?'

'Yes, sir.'

'Heard any more from the hospital?'

'Not yet. She's back from surgery but she's still critical.'

'Have you found the murder weapon?'

'Not yet,' Charlie said. 'I was just telling my team that we have to find it. We'll need it to make our case.'

'To make the case?' Charlie could imagine him in the meeting, the top brass listening to every word, every nuance. But he wasn't going to lie just to please the assistant commissioner.

'Charlie, she had his head in her backpack, for God's sake.'

'We still need a murder weapon. I want to get the search started tonight but my boys reckon the local plod are dragging their feet.'

'I'll make some calls. Anything else?'

'Not at the moment, sir.'

'Right. Get this sorted, Charlie.' He hung up. Charlie put the Nokia back in his pocket.

'What about the girlfriend?' he said to Grey.

'She's still in shock. Not making a lot of sense. From what we could make out, she was already inside the house when it happened, Williams was still on the front steps. She saw someone come up behind him, out of nowhere were her words, grabbed him from behind and slit his throat. Sawed his head off right there by the marble lion.'

'What did she do?'

'Just froze by the sounds of it. Most people would, I reckon.'

Charlie thought about Meg Lennox tossing the bin liner at him with Williams' head inside. How long had he stood there? Five seconds, ten? Long enough. *Most people would.*

'Description?'

'All in black, said she couldn't see her face, she kept her helmet on the whole time.'

'Must have been a lot of blood.'

'I suppose so.'

'No suppose to it, sergeant. The stuff goes bloody every-where. You know this. It's like a firehose, right?'

'Yes, sir.'

Charlie couldn't stop thinking about her holding out that bin liner. Yes, it was late in the evening, she was all in black, but he could have sworn there wasn't a speck of blood on her.

'Did we find the cabbie?'

'Said he didn't see anything. Dropped them off, drove away, didn't look in his mirror.'

'She must have been waiting for him,' Singh said. 'Plenty of places to hide the bike. Did for him, then took off, just as you and Lovejoy got here.'

'There's a security camera up there,' Charlie said, nodding towards the roofline.

'Someone cut the wires.'

'She knew what she was about,' Singh said.

'So we can't actually prove it was her that did it,' Charlie said.

'But she had Williams' head in her backpack, guv,' James said.

'So everyone keeps telling me. But if she lives, *if*, and this gets to court, she could say she found it in a skip bin and decided to take it home and hang it on the wall as a conversation piece. Sorry, but this is not finished. No one saw her *face*. We need a visual, or we need CCTV, or we need DNA, or we need the murder weapon with her DNA, or her fingerprints, something. Where's the girlfriend now?'

'Still at the hospital.'

'Have we got someone with her?'

'Lubanski's there. But, like I said, sir, I don't think the girl-friend's going to be much help.'

Charlie shook his head, thought about going home and leaving them to it. No chance of that, there was a mountain of

343

paperwork waiting for him back at Essex Road, and he needed to have a chat with the union lawyer about what had happened, in case the DPS came sniffing around.

And all they had on Meg Lennox was circumstantial. Mark Williams might be dead but there were a hundred more out there just like him who would rip the case to shreds in court.

Charlie headed back to his car. 'No free drinks down the pub just yet fellas,' he shouted at them over his shoulder. 'This isn't finished.'

DAY 12

CHAPTER FIFTY-SIX

Tom Miller answered the door. He was back in his wheelchair, wearing his check shirt and army shorts; a reasonable disguise, Charlie thought. The bionic superhero he saw at the hospital the previous night was gone.

Tom sighed when he saw it was Charlie, turned the chair around and went back inside. Charlie followed.

'No prosthetics today?'

'I don't like to wear them about the house. I'm more comfortable in the chair.'

'You looked like you'd had plenty of practice in them.'

'Yeah, but this way I get to sit up the front at the football.' He said it straight-faced, Charlie supposed it was a joke. 'The wonders of carbon fibre and titanium. Suppose I'm lucky, in a way. My body will get older and degrade but there's part of me that's going to get newer every year.'

He wheeled around in his den, spread his arms.

'So, what now?'

'Have you spoken to the hospital?'

'The doctors say they're optimistic. You must be pleased. Nothing worse than standing a dead woman in the dock. Not much satisfaction in that.'

'As it stands, there's six people dead. I didn't want there to be another one.'

'I thought bodies were your business.'

'Mr Miller, your sister has been directly responsible for three of those deaths and indirectly responsible for the others.

So, let's dispense with the attitude, can we?'

'If that's what you want.'

'Where's Mrs Miller?'

'She's not dealing too well with this. Her doctor's prescribed her some meds. She's upstairs asleep.'

They stared at each other.

'You can't prove it was Meg that did it. She could have had help.'

'Did she?'

'How would I know? Have you asked Williams' girlfriend?'

'Said she saw a figure in black come towards them with a knife. That's about it.'

'That must be frustrating. What about the cabbie?'

'He'd already driven away, didn't see anything either.'

A half-smile. 'Someone must have seen something.'

'You'd think, wouldn't you?'

Charlie's eyes were drawn to the wall behind Tom's head, the photograph of Tom, Gordon Lennox and Joe Cole, arm in arm. It was the same one he'd seen during their search and seizure at Gordon's place.

'Tom,' he said. 'Mind if I call you Tom?'

'Yeah, I do. It's Mr Miller to you.'

'All right, Mr Miller. We know you're not telling us everything. So, let me put my cards on the table. My DCI wants to charge your sister-in-law as soon as she wakes up, but I said to him the same thing you just said to me. We can't prove she did it. She's an accessory, bang to rights, but was she the cutter? Like, why was there no blood on her clothes? There would have to be some. You must know what it's like. Did you ever cut someone's throat yourself?'

'You mean, in the army?'

'Where else would I mean?'

'That's classified information,' Tom said.

'Must be like a fire hose. Blood would just go everywhere. Of course, there was a fair bit of blood on her by the time

348

we got her to the hospital, the forensic people are testing her clothes now. But what if it all belongs to her? That would raise questions.'

'And they're the sort of questions that would be raised by a good defence council. Anything can happen in court. Believe me, I know from bitter experience.' He spread his hands. 'Why are you here, inspector?'

'I just wanted to ask you if you thought it was all worth it?'

'Was what worth it?'

'The revenge.'

Tom swung the chair around, pointed to the photograph of a little girl on the mantle, hugging a soft toy. There was a small vase of flowers beside the picture. It was a shrine, of sorts. 'Was it worth it? Better ask Zoë. Anything else?'

'One other thing. Do you have blades?'

'Blades?'

'Yeah, you know, the running blades the runners wear in the Paralympics.'

'No. Why?'

'Just a thought. I bet you were proper fit in the army though, right? Had to be.'

'Fitter than most.'

'Probably still are by the looks of you.'

'Try not to get too flabby. Got a gym out the back. Look, your blokes have been right through this place. I've got nothing to hide. If there's nothing else, inspector, we'd like to be left alone.'

Tom heard his wife calling from upstairs. 'Who is it, Tom, what's going on?'

He wheeled into the hallway to answer. 'It's all right, sweetheart, I've got it. Nothing to worry about.'

Charlie reached for his phone, took a photograph of the picture on the wall, the one of Tom with his SAS mates. He put it back in his pocket and followed Tom into the hallway.

'I'll let myself out,' he said, and left.

CHAPTER FIFTY-SEVEN

Charlie couldn't face the paperwork this morning. It kept mounting up; the fallout from the last twelve days wasn't going away any time soon. There would be a massive internal enquiry, and everyone on Gold Group was scrambling to find a scapegoat for all the perceived errors.

The DCI was winding the case down. They had Meg Lennox; Gordon Lennox was dead; and Tracy Lennox was under round-the-clock surveillance. She was now on suspension while her recent conduct was investigated by the DPS. Meanwhile, the media circus raged on, journalists feeding on every little morsel of information like sharks attacking an injured whale. Charlie was heartily sick of it. He was glad the DCI was in charge, happy for someone else to take the heat.

An extraordinary search in a one-mile radius of the murder scene in Guildford had failed to recover the murder weapon. Initial results from the laboratory at Lambeth weren't encouraging either; how could Meg Lennox have murdered Williams in such a brutal way and not have his DNA on her? Didn't make sense.

Gold Group's problem was that neither of the other two people they had so far identified as suspects in the inquiry had been anywhere near Williams when he was murdered.

Parminder tapped on the door and came in.

'I've got what you were after,' she said. She put a photocopy of a map on his desk, there was a red circle with GPS coordinates written beside it in black felt-tip pen.

'You found it?'

Charlie had sent Parminder the photograph he had taken on his mobile phone at Tom Miller's house, the picture of Tom, Gordon and Joe Cole, arm in arm.

'Your guess was right, it had been on Lennox's Facebook account at one time. He deleted it in May.' She shrugged. 'But once it's on the web, it's never truly gone.'

'Good work.'

'It was first posted back in July 2013, when Facebook was still cool.'

'A few months before they went to Helmand.'

'I checked the geotags on the image. This is where it was taken.'

Charlie looked at the map. It was a small farm in Essex, between Harlow and Bishop's Stortford. 'I wonder why he lied to me?' Charlie said aloud.

'Who, guv?'

'Tom Miller. He told me it was taken in Afghanistan.' He peered closer at it. 'I believed him at the time. I mean, you can't really see anything in the background, I suppose. Just the jeep. Anyone can have an old khaki jeep. Can you check who owns this farm for me, Parm?'

She slid a piece of paper across the desk, she was already well ahead of him. He read it through quickly. 'Joe Cole owned this place?'

'It's just a few acres with a rundown farmhouse. His father left it to him when he died in 2010.'

'Where's his mother then?'

'Over in Acton. Want her address?'

'Yes, please. I think we should have a word.' He got his jacket and went out to find Grey. He felt a muted thrill. He hoped he'd found the missing part of the puzzle.

'I owe you an apology,' Grey said, as he drove out of the yard.

'Look Matt, I don't mind anyone calling me out if they think

351

I've done the wrong thing,' Charlie said. 'But you should have kept it between us.'

'I know. I was out of order. I'm sorry.'

'Apology accepted. Let's say no more about it.'

'My wife. She likes you, you know. After she met you at the lunch. She thought you were all right.'

'You're lucky. She's your biggest fan.'

'It's good to have one, at least.'

'Is that the reason for the apology? Did she put you up to it?'

'Maybe. She said I read you wrong. She's got a pretty good radar about these things.'

'Most women have, sergeant.'

Amanda Cole didn't live that far from Charlie, though in a bit more style. From the outside it looked like just another grim conversion; the place could have been council offices once. After they got buzzed in, they took the lift to the top floor. Mrs Cole owned the entire floor and had the proper industrial look going on; there were what looked like Peruvian rugs hanging on the bare brick walls, odd bits of steel and copper that were probably worth a fair few quid at artists' galleries, a giant poster of a music festival from the sixties. It was open plan, with hanging lights that looked like UFOs from a budget sci-fi movie, concrete floors, and a 180-degree view of Acton Town, which was as pointless a view as Charlie could imagine.

She had thick bifocals that lent her an owlish look, and wild grey hair with purple streaks. She was dripping with gold chains and bracelets, looked like one of those gallery owners in Muswell Hill who charged you ten quid for a painted log.

But when she spoke, the illusion was immediately shattered. Her voice broke and she grabbed at Charlie's arm. 'This is about Gordon, isn't it? That poor man. When I read about it in the papers I cried and cried. None of those boys left now, except Tom. They were good boys. Such a waste.'

Charlie disentangled himself as gently as he could. He showed her his warrant card and introduced DS Grey. 'We're sorry to intrude. As I said on the phone, we won't keep you long.'

'Would you like a cup of tea?'

Oh, Christ no, Charlie thought. The last thing. 'No thanks, Mrs Cole. As I said, we don't want to keep you.'

She led them to a large sofa at the other end of the room, white leather and steel. It was bigger than his car. Mrs Cole sat on one end of it. 'How can I help you?'

'It's about Joe.'

'Joe?' She got teary again. 'My Joe's dead.'

'I know. What I wanted to ask you about was the farm, up near Bishop's Stortford.'

'That old place. What about it?'

'We've done some checking, and it seems that your son left it to Tom Miller. In his will.'

'What about it?'

'We don't understand why he had it, why your husband didn't leave it to you.'

'Is this important?'

'It could be.'

'I don't see how.'

Charlie smiled and waited. Silence was always the best question.

'Oh, I didn't want that old dump of a place. No one's lived there for years. My husband, God bless his soul, he was left it by his uncle, it's not much.'

'Your husband's dead now?'

'The big C. Five years back. What is all this about?'

'Did it surprise you that Joe left it to someone outside the family?'

'There was no one else to leave it to. And they were real close mates, all those boys. I mean, look at the things they went through together. I suppose Joe must have thought it would help him out. After what happened, you know.' Amanda Cole looked from him to Grey and back again. She looked bewildered. 'Come on, now. Why are you asking me this?'

353

'We're trying to tie up some loose ends.'

Grey leaned in. 'Joe was married, wasn't he?'

'The cow left him. A lot of them do, don't they? Took the little girls with her. I hardly see them any more.'

'Why did she leave?'

'Same reason they all do. She said he'd changed, but I didn't see it. Anyway, even if he had, it's supposed to be better or worse, right? Help him through it. It's what a wife does. Not her. Selfish bitch.'

'He committed suicide not long after she left?'

'About six months after.'

Charlie took over. 'Mrs Cole, you were the one who identified the body. In the morgue?'

'Why are we talking about this?'

'Are you sure it was your son?'

Her expression changed, she clung to the arm of the sofa as if they were on a ship and a large swell had just passed underneath. She looked actually seasick. 'What are you saying?'

'Did you see Joe's face?'

'It was all mangled up. He fell onto the rocks. I couldn't stand to look, you know. But they said it was him. It must have been him. I recognised his watch and his jumper.'

'But you didn't actually see his face?'

'There wasn't anything left to see.' She started to hyperventilate. Charlie took her hands, turned to Grey. 'Better call an ambulance,' he said.

CHAPTER FIFTY-EIGHT

'You can't tell my dad I was here,' Jamal said. 'He'll go fucking mental.'

Lovejoy smiled at Jamal, then at the social worker sitting next to him, trying to put everyone in the room at ease. It wasn't easy. She wanted to shake Jamal and shout: *Hurry up and tell me what you saw!*

He was wearing trendy street gear, a Tommy Hilfiger t-shirt, a C. P. Company hoody. He was trying to look Bronx, even though his father was an investment banker from Surrey. He said he was fifteen, but Lovejoy had him thirteen tops.

'Why don't you tell us what you know, and we'll take it from there.'

Jamal looked at her, then at DC Khan, sitting beside her, ready to take notes. He fidgeted a bit. 'I don't want to get into any trouble, all right?'

'You can't get into trouble for telling the truth,' Lovejoy said, and hated herself for it. No one believed that any more.

Poor kid. He had the whole ghetto roll thing going when he walked in, and now he looked like he was going to cry.

'What made you go to the police, Jamal?'

'I heard about what happened like. To that bloke. Got his head cut off, didn't he? That ain't right.'

'No, it's not.'

'Can't sleep thinking about it.'

'What was it you saw, Jamal?'

Lovejoy had given him some water in a polystyrene cup when

355

he'd first come in. He sipped at it like he thought it was poisoned. Finally, he got together the courage to say his piece. 'Look, that afternoon, I was with my bro Luca, we were down the trees by the golf course, like. There's a footpath down behind our house.'

'What were you doing down there?'

A roll of the shoulders. 'We was watching shit on Luca's phone. We go down there after school, no one can see us, right?' He kept staring at the desk, wouldn't meet her eyes.

'There's no law against doing that, Jamal.'

'If my dad finds out, there will be.' He fidgeted in his chair.

'What happened?'

'Saw this bloke. He was acting weird. We was dead scared, he was coming right towards us like, he looked like Captain America. And it was getting dark and everything.'

'Captain America.'

'Yeah, you know, he was like all in black, and he had a helmet on. Couldn't see his face at first.'

'Go on.'

'He had a backpack with him. He took off his, like, jump-suit, and his helmet, and put them in the backpack. They was covered in blood. Then he took off running again.'

'What was he wearing under the jumpsuit?'

'Just like running gear, and that.'

'Did you get a good look at him?'

Jamal shrugged. 'I suppose.'

'Perhaps you could help us put together an E-fit picture. Do you know what that is? Perhaps you've seen them on television. We use a computer program to put together a picture of some-one from your description.'

'It's really cool,' Khan said.

'All right. I suppose.'

Lovejoy leaned back in her chair. Who to tell first, Charlie or the DCI? 'Jamal, after that, do you think you could write this all down for us? DC Khan here will help you. He'll get it printed up and then if it sounds right, you can sign it for us.'

'I can't do that!'

'It's very important.'

'I tell you what's very important, what's very important is my dad doesn't fucking kill me, and he will if he knows me and Luca was watching . . .'

He stopped. Lovejoy waited him out.

'Watching shit.'

An hour later, Lovejoy had an E-fit of the man Jamal had seen by the golf course, stuffing blood-soaked leathers and a full-face bike helmet into a backpack. When Parm saw it on her laptop she showed Lovejoy the photograph of Miller, Lennox and Joe Cole she'd retrieved from Lennox's Facebook account and pointed to one of the three men.

'It's *him*,' Lovejoy said. 'That's Joe Cole.'

CHAPTER FIFTY-NINE

'What are you looking at?' Grey said, glancing over at Charlie in the passenger seat. 'Are you on the Arsenal website again?'

'That bloody shower. Drew at home with Wolves. No, I'm on my Kindle. I'm reading *The Art of War.*'

'What is it, a novel?'

'I'm at work, sergeant. I don't read novels at work.'

'What is it then?'

'It's by a bloke called Sun Tzu. He was a Chinese general from 500 BC. And it's about what it says on the tin. The art of war. Tom Miller had it on his bookshelf. I decided to download it, read it for myself.'

'Any good?'

'Maybe,' Charlie said.

They turned off the M11 onto a B road. Soon they were rattling across cattle grids, tall hedges crowding them from either side. Charlie saw a sign for fresh eggs, leave the money in the tin. He decided he'd get some on the way back.

'Does it have any bearing?' Grey asked him.

'Well, see, that's what I'm wondering. I thought it would all be about tactics, logistics, supply lines, terrain. But it's much more basic than that. This Chinese geezer reckons that warfare is basically the art of deceit.'

'Example?'

'Bait and ambush. Point your enemy where you want them to go. That sort of bollocks. Have you ever felt, sergeant, in the last two weeks, that you've been led around by the nose?'

'How do you mean?'

'First the Millers give us an alibi, then we find out Mrs Miller has been driving around late at night, around the time Grimes was murdered. So, of course, we bring her in. Then, when Barrington gets offed, Tracy Lennox goes missing, and her brother wanders up and down the high street not half a mile from our murder scene, they make us look at them. Then the other sister finally shows up, we know she was involved, but was she the killer? Every step of the way we've had bright shiny crap waved in front of our eyes. What if the whole family was in on it?'

'All of them?'

'They're the distraction. The deceit. Do you get the picture?'

'But who's been doing the murders?'

'Well whoever it was, they were elite, and they were organised. They knew where all the CCTV and ANPR cameras were, because we never got a good trace, ever. And they were physically fit, because if they weren't the one on the motorbike, they must have legged it away from the murder scene without getting caught.'

'Fit as a bloke trained to run ten miles through the moors with a seventy-pound backpack. Someone like that?'

'That's what I'm thinking.' Charlie's mind wandered, slipped into neutral. He was bone tired, he'd been on autopilot for almost two weeks now and exhaustion was getting the better of him. But at last things were finally starting to make sense.

'Are you thinking what I'm thinking?' Grey said. 'That this Joe Cole might still be alive?'

'The theory seems to fit the facts.'

'Should we get back up?'

'For a dead man? Let's see if I'm right, first. But if there's anyone at this farm, we get the weapons squad to do the hard stop then.'

Grey stopped at a railway line, the lights started flashing, and the red and white gates came down. A few minutes later an express train hurtled through the crossing, their car shook from the backdraft, and Charlie jerked upright, startled.

Grey looked at him, surprised, a little amused. 'You all right, sir?'

'Don't call me sir, I've told you, don't be so bloody formal all the time. Everyone else calls me guv or guv'nor. And yes, I'm all right. I just don't like trains. Bad memories.'

Bad memories of a little kid with big ears and ginger hair. Too nice, and too gentle, by half.

He sat at the breakfast table, his fists clenched in front of him. He thought they'd be pleased with him. All the things he'd done, for his country, for Tom.

Instead they sat there, heads down, wouldn't even look at him.

'It's over,' he said. 'We can be a family again now.'

Not a smile, not even a glance.

He stood up, smashed his fist on the table. The spoons rattled in their bowls and sugar spilled on the table.

'What do you want from me? You should be proud. Proud. I did what everyone else was *afraid* to do!'

Half a mile down the road from the crossing, they found the farm. Grey turned off the road and Charlie got out; there was a padlock on the gate, they'd have to go up on foot. His Nokia started ringing in his pocket: Lovejoy. She'd have to wait.

'Shall we check it out, guv?' Grey said.

Charlie smiled. Finally, he'd got the idea. 'Are you sure about this?'

'I think you're right. We should scope the place before we bring in the cavalry. Look pretty silly if there's no one there.'

'All right.'

They vaulted the gate and started up the drive. Charlie could see the old farmhouse through the bare winter branches of the elm trees. The place was run down, two storeys; there were pebble-dash walls and a wooden door, the bright blue paint peeling off in strips. He stopped, looking for signs of life. There was an old Kombi van, gone to rust, a caravan, a skein of smoke rising from the chimney.

Grey was about to say something, but Charlie put a hand up, signalled for him to listen. Someone was in there, shouting at the top of his voice, proper going off their nut.

'Get some back up?' Grey said.

'Definitely,' Charlie said. 'Look out.'

Someone came banging out of the house, roaring. Charlie took a few steps forward to hide behind the nearest tree. Grey did the same, grunted, and went down, flat on his face.

'Sergeant?' Charlie said. Grey didn't move. 'Matt?'

The man on the veranda was lean and muscled, he had long hair and a beard. He seemed to be yelling at nothing. He kicked the door frame and went back inside.

'Matt?' Charlie said.

He knelt down. Grey didn't move. The end of a crossbow bolt protruded six inches from the middle of his spine. Blood had flowered on the back of his jacket, a pool of it lay around the wound. Grey's head was turned to the side. He looked surprised. His eyes were half-lidded, already glassy in death.

Charlie looked down, saw the tripwire tangled around Grey's shoe. Charlie was on the left and had run off the path to find cover; Grey had been on the right, stayed on the path, and tripped the wire. Life and death was as simple as that.

Charlie looked up at the house. He could still hear the yelling.

He knew what he had to do. He went back to the car, called it in: officer down, armed response required. He was told to stand by.

Stand by.

Charlie thought of all the times he had stood by in his life. The last time was when he was about sixteen and he stood by while his father beat up his mother. The time after that he had waded in and resolved the situation himself.

He thought about Grey lying up there on the muddy track with a fucking cross bolt through his chest and he thought about having to tell his wife what had happened to him.

He set off back up the track. If that was the way this fucker wanted to play it, then he'd have to kill him too, or he'd never sleep at night again.

CHAPTER SIXTY

Charlie avoided the path and Grey's body. He went up through the trees, inching his way, watching for more tripwires, past the caravan and the old VW Kombi. There was an axe embedded in a chopping block, some rusted children's toys, a tricycle and a rusted swing set. An ancient khaki jeep was parked under the lean-to, he reckoned it was the one he'd seen in the photograph on Tom Miller's wall.

The door was still wide open. He took a step inside.

There was a passageway with cracked slate tiles, and a wooden staircase led up to the second floor. He could see straight down the passage to the kitchen, there was a ceramic hob and oven, a washing machine in one corner, a wood-burning stove.

The long-haired man was leaning on the kitchen table with his bunched fists, screaming at the three empty chairs. There was a sandwich on a plate in front of each table setting. The man was wearing a sweat-stained Nike shirt and running shorts. He looked vaguely familiar.

He looked up at Charlie and the expression on his face when he saw him, it wasn't anger, it wasn't hate, it was more like surprise and mild annoyance. 'What the fuck do you want?' he said.

Charlie realised why he was so familiar. He was Gordon Lennox's labourer. He'd met him that day when he and Grey had gone over to the renovation at Larkhall.

Nice shoes.

All that hair and the scraggly beard, he looked nothing like the Joe Cole in the picture.

Charlie pointed to the empty chairs. 'There's no one there,' he said.

'What?'

'Joseph Cole, you are under arrest for the murder of Michael Grimes. You do not have to say anything, but it may harm your defence if you do not mention when questioned something which you later rely on in court. Anything you do say may be given in evidence.'

'Are you out of your fucking mind?'

'And you killed my sergeant.'

'I did no such thing.' He looked over Charlie's shoulder to the door. 'Oh, that.'

Charlie took a step towards him. Cole got something from behind the door and suddenly there was a shotgun in his hand. He fired. It was like a cannon going off. Charlie instinctively threw himself on the floor.

He lay there, waiting for the pain. When it didn't come, he rolled over on his back and looked down. No blood, nothing. But there was plaster everywhere, a choking cloud of white dust. Cole must have pointed the barrel upwards at the last moment and blown a hole in the ceiling.

Charlie scrambled upright. Cole had gone out the back door, he could see him running down the hill, balanced, easy, the shotgun in his right hand. Without thinking Charlie ran out after him.

CHAPTER SIXTY-ONE

He makes it look so easy, Charlie thought. Cole was loping down through the trees, towards the railway lines at the bottom. Charlie slipped in the mud, tumbled a few yards, got up and kept going, but he knew the bastard was going to get away. He saw him heading towards the wire fence at the bottom of the property. Cole vaulted over, one hand on the top wire, piece of cake.

Charlie was out of breath when he got there, leaned on the wire, exhausted. He looked up, saw Cole standing on the other side of the railway line, the shotgun in his right hand, held loosely at his side.

'What do you think you're doing?' he said.

'You killed my sergeant,' Charlie said.

'You can't go after someone with a shotgun when you're unarmed. It's madness.'

'No madder than what you did,' Charlie said, and he put one foot on the wire and swung his other leg over. He landed none too gracefully on the other side and straightened up.

'I don't want to do this, but you take one more step and I stop playing nice.'

Charlie hesitated. He looked at the shotgun. He couldn't turn back now, but he didn't want to die.

'What's your name again?' Cole said. 'You told me that day you came to talk to Big Gordie.'

'Detective Inspector Charlie George. Charlie.'

'Well, Charlie, do you know what one of these things does

to a human body? You don't get a flesh wound like you see in the movies. A shot gun blast, it's not just one bullet, it's a spray of metal, blows whole chunks of you clean out. At this range, one barrel and you'll look like hamburger mince. Two will blow you in half.'

Charlie heard a whine in the rails. There was a train coming.

Cole heard it too. 'Now, do I shoot you before the train comes or do I wait till it comes through and then take off?'

'Whether you kill me or not, it's over. I've called it in. In about ten minutes the whole county will be full of helicopters and sniffer dogs. This is it, mate.'

'Well, why don't you wait for them, you mad bastard? Why run after me like this?'

'Because of my sergeant.'

'So you think you've found something worth dying for, have you? We've found some common ground.' Cole took a step towards him. 'I found something worth dying for, too. It wasn't king and country, it was my mates. Just like you.'

'Tom Miller.'

'Lost both his legs over there and what does he get in return? Some fucker kills his kid and does he get justice? No. He gets *pissed* on.'

'What was my sergeant then? Collateral damage?'

'No, you don't get to decide how this conversation goes, Charlie. I'm sorry about your offsider. That was never meant to happen.'

'Well, he's dead anyway, whether you meant it or not. He had a wife and two kids. You happy about that? Oh, and she's in a wheelchair, too, same as your mate.'

Charlie thought about rushing him and decided that was suicide. He'd blow him away before he even got three paces. But he couldn't turn back either. Just keep him talking then, till the cavalry arrive.

Everything was coming together in his head; Meg hiding out here in the caravan since she'd gone AWOL, helping Joe with the whole plan; burner phones to coordinate with Gordon and Tom and Tracy, carry it out like, yes, like a military operation. *If you make your enemy look the wrong way, you have the greatest chance of success.*

The knife Joe used, he'd bet a month's pay that was back there in the house somewhere. A *pesh kabz* like Tom Miller's, like Tracy's, sliver missing from the blade. It would match the fragment they found in Grimes' kitchen floor.

'Why Meg?' Charlie said.

'It was her plan. She's the smart one. You think Gordie came up with this? Or me?'

'Were you and her . . . ?'

'After the missus left. Yeah.'

'Look Joe, I know how you feel, but you've made your point. Put the gun down, let's end this right here. There's no point in going on with this.'

'You know how it feels, do you? Prove it to me. Because if you can't, then I'm going to blow you away, right here, right now. So, tell me, Charlie. Tell me you know how it feels.'

There were sirens, but they were still a long way off. The rails were shivering, he looked around, there was a bend about a hundred yards from where they were standing, couldn't see much beyond it because of a stand of beech trees. The train couldn't be far away.

'My brother, Liam.'

'What about him?'

'I was sixteen years old. I left home. I'd had a fight with my old man.'

'An argument?'

'No, a proper fist fight. See the scar there, over my eye. He had a threepenny-bit ring, worked like a knuckle duster.'

'He beat you up.'

'No. Not this time. He got one shot in then I took him apart. I was pretty handy in those days. But I couldn't stay around at home after that.'

367

'Where did you go?'

'I dossed down at a mate's house until I found a place of my own. Got a job, rented a bedsit in Hackney.'

'Is that the story?'

'No.'

'Spit it out then.'

Charlie had never told anyone before, perhaps because no one had ever pointed a shotgun at his midriff before and made him tell it.

'Liam rang me at my work.'

'How old was he?'

'Not old. Fourteen.'

'What did he want?'

'He said he wanted to see me. He said it was important. So I said I'd meet him outside the betting shop down the high street, after he finished school.'

'But you were late.'

'Yeah, I got on the bevvy with some of my mates and they were taking the piss, said I couldn't hold me beers, so I had a couple more, thought he'd wait for me. I was half an hour late.'

'And he didn't wait?'

'No. He went down the railway line and stepped in front of the 5.17 to Southend.'

'And if you'd been on time and talked to him, you think maybe he'd still be alive.'

'Maybe. I'll never know what he wanted or if I could have made a difference.'

The whine was getting louder. He saw it now, an express, another ten seconds, maybe less, and it would be here. If he was going to cross the rails to reach Joe, he would have to do it now.

This must have been what it was like for Liam, he thought. You heard death coming, humming like some giant insect, you looked up, and there it was, the front of the train, the windscreen at the front like giant eyes, then a great roaring, smashing death.

What made him step out? How could he do that?

Cole lowered the gun. 'That's a sad story,' he said.

The driver had seen them, but a little too late, pounded the horn in one long shattering blast. The wheels screeched on the rails as he applied the brakes.

'I often wonder,' Charlie shouted across the lines, 'what was going through his head when he stood in front of that train.'

'I know exactly what went through his head,' Cole shouted back. 'The 5.17 to Southend.'

And he took two steps forward and then he was gone.

CHAPTER SIXTY-TWO

Ten days later, Oxford

It started to rain as they came out of the cathedral. It was the perfect day for a funeral; grey, overcast and wet. Charlie stood on the grass in his dress blues aching for a fag. He watched the DCI and the police brass, all in full ceremonial fig, follow the family out of the church. He couldn't wait to get this over with.

He kept seeing Grey lying face down in the mud and leaves, a bolt through him. He supposed he'd never stop dreaming about that, even when he had his eyes open.

The cathedral and grounds were packed, police officers from all over England had showed up, not just Metropolitan police. He had been a bit of a loner in his short time at Essex Street, but the whole world had turned up for his last hurrah. A lot of the general public were there as well, lining the route of the cortège; a few of them were even crying.

They didn't even know him.

It was a big crowd, but there was an eeriness about it, everyone speaking in hushed whispers. The bells were tolling. Give me strength, he thought, I have to get out of here.

He saw Lovejoy; she came over holding an order of service, Grey's picture on the front. He noticed that she was still limping a bit. 'Guv.'

'Hello Lovejoy.'

'Lovely service.'

'Yeah, it was nice, as funerals go. Never been to one that cheered me up though.'

'The DCI spoke well.'

Charlie nodded. Grey would have loved all that, one of the old boys bigging him up like that in front of the Home Secretary. Although he would probably have preferred being alive a whole lot more.

'Got everyone here.'

'A regular *Who's Who* of London.'

Whitney came out of the cathedral, her children either side of her chair, surrounded by her family.

'He had a lot of family, by all accounts. Her, too.'

'Good. She's going to need them.'

She was immediately surrounded by mourners, all of them wanting to shake her hand. The police commissioner was at the front of the scrum, the Lord Mayor of London was in there as well. Whitney caught Charlie's eye and headed over. He heard press cameras clicking and whirring. Oh Christ, Charlie thought. This is it.

She stopped in front of him, and looked up into his face. She looked utterly dignified, no running mascara, no red eyes. She would save the tears for later, like a good cop's wife. She held out her hand and he took it. 'Thank you for coming, Charlie,' she said. 'Don't you go blaming yourself.'

Charlie nodded. He felt like he'd swallowed a bloody great stone. He couldn't speak.

'I heard what happened. It couldn't be helped. I'm proud of both of you.'

What could he say to her? I'm sorry for your loss?

She turned and wheeled away.

'Well,' Lovejoy said. 'Amazing.'

Charlie nodded, still didn't trust himself to speak.

'Are you going to the crematorium?'

Charlie shook his head, took a few moments to pull himself together. 'No, it's private. Only immediate family. Who's that over there, Lovejoy? That your boyfriend?'

371

'Do you want to come and say hello?'

'Don't think so. Don't want to keep my plus one waiting.'

'Who is your plus one? Do I know her?'

'Ben. My brother. We're going to visit Ma after this and then we'll probably find a bar. He said I needed to get hammered and he's probably right. By the way, how's Charlie?'

'He's fine. You'd never know there was ever anything wrong with him. Harry is teaching him to play fetch with a tennis ball.'

Good for Harry. Still, that hurt. He was my dog first, Charlie thought. It was my car he shat in, and my packet of biscuits he scoffed that first night. Still, that was life. If you didn't hang around, you lost first dibs. That was the rules.

'When are you back, guv?'

'Don't know if I will be, not until after the DPS are done with me. Besides, I don't know if I want them to clear me this time. I've used up all the petals on my four-leaf clover.'

'You'll be back,' she said.

Charlie said he'd see her sometime, and headed through the crowds, found Ben waiting on the other side of the green. His girlfriend was with him, she had an arm around Rom, who looked lost inside his hooded puffer jacket. He had a surgical mask on his face. Flu season was starting.

'All right, Charlie boy?' Ben said.

'Thanks for coming, mate.'

'Took the whole day off work for you. That means you owe me about ten thousand quid. Come on, my son. You look like you need a drink.'

It started raining harder and his dress blues were soaked. He felt like shite, he didn't have anyone to go home to, and he didn't know if he still had a job.

Still, he was alive. That was something. Even on a wet Thursday afternoon in Oxford.

ACKNOWLEDGEMENTS

Another huge thank you to Krystyna Green, my editor at Little, Brown, for keeping Charlie in a job. I create the bodies, but you sanction the murders. Thank you for your boundless enthusiasm in bringing Charlie to life.

Many thanks again to my desk editor, Rebecca Sheppard, for getting me through each step of the editing process and keeping me on schedule.

Thank you to the wonderful Charlotte Cole, who did such a great edit on the manuscript – thanks again for writing that timeline – and for making sure there were no heatwaves in November.

Thanks also to proofreader Rachel Cross, who picked up the last of the typos. Let's hope there aren't any more!

And to my amazing Beta readers: thanks Jess, it's so useful having a daughter with a degree in English Lit! And to Lise . . . for all the pages you screwed up and threw out the window, for all the long Sunday afternoons going through the draft line by line, and for your endless support and encouragement. I think I need you to give up your day job, sweetheart.